W9-BAF-067

THE STYX

Also by Jonathon King

The Blue Edge of Midnight
A Visible Darkness
Shadow Men
A Killing Night
Eye of Vengence
Acts of Nature

ISBN 978-0-9817036-5-7

This book is a work of fiction. References to real people, events, establishments, organizations, or locales are intended only to provide a sense of authenticity, and are used fictitiously. All other characters, and all incidents and dialogue, are drawn from the author's imagination and are not to be construed as real.

Published by
Middle River Press
1498 NE 30th Ct.
Oakland Park, FL 33334
middleriverpress.com

Second Printing
Printed in the USA

The Styx

Jonathon King

2009

Middle
River
Press

THE STYX

Chapter 1

Always the women came first. Once they knew it was safe, that it wasn't something contagious, that there wasn't something violent still flying around: bullets, blades, fists. When it was a so-called natural death, the women were the first at the door, tapping lightly and calling out the name of the son.

"Michael? Michael, luv? It's Mrs. Ready from down the way. Come to help you. Please now. Open up and let us in, lad."

When death befell one of their own, someone like them, the word would pass through the slum more quickly than a gutter fire. And when it was another woman, a peer, an Irish mother, it was like a looking glass of their own inevitable demise, and Jesus, Mary and Joseph, it had to be put together in the way only a woman could.

Michael got up from the straight-back chair and went to the knocking at the door without turning his head from his mother's face, like she might still awaken and bark a command or call out: "Aye, who's it now?"

He had been staring at her dusty profile for only an hour or so now, ever since the local doctor had pronounced her dead and walked back down the tenement stairs. It was not like the vigil he'd sat for the three days she'd lain there, her cough rattling in her tiny chest like broken glass in a paper bag, sweat pouring off her brow in such gouts he swore the wet cloth he dampened from the washbasin was itself drawing the perspiration from her skin. The rag would go on cool and damp and come away hot in his hands as he rung it out.

"It's a fever, Mama, it'll break soon," he'd kept repeating.

"I know it will, Danny. I know. I'll be up in a bit, son. Just a bit." She'd mistaken him for his older brother, the one who'd left.

But they were the very same words she'd said to him for as long as he could remember when it was he in the bed with the croup or that one winter with pneumonia. She was his mother, always there. But now she was thirty-nine, ten days from forty, and he was twenty-three. It was a role reversal that would have seemed surreal but for the reality of the pain that tore at him.

"She's gone now, Michael," the doctor had said to him at dawn. "Gone to the Lord, bless her soul."

He'd listened, without taking his eyes away from his mother's face, as the doc packed his bag, closed the door behind him, and clomped down the narrow staircase in his old shoes. How many journeys does that man make a day on these tenement steps, where the denizens of the Lower East Side fall every hour, like grains of sand, only to be replaced by another wave of immigrants washed ashore? What's the Lord got to do with it?

And then the women came. Michael answered the tapping, stared out at Mrs. Ready and a tight clutch of others; he recognized Mrs. Brennan, his best friend's mother, and Mrs. Phelan, from above the bakery, and another he barely knew. They were bundled in winter coats and dark hats and were carrying baskets the contents of which only they knew.

Mrs. Ready stepped into his space and looked up into his eyes, and for the life of him he didn't know how to react. The woman, not much older than his own mother, put her palms to his cheeks. "We know you're hurtin', Michael. But let us do what needs doin'. Go downstairs now to the street and get some air, lad."

He watched the others move in, sliding immediately to the bedside, dark hens come to cluck and perhaps to weep over another. When Michael said nothing and just stood with the door open, staring, Mrs. Ready came back to him, picking up his coat on the way and draping it over his shoulders.

"Go on now. We'll find our way," she said and gently ushered him out.

Outside it was barely eight a.m. and the street unusually full. Michael stood on the steps of their tenement and looked about as if he hadn't lived in the building for most of his life. These were the streets where he and his father had walked hand in hand on Saturday mornings to the poultry shop on Pitt Street. The once-a-month chicken had always been Michael's choice. Then his father was gone. These were the streets where he and his brother had chased and been chased by a dirty flock of Irish kids, dodging the wagons, scrapping after spilled produce, finding ways to entertain themselves, be it a stickball game or gawking at some irrelevant gang fight. Then Danny was gone. These were the streets where his mother had a magical touch for finding the deals for food and bartering for work and cajoling a city worker for word of an inoculation program or infestation warning, all the things that kept them alive. And now she was gone too. "You're going to watch me die of a broken heart," she'd told him three days ago through lips cracked with the heat of her fever. "Don't let anyone tell you it can't happen, m'boy. Aye, it's a sure malady when you lose your husband and your son."

"You haven't lost your son, Mama," Michael told her. "Danny's coming home when he finds his treasure, and I will always be here with you."

Now the street scene seemed unrecognizable as he stood with his hands in his pockets, eyes reddened from grief and lack of sleep and mind gone so numb he didn't hear the man in front of him until the elder fellow took his sleeve.

"Michael! Michael Byrne," the man was saying. "It's me, James Brennan, Jackie's father."

Michael shook his head while Mr. Brennan was shaking his hand, and both actions seemed to pull him back to reality.

"Sorry, Mr. Brennan. Sorry, sir. I was just—"

"Don't even say it, lad. We're the ones'er sorry for the loss of your dear mother. Jackie told us how sick she was and all."

The elder man had looped his arm through Michael's, as a gesture of both moral and physical support, considering his dazed state. The morning air was still near freezing, and Michael had been just standing there on the stoop, staring out at the cold dankness of the city.

"We've already taken up a bit of a collection, Michael. We've got a coffin maker from Hanlon's, and we'll get the wagon arranged for three this afternoon," Mr. Brennan was saying. "It'll be a fine send-off, lad. No worries now, OK?"

Michael watched a coal wagon creak by in the street, pulled by a haggard old mare, tired before the day had even begun.

"A wagon?"

"Aye, out to the cemetery over in Brooklyn, son," Mr. Brennan said. "Unless you've got other plans. Maybe a special arrangement with St. Brigid's?"

Michael hadn't been to St. Brigid's in ten years. His mother had been devoted to the old famine church on Avenue B, a rock for Irish immigrants like themselves. But she stopped going to services after Michael's father had gone and instead took to cursing her religious tenets on a regular basis, blaming God for leaving her damned and in the grips of hell over the past few years. Cemeteries in the city had been banned years ago as land became scarce. The rural fields of Brooklyn had become the resting place for the modern dead.

"Uh, no, sir. No, the wagon is fine, sir. Thank you, sir."

The two stood there together, watching out over the street, Mr. Brennan stamping his feet in the cold, Michael blinking his eyes as if taking shutter photos of a world he didn't recognize anymore. On several occasions men or women with faces he should have known came up and offered their condolences. The men shook his hand, clasping it with both of theirs as though he'd come through some sort of initiation of pain into their world of adulthood. The women simply took his hands in theirs and looked into his glossy eyes with a knowledge he had never seen before.

Yes, his father was gone, but there had never been condolences given like these. Yes, his older brother had left, but it was an absence of his own making, a choice even. Now Michael was the only one left, a position that harbored this sympathy in others but only froze Michael for now.

"Ah, there, boy. The ladies are finished," Mr. Brennan finally said and turned Michael back to his own entryway. The four ladies were descending the steps, moving in a dark pack. Again Mrs. Ready took his hands.

"She's ready, son," the woman said. "If you'll just sit with her now, we'll start spreading the word and you can greet the well-wishers. We'll make sure you get some food in you, too, Michael."

She then turned to Mr. Brennan.

"The wagon has been arranged?"

"Aye. Three o'clock."

She patted Michael on the sleeve. "We'll be back, son. You won't have to do this alone."

When they'd gone, Michael made his way back up into his flat. Lying on the bed, his mother's corpse had been transformed. The women had found her black dress, had apparently spongebathed her and changed her clothing. They'd used some kind of scented water. The room smelled of flowers instead of sweat and mold and sickness. They'd left two extra kerosene lamps to help brighten the room. All had been carefully posed: his mother lying square in the middle of the bed, her black church shoes buffed and tied, her dress unwrinkled and tucked just right along her thin body. Her hands were folded on her chest, the fingers interlaced, the ring his father had given her before they even left Ireland on her finger and turned prominently upward. Her eyes were closed, and the grimace of death had been replaced by simple manipulation of skin going slowly into rigor. The women had used perhaps their own makeup to cover her mottled gray face and had added just a whisper of rouge. Still, when Michael looked down at his mother, her face seemed to be melting; the bones of her cheeks and nose looked as if they would expose themselves as her skin slackened. The women had added some color to her lips to keep them from going dark, but even with the faux stoicism they placed on her face, she seemed a puttied version of herself.

Michael washed himself and dressed in the best clothes he had, a pair of corduroy pants, a shirt that could still pass for white, and a threadbare jacket. He took up his post in the straight-backed chair again and listened for the inevitable sound of footsteps up the stairwell.

The Sheehans from the butcher's shop down the block came. The Huntaways from next door. The Flannigans from the tavern. Couples his mother's age that he barely knew came and pressed coins rolled in pieces of cloth into his hand. Women brought pots of stew and sweetbreads and placed them on the only table in the room. Three young boys came with flowers. Michael didn't know their names. "They went out and got them from the professor up on Tenth Street who grows a garden," their father said. Michael nodded. He and Danny had done the same when they were that age and old Mrs. Clancy died, but he didn't remember them asking first. He caught himself wondering if it was from the same garden. So long ago.

Near the end of the prescribed two hours of visitation, one of Danny's old friends showed up. Ian Cronin. Ian and Danny had been thicker than thieves until Cronin had joined the police.

"Aye, Michael," Cronin said, taking Michael's hand. "Heard about yer mum. Sorry." Cronin was an officer up in midtown, and Michael kept the surprise out of his eyes. He hadn't seen Cronin since long before Danny disappeared, and even though Cronin and Michael had both been officers back then, they rarely crossed paths. Cronin's head was lowered, maybe in reverence to the moment, but Michael had a sense that Cronin was hesitant to look him in the eye.

Still, Cronin did the dutiful thing, stepped up to the bed where Michael's dead mother lay and made the sign of the cross and then knelt and whispered a blessing. Then he stood and turned to Michael and took his hand again, but this time there was an envelope in his palm.

"Sorry again, Michael," he said. "I should have come sooner."

Michael looked at him quizzically but only nodded and folded the envelope into his pocket.

Afterward, the women stepped forward again, gathered together the food and then took Michael by the elbow and escorted him down the staircase. Four men with tools in their hands and slats of fresh-hewn pine under their arms passed them going up.

Michael ate out on the stoop, barely tasting the food. The women kept passing plates to him and then reloaded each time he refused more. As he ate he could hear the tapping of nails upstairs and the low voices of the men singing an Irish dirge that he could not place.

At one o'clock an empty wagon pulled by two unmatched horses clattered up to the curb. As if that was their signal, the men from upstairs carried the coffin down the stairs and slid it carefully into the back. Also on that seeming signal, some two dozen people from the neighborhood queued up along either side of the wagon. Jonas Ready stepped up next to Michael and, with the tact of a fine waiter, got him up and positioned behind the jury-rigged hearse. From the inside of his coat pocket Mr. Ready withdrew a flask that he passed to Michael. The whiskey went down like a jolt but could not bring a tear to Michael's eyes. The long night and morning had done that, and he had nothing left. He took another long swig to be sure, and then Jonas Ready gave the wagon driver a tip of his hat and the entire ragtag procession began, more tactful and reverent, stoic and proud, hopeful and helpful to the memory of Michael Byrne's mother than its members ever were when she was alive.

Chapter 2

She took the news of it from the night air, in the odor of hot pine sap bubbling as the trees burst into flames and in the smell of dry plank wood charring in fire. She stood on the back porch of the luxurious Palm Beach Breakers overlooking the ocean and turned her face to the north, and the scent on the breeze furrowed her brow.

"What is it, Miss Ida?"

The young woman had picked up on the look in Ida's face. She was perceptive that way, unlike others of her kind. It was why Ida liked the girl. But though she might be good at detecting emotion in the careful faces of the hired help, the girl did not have a nose for burning wood floating on salt air. The old woman did not turn to the girl's question and instead kept her head high and her eyes focused on the treetops at the dark northern horizon, searching for a flickering light. She drew in another deep breath for confirmation and then began to move off the painted steps of the hotel.

"Miss Ida?" the young woman said. Her long dress rustled as she hurried down to catch up. "What is it?"

The old woman was still scanning the trees, her eyes showing only a hint of anxiety, but the girl could see moisture welling in them.

"I'm sorry, ma'am," Ida May Fluery said without breaking stride, "but I believe they are burning my home."

The two women walked quickly down the broad walk and around the northern side of the hotel: Ida May Fluery, the head housekeeper at the Breakers, and Marjory McAdams, daughter of a Florida East Coast Railway executive. The one in the lead was a small black woman in a dark work dress with a white apron to mark her employment. Folds of her skirts were in her fists, and her hard leather shoes were flashing across the crushed rock of the service road. Struggling to keep up, Marjory McAdams was also in a dress, but one of considerable fashion and not made for running. Thom Martin, one of the Breakers' bellmen, was smoking under the hotel's portico when he took note of them and would have been quite willing to watch the younger woman's ankles as she hiked her dress to keep pace until he recognized who she was and the direction both were heading.

"Miss McAdams," he called out as he ditched the cigarette and hustled after them. "Uh, Miss McAdams, ma'am?"

Neither of the women turned to him until he had run to catch up and again called out Marjory's name.

She finally spun on him and appeared surprised, but turned instantly in control. "Mr. Martin. Fetch us a calash, quickly, please. We need to take Mizz Fluery home." She kept moving with the older woman.

The bellman stopped jogging but still had to lengthen his walking stride to keep up with them. He hesitated at the request but had to consider it, coming as it did from a superior's daughter.

"Uh, ma'am, there's no one down in the Styx tonight, ma'am," he said, trying to be pleasant and deferential. "They're all across the lake at the festival, ma'am. I, uh, could get a driver to take you all over the bridge to West Palm."

The elderly woman had yet to either acknowledge the bellman or slow her stride. But Marjory McAdams snapped her green eyes on the man and sharpened her voice:

"Either get us a calash, Mr. Martin, or I shall fetch one and drive it myself, and you know, sir, that I am quite capable."

The bellman whispered "shit" as the women continued on, and then he turned and ran back toward the hotel.

They were already onto the dirt road leading through the pines and cabbage palms to the northern end of the island when the thudding sound of horse hooves and the rattle of harness caught up to them. Marjory had to take Miss Fluery by the elbow to pull her to the side as Mr. Martin slowed and stopped next to them. Without a word they both scrambled up into the calash before the bellman had a chance to get out and help. As they settled in the back, he turned in his seat:

"Miss McAdams, please ma'am. All of us was asked to stay out of the Styx tonight. It might be best..."

"Mr. Martin, can you not smell that smoke in the air?" Marjory said, meeting his eyes. Martin turned to look into the darkness, even though the odor of burning timber was now unmistakable.

"Yes, ma'am," he answered, without turning back to face them.

"Then go, sir."

"Yes, ma'am," he said, and snapped the reins.

The horse balked at the darkness with only the light of a three-quarter moon to guide it, but it moved at the driver's urging. Miss Fluery kept her eyes high and forward and could see the gobs of smoke that caught in the treetops and hung there like dirty gauze. In less than another quarter mile, she stood up with a grip on the driver's seat, and Marjory could see the new set of the woman's jaw. She too could see flickers of orange light coming through the trees as if from behind the moving blades of a fan. Despite his reluctance, Mr. Martin urged the horse to speed.

"It may only be a wildfire," Marjory said carefully, but the old woman did not turn to her voice of hope as they pressed on.

Minutes later the carriage slurred in the sandy roadway when they rounded a final curve and came to a full stop at the edge of the clearing. The horse reared up in its traces and wrenched its head to the side as the heat of some two dozen cones of fire met them like a wall, and the white, three-quarter globe of the animal's terrified eye mocked the moon.

Marjory had been to the Styx before, having talked Miss Fluery into letting her walk the distance to see some new baby the housekeeper had described. Marjory knew she was defying all social rules, but her inquisitiveness had long been a part of her character. The Styx was the community where all the Negro workers—housemaids, bellhops, gardeners and kitchen help—lived during the winter season, when the luxurious Royal Poinciana and the Breakers were filled with moneyed northerners escaping the cold.

Marjory had not been shocked by the simple structures and lack of necessities in the Styx. She was not so naïve and sheltered in her family's mid-Manhattan enclave not to have witnessed poverty in New York City. She had seen the tenements of the Bowery and had secretly had her father's driver, Maurice, take her through the infamous intersection of Five Points to witness the sordid and filth-ridden world of the Lower East Side.

The Styx was, by comparison, quaint, she had justified. The shacks of the workers were made of discarded wood from the Poinciana's construction and slats from furniture crates and shipping cartons. Some were roofed in simple thatch made with indigenous palm fronds, others in sturdier tin. Miss Fluery had told her that two winters ago, one of Flagler's railcars had jumped the small-gauge tracks to Palm Beach Island and collapsed into splinters as it rolled down the embankment to the lake. Given permission, the black workers had scavenged the debris, and the car's tin roof ended up covering six new homes in the Styx.

On this night the thatch roofs had become little more than cinders floating up on hot currents into the air. The tin ones were warped and crumpled by the heat like soggy playing cards. As the women and driver watched, the Boston House rooming home fell in on itself, sending up a shower of glowing embers and a billow of dark smoke.

Ida May had not loosened her grip on the driver's iron seat handle and had not turned her face away even as the heat scorched her old cheeks. Marjory put her hand on the woman's arm.

"Mr. Martin said everyone has gone across the lake to the fair, Miss Ida. Surely no one was at home. Surely they're all safe."

Fluery looked into the flames of her home, which had stood at the prominent crown of the makeshift cul de sac, and listened to the sound of clay bowls shattering in the heat and ceramic keepsakes exploding into hot dust. She did not acknowledge the girl's words. Marjory was a young white lady from the North. She could not discern the smell of linen and Bible parchment burning any more than she could recognize the odor of charred flesh. But Ida May Fluery knew that smell. The news of death was already in the air.

No, they surely are not all safe, Ida thought. And just as surely, she thought, whoever it is, someone has murdered them.

The rest of Ida May's neighbors would hear the news by word of mouth, and it was as rapid and frightening and as unpredictable as the flames themselves.

Mr. Martin rattled back through the woods at an axle-breaking speed to the hotel as much to report the fire as to pull someone of more importance into the situation. He left Miss McAdams and the old house woman at the edge of the burning shantytown. They had refused to budge when he begged them to come back with him, for there was nothing they could do before daylight. The place was destroyed. The fire had already swallowed everything it wanted and had not made the jump from the clearing to the trees. The old woman had acted as if she hadn't heard him and just stood there with those damned spooky eyes of hers glowing. Miss McAdams couldn't convince the old lady either. Finally, in frustration, Martin snatched a kerosene lantern off the left side of the carriage and held it out to her.

"At least take this, ma'am," he said.

Instinctively, Miss McAdams reached out for the lantern but stopped herself when her eyes lit on the glow of the flame inside. It was a look, not of fear—Martin doubted that this young woman feared anything—but some deeper angst. The driver himself balked at the look and began to withdraw the offer. Finally it was the old woman who stepped forward and grabbed the lantern from Martin's hand and then turned without a word.

Christ, he thought, what was a man supposed to do? And he yanked at the reins, turned the carriage round, and then whipped the horse violently into a gallop.

When Martin scrambled off the driver's seat at the front steps of the Breakers, the head liveryman was already up with his arms crossed and a stern look fixed on his face

"Jesus glory, Tommy. Hold on, boy. You're going to shake that rig to pieces."

Martin pulled his hat off in deference to the liveryman, who was considered a superior to all the valets and housemen and some say had been given the job by Flagler himself after serving the railway baron as a sort of sergeant at arms on his early trains into Florida.

"It's a fire, Mr. Carroll," Martin said, trying to control his voice. "In the Styx, sir."

Carroll turned his massive head to the north and then back on the young man before him.

"Were you not told that no one was allowed in the Styx tonight, Thomas?" Carroll said, and the young man could not meet his eye.

"Yes, sir. But—"

"Then why the hell were you out there, son? And why aren't you over the bridge in town where you could be chasin' some local young lady at the fair instead of snootin' around in dark town?"

"I was taking Joe Shepard's late shift, sir. But—"

"But what? You lost a bet to Shepard in a dice game and now you're trying to add to your mark of stupidity?"

Young Martin was getting used to being ignored and berated this night and could not take his eyes off the toes of his boots.

"Don't worry about some fire in the Styx," the manager said, easing up on the boy. "It's none of your concern."

"But Mr. Carroll, sir. Miss McAdams and the old house woman, the one in charge of the maids. They're both out there, sir, and sent me for help."

The manager stared at the boy like he was trying to hear the statement with his eyes. Then he cursed once, spun on his heel and banged up the staircase. Before disappearing through the big front doors of the lobby, he turned and ordered the young bellman to take the carriage to the livery "and cool that damned horse down before it catches a cold."

In the stables Martin shared the story with the livery watchman. Two Negro stable boys repairing harness in a back room overheard the words "Styx" and "fire," and one scrambled through the back stalls and headed on foot to the bridge to the mainland. And thus the news traveled in both directions, to the unofficial governors of Palm Beach and to the families who had paid a terrible price as they ate free ice cream and spun laughing and shrieking on carnival rides, oblivious of their fate.

Chapter 3

Eight o'clock on a November night and the alcoholic braying of JackBrennan was spraying out into the cold air of Manhattan's Lower East Side: "All hail Detective First Grade Michael Byrne on his bloody leaving from the New York City Pinkertons with all his teeth intact like the smile of a teenage whore whom we should all be so lucky as to meet tonight."

"Hooray!"

Byrne raised his pint, smiled his sheepish smile, which only exacerbated his old friend's ribald comments, and joined a half-dozen men in downing their ales in a long single draining. The end task was met by the slamming of glasses on the bar of McSorely's Pub, the shuffling of chair legs on raw wood floors and a call for another round. Byrne looked over the heads of the young men he'd helped train and then commanded. In the dull flickering light of McSorely's electric lamps, they looked an almost civilized bunch. None of them over five foot eight, except for big Jack. None over 150 pounds. In the dimness you couldn't see the dirt at their neck collars or the worn seams of their waistcoats and trousers. But their hand-cropped haircuts were all the same, short and sharp. And without looking, Byrne knew they all wore polished brogans on their feet, some of them wearing proper footwear for the first time in their lives. The shoes had been provided by the company, of course, and were the same style as those Byrne had on his own feet. The haircuts and boots were requirements of their employment with the Pinkerton security company and set them apart from the street thugs and gang mobs. These were boys selected by the keen eyes of company scouts and their connections from the streets. They were a chosen few, perhaps selected because of a light of intelligence in their eyes, maybe because of a sharp, almost feral knack for survival through their wit, maybe because of a natural athleticism that set them apart in a fight. They were neighborhood kids like Byrne, rough-hewn from the tenements yet gilded with some touch of potential.

Byrne had picked some of them himself, only a couple of years after he had been so singled out. An organization like the Pinkertons needed such young men—those with knowledge of the corners and garbage-strewn alleys of the city, those with an ear for the mixed languages of the streets where plans were set and crime was hatched.

Byrne reached down into the pocket of his trousers to feel the folded paper note once again, as he had dozens of times in the past several days. He wasn't sure why he carried it. He had already memorized the words in the telegram that Ian Cronin had passed him on the day of his mother's death:

> *mikey... it is time for you to join me... i will soon be taking a grand piece of property in Florida... i now have riches and land, what da always wanted... the rail tickets and money enclosed should get you and mother to west palm beach... i will meet you whenever you arrive...your big brother, Danny.*

The telegram was the first time he'd heard from his brother in three years. Danny the first-born child. Danny the chosen one. Danny, supposedly the smarter of the boys and crowned as bearer of the family name. But after their father had died, Danny had turned sullen and angry and violent. His way of charming and schmoozing even the most cynical of the city dwellers of their last nickel or shoelace or pint had been his greatest talent. But you needed a pleasant twinkle and a bright patter and a patience to work such a magic, and Danny had lost all of that after seeing their father work his fingers stiff and his knees to creaking and his dreams to dust only to die in the muck and horse droppings of the street. One night after the old man's passing, Michael came awake in their bed, and in the gray darkness he'd watched Danny move about the apartment, dressing and gathering his things. He watched his brother move like a shadow and bend and kiss their mother's quiet cheek. He'd squeezed his own eyes tight when his brother came back to their shared mattress and touched Michael's foot in a gesture of good-bye. He reopened his eyes in time to see Danny go to his parents' dresser and take their father's silver fob watch—the precious one with the blue steel hands and his initials scrolled on the back—from the top drawer. It was not a theft. The watch had been willed to Danny and was his right. The last Michael saw of his brother was a final peeking eye when he carefully closed the door behind him as he'd often done when escaping into the night, but this time he'd gone and never returned.

The thoughts came again as Byrne touched the edges of the folded telegram in his pocket, rubbing the now soft edges with his fingertips. The tickets and money Danny referred to of course never made it to Michael. The telegram had been sent originally to his old New York Police Department substation. From there it had gone to a former sergeant, who passed it on to Ian Cronin. Michael had not opened it until after his mother's burial, when he was back and alone in the empty walkup. He'd read it as he sat on the edge of the bed and carefully folded it and put it back in his pocket, and there it burned, stirring his anger at the brother who'd abandoned him, swelling his resentment for being left to care for their mother alone. He'd given up on Danny's return and damned his brother's memory when Danny came creeping into Michael's dreams at night. So why was he still carrying it? Why had he been so eager to jump at the offer to work a train going south in the morning? To see if it were true, this promise of land and money? Or maybe to ring his brother's neck if he could catch up to him? He'd gone to the telegraph office in midtown and asked the clerk to reply to the origin of the telegram:

Danny... coming to meet you... ma is dead...mike

Byrne questioned the terseness of the message now, the bluntness of it. But tough shit. Danny had tossed enough hurt at his family to deserve a bit of it back. He'd kick Danny's ass when he found him, he swore he would.

"Aye, Michael, here's to you," came another booming voice from yet another corner of the pub, and Jack Brennan again swaggered over and lifted his glass. "To the sharpest and the most civil among us lads," he hollered and tilted his head to Byrne. "And the most dangerous and merciless with his whip of steel."

Byrne raised his beer with the rest and smiled his smile and nodded his thanks and never said a word to anyone of his brother's telegram. To them Byrne was leaving, nothing more. Leaving New York would seem like falling off the edge of the world to the men. Just the thought of such a move would set them bragging about their wretched lives to whatever extent needed to cover their fear of leaving the Bowery, or Alphabet City or the Gas House District. None of them had ever set foot out of the neighborhoods. Yes, Byrne's sought-out reassignment would seem a retirement to them, and in a way he used the same term to try to fool himself and justify his mission. He'd become the old man of Pinkerton squad number eighteen, he'd say. At his age he was over the hill. It was time to let the younger bulls begin their rule, except of course at the top of the company, where the big-bellied commanders and sharp-faced businessmen ruled the overall. But those heights were no place for a neighborhood kid like Byrne to climb, nor did he personally care to try. Tomorrow he'd take his newly acquired rank of detective and report for duty on a new railway line built by Henry Flagler, the oil magnate whose Manhattan mansion had been guarded by the Pinkertons for years. Tomorrow he would be headed toward a great unknown called the state of Florida.

But tonight Michael Byrne was here at McSorely's working his way toward alcoholic oblivion when a sudden rush of cold air from the front door of the tavern blew through and an immediate wave of commotion was started by an ungainly local urchin named Screechy.

Everyone knew the lad from the unhealthy look of his dull, copper-tinged hair and the high, raspy sound of his voice. The hair was discolored from a lack of nutrition, and the voice had developed from an infancy of wailing for a mother who never responded. The combination should have killed the child before he was a toddler, but some impossible gift for self-preservation had saved him for the streets.

"Come on, then, Michael," big Jack yelped into Byrne's ear while grabbing him by the coat sleeve. "Screechy says the Five Points boys are havin' it out with the Alphabet City Gang over in Tompkins Square Park."

Screechy. Every time Byrne saw the kid, he thought of Danny: the same feral nosiness, the same lust for everything in the streets and how it worked, especially the ways of the cons, the hooks, the pickpockets and hustlers. Screechy was Danny fifteen years ago, and like Danny, he had the ability to pull you into a place you shouldn't be going.

Most of Byrne's troop was already starting out the door, reinforced by their drunken buzz, following after the smell of adrenaline and violence. When Byrne hesitated, his old friend gave him that practiced look of impish amusement. "Just for a look-see, eh? Not that we have to get into it, you know?"

Out in the street, the cold hit them all in the face. It had been near fifty degrees inside McSorely's, the place being heated by a single fireplace and the body temperature of a couple dozen men, but out here the temperature was below freezing, and the lot of them thrust their hands into their pockets and moved more or less as a group down Seventh Street east toward the park. By the time they'd reached Second Avenue and passed under the El, the frosty air had sobered Byrne enough to start him second-guessing his decision to come along. In the light of the dim electric lamps on the avenue, he could see the plume of his own breath and feel the hairs inside his nose crinkle with cold.

"What the hell, Brennan," he said, "has happened to my going-away party?"

Half said in jest, the comment seemed to float in the darkness over his big friend's head as they made their way down the next block. Brennan's nose was up in the air as if sniffing at a trail to a feast. The big man stayed quiet, matching the quick steps of their group ahead until they crossed First Avenue and heard a human howling in the distance. From his higher vantage point, Brennan spotted torch flames in the distance.

"Your party has just become a bit more interesting," Brennan said, turning to his commander with a glint of excitement in the widening whites of his eyes. At that the lot of them broke into a jog, their matching brogans slapping the uneven cobblestone of the streets and heading for the edge of Tompkins Square.

At the first cry of impending violence, they stopped. Despite the efforts of the city when it revamped Tompkins Square Park to bring an open space to the jumbled stacks of tenements and street markets of the Lower East side, the place at night was nearly as dark and shadowed as the alleyways around it. The new electric lights at all four corners did little more than add a Luciferian flicker to the winter-bared trees inside the square. Some of the men went to their haunches, a tactic Byrne himself had taught them. Still, he and big Jack remained upright, using the night sight they'd gained from their childhoods on these streets to make an assessment.

"There, on the left," Jack said, his finger pointing to the north side of the park, where they could now make out the flame of a torch.

"Aye and there on the south side," Byrne said, pointing out the torchbearer on the opposite side.

With that little light as a backdrop, they could see the outlines of bobbing heads, but the number was impossible to count. They could also make out the occasional flash of metal, maybe a pipe, maybe a long blade.

"Could be a dozen a side, maybe more," Jack said. "Five Points boys to the south."

Brennan could hear the disgust in his friend's voice. The Five Points Gang had been growing in viciousness and number since both of them were kids. If Brennan and Byrne had not been saved off the streets by a well-meaning New York City cop, they would have been sucked into the gang life just like the others they grew up with in the Gas House District. And the Five Points gang would be their natural enemy.

But from here they stood back and watched the dark gap between the torch flames begin to close, step by step, the silence of night now starting to fill with the shouts and curses of gang members stoking for the fight. When they heard the first guttural thump of flesh against flesh, all of Byrne's crew came to their feet, squinting into the dark to their right. Byrne knew the tactics of the Five Pointers. They would have sent some of their gang out to either side of the park's edge to flank the Alphabet City boys.

"Aye, ya little bastard," came a shout followed by the rustling of fast feet in the dry winter leaves. The Pinkertons now stood tall and almost instinctively closed ranks, shoulder to shoulder as the sound came closer. Then as if from behind a black tree came the rolling form of a small human being, spinning, head over hips and then gaining its feet for only a second before the man chasing behind sent a boot crashing against the boy, knocking him again to the ground.

"Ya shite! You warned 'em ahead of time didn't ya, ya little prick?" the big man yelled, recocked his leg, and sent another toe into the boy's ribs. A muted squeal of pain came out from between the child's teeth, and from ten yards away, Byrne recognized the tousled mop of reddish hair. "Screechy," he called out once before bounding up over the curb and into the park.

The Five Pointer's leg was again at the ready, and the boy had curled to a ball, his elbows over his ears to protect his head, when the whipping sound of thin metal swept through the cold air and a shaft caught the gang member on the outside tendon of his support leg and dropped him like a sack of grain.

"Christ, Screechy, you should know how the hell to keep out of the big boys' brawls by now," Byrne said, standing over the both of them now with a metal baton in his hand that he'd pulled from his waistcoat. The boy peeked up at Byrne between skinny forearms, and a smile started to come to his eye but quickly changed when they both heard the rustle of leaves. The Pinkerton detective's baton was still pointing down when a fist crashed toward his temple.

Byrne rolled away at the last second and the punch caught him but had lost most of its force. The quick move also caused his attacker's weight to carry him past Byrne, who used his pivot to bring the baton across the back of the man's head. The man went face first into the dirt. But a companion was on Byrne immediately. Reinforcements had followed, but so too had Byrne's Pinkertons and the row was on.

He woke, as usual, freezing his ass off and dreading the darkness that would surely greet him as soon as he could pry his crusted eyes open. Byrne pulled the blanket tighter, curled his shoulders in, and felt the pull of his clothes against the bed linens. He found the strength to move his feet and was relieved to find that he had at least taken off his brogans before climbing into bed. Yet he still winced at the thought of putting his feet to wooden floors that were chilled like pond ice and then slipping his feet into frozen shoes. Which, then, he thought, was going to be warming which?

He finally gained the willpower to force open his right eyelid and spied the dull light seeping through the eastern window of the room. But when he squinted, he felt the small crackle and pull of blood-caked skin at the side of his face and quickly recalled the slam of a fist against his temple last night, his own retaliatory swing of his baton, and the blur of adrenaline and the scrape and shove and wrestle of bodies and shouts and whistles of a familiar chaos.

Christ! He let his fingers come out from under the blanket and immediately probed around inside his lips, touching and counting his teeth, feeling for unnatural gaps and then recalling big Jack's toast to his smile, before the row, before he and his boys had left most of the Five Point flank men lying in the rotting leaves moaning from the precise whippings from batons. None of his own men had suffered more than minor bruises, and to avoid any more confrontation, they'd grabbed Screechy by the scruff of the neck and hauled him back to McSorely's and forced him to drink a pint of lager and ordered several more rounds for themselves.

"Aye, Michael," Brennan had said, "my forewarnin' to anyone worth a listen about that steel whip of yours shoulda reached that Five Pointer puttin' the boot to young Screechy." Brennan had leaned in conspiratorially. "And I swear I heard Danny's voice comin' out of your own mouth when you sent the boy packin'. Just like your old brother done to you when you were just a straggler on the gang fights."

Byrne had tipped his last mug to mark the memory. He barely recalled making his way in the dark with Brennan to his tenement south of Hamilton Fish Park. There was a blurred recollection of hugging his mate in a farewell while the both of them stood staring at the lights strung above the newly finished structure of the Williamsburg Bridge.

"You get out, you lucky bastard. Get out of this city before the bloody rats eat us all," Jack Brennan had said. "Go on to Florida, wherever the hell that is, and make a life for yerself away from this place."

Now it was his day of leaving. Yet he did not bolt from bed. He had plenty of time. Late morning train out. He lay still instead, watching his own breath stream out in jets of white into the single room. He did not move his head, putting off what he knew would be some pain from the fracas of last evening. He shifted his slowly improving eyesight to the door opposite. The locks were set. Maybe he had not been as drunk as his pasty mouth indicated.

He lay there several minutes, planning what he'd have to pack—a few articles of clothing that he'd splurged on by having the washerwoman downstairs clean and hang out to dry. He stared at the old dresser drawer where inside a small leatherette held several keepsakes, including the papers his parents had kept and their documents from Ellis Island, their photographs blurred to sepia with age. And once it held his father's watch. The sight of Danny slipping it out of the drawer the night he left came into Byrne's head again. When their father died—their mother told them he'd been crushed under the wheels of a delivery wagon on his way to his job as an apprentice steamfitter—Michael had known that she'd lied. He was convinced that his father was alive because he knew the old man never went anywhere without the Swiss-made watch that he'd brought with him from Dublin and rarely let out of his sight.

Byrne shifted his eyes again, looked up to the eastside window in the room and tried to will the light of a late sunrise in through its dirty panes. He thought of how proud his father had been to move them to the second floor of a building where they'd started out in the rat-infested basement, then to the fourth floor top where the rickety stairs and lack of heat was the next stop for the poorest. Year by year his father had muscled and scrapped and used that optimistic smile of his to make friends, find connections, and get into a better job. The steamfitter job was one he'd been vying for, one to pay the forty-eight dollars a month they'd need to rent a flat farther north in a better neighborhood. But after two years, the old man had started to change. The smiling eyes began to go dull at dinner. The full throated Irish brogue that told wonderful stories at night went hollow and finally quiet. One night, Michael had risen from his cot to use the tenement's hallway bathroom and saw his father sitting up, staring out the only window of the corridor at a view that contained only the brick wall of the building next door. His parents never argued those last two years. No complaints from his mother. No recriminations from his father. Then the man who'd broken his back, and perhaps his soul, to raise them was gone.

Byrne could see the vision of his father that he'd formed in his own head afterward, the one of his sinewy, 140-pound body lying in the middle of the filthy street, the indentations of horse hooves carved into his skin, his legs twisted at impossible angles. But in the vision, now a million sleepless nights perfected in his mind, Michael never saw a mark on his father's face, never a change in his absorbed and intelligent eyes.

Of course, Michael had never really seen the body, had in fact never been to a funeral ceremony or a graveside. All he and Danny were left with was the watch, the only thing of value their father had brought on the coffin ship from Dublin, with its plain ivory face and oval halo of silver. And that's how he knew his mother had lied.

Byrne gathered himself—he hated the cold—and then flung back the blanket and stood. The cold wood floor stung as he knew it would. He'd gone to sleep last night with his pants on, and they would have to do for his journey. To his surprise he found that he'd actually taken off his shirt and hung it on the bureau. But when he held the bone-white garment up, he could see even in the bare light that there were blood stains at the left shoulder, and that wouldn't do. He reached into his pocket, came out with a stick match, and lit the kerosene lamp on the bureau top. The flame crawled up the mirror before him.

The reflection was of a man with dirty-green eyes and high cheek bones. The aquiline nose was slightly bent, broken only once by a beer bottle, and the ears were somewhat large but pinned back as if in perpetual full charge. There was a dark streak running down the left side of the muscled cables of the neck, which appeared to start somewhere inside the light brown hair. He followed the trail up to a slick, sticky mass just above the ear. He touched the spot with his fingertips and could feel the sharp flash of open nerve endings but did not flinch. Byrne had always had an unnatural threshold for pain. He probed around the area a bit before determining the wound was minor and then went to the large metal sink that had been installed only a year ago, when plumbing came to the building. He'd run a basin full of water and set it inside yesterday, not trusting that the pipes bringing water to the second floor would not be frozen in the early morning. Indeed, he now had to crush the top skin of thin ice on the porcelain, and then he dipped a rag and began cleaning the rip in his scalp that had likely come from a ringed fist or some lucky swat of a length of pipe during the fight last night.

He gathered the rag and the basin, moved to the bureau top and began washing his face with the now blood-tinged water. The crusted scrape on his left cheek came clean though raw, and the grime of soot, constantly in the city's polluted air, wiped off as well. He found both a bar of lather soap and a small bristle brush and lathered up his slight whiskers. He then bent to retrieve the single-bladed knife he always carried in a sheath strapped to his ankle. The instrument was small enough for concealment and had many uses, some routine, some that just happened to come along. He shaved himself clean. He would be meeting his new bosses today. Better to present his best. When he'd finished, he cleaned the blade and put it back in its holster and then packed everything he owned into a single old leather satchel. The fact that he had so little made no impression because no one he knew had much more. He donned the warm coat given to him by the same Pinkerton supplier who gave them all their shoes, took one last look around the apartment, to absorb its memories and its lessons, and locked the door behind him. The landlady would know soon enough, when the rent was due, that he was gone.

Outside, an early morning gloom was on the day, though it was always hard to tell whether it was the cloud cover or the density of coal smoke and ash hanging in the air. When Byrne stepped off the threshold, he nearly bumped into old Mrs. McReady, who was mumbling and moving her equally old produce cart into position for the day. The woman was bundled in layers of dull and worn clothing that as far as Byrne could tell never varied, whether worn in the heat of summer or the freezing nip of winter. He had known the woman all his life and long before she'd lost her mind.

"Pardon, Mrs. McReady. Didn't mean to startle you," Byrne said, using a touch of the old country in his voice for her, a holdover that he tried to avoid when speaking to anyone in the city who might take a dislike to him because of his heritage.

The woman looked up into his face with milky eyes and an illusory recognition.

"Danny, me boy. Good mornin' yourself and how is it you're so late gettin' off to school?" she said, mistaking him for his brother as she always did and chastising him though he had not been school age for a good ten years.

"No school today, Mrs. McReady, and it's me, Michael."

The old woman huffed at the correction, whiffed her hands in the air and turned to wrestle with the handles of her cart, the diameter of wooden posts thicker than her own tired legs. Byrne swung his satchel over his shoulder and helped her move the cart to the position where it had sat every day for two decades.

"Bless you, Mikey, but don't touch my cart again, boy, or I'll tell your mum and she'll whip you solid," the old woman snapped. Byrne would have laughed at the threat but for the image of his mother that instantly jumped into his head. She had never touched him in anger, and in her last years she'd barely had the strength to stand.

"I'd appreciate you not telling her, Ma'am," he said to Mrs. McReady.

"Aye, this one time, boy." She reached in under the canvas that covered her cart and withdrew a small green apple and pressed it into his palm. "Now get on with you, you'll be late for school."

Byrne hugged the old woman, squeezing the rumpled bundle hard, but was still unable to feel the bones hidden somewhere inside that magically kept her upright.

"So I'm off," he said as she stood there, her eyes gone vacant, looking befuddled and slightly stunned by the odd recognition of a man's arms around her if only for a second.

Byrne started north on Pitt, the sky in the east showing just a smoldering of light as if the sun were being held down by some giant gray fabric. The air was moist and the cold penetrating. The only advantage of winter was that the garbage and sewage in the streets were frozen, which kept the stench at a minimum. Though the streets were still empty of people, Byrne walked along the edges of buildings, head down and eyes up. By habit he knew that in these neighborhoods you did not draw attention to yourself regardless of your errand. As he skirted the western edge of Hamilton Fish Park, he could make out the huge arch of the gymnasium, the place where New York Police Captain John Sweeney had found him and big Jack and others when they were boys and drafted them into a yet unofficial junior police crew. It was in that gym that Byrne had learned the use of the telescoping baton. Captain Sweeney had given him rudimentary anatomy lessons, nerve points on the human body, weak spots where grown men could be struck and quickly rendered harmless. That knowledge and Byrne's own mechanical perfection of the balance and design of the steel baton had impressed Sweeney and had saved Byrne's ass more than a few times on the streets.

When he and Jack Brennan were seventeen, Sweeney pulled them aside and told them he could pave their way into the city's police department. The pay would be minimal, but they'd have a chance at regular jobs, a perk that few like them could get without being beholden to the neighborhood bosses.

"You're smart boys. You know the streets and the characters out there. We need young men like yourselves to tap into what's going on so we can clean out some of the vermin, you know."

When Byrne took the offer to his brother, Danny scoffed in his face.

"I'll make more money in a week on Broadway than you will in a year," he said, and Michael knew it was true. By then Danny was working as a barker out in front of the follies and running a gambling table in the basement of the place at night. Since they were kids, Michael had tagged along but only watched, careful to stay out of slapping range of his brother's hand but soaking up the atmosphere, the gestures, and the faces of pimps and prostitutes, opium sellers and dice shooters. He could still recall the day Danny was up on his soapbox while Michael sat on his heels in a nearby alcove. In his memory, he was filing away the details, the way his brother used his arms and hands to articulate his pitch, the voice he used, so different from his normal conversational voice, the eye contact, picking out the potential buyers from those too smart or too conservative to take a chance. He memorized what clothes Danny wore, gaudy jackets and vests Michael had never seen at home that were either borrowed from other barkers or kept somewhere secret so their parents wouldn't know. But when Michael's eyes got to his brother's feet, he noted that Danny was wearing mismatched socks—one checkered and one blue—and when he looked down at his own feet, he was wearing the exact same pair—one checkered and one blue.

Somehow, seeing Danny up close shielded him from the allure of it all. Instead Michael watched and memorized faces, names, the knowing winks, and the strange vernacular of a dozen languages and accents.

He may have admired his brother's way of dealing with the streets, but when Michael and big Jack got the chance to join the police, they both got hired on the spot with Sweeney's recommendation. They did some minimal training and were sent out as fodder to manage the traffic on Broadway, dancing in between the horse wagons and push carts and the pedestrians moving to and from the El and plowing beneath the iron structures. After the day's street duty, they'd be called in as muscle in the so-called vice sweeps of the west side of Manhattan in Hell's Kitchen or to quell skirmishes between their own Irish brothers and the Negroes living nearby in the San Juan Hill section.

After three years Byrne knew he was not made for the job. He lacked the ruthlessness of his sergeants and shrank at the orders of the ward bosses who called for the outright beatings of citizens who Byrne could plainly see simply couldn't afford to live in the neighborhoods or were of the wrong ethnic persuasion to stay there. He was also too adept at recognizing the graft and payoffs being made to authorities on a regular basis, a detailed accounting of which he'd brought to upper command, only to be told to put his sharp eyes and ears to better uses and keep his Irish yap shut.

It was Captain Sweeney who saved him yet again and got him assigned to a special unit that was assembled to provide security against looting during the massive reconstruction of the Grand Central Terminal on Forty-second Street. There Byrne's eye and ear for both graft and outright theft gained the attention of the private contractors, who cared more about their money than the ethnicity or social standing of those ripping them off.

When the Pinkerton agency made inquiries about hiring him away from the police two years ago, Byrne didn't hesitate. Now, after receiving Danny's telegram, it was he who'd gone to the agency bosses to ask them if he could have a position on a security team for the railroads. They'd been surprisingly quick to assign him. He now had an eight o'clock appointment on board a southbound train to Washington, D.C., and points beyond.

So it was that Michael Byrne, the last but one of a New York immigrant family, found himself walking across East Houston in the chill dawn, skirting a short line of Colonel George Waring's sanitation wagons. There he slowed to watch a group of men in white uniforms who were armed with ropes and a jury-rigged slide as they loaded the half-frozen carcass of a horse that some unlucky freight man had left where it dropped. Normally the crew would be shoveling black snow, a mixture of ice, garbage and refuse that was piled alongside the street, which would then be dumped in the East River. A dead horse was an occasional break in the routine. Byrne passed quietly and made his way west on Houston. His plan was to slide along the northern edge of the Bowery—better to avoid any trouble with the gang boys there who no doubt wouldn't be awake and out of their dens as of yet, but why take the chance. In the now dull light he could see the raised rails of the El running above Second Avenue. He estimated he had four miles to negotiate to reach Grand Central but turned up First Avenue anyway. He wanted to walk his city one final time.

Heading north, he lengthened his gait on the wide sidewalks, absorbing the signage of a hundred businesses as he passed: a cutter displayed a giant pair of scissors at Third Street; a sausage maker had a huge wurst protruding from his first-floor shop at Fourth. At St. Marks Place the family crest of the Medici family with its three gilt balls indicated a pawnbroker. Byrne stopped at the intersection and looked east, where he could now see the skeletal trees of Tompkins Square, and he touched the side of his face with his fingertips where the bruise from last night was still tender, but he smiled at the recollection of his wand against the back of the head of a Five Pointer.

The farther north he marched, the better the business venues. Still, most of them had adopted an Old World style of hanging their signs out over the sidewalks to gain attention: an enormous pair of eyeglasses advertised an optician; an outsized cutout of a violin, a musical instrument shop.

Soon he began to move through areas where he rarely traveled unless on police business and where, as a citizen, he didn't belong. Large, multistoried homes of stately architecture adorned the side streets, although age and the city's constant soot and pollution had stained their facades. Even the rich could not partition off the air. Past Fourteenth Street, he glanced west and could see the buildings of Stuyvesant Square Park, named after one of the richest patriarchs of the city, where he had once delivered a man of means to the New York Infirmary after a beating in a brothel down on Bowery. It was all done quietly, of course, but despite warnings from his superiors, Byrne had never forgotten the man's name and had tucked it away for some future use.

His ability to remember even the most mundane details was something Captain Sweeney had both praised Byrne for and warned him against.

"You've a sharp mind, lad. Wasted down here and truth be told, wasted in this department, considering. Mind that memory of yours doesn't get you in trouble, Michael. Some things are best forgotten in this godforsaken life. The reason you're here, hell, the reason we're all here is to forget the past and move on to a better future, boy. Don't let what's already happened get in the way of what can be."

Byrne had listened intently to the man's lessons. And as was his nature, he would never forget a single word, or anything else that cared to strike his mind.

Within another mile, he began to feel anxious, a shiver of nerves running into the muscles of his upper back. Ahead were the red brick walls of Bellevue Hospital, the notorious house of the mentally deranged. Byrne had not forgotten a single whispered word that he'd overheard between his mother and neighbors after his father's disappearance on a winter day years ago.

"Screechin' like a madman, he was, Ann Marie."

"Wild as a cut beast one minute, starin' inta the afterworld the next."

"It was in his eyes, luv. Ya can't deny that. His mind was gone."

"It's the best, Ann Marie. Before he turns on ye and the boys."

"Three times this month, Ann. Naked in the freezin' street. He's insane, woman. Deal with it."

His mother always denied it. She would never admit that she'd had their father, her own husband, committed. The tale told to her sons about their father's accident on the street had been her story, and she stuck to it.

But after he'd been made a cop, Byrne would ask for his father by name at Bellevue and a dozen other madhouses in the city whenever he was in a district on assignment. He tried to make it sound official, as if he were investigating a crime. The intake officials would sometimes pretend to go through the lists, finally looking up to give him a raised eyebrow that only meant that for a bit of a bribe they might have someone who fit the description. He'd even paid a couple of times at first, only to have some poor bugger marched out who was a foot shorter or some dark-skinned European who would no more pass for Irish than an African slave. But even the old white-skinned wretches they'd bring forward, Byrne could always tell by the eyes. He would know his own father's eyes if he saw them again, even if Da had gone insane.

Today he had to march on. Was he giving up the search for a father who he still believed was lost if not dead? Yes, he supposed he was. He had someone else to search for now, and a train to Florida was a portal to that quest. As he walked north, the smell of the East River blew in, an air salty and fresh mixed with the refuse and excrement piled along its banks. He took out his own cheap watch and checked the time: seven fifteen. The sidewalks around him were already starting to b usy up with pedestrians, their nostrils blowing steam as they made their way through still freezing temperatures. They were mostly laborers at this time of day, men in the trade uniforms of construction and iron workers and steamfitters moving west as he was now along Forty-second Street. Within two blocks he could see the enormous train shed of the new Grand Central Station rising up at Lexington Avenue. The glass and steel construction dwarfed everything around it, and it was not yet finished. Already Byrne could hear the clanging echoes of iron against iron, the dragging friction of hard stone being moved. He went through the instructions in his head: meet with Pinkerton detective Shawn Harris on lower track three aboard the southbound train to Washington, D.C.

Byrne had worked the station as a cop when it was in different stages of construction, but when he entered the enormous waiting area this morning and looked out from the staircase, it was still bewildering in size and scope. Sixteen thousand square feet of chiseled and carved stone and marble, and across the way a cast-iron eagle with a wingspan that had to equal the length of any wagon on the street outside. Byrne stood a full five minutes, staring at the movement of people below, appearing in miniature like insects scurrying to assignments unknown. Unconsciously, he reached inside his coat and touched the shaft of his baton. He could not help but think of himself as like them, impotent BBs in a boxcar, as he moved down to join them.

At an information kiosk he was directed to the southbound Hudson River Railroad line below. In the bowels of the building, the noise created by the massive steam engines and their giant wheels screeching along steel rails was an assault on the ears and caused Byrne to narrow his eyes in a grimace. Making his way by the directions given, he had to search through clouds of smoke and steam to find the numbered markers and letterings. He stopped a uniformed railway worker and shouted in his ear "The Flagler departure?"

In response he got a finger wagged in a northerly direction, and of the response shouted back, the words "number ninety" were all he could make out. With his shoulders hunched as if to shield his chest from the onslaught, Byrne made his way down the platform, dodging the wheeled wooden carts of baggage handlers and the occasional geyser of steam spurting from the undercarriage of the train until his attention was snatched by a handsome forest-green railcar with a gilded "90" on its façade. He took a step back to take in the entire car. Above the row of windows, the name Florida East Coast Railway flickered in the same gold lettering. It was Flagler's private rail car. Since Byrne couldn't determine by sight which end of the train car held the back door, he approached the northern end and put one foot onto the iron stair step. When he stood up, his nose met the knee caps of a large man balefully staring down into his face.

"My name is Shawn Harris," the man said. "And you had best be one Michael Byrne, lad. Or your ass is mine."

After he had assured the estimable Mr. Harris that he was indeed Michael Byrne, he was allowed to board the train "after you wipe the grime and shite from those company shoes, m'boy. We don't allow that part of New York City to travel aboard Mr. Flagler's railroad."

Once his soles were passable, Byrne climbed up the wrought iron stair and joined Mr. Harris inside the car. The warmth was the first of several surprises Byrne encountered as the two men entered.

"This, lad, is number 90," Harris said with a sweep of his giant paw. The grand movement instantly struck Byrne as out of place for a big Irish thug of a former cop. But he soon understood the man's pride.

The interior walls of Mr. Flagler's private car were paneled in a light-colored satinwood and framed in hand-carved white mahogany that even without the aid of the electric lamps gave the place a feel of sunshine that was the polar opposite of the dark, polluted gray of the city Byrne had just walked through.

Passing through the sitting areas and a desk surrounded by shelves of books with gilded bindings, Byrne was aware that he'd unconsciously pulled in his elbows and turned his hips so as not to come even close to touching anything. The furniture was upholstered in decorative floral designs of greens and gold, mirrored in the carpeting and curtains. Harris looked back with a raised eyebrow and warning tip of his chin to the gleaming bronze chandelier as he maneuvered his big head around its cut glass. Byrne looked up, even though he knew his own height did not put him in danger of touching the object, but he noticed when he did that even the Empire ceilings of the car were green and decorated with gold leaf. His mouth must have been hanging open, for Harris cleared his throat and winked at the younger man's show of amazement. As they passed through the dining area, Byrne saw the fireplace, flames dancing at a low level, which explained the warmth of the place. He'd barely had time to take in the opulence when Harris opened a door and they both stepped out onto the open balustrade at the opposite end of the car. The shot of cold in his nostrils caused Byrne's eyes to water, and Harris let him take a second to adjust.

"That, my young detective, is Mr. Flagler's sanctuary, and our number one duty is to keep out anyone that don't belong inside.

"Mr. or Mrs. Flagler or his chief, Mr. McAdams, is consulted directly before any person is allowed to enter. You screw that assignment up, lad, and you'll be off the train regardless of whether she's stopped or still movin', eh?"

"I understand, sir," Byrne said, giving the sergeant due respect even while still measuring the man.

"Good," Harris said. "We run shifts on the fore and aft platforms when we're stopped for loading or unloading and especially when we spend anytime overnight on a side track for any reason. "Mr. Flagler considers number 90 to be his hotel room on the road, so that's the way we protect it and him."

Byrne nodded, absorbing as he always did, and then working out a response if one was called for.

"Protect from who?" he finally figured it best to ask.

"Ha!" Harris gave a snort, which Byrne was soon to realize was his standard guffaw at all things he understood and felt others didn't. "From the same goddamn scalawags and supposed business moochers that you guard him from in the city, boy. 'Cept here they're more brazen cause maybe they think since they're on the same train as he is, that he's like their neighbor or something. Most of these wags wouldn't dare walk up to the man's house or office in the city but think they can come right through the train cars to his door and tap him for an audience."

As a cop, Byrne had indeed once been ordered to provide "security" for the Flaglers' mansion on Forty-second Street, just a few blocks west of Grand Central, on a night when a crowd of so-called protesters had gotten their courage up to march against the rich and powerful. After a minor scuffle with a knot of the more drunk and aggressive of them, it had been one of the more boring nights he'd spent on the police force. Yet he knew even now that the small legend of that night had somehow led to this very day.

"Then there's the beggars and assorted nasties who try to push their way through when we're at some common rail stop along the way down South," Harris said. "But I don't figure that's going to be a problem for you, eh, Byrne."

And there it was. Proof of what wouldn't be said to him directly when his Pinkerton commander came and gave him this assignment.

Harris was giving him that wink and a grin that meant he wanted the story from the origin. Byrne pretended he didn't understand and simply nodded.

"Oh, come on, lad. At least show me this little piece of weaponry I've heard bragged on by men I'd have to admit aren't easily impressed."

Byrne had already anticipated the inevitability of the request, and in a motion like a magician's flick of a satin scarf, the baton flashed up in his hand with a whisper and was instantly in front of his face, bringing Harris' eyes up to meet his.

"I heard there were six men, big men, mind you, lyin' in the gutter outside Mr. Flagler's house within less than a one minute round," Harris said, focused on the short steel wand. "Boys said you never skinned a knuckle, never drew your gun."

"There were only four," Byrne said, and then with a snap of his forearm, the baton telescoped to three times its length with a sound like a switchblade being opened. "And they weren't that big."

The display did not make Harris jump, only his hand moved, tucking quickly into the thick breast flap of his coat.

"Aye," he said, now measuring the piece of steel from its tip to Byrne's fist and then looking back up to the younger man's eyes. "Let's get you back to the caboose, lad, where we'll have some breakfast and I'll fill you in on the rest of your duties before he himself gets here."

Byrne jumped down from the steps onto the platform, landing lightly on his toes. He could feel the big Irishman's eyes on the back of his shoulders and knew it was he who was now being measured. He retracted his baton and tucked it away in an inside pocket where it would be easily accessible.

Chapter 4

It was barely eight o'clock and the sun was already heating the back of Ida May Fluery's indigo blouse. She could feel internal heat rise to the collar at her throat and spread up to the perspiration beading on her wide dark forehead. She was standing on the very same spot where she had so often stood—at the head of the cul de sac in the Styx, organizing if she needed to, greeting when she wanted to, and cajoling when she had to. But this morning there was no shade on the hard-packed sand in front of what had been her home. The tree cover was now blackened and bare, the sun streaked through still rising wisps of brown smoke. This morning Miss Ida was giving out prayers and consolation in whispers and small tight hugs to the residents of her community.

Ida had not slept. She'd remained up throughout the night, helplessly watching until the flames that consumed every dwelling in the Styx had finally eaten all they could and then settled down as coals glowing like lumps of living, satisfied evil.

Last night when word jumped across the railroad bridge to West Palm Beach that the Styx was burning, a handful of her neighbors made it across the lake before some official closed off access to the island, stating that only firefighters were allowed across. No one, of course, in any such capacity ever arrived at the site of the blaze. Ida was there. So too were a couple of the stable boys and three cooks who were on duty at the Royal Poinciana Hotel on the lakefront a mile or so away. The boys had made foolish attempts to run in close to the flames to rescue things they deemed valuable. The women simply stood and watched and wept. By sunup an assistant hotel manager, a Southern white man of indeterminate age, had arrived and gently herded the onlookers back to the Breakers with the promise of food and clean uniforms and then with equally gentle words reminded them that they still had to report for work today.

When the manager stood in front of Ida May, she seemed to look straight through him.

"Mizz Ida," he said quietly, "ya'll going to have to supervise your people back at the hotel, ma'am."

Her eyes were not those of some unfortunate in shock but those of a woman who could envision her duties on some chalkboard slate only she could see.

"I will do my supervising from here, sir," she said, tempering her manner so as not to sound like she was giving the orders. "May I suggest, sir, that when folks are finally allowed to cross back from West Palm, you could please have a few at a time come out to their houses. I will make sure they can see what they need to see, sir. Then I'll get their work schedules right and send them back. Will that be acceptable, sir?"

The assistant manager seemed to focus on something slightly beyond the crown of her head while he considered how to explain it to his own superiors and make the plan his own.

"I'll take these folks with me," he said. "And send the next directly."

When he walked away, Ida took up her spot in front of the ashes of her house and supervised the comings and goings. She watched the disbelieving expressions of each of the new arrivals as they approached the blackened cluster of charred timbers and ash. And when the faces broke with despair or with anger, she passed her whispers of strength or possibilities along.

"Gone be alright now, Mazzie. You safe, that's all that matters. Right?"

"Careful now, Earl. You know the Lord don't take anything ya'll really need. You know that, Earl. Right?"

"It's OK now, Corrine. Come here, give a hug, sweetheart. Your children are all safe, right? They with you and that's everything, you know?"

After an hour or so, that particular group of neighbors would straggle back from their individual tragedies, their skin smeared with soot, the men carrying the head of some metal tool or heat-warped tin box, the women with a scrap of seared cloth, a blackened iron cook pot or an empty, charred picture frame.

Marjory McAdams was aboard the third wagonload to arrive. She had left the Styx while it was still dark and the sparks of the fire were just beginning to settle. She'd waited there with Ida May for hours after young Thom Martin had left in the calash, promising he'd soon return with help.

"I cannot believe someone hasn't responded," she'd said in the middle of the night, looking expectantly back down the road to the hotel as if a fire brigade would surely come swinging round the corner at any second, as it would if the Styx were midtown Manhattan. Ida May had ignored her comments, knowing the truth and thus the futility in the young woman's expectations. Marjory had finally given up trying to talk Ida into returning to the hotel with her and had marched off on foot. When she returned now, she had not changed her clothing, which was still soot stained. Her face had been hastily wiped clean, but she had not even taken the time to change her shoes, which were dust covered, as was the bottom eight inches of her skirt. In the light of day, the destruction before her had changed from the smoky blur of varying shades of gray and black to the stark outlines of broken angles and spires of charred wood pointing oddly up like giant corroded fingers. The rising wind from the ocean had just begun to sweep the brown wisps of smoke from the surrounding treetops. Marjory waited until the new arrivals passed Miss Ida's consoling whispers and then watched them as they walked into the remains, their heads moving back and forth, taking in the alien sights and saying nothing. When they had all wandered off, she approached the head housekeeper, softly cupped her shoulder and bent her cheek to the woman's grayed and soot stained head.

"I have heard that everyone has been accounted for, Mizz Ida. Everyone is alive. Thank the Lord that the fair drew most everyone across the lake. That in itself is a blessing."

The old woman did not move her head, neither away from nor into the consoling hug of the young white girl. Her only reaction was a slight movement of her cheeks, which sucked in as if a small taste of bile had entered her mouth.

"My father says Mr. Flagler is on his way from New York City this very day," Marjory said. "You know he'll take care of you all. He's a good man. My father said there is no doubt that he will find quarters for you either at the hotel or across the lake, so don't you worry."

Ida did not respond. She had been across the lake many times to the new city of West Palm Beach. The cheap, tossed-together buildings did not bother her. And the few merchants there were just starting out, so they were not yet profitable enough to turn away colored folks with money to spend. Ida had even gone to a service there at the Tabernacle Missionary Baptist Church, which was a simple wood plank structure built on pilings on a plot of scrub pines at the edge of the town. She recalled the preacher as young and full of a heartfelt passion. So the idea of moving yet again was not something she feared. Ida had made new starts before. This would be no different from her families' move from Charlotte when the Abernathy family began buying up farm acreage to expand that city, or in Savannah years later, when she'd been displaced by a new mercantile warehouse being built near the waterfront. As a woman whose family had always worked for others, Ida May Fluery knew the rules of the real world: when money comes to a place, those who are not owners are pushed aside.

Her natural skepticism, born of nearly sixty years of experience, told her this situation was no different. No different, that is, until screams started sounding from the far depths of the Styx.

The horses were the first to hear. Just as they started to pull away with a wagonload of residents, the team's ears pricked up at the unnatural sound, then their nostrils flared and they balked in their traces.

Miss Ida may have picked it up next and mistook the high, keening noise as some kind of animal cry. But the third wail, closing quickly from the east, caught the attention of everyone at the clearing and all of those in the wagon, and they all turned their heads.

"What in Christ's name now?" said the driver.

In the distance the image of Shantice Carver could be seen stumbling into view, and Miss Ida let a snort escape through her nose. Marjory looked over in surprise as she had never witnessed a derogatory utterance come from the woman in the two years they'd known each other. The young Carver woman was in a half jog, her arms bent at the elbow and hands up in her face as if to cover her eyes from some horrific sight, yet her fingers were splayed enough to allow her to see where it was she was running to. With her arms in such a position, she seemed to toddle more than run, and the high-pitched noise coming from her mouth gradually turned from unintelligible screeching to words: "Theysaman, theysaman, theysaman…"

No one moved to meet her, but the anguished cries seemed to pull Marjory out of her initial shock, and she alone stepped forward. She realized the distraught figure was certainly more than a girl, and from the bouncing of her bosom was more in the line of a young woman. Still, she took the poor thing by the shoulders and allowed Shantice to bury her face into Marjory's own neck as if comforting a child.

"It's OK now, it's OK."

Despite the tableau of emotion, those in the wagon were now only mildly interested, as if they had seen such a display before or had reason not to feel much compassion for this one of their own. But Miss Ida relented and walked over to the embrace between the two women, which had gone on long enough to have become an embarrassment.

"All right, Shantice. All right," Miss Ida said with a voice not exactly comforting but still understanding of the situation. "It's a hard time for everyone. What has you so all tore up, girl?"

At the sound of Ida's voice, the woman stepped back away from Marjory, and again her fingers went fluttering up into her face.

"Theysadedman, theysadedman, theys…"

"All right, all right, now slow down, woman. Cain't nobody understand what you're trying to say with all that screechin'. You take a good long breath now and slow down." It was obvious that the woman had taken stern orders from Miss Ida enough times in the past to nod her head and immediately start to suck air into her mouth and begin to swallow. Her next words were both several octaves lower and decibels quieter.

"Mizz Ida, ma'am. They is a dead man yonder near my place."

This time those listening in the wagon began to rise and jump down on the ground. The driver was now too entranced himself to complain though he stayed in his seat.

"All right. All right, Shantice," Ida repeated. She reached out to take the woman's shaky hands in her own and covered them as if calming both Shantice's heart and her own.

"Who is it, Shantice? Tell me who it is that's dead?"

Now the small group was stone silent, waiting for grief to slap them.

"It's a stranger, ma'am," the woman called Shantice said. "I ain't never seen him before, ma'am, honest to God."

Ida's brow furrowed in skepticism, a reaction that caught Marjory by surprise as much as the woman's plea for believability.

"Now, Shantice, get yourself together, woman. You know every man in the Styx and most every other man on this here island. You think hard who you seen out there," Ida ordered the woman.

"I ain't never seen him, ma'am. God's truth. He's all burnt up, an he gots money ..." At this point the woman's hands started back to fluttering and her voice began to cry and climb. "He gots money in his mout," she finally said, her fingertips now dancing near her own lips.

With the new information, Ida shook her head with incredulity and started to turn back into the group as if this tale was a child's exaggeration that went beyond belief at a time already full of unbelievable events.

"An he's white, Mizz Ida," Shantice blurted out, her words catching the elderly woman in midstride and freezing everyone within hearing distance. "It's a dead white man."

Chapter 5

The train was ready when Flagler was ready.

After a breakfast of hot oatmeal and weak coffee, during which his new supervisor gave him his duties until such time as they were out of the city, Michael Byrne was positioned at the head of Flagler's car number 90, where he was instructed to "stand ready like a Pinkerton man and don't let anyone approach while Flagler and his wife are boarding."

With a newly requisitioned knee-length woolen coat, Byrne stood rather comfortably in the cold, his hands clasped behind his back like he'd been taught as a police recruit, only moving up and down the loading platform. No one was within a car's length of number 90. The other passengers and material being loaded were up the tracks where the less glorious coaches and boxcars were aligned.

Byrne cut his eyes to the north when a contingent finally arrived out of the clouds of steam. Flagler was not difficult to pick out. He was the one in the middle, wearing a dark suit without an overcoat despite the cold. He was of average build—about five foot seven and a thin 140 pounds—despite his reputation as a giant of the business world. His most distinguishing feature was his full head of snow-white hair and a thick broom mustache to match. His back was straight, his chin held high, and his gait was best described as leisurely. He moved at a slow pace, though not because of any obvious infirmity. He was simply not a man in a hurry, nor one who needed to be.

Byrne knew little about the man other than he was rumored to be in his late seventies and had long ago become rich as the partner of John D. Rockefeller when the two of them established the Standard Oil Company. His was a station of the upper class that a man like Byrne did well to stand out of the way of and at attention to. Flagler's world was nothing that a working-class mick such as Byrne could ever understand, nor would he want to. They're different, the rich, and so be it.

Walking a half step behind Flagler was a woman who Byrne assumed was his wife. He was careful to only glance at her so as not to catch her eye, and he noted that just from her profile she looked many years younger than Flagler and was dressed in the fine conservative style of a woman of means. Her skirts were not flowing; her coat was not of ostentatious fur or fabric. Her dark hat was certainly large but plumed with only a small shaft of feathers of a kind Byrne had never seen even though he'd stood guard at several dignitary functions or special performances at the Metropolitan Opera.

Following behind the couple was Flagler's personal valet and a phalanx of business types carrying briefcases. And then the porters wheeling an entire baggage cart loaded with luggage. Harris nodded in greeting to Flagler and then helped Mrs. Flagler board. Then the couple disappeared into their car. Byrne would barely even glimpse them for the rest of the trip.

He and Harris helped load the baggage, and within ten minutes of Flagler's arrival, the train whistle ripped through the enclosed space under Grand Central Station and the train pulled out.

Hours later Byrne's eyes were still watering, and it was from something besides the cold. The train was only minutes out of the rail yards at Jersey City, heading south. There was something foreign in the air that seemed to sear the insides of his lungs when he took deep breaths. He was stationed at a designated spot at the forward door to private car number 90, where Harris had placed him.

"No one goes past you without Mr. Flagler's personal word," Harris had instructed. "I'll be back once we get under way again and take you on a bit of a tour."

So Byrne stood on the outside platform and found that if he inched his back close to the adjoining car in front, he was able to withstand the cold by hunkering down into the turned-up cowl of the coat and burrowing his hands deep in its pockets. The morning's events—seeing Flagler and his entourage close up, the glimpse of the rich interior of the private train car that he was to guard and the melancholy sight of New

York City fading behind them—had spun so quickly in his head that he was just now able to use the minutes alone on the platform to assess his decision to take on this assignment.

If he was to be nothing more than a bodyguard for Flagler and a watchman for his rail car, then he'd made a mistake. The work that he'd done for Captain Sweeney—putting together the names of certain Tammany bosses and politicians and documenting their travels to and from the opium dens and brothels of the Lower East Side—had come with the promise of a certain career. Sweeney had been impressed by young Byrne's ability to write, a skill not learned through schooling but from pure memory and copying of words and phrases picked up from newspapers and signage on the streets and the handbills that Danny was sometimes paid to give out. Sweeney had then been shocked further by Byrne's photographic memory of faces and seemingly flawless ability to attach names to such faces.

The young police officer's lists and detailed observations had, according to Sweeney, been invaluable in the department's battle against corruption, but the changes would be slow in coming. At one point, the captain had said it was too dangerous for Byrne to stay in the department. Thus, the Pinkerton offer.

The arrival of Danny's telegram had been an additional push and had given him this Florida destination, and Sweeney encouraged it.

"A perfect solution. Go south into the sun for a while, Michael," Sweeney said. "It'll be like a fine vacation and then you can come back home when things calm down a bit and these bastards from Tammany Hall are out on their arses. Then we've got a job waiting for you, son."

But now he was second-guessing, watching the buildings of Jersey City shrink down with each mile and the landscape becoming greener and more expansive than he'd ever witnessed as a city boy. Florida seemed a foolish dream now. What if he couldn't find his brother? What the hell would he do in the sun anyway? Only rich New Yorkers or people with tuberculosis went to Florida seeking a place to stay warm and breathe more easily. As if the thought alone caused it, Byrne bent over in a coughing fit, and as if on cue Harris nearly knocked him overboard coming through the door to the other cars.

"Don't be afraid of it, lad," Harris said, again sporting the smile that said, I know what you don't know. "It's the air, son. Your city lungs'll have to get used to it."

Byrne straightened and spat down onto the rail bed rushing by below.

"Why," he said, wiping his mouth with the back of his sleeve. "What's in the air?"

"Nothing," Harris said, now starting to laugh. "There's nothing in it but clear, clean air the likes of which you haven't taken a breath of since you were born in some Irish tenement, what with the soot and smoke and rubbish stink of the place.

"It's like a taste of pure water that you pour into your mouth for the first time. It's so different, your body isn't ready for it. Keep breathin', boy. It's good for you."

Byrne took a shorter breath, but his eyes were on Harris, and the burn of his deprecating tone was running up into Byrne's ears.

"You're name isn't Harris, is it?" he finally said, his eyes holding the big man's.

The older detective lost his smile.

"It was O'Hara when my father and two sisters got to New York in 1860, lad. The old man figured it was better changed unless you wanted to starve with the rest of the Irish. You might do well to consider it, Byrne," Harris said. "Now, let's take a walk."

Harris led the way, passing slowly through the first passenger car, touching the top corners of each seat as he passed. The gesture was made not to collect his balance—his experience of walking through the rolling train was like that of a seaman, and he rarely wavered—but to signify some sense of ownership to the riders he seemed to study one at a time.

Byrne followed, but his sea legs were not yet established. He pitched side to side with the sway of the cars and twice bumped into the shoulders of men sitting on the edge of the aisle.

"Pardon me," he said both times.

When they left the first car and stood on the outside connecting platform, Harris lectured him.

"Don't ever offer apologies, lad. You're security here, and the likes of them know that just from the look of you." Harris tipped his chin back toward the car. "A little respect goes a long way if somethin' should occur. It also warns 'em if they start to think they can cross you. You know what the uniform does on the street? It's the same here. You want them to know you're Pinkerton."

Byrne knew the tactic: force and bully. It was not a method he preferred. His best work was done undercover, working the sidelines and shadows. He did not fear direct confrontation; the steel whip in his hand was more than effective, but he liked the advantage of observing trouble before jumping into it.

"Now let's see that talent of yours that Captain Sweeney bragged on to get you there," Harris said. "I'll go through the next car. You follow in five minutes and I'll meet you on the next platform."

Byrne waited until the door closed on Harris's back and then slipped his watch from his pocket and checked the time. He watched as the landscape out in the midmorning sun changed to bare winter trees and chilled brown shrubbery and the occasional rail siding flashing by. He closed his eyes and took a deep breath of the air, and this time he held it without choking. The smell was of leaves decomposing on the ground, not unpleasant like the odor of rot, but something simply changing and refueling the soil. It was a sensation completely foreign to him.

When the five minutes had passed, Byrne opened the door to the passenger car and walked through at a pace that was unhurried but not so slow as to draw attention. No one fails to at least look up as a stranger passes by in such close quarters, but what they notice, and what each one remembers, is the key. Captain Sweeney had obviously passed on word of Byrne's ability.

When he stepped out onto the open platform, Harris was waiting with a smarmy grin on his face, arms folded across his broad chest almost in the manner of a challenge.

"OK, lad. Tell me what you saw."

"Twelve passengers," Byrne started, "Seven men and two women in their midtwenties. The women are both married. Three children, two of them girls. The younger of the women with her son is nervous enough to be holding her St. Christopher's in her left hand. Her shoes are the kind a woman who had several miles and days to go would wear. The other woman is wary of men. She keeps cutting her eyes up at the old guy up front and flinched hard when I came even with her shoulders. Her clothes make her a social elite. If she's going to Philadelphia, her husband is probably a businessman."

Harris had stopped grinning and stared at Byrne's eyes.

"And the gentlemen?"

"Not a farmer among them," Byrne started. "The three by themselves are salesmen is my guess by the worn threads on their jacket cuffs and the resoled shoes. The valises they have are probably filled with samples and clean white shirts.

"The three fellows facing each other in the middle are interesting. They're playing three-card monte, but there's no money being exchanged. It looks like the two on the north seats are actually teaching the scam to the other. By his accent, he's probably a Pole from Brooklyn. I'm not sure about the document briefcases they all seem to be carrying. But shysters sometimes all look alike even when they aren't trying. "

By now Harris had raised that spiked eyebrow of his and had dropped his folded arms to rest on his newly relaxed belly.

"And the last?" he said.

"Older man." Byrne hesitated, picking his words. "A poor man's version of Mr. Flagler himself. The cigar wallet in his suit coat pocket. Three rings, one with a nice stone. The shoes are new and expensive, but the collar of his shirt is too off-white for professional laundry. That briefcase he's got next to him has a lock on it; never seen one of them before."

Again he hesitated.

"Is that all?" Harris said.

"The old guy was studying me as much as I was him. Nothing gets past that one. Reminds me of Sweeney himself."

"Aye," Harris said. "And the old captain didn't let you slip past either, did he now. Right as rain he was with the likes of you, young Byrne. Talent as advertised. Now I'll have to worry about you takin' my own job."

Byrne did not blush at the compliment. He'd been asked to demonstrate his photographic memory before and he had not shown Harris even the beginning of his abilities.

He was later to learn that the women were indeed wives, one of a Philadelphia investment banker and the other meeting her husband who was homesteading a piece of land in Florida. She would continue with them for the entirety of the trip. The salesmen were just that, men working the connections between New York and Philadelphia. The three budding card sharks were "binder boys," as Harris called them. They were young men who'd put chunks of money together through whatever means: beg, borrow or steal. Now they were headed for Florida and the promised land of booming real estate. Harris again explained that these three would join a growing number of speculators who had found early on that previously useless land in the newly blossoming cities along Mr. Flagler's rail line was gaining in value by the day.

"The crooks'll get a stake from some business type in New York and come down and buy a binder on the sale of a piece of land and then slap away the mosquitoes while the price keeps risin'," Harris said.

Harris explained that a binder was a nonrefundable down payment that required the remainder of the cost of the land to be paid within thirty days.

"They might swat the insects for twenty days, maybe even twenty-eight before they sell it again before the final payment is due. And the profit, m'boy. You ain't never seen the price of land climb the way it does in Florida.

"I watched a binder pass through six hands before the last fool got caught holdin' the bag with no more buyers around. But hell, this is just the beginning of these rascals. That group is goin' to the end of the line in Miami, and believe me, they're playin' three-card monte with land deeds down there, lad."

Byrne filed the information away. It takes money to make money, unless of course you're a thief or taking advantage of someone else's cash. Those weren't hard lessons to learn on the streets of the Lower East Side. They were also lessons he'd watched his brother employ on a regular basis. If they were three of a kind in the business of fleecing someone, maybe they had run across Danny in their travels. Michael would find an acceptable time and place to speak again with that group.

"And what about the gentleman?" Byrne said, wanting the same background on the older man who had eyeballed him.

Harris tried to straighten his face to give a flat look that was a mighty effort for a rough Irishman.

"Faustus," he said. "Stay clear, Byrne. He'll be tryin' to recruit you to some unholy religion that'll lead to trouble that we have no part of and no relation to. Leave that sleepin' dog lie, hear?"

Byrne was ordered to again take up his post on Mr. Flagler's car while they made a short stop at the North Philadelphia station where the Germantown and Chestnut Hill lines merged. Soon enough they crossed the deep-running Schuylkill River and merged into yet another line. Byrne watched the landscape change yet again as they approached the city and caught sight of charred destruction. It became evident that the main rail station had recently been destroyed by fire, and although the tracks had been cleared, the scent of charred and smoldering wood was still in the air. Byrne coughed and thought of his new sensitivity to clean air and how quickly one could recognize the sullied version.

Byrne climbed number 90's outside ladder. From a vantage point over the roof he could see the French Renaissance building of city hall growing in the distance, with flags aflutter at several cornices surrounding the spire at its middle, where a statue of William Penn stood impossibly high in the sky.

When the train pulled slowly into Philadelphia's center city stop at Broad Street, Harris jumped down and gave Byrne a hand signal to do the same. They oversaw the uncoupling of Flagler's car and its positioning on a side rail, where it would sit alone like some elegant museum piece while the smoke and ash and soot of the rest of the rail yard swirled round it.

Byrne stared wide eyed at the grand towers of the Masonic Temple across the wide street.

"The exterior you're looking at is built of Cape Ann syenite, which takes its name from Syne in Upper Egypt, where it was quarried for monuments by the ancient Egyptians," a deep voice said. Byrne turned to see the man called Faustus standing just behind him, worrying on a pair of calfskin gloves. "The other sides are of Fox Island granite from the coast of Maine. Each stone, in accordance with Masonic tradition, was cut, squared, marked and numbered at the quarries and brought here ready for use."

"Is that so?" Byrne said, turning his head back to the Temple but admonishing himself for not detecting the man's presence earlier, "Mr. Faustus."

Despite the use of his name by a complete stranger, the elderly man did not miss a beat.

"Amadeus Faustus," he said, extending his gloved hand. Byrne shook it. "She was dedicated on Friday, September 26, 1873," Faustus continued. "The eighty-seventh anniversary of the independence of the Grand Lodge of Free and Accepted Masons of Pennsylvania."

This time Byrne looked directly into the man's light-gray eyes, holding them. Was this the pitch of recruitment that Harris had warned him against?

"Thank you, sir. I will not forget," he said.

Faustus did not disengage his look. He reached into his vest pocket.

"I have no doubt of that, young man," he said and flipped a large coin into the air in Byrne's direction. Byrne snatched the object with a movement and speed like that of a snake strike. His reaction was habit, formed from hours of practice at a game he and Danny had perfected. Since they'd been kids on the street they'd passed idle time by positioning three coins on their forearms and then in a motion tossed all three into the air in front of them. The goal was to snatch all three out of the air, individually with separate strikes of the hand, palm down, before the last coin touched the ground. They'd been working on four coins when Danny left New York.

Byrne turned the coin in his hand and slipped it into his pocket.

"Not going to bite it to test its quality?" Faustus said, passing him in the direction of the entryway to the Temple.

"No sir," Byrne said. "That would be crass." He heard a sharp whistle from the direction of number 90 and hustled back to Harris's side.

"Mr. Flagler will need you to escort him to a business meeting, lad, while I accompany the missus to Wanamakers," Harris said. They squared their shoulders in the direction of the departing Faustus, watching after him. Byrne showed the detective the coin the old man had tossed to him.

"I don't recognize it," Byrne said. "Worth anything?"

Harris looked at the markings on the metal and laughed.

"Not a penny," he said. "It's an old Confederate fifty-cent piece re-strike, lad. Not worth the metal it's stamped on. Useless, just like the man who gave it to ye."

Chapter 6

By midmorning there were more white people in the Styx than had ever set foot there at one time before.

Mr. Wayne T. Pearson, the manager of the Poinciana and the Breakers, had arrived with his assistant. At first he'd simply been riled by the lack of a consistent staff at the hotels as the Negro workers had begun taking turns surveying their burned homes and sifting through the ashes for anything they could salvage. But when reports that the body of a man, a white man, had been found in the debris, Pearson was compelled to investigate. The fire had now become an urgent matter of rumor control.

Since it was his wagon being used to transport the black workers, Mr. Carroll, the head liveryman, was also there. Thom Martin had relayed word of the white man's body, and that news, as well as blatant curiosity, had pulled Carroll to the place as well. And then there was Miss McAdams, who had not left Ida May Fluery's side.

When Mr. Pearson arrived, the rest of the group was still standing near the rear of Shantice Carver's burned-out shack, and they parted as if his substantial chin were the prow of boat.

Pearson did not say a word, only reading the eyes of the gathered people who glanced back at a flame-darkened lean-to. It was indication enough where the focus of the day lay. He stepped beyond the gathering and looked down on the corpse of the dead man. The body was stretched out on a platform of wood and protected to a degree by the roof of the lean-to, which had obviously been used to store kindling and firewood. Pearson surprised the onlookers by going down on his haunches to get a better view. His assistant initially tried to follow suit but blanched at something—the look of the dead man's partially scared face or maybe the smell of burned flesh—and quickly abandoned his boss for a nearby tree trunk on which to retch. Pearson did not react. He was an older man and had seen battle in the Civil War as a teenager. Dreams and visions had visited him many times since. This experience was a mild dose of death.

Before him lay a man who appeared to be in his late twenties, broad of shoulder and tall, probably five feet nine inches. The body was dressed in a dark-colored blouse, possibly of some kind of linen or even silk, which appeared to have actually melted in spots and adhered to the man's skin. His trousers were of a style befitting an evening suit. His shoes were definitely made for a more formal affair than one this place might offer. Despite the disfiguring burns to the man's face, Pearson could see high cheekbones and remnants of a mustache that was indeed partially wrapped around a roll of singed U.S. paper currency protruding from the corpse's mouth. Pearson was unable to determine the denomination of the bills. Some six inches below that, where the dead man's Adam's apple should have been, was a blackened hole. Though his past experiences had been with wounds created by musket balls, Pearson had no trouble discerning that a bullet had been fired into the man's throat.

The manager finally stood and stepped back to give the site a more thoughtful survey, noting the near total destruction of anything flammable, including the four walls of the nearby shack. He took a folding knife from his pocket, approached the corner of the lean-to and took a deep carving from the wood and examined it. As he suspected, the wood, probably salvaged from some shipwreck or washed up on the beach from a floundering barge, was Dade County pine, a wood known to be so hard and strong that it was nearly impossible to drive an iron nail through it. The wood's properties also made it impervious to only the hottest of flame, and it had indeed sheltered the dead man's body instead of hastening its total consumption by fire.

"Does anyone recognize this poor soul?" Pearson finally asked aloud, looking specifically at the livery supervisor and young Martin and then at his own assistant. "Percival? Step up here and take a look."

The assistant hesitated at the request and only jerked his knee as if his foot was railroad spiked into the dirt.

"For God's sake, son, it isn't diseased, it's only dead," Pearson said, and the younger man finally did manage to take a closer look but only shook his head in the negative and then backed off.

"Has anyone gone across the lake to inform the sheriff?" Pearson then said, again looking only at the white people in attendance.

"Uh, I believe, sir, everyone was waiting on you, sir," Mr. Carroll said.

"Well, I am not the coroner, Mr. Carroll. I am only a hotel manager. I suggest you go fetch Sheriff Cox and let him do his job, and as for the rest of you, we have guests at the Poinciana and the Breakers who need not know anything of this." He finally eyeballed the Negro members of the group. "And should I find that those vacationers have heard of the details of this incident, then I will surely know from whose mouths those details came."

All of the workers were now nodding their bowed heads under their manager's baleful eye and starting to take small, nearly imperceptible steps away from the space as if Pearson was wrong about the diseased nature of the scene.

"Meantime, I do commend you, Mizz Fluery, for your impromptu scheduling in the face of this adversity, but we do have a hotel to run.

"And Mr. Carroll, I do suggest that after summoning Sheriff Cox, you make sure that nothing, and I do mean nothing, changes here before he arrives."

The manager then turned on his heel and stepped over to Miss McAdams, offering her his crooked arm.

"You, Miss, may return with me in my carriage," he said, with a look that was not meant to be challenged.

The ride to the hotel was made in silence. Pearson and Marjory McAdams sat in back, looking out opposite sides of the carriage while the manager's assistant sat up front with the driver. When they reached the turn to the Breakers' entrance, the assistant glanced over his shoulder for instruction. With a flip of his wrist, Pearson indicated to veer right to the Royal Poinciana. Before protesting that her accommodations were in the beachside hotel, Marjory caught herself and kept her lips sealed. She'd been in trouble before when she was discovered doing something "untoward" and knew it was useless to react to anyone other than her father.

She sat back in the carriage with her hands folded in her lap and stared out at the meticulous landscaping of hotel grounds. It was now nearing noontime, and the temperature had risen to the midseventies. The breeze from the ocean had also increased, and a scent of salt tinged the air. Couples were out walking along the wide, crushed-stone avenue, parasols raised against the sun. Others were bicycling toward the ocean. It was a quaint policy that no other vehicles were allowed on Flagler's hotel properties, certainly not the motorized kind that some of the wealthy guests from the North had recently been infatuated with. When Flagler's train pulled across the lake bridge to deliver his guests to what was now the largest resort hotel in the world, the noise of machines was something the oil tycoon's influential friends would not be bothered by. As an accommodation, guests moving about the island could be conveyed any distance in the hotel's "Afromobiles." These contraptions married a bicycle to a large wicker chair in which guests could ride while a valet peddled from behind, taking them to any destination or simply for an hour's ride about the property. These convyances were publicized as Afromobiles because most of the valets were Negro men.

As they passed three of these, Marjory looked carefully at the drivers, trying to discern from the look on their faces whether they knew what they had lost in the fire or were concerned over where they would sleep tonight. But their looks were as impassive and unemotional as if the men were part of the machinery they propelled. Marjory turned her eye to the rows of coconut palms that gracefully lined the avenue. Only the tuned ear heard the dead fronds in the tops, dried and scratching in the wind. She counted them, trying to distract herself from imagining the destination Mr. Pearson had in mind and in order to keep her mouth from getting her deeper into trouble. Instead, she speculated on who might identify the body now lying in the Styx, awaiting the sheriff, whose reputation preceded him as a man who was ironhanded when it came to keeping the sometimes boisterous rail workers in line during their off-hours on the mainland and also making sure nothing that contained a whiff of illegality or violence should cross Lake Worth onto Palm Beach Island's fantasy getaway. She'd met the sheriff once, at a social luncheon, and he struck her as someone as false and vulgar as the cheap cologne he wore at midday.

When they finally pulled into a turnabout at the rear of the massive Poinciana, a livery boy took the horses by their bridals and a valet helped Marjory and Pearson down. In the side yards off to the north, Marjory could see a small gathering of ladies and gentlemen watching what could only be Roseann Birch, in full Victorian skirt and in full swing, hammering a golf ball out into an open field from a tee specifically built for the driving range. Roseann, a stout and irrepressible woman in her fifties, was the wife of an extremely rich banker in New York City, and Marjory had seen her harrumph and flick off any man who questioned her participation in any activity at the hotel, be it golf, tennis, competitive swimming in the salt water pool or even skeet shooting.

"Men are simply boys with toys. The only deadly sports I stay away from are politics and real estate," she was famously known for saying aloud in mixed social settings, after which she usually downed a mint julep in one swallow, her eye challenging any man to match her estimable ability to consume alcohol.

Marjory followed Pearson up the marble stairs. As they crossed the expanse of the hotel's grand lobby, Pearson's heels clacked over the inlaid Italian tile, and every employee and nearly every guest tipped their heads in deference to the manager and half also made notice of Marjory. The men that she knew through introductions by her father indeed made it a point to touch the brims off their boaters and greet her by name as she passed. She greeted them by name if she remembered and by a subtle smile if she did not. Some of the newer guests were gaping up at the ornate frescoes on the ceilings or at the arrangements of bright orange bird-of-paradise flowers shooting erotically from their boat-shaped cocoons and accented with their deep-blue tongues. The new arrivals always tickled Marjory with their awe of Florida's tropical surprises, unique regardless of the guests' moneyed stations or wealth of travel experience.

At the front desk Pearson simply laid his hand on the polished onyx countertop and a sheaf of telegraphs and messages was placed in his palm. He moved on without glancing at them. Even though the manager had still not vocally indicated their destination, a bit rude by most standards, Marjory refused to ask, but she could tell by their path through the hotel and past the open lounges that they were headed toward Pearson's office.

At the oak door of the manager's suite, Pearson acted the gentleman, opening it and allowing her to enter first. He employed no secretary, passed through the outer office without breaking stride, opened the door to his inner sanctum for Marjory, but stopped his assistant with a single glance and closed the door behind him. Marjory glanced back at the gesture and set her jaw. In mixed company, most especially a man with an unrelated woman, a door closed in private was an unusual occurrence.

"Please, sit, Miss McAdams," Pearson said, moving around to the business side of his massive desk. Marjory remained standing, turning away to face the fireplace. The hearth was cold and whisked clean of any ash. It was winter, but rarely did the temperature fall low enough for a fire, especially not in an office that would be used only during the daytime. She glanced at the photographs and framed certificates that lined the mantel. They all had to do with the building of the Royal Poinciana. None held any hint of the personal Mr. Pearson.

"I have here, Miss McAdams, a telegram from your father."

She turned at the pronouncement.

Pearson slid the typed paper across his desk, the surface of which was immaculately clean and without a single other object on its polished surface.

"He has asked that you remain in your suite at the beach hotel and await his arrival tomorrow on the afternoon train. He asks also that you refrain from any further contact with the situation in the Styx and not to speak of it to any of the other guests."

Marjory stepped across the room and laid her fingertips on the stiff paper of the telegram. She knew that the Florida East Coast Railway stations each had telegraph offices and that messages were delivered twice daily, a staple for the businessmen clientele at the hotel, who were convinced they could not be out of touch with their various holdings in New York and elsewhere during their travels.

She picked up the telegram and without reading it slipped the paper into her pocket.

"Are you in the habit of reading everyone's correspondence before delivering it, Mr. Pearson?" she said, knowing she was on thin ice with the manager. But maybe that's what one does in Florida, where there is no ice, she thought, dismissing the gravity of her disrespectful tone.

Instead of becoming angry, Pearson showed no emotion.

"Yes," he said, and Marjory swore she saw the slightest sign of a grin at the corner of his mouth.

The statement caught her speechless. The brazen possibilities, as well as the potential opportunities of such actions by the manager, only began to form in her head.

"I shall make sure that my father is aware of the policy," was the only retort she could form.

"I'm sure the information will be moot," Pearson said. "As it is he who instructed me to the policy when I was hired for this position."

Unlike with her father and many of his friends, Marjory couldn't tell whether this man was lying. He kept his gray eyes as unreadable as a washed slate.

"You may go," he finally said.

She formed a vitriolic response behind her tongue, but held it. She spun on one heel and walked ever so carefully toward the door but stopped and again faced the desk.

"Did you recognize him, Mr. Pearson?" she said. "The dead man?"

The manager raised his head and looked up through his eyebrows, but hesitated for only a beat.

"You were there, Miss McAdams, when I asked if anyone recognized the unfortunate soul."

"Yes," she said. "You asked if anyone else recognized him, Mr. Pearson. But you didn't say whether you did."

There was now a twitch in the manager's cheek. She had perhaps gone too far.

"You may go," he repeated.

Marjory pinched both sides of her skirt and performed a slight curtsy.

"Yes, sir," she said and stepped out of the office. Only later did she wonder where the Southern accent of her "Yeas sir" had come from. She was sure that it came across as if she were a slave obeying the demands of the plantation owner. She would be in even deeper trouble with her father if that indiscretion was also communicated.

Marjory made her way outside, onto the hotel's wide colonnade, a broad, covered porch lined with rocking chairs that overlooked the emerald-green lawns. A few women perched in the chairs, dressed in their Victorian finery, chatting side by side or simply working their embroidery in their laps while enjoying the breeze. Two men in seersucker suits, straw boaters and the white shoes typical of dressed-down vacationers smoked cigars and talked in low voices near one of the white columns. But most of the hotel guests were in the distance in the Coconut Grove, seated at linen-covered tables under the shade of the palms. The hotel orchestra was playing. Marjory could make out the strains of a Sousa march, "The Belle of Chicago" or "The Bride Elect," she could never tell them apart. She moved to an isolated spot along the rail and took the telegraph from her pocket.

> *my dear Marjory… arriving noon train Wednesday 13… please, please behave and remain charming… will call on you at beach suite in due time to discuss recent matter… until then hold your own counsel… pp.*

Confined to my suite and ordered not to speak to any of the guests of the burning of the Styx and the death of a white gentleman found with a roll of money in his mouth indeed, she thought. It says no such thing! Pearson's reading of the telegram was typical of a military man's ciphering, strict and strident, black and white. It's a wonder the North won the war at all with such men at the switch.

Her father was asking for her best manners because with him gone, she was the only representative of the family on site. Rather than banning her from discussing the situation, her father knew of her inherent inquisitiveness and no doubt wanted to speak with her about the events to gain as much knowledge firsthand before others in his employ.

That was a far stretch from the angered and distressed accounting offered by Pearson. The true meaning of the message was only reinforced by the signature, pp, which was the endearment "Pa Pa" that she had used for her father since childhood.

Marjory tucked the telegram back into her skirts and looked out onto the grounds. The man was after all very well regarded by her father and Mr. Flagler himself. She closed her eyes. Asking him out loud if he'd recognized the dead man! My God, girl, what were you thinking? Still, he had not confirmed or denied, had he? She ordered her emotions and took account of what she'd witnessed at the Styx. In her mind's eye she marked off the length of the lean-to, from where the heels of the corpse lay, all the way to the head. She was astonished that the fire hadn't consumed the entire mess. She had seen the singed mustache but hadn't dared to look closely at the face, burned as it was. She squeezed her eyes tighter.

It would be best at this point to describe the man and the situation to her father when he arrived tomorrow in simple, vague terms. Was it possible that he would recognize the victim? She didn't think so. Such a man was not the kind her father would have been acquainted with.

Marjory still had her eyes closed when the orchestra struck the opening chords of "After the Ball" and she opened them and looked out toward Coconut Grove. Maurice, the orchestra's conductor, was certainly dancing at his own boundaries, she thought, by playing the popular Tin Pan Alley tune. Then her eye was caught by a dark knot of men moving up the walkway toward the hotel entrance.

There were three, but only one mattered. He was the shortest of the group but the most imposing. The others were as accessories, flanking the substantial girth of Sheriff Maxwell Cox. No one, Marjory thought, could forget the notorious sheriff after even a single glance. Cox was an imposing keg of a man, almost inhumanly broad in the chest, with muscled arms and back curving down from his thick shoulders like oak slats on a barrel. His trunklike legs and hips moved as one, creating a rolling motion, and she couldn't help think that if he fell, he would surely continue to roll like a massive bowling ball to his destination. Marjory involuntarily put the tips of her fingers to her lips to stifle a laugh. Sheriff Cox was not a man to take as a joke.

She continued to watch the sheriff and his dark-suited entourage move up the walkway to the main entrance of the hotel. She had no doubt that their destination was the very office she'd just left. Cox was the leading law enforcement officer in all of Dade County, which encompassed everything on the east coast from Sebastian Inlet on the north to the new village of Miami on the south. The sheriff had recently been spending more and more time in West Palm Beach, where money and influence was flowing in on Flagler's coattails. Pearson's orders to bring him to the island had been followed with haste, and now the big man was here to set things straight. Cox's Southern past came with a reputation of being particularly harsh when it came to Florida's migrant population, and the very whisper of a white man found dead in a Negro community would have inspired him to inject his authority without wasting time.

Marjory watched the procession and caught the lyrics of the tune being played for those at tea in the grove, most of whom were no doubt oblivious to the burning of an entire community only a couple of miles from their afternoon merriment:

After the ball is over, after the break of morn,
After the dancers' leaving, after the stars are gone,
Many a heart is aching, if you could read them all—
Many the hopes that have vanished after the ball.

Chapter 7

It was the darkness that stunned Michael Byrne, kept him awake and outside on the platform of the caboose staring at the flat blackness of a moonless night. He had never encountered such a lack of light, a total void like a black painted panel of nothingness for miles and miles at a time. He could only imagine the silence because the train's own mechanical huffing and grinding and clacking overwhelmed all else, but he knew it was out there in that blackness. That unchecked silence made him think of that barroom conundrum: if a tree falls in the woods and no one is there to hear it, does it make a sound? He could also only imagine the lack of movement as he stood on this platform and its constant rocking, back and forth, over the uneven and frequently dipping rails. But out there, he could see no tilt or rumble, push or shove, rise or fall. He might have been mesmerized. He might have even been a bit scared. But he wasn't sleeping. This moving landscape was too strange and awesome for a young man born in the constant sidewalk swirl, cacophonic sound and unavoidable light of the city.

After Henry Flagler's business meeting in Philadelphia and after his wife's numerous boxes and cartons and purchases from Wanamaker's were loaded, their private car was moved back onto a main track and switched onto yet another southbound train.

"This is one of Mr. Flagler's own FEC trains," Harris said. "Straight to Jacksonville now, lad, no stopping unless Mr. Flagler himself asks."

When they hit Washington, D.C., Byrne's view was restricted to what he could see when the train stopped briefly to take on passengers at the Pennsylvania railroad station at the base of Capitol Hill. Still, in the late afternoon light, he could see the glowing white dome of the Capitol building to the east and the towering Washington Monument to the west. He recalled a night at McSorely's when a traveler described the monument as a giant spear shooting straight up into the sky, the tallest structure in the world, although some equally drunk Frenchman argued there was a taller tower in Paris that had been built for the World's Fair. After seeing the marble shaft in the distance, Byrne would now have to side with the traveler, but that night he and the boys had a laugh when the man and Frenchy got into a fistfight over the whole affair and ended up out on Seventh Street lying in a gutter of frozen horse urine, which no one would argue was the lowest point in the United States.

The train rolled south for the rest of the evening and night. Byrne and Harris took turns walking the cars, again running surveillance on new passengers. "Puttin' 'em in the iron sites," Harris called it. But there was no one of interest. Another family was aboard, this time with the head of household in attendance, a businessman from D.C. whose shrewish wife stared at the side of her husband's face when another woman passenger walked through to see whether he would look up from the papers he was reading. Two new men traveling alone had taken places in the club car. One was working at a flask in his coat pocket, surreptitiously sipping from the neck of the bottle. He'd be unconscious before eight o'clock, Byrne determined.

Mr. Faustus had reboarded. He winked once when Byrne passed through the sitting car. But Byrne avoided the subtle invitation to stop and talk, albeit with great reluctance. There was something about the old man's interest in him that was palpable, or maybe he tested everyone he met on the train. Perhaps he'd even met Danny. Byrne wanted to pick the old man's brain, find out more on his own rather than judge the man based only on Harris's cryptic appraisal. But for now Byrne would wait, as the sergeant had warned. Instead Byrne moved along and chose the binder boys as his intelligence target.

"Evenin', boyos," he said to the group and slid into a seat without asking.

The three glanced at one another, and then the oldest looking of the team slid over a bit and said: "Free country, mate."

"You're on from New York, eh?" Byrne said, using his accent from the street, not kissing up, but unashamedly trying to take advantage of a connection based on Harris's information.

"Brewer's Row in Bushwick," said one. He was German looking. Byrne checked his hands, small and uncalloused, his eyes clear and smart under high cheekbones. Might be the smartest of the bunch, Byrne thought.

"Cherry Hill," said the swarthier one. Italian, Byrne guessed. Scar on his cheek, possibly from a knife cut. His were shifting eyes, working his peripheral vision, expecting someone to come up behind him in a strange place.

The older one was looking at his mates. Byrne figured he was calculating his own answer. He was displaying an easy, knowledgeable air—strike up conversation with a stranger without a problem, feel him out for something to take advantage of. He'd be the one calling marks in off the street, reeling in the rubes for a game of three-card or into the brothel for a turn. He'd be the one most like Danny.

"Tenderloin, my friend," he finally said like he'd pinned a flower in his lapel. "And you?"

"Gas House District," Byrne said and then made careful eye contact with each one of the men. It might have been a declaration of battle if the conversation and demarcation of neighborhoods had been taking place on the streets of New York. But the need for piss-marking their territory was absent here on a train to a place called Florida. They all had something in common, an adventure into an unknown where none of them had allies.

"A Pinkerton from the Gas House," the older one said, looking down at Byrne's shoes.

"That obvious?" he said, not bothering to dispute the fact.

"Them brogans are like a badge, Pinkerton. Anybody with a brain on the street knows that, my friend."

"That they would, my Tenderloin friend," Byrne said, straightening out his legs, crossing his ankles out in the aisle and getting comfortable. "So boyos," he said. "tell me about your game."

"Don't tell me a Lower East Side Pinkerton needs a course on three-card monte," the smart one said.

Byrne crinkled up a grin at the side of his face. "Wouldn't tell you that, my friend. It's not the card game I'm unfamiliar with," he said, nodding at the leather briefcases tucked beside each man. "It's the real estate business."

The Italian's hand was the first to go to his case, almost unconsciously placing his palm across the flap. Byrne guessed him to be the poorest of the lot and most likely to be one of those Harris had said would have borrowed the investment money from his family and friends to make a killing in sunny Florida.

"I'm not interested in the money, boyos," Byrne said, raising his palms toward them. "Only interested in the game."

The older one eyed him. "Never trust an Irishman who says he's not interested in the money," he said and then let his own grin take a corner of his face.

"Indeed," Byrne said, and they smiled together and some sort of curbside trust was entered into.

"The premise ain't much different from playin' the streets," Tenderloin said. "Buy somethin' from the market down on Watts and then run it up Broadway and sell it as new for a profit before the yuks up there seen it."

Byrne nodded. He and Danny had done the same thing as boys, snatching up new cloth their mother had acquired and running it up to a seamstress in mid-Manhattan, where they got twice the price.

"The market for land is brand new and strong as hell down Florida. The place is near empty, land spreadin' out like a green jungle and just waitin' for people to come work it or live on it," the older one continued.

"Not much different from north Manhattan Island when your old da, and mine, got to America, right?"

Byrne started to react to the mention of his "old da" but since the man from the Tenderloin had tossed his own family into the mix, Byrne let it go as an unintended slur.

"You need money to make money, right, Pinkerton? So you use what money you have and buy up a chunk of land that looks like it's gonna be in the center of town in due time, and believe me, the times run damn fast down in Florida.

"My first trip down, Palm Beach was a pimple on me mum's ass. Now the bloody place has a palace on the shore, and it's spillin' across the lake to what they're callin' West Palm Beach. The county surveyor already whacked the place out into mapped lots and streets while it was still farmland. Sound familiar?"

Tenderloin nodded to his companion from Bushwick.

"Just like Brooklyn," he said.

"Right-O," said Tenderloin. "And while the Vanderbilts got the east shore line for their mansions early, the rest of 'em got the Cross Roads."

Byrne sat back and watched the trio's eyes, especially those of the Italian. Were they optimistic boys, or angry ones? He knew that the man he was paid to be guarding was not only considered an oil magnate and a railway magnate; the phrase *robber baron* had also been used to describe him. Flagler had built his destination hotels down the east coast of Florida at a time when there wasn't a damn thing south of Jacksonville.

"Not that you've got anything against the ones first in line," Byrne said, not even attempting to be coy. The man from the Tenderloin began to laugh.

"Hell no, Pinkerton. We ain't got nothin' but admiration for your boss Mr. Flagler back there in car ninety." He then leaned in conspiratorially. "People bigger'n us been following the old gent around for years, tryin' to figure where he's going next so's they could jump up the price of their land or buy it out before the mighty Flagler arrives.

"Fact is, the old man did it himself the same way. Promised to take his railroad all the way to Miami, he did. Even the state legislature knew money and progress would follow. They gave him eight thousand acres of right-of-way for every mile of track the old fella built. He'll have millions of acres free of charge by the time he's through."

Numbers had never been Byrne's strong suit, but he was no fool. And he now realized his estimate of the shyster from the Tenderloin district was far too low. The man had done his homework.

"Don't matter who's first," he said. "There's plenty of Florida to buy and sell. The railroad and new hotels just make it easier for the pigeons to follow, if you get my drift. No, Pinkerton, we got no quarrel with old Henry, long shall he live."

Tenderloin reached into his jacket for a small flask, a gesture followed by the other two, and the tiny mob tossed back a toast.

"It's not the likes of us small-timers you've got to worry about, Pinkerton," he said. "It's the big players like the highfalutin Mr. Faustus up there in the smoking room you should have your eye on. He's more of a danger than any of us will ever be. Listenin' to his Peter Funk sermons on the right way to live will lead ya to doin' nothing but starvin' to death while he builds his church on your back." Tenderloin bobbed his head once, statement served. Conversation ended.

Byrne had risen then and unconsciously slipped his hand into his pocket where his fingertips found the Confederate coin. He wasn't worried about Faustus quite yet. He'd heard his brother do the carny barker's routine and the preacher's harangue and the bait-and-switch patter enough to spot a puller-in. No, Faustus would be one to watch, but right now Byrne figured he'd ingratiated himself enough with these lads to ask his question:

"So, you boyos ever run across a man name of Danny Byrne?"

The three looked again at one another. Admitting to a Pinkerton to knowing a man who wasn't present was not something any one of them would do lightly. It would be akin to ratting someone out on the streets, and it always stank of trouble that could come back on you.

"About my size," Byrne pressed on. "Bit more red in his hair and a couple years older."

The one from the Tenderloin studied Byrne's face with even more intensity than before.

"People change their names down in Florida," he finally said.

"Aye, and elsewhere," Byrne replied and added a grin.

They all nodded in assent.

Byrne tipped his head goodnight to the group.

"Any time," said Tenderloin, extending his hand. "Gerald Haney."

Byrne took the hand and shook it. "Michael Byrne."

"Oh, then it's a relative you're lookin' for," the binder boy said, changing his tone a bit, but still wary, as if he was gathering his own intelligence.

"My brother," Byrne admitted, not knowing why he suddenly felt he'd been too forthcoming.

"Well, then, we'll keep an eye out," said Tenderloin and tipped his own chin in goodnight.

Now, from the platform of the caboose, Byrne looked out on the matte of blackness behind them and had the overwhelming feeling that the train he was on was the only living thing in the night, roaring through an uneasy nothingness. It was an odd, sliding community, he thought, filled with people strange and familiar at the same time. When he woke in the morning light, he would be in Florida, land of sunshine and honey, he'd been told. But somehow he was increasingly doubtful of that description.

"Jacksonviiiilllle. Jacksonville!" the voice called out, penetrating Michael Byrne's head and causing him to jolt up off the lower cot and reach for his baton, which was always tucked beside him. The caboose was empty but for the sunlight streaking in through the side windows. The other train workers were long gone, including Harris, who had the morning shift anyway, but Byrne was still surprised that he had slept through the dawn. He swung his legs over the edge of the cot, and when his feet hit the deck, he felt the purr of the machine beneath him. Through the soles of his feet, he could feel the vibration of the engine, like the deep snore of a large animal, but no movement. They'd come to a full stop, and he couldn't believe he hadn't awakened.

He dressed quickly and poured himself a cup of coffee that Harris must have made on the small wood stove. It was still hot, but he found himself looking into the mug, confused by the lack of steam and the new feel of sweat filming on his face. He turned to one of the sliding side windows and found it wide open. Even before he opened the rear door, he noticed the collection of coats still hanging on the hook and then stepped through to the platform. The rail station was relatively small, a single track and two turnouts. He found it curious to see the remnants of another set of tracks running parallel that were narrower and definitely of a different gauge. He leaned out over one side and took in the small wooden station building and the plank platform that appeared aged in a way that brought dry bones to mind. He found himself squinting in the too bright light and used one hand to shade his eyes and check the position of the sun. It was barely fifteen degrees up in the sky, so it couldn't have been past nine in the morning, but the orb seemed far too close to be natural. He spotted a handful of workers wheeling a cargo of crates and barrels from a loading dock and noted that all of the men were wearing sleeveless shirts and hats darkly stained with sweat. He found himself again wiping his own damp forehead with the back of his hand and whispered, "Jaysus, it's hotter than Hades."

Byrne was just taking a deep breath of the heated, new-tasting air when he heard Harris calling his name from the interior of the caboose.

"Rise and shine, lad. You've got fifteen minutes to get ready for a bit of a side trip." They nearly collided at the back door. "Mr. Flagler has decided to take an excursion to Jacksonville Beach with some of his business friends and interested passengers, and you'll be needin' to go along."

"Right," said Byrne, starting to cough on the lungful of moist air.

Harris was smiling.

"Aye, bit of a new climate for you, boy. But you'll get used to it. Some folks pay a pretty penny to come down here and breathe this stuff, and I'm givin' you the chance to sample the best of it if you'll just get your arse in gear.

"Right," Byrne said again, already moving about the cabin, pulling a cake of shaving soap and his sharp knife from the sheath on his calf.

"Mr. Flagler wants to take a look at just what the new spur he built to the beachfront has bought him," Harris said, pouring himself a cup of coffee from the metal pot. "You'll be ridin' a work train over that's meant to haul in material from the coal and lumber docks. The cars should be empty, but there's still a gang of state convicts the company leased to do the hard haulin', and they ain't exactly a friendly bunch. I don't want the boss out there without one of us nearby just in case somebody gets pissy, mind you."

"Right," Byrne said a third time, buttoning his shirt and slipping on his suspenders. He rinsed off the knife and slipped it back in the sheath, rolling his pants leg back over it, and then reached for his coat.

"I wouldn't suggest takin' that," Harris said, that know-it-all grin once again coming to his face.

Byrne removed the telescoping baton from inside the coat and slipped it down into his hip pocket. As they started out the door, Harris stopped, reached up into a baggage rack, brought down a small cloth jockey cap and handed it to Byrne.

"Only a fool walks around in the Florida sun without a hat, m'boy," Harris said and continued out the door.

Byrne noticed the immediate advantage in having a brim to pull down and shade his eyes. He'd never experienced such sunlight: intense, clear and blinding if one didn't keep it from glancing directly off the face. He scanned the surrounding rail yard. It seemed nearly as busy as that of the Philadelphia stop but in a different manner. Here, building material and supplies were flowing. Flat cars were being stacked with lumber, and men wheeled crates up ramps into the adjoining box cars. The heated air was pungent with the odor of sawdust and raw earth and sweat. Byrne was standing near Flagler's car and stepped closer to number 90 when he heard movement at the door. Without forethought he inadvertently moved into the shade created by the train car and felt the temperature of his exposed skin immediately start to cool. "Only a fool stands in the direct sun when there is shade available," he whispered under his breath. Harris could have taught him more than just the hat trick.

When Mr. Flagler finally appeared in the doorway, he was wearing a suit of light wool, a collar shirt and tie, and an odd pair of darkly shaded spectacles of the likes Byrne had never seen. Flagler stepped down spryly and began immediately across the station decking, headed south. He was, Byrne would soon learn, in business mode, his bearing straight and purposeful, his eyes set straight ahead but still absorbing all around him. Byrne fell in behind the man and shortly realized that, like some kind of pied piper, Flagler began to draw suited men from the offices and doorways, men who were seemingly trying to draw his notice or simply gather some of the great man's luck or brilliance by trailing in his wake. The gathering made Byrne nervous, and he slid his hand down in his pocket where he fingered the metal baton. But the men kept their distance, greeting Flagler with good humor and welcomes. They all appeared to know his destination, and no one stepped out in front of him. After crossing thirty yards of limestone rail yard, the entourage approached another set of tracks, where an engine with only two cars attached sat waiting. Byrne could see from the grime and soot, with which he was intimately familiar, that this was a working engine and looked odd hauling the clean passenger cars that appeared to have been hastily brought on line for the occasion. Flagler was greeted by a man in a business suit who looked uncomfortable in the getup, and Byrne heard him introduced as the shipping yard manager. Flagler shook the man's hand in a friendly manner and smiled, the first time Byrne had seen him do so, and the men all round seemed to physically relax. But when the manager motioned for Mr. Flagler to be the first to board the first car, Byrne stepped up to his boss's side.

"If I may be allowed, sir?" he said.

If the railway baron was caught unawares, he showed no sign, only coolly raising one white eyebrow before responding:

"I do not think it necessary, this being my own property, Mr. Byrne. Yet it is your job, I suppose."

"Yes, sir," Byrne said and then clambered up the steps and went swiftly but efficiently through the rail car, eyeing every possible hiding place and corner before returning and then dropping again to Flagler's side. The man simply raised his eyebrow again in question and then returned Byrne's nod of affirmation that it was safe to board. Byrne stood at the door stoically but carefully memorized the dress and facial features of a dozen men as they climbed the stairs and any lump or pull on their coats or pants where guns or knife handles might be concealed. The shipping manager was the last.

"Is there a reason, young Pinkerton, for such scrutiny?"

"Mr. Flagler is an important man," Byrne said dryly.

"No news in that, Pinkerton. And getting more important by the day, I would venture."

"Board!" the manager yelled out toward the engineer in typical trainman's manner and stepped up into the car. Byrne let thirty feet pass and then grabbed the next car's metal banister and swung himself up onto the entire moving mass.

From the grated platform at the rear of the short train, Byrne watched the city of Jacksonville spread out. Harris had told him that before Flagler, the town was the southern terminus of all rail traffic. Byrne found it unimpressive—some brick buildings and facades, some stone-paved streets but curiously no street lights. Most of the place was dominated by wooden structures and wagon traffic and the rail yards. As they moved east, the view widened and he realized what was missing. The sunlight was unimpeded. Yes, it was hot, he could feel the sweat under his vest move in a single trickle down between his shoulder blades, and twice already he'd mopped his forehead with the hat Harris had given him. But Byrne soon realized it was the air itself that seemed to glisten with a purity he had never experienced before. The place was absent the smoky haze that always hung in New York. He had once listened to a watchmaker at McSorely's talk about being fitted with a new pair of spectacles to correct his deteriorating eyesight. He described the new lenses as creating such "sharp, colorful and detailed vision that it was as if the entire world was reborn." A couple of the fellows at the bar asked to try them and only winced and became dizzied by the experiment. Now Byrne thought that this present view was what the watchmaker must have experienced. He doubted that anyone could wince at anything so crystal.

Soon Byrne felt the angle of the train change, and he swung his torso out around the corner of the car to see that they were slowly mounting a bridge that spanned a river called the St. Johns. The small freight bridge was nothing to compare with the Williamsburg Bridge at home, but neither was this river anything to compare with the East River. Byrne stared down into what was obviously water—he could plainly see small boats moving with the current. But he was confused to see that the shadows of those craft followed slightly behind with the angle of the sun. When he leaned over and checked the bridge supports below, he witnessed the same phenomenon, shadows from the stanchions were stretched out from the base. He at first thought it was some sort of optical illusion until his staring determined that the shadows were actually rippling and he was finally convinced that the water itself was clear. The shadows were playing along the white bottom of the river itself. He had never seen water so clean.

Once over the bridge, they picked up speed across what appeared to be a dry peninsula of scrub plants and low trees of a variety again foreign to Byrne. After some thirty minutes he heard the sound of the train whistle and felt the shift in momentum to slow. Again he leaned out to see ahead and was once again greeted by a sight unequaled. Now before them on the horizon was the Atlantic Ocean in a shade of blue green Byrne had seen only in samples of the colored cloth his mother had once sewn in their tenement as piecework for other women's dresses. His neck began to ache as he held himself out over the railing, and in frustration he decided to climb the carriage ladder to the top of the train car so he might look forward and out on the view. From the higher point, with the wind in his face, Byrne was mesmerized. The vista of water changing color from cyan to turquoise to teal and then to steel blue out at the very edge of the earth was stunning. Along the shore was a foam line of cream and then the white of sand beach that made him squint at its brightness and think quickly of Flagler's odd-looking shaded glasses.

The tracks became lined with loading platforms and tin-roofed storage sheds, where stacks of lumber waited. Byrne noted the scent of fresh-cut wood, the bite of turpentine, but also something else that dominated and reminded him of the fish markets back home off Water Street.

His attention was quickly caught by a group of workers ahead. They were a gang of men sweating under the direct sun, hefting railway ties as part of a secondary track siding. All of them were dressed in worn and tattered gray trousers with a stripe in the leg seam. On their heads they all wore striped hats the kind of which Byrne did recognize. Prisoners. He had seen the same headwear on work crews from the Tombs. He looked now with more scrutiny at the edges of the group and finally spotted the guards: two men, standing easily to the east and west, both cradling rifles in their arms. Byrne quickly moved down from the roof, entered the car below and made his way to where Flagler was entertaining, or being entertained by, his business associates. The well-dressed men were standing loosely, their hands in their pockets or thumbs in their vests, all seemingly held in rapt attention by whatever Flagler was saying. The old man himself would speak a few sentences and then bend at the waist to look out the window and appraise whatever it was he could see. The train was moving slowly, and when Byrne also bent to look out the window, he noted that not one of the working men looked up or took notice. The worlds of the men inside and out were a universe apart. It was not unlike the thousands of gaunt, starving faces Byrne watched and recorded every day of his life in the tenements of the Lower East Side and those nouveaux riches he would later watch over as a barrier cop as they entered Delmonico's at Fifth Avenue and Twenty-sixth Street. He was pondering the feeling that his past seemed to be following him when the train began to slow further. He looked to the east to see that the engine was now moving out onto some kind of a pier, leaving land behind. He made a quick assessment and decided that with only those aboard to accompany him, Flagler would be safe. With the train starting to move out over the sea, Byrne stepped onto the stair step and then jumped down onto the rocky ground.

The sound of his feet sliding in the flint bed of the railway attracted the attention of one of the prison guards, who swung his rifle. Byrne raised one hand, tipped his hat politely and dusted his trousers with the other. With a quick glance at his clothing and shoes, the guard became satisfied that no alarm was needed, nodded and turned back to the gang work. Byrne was pleased that the guard didn't bother with even a cursory questioning. He would have hated to admit he was intensely fearful of being out over water and his motivation for jumping from the train was not just that he thought Flagler was safe.

The train had stopped at the end of the pier, and Byrne counted three ships that were lashed to the northern side of the dockage. Two were three-masted clipper ships that must have measured some 130 feet in length. Their sails were down, and Byrne noted the davits built along Flagler's docks that were used to reach over and haul off the lengths of lumber being imported into the state to build not only Flagler's new hotels but also the commercial buildings and homes that cropped up around them. Byrne had seen the same type of sailing ships along the East and the Hudson Rivers that flanked New York. What he had not seen in New York was the vision he now took in from the south. The aqua water was even clearer and cleaner from this vantage point. He stared at the ribbon of white ground being brushed by the waves and leading up to the low tangle of scrub brush. Considering the stacks of wood plank behind him, it seemed no surprise that trees would be afraid to grow anywhere near here. But it was the white ground that intrigued him, and against his better judgment to stay near Flagler's train, he moved down the embankment to the flat stretch leading to the water.

Byrne had seen sand before, used in concrete filler or mixed with mortar for brickwork. He had seen powder before, on the dressing tables at a brothel when he was part of a police raiding party in the Tenderloin district. He had never seen the two mixed, and that's what he found himself standing on. The sand was so fine he was at first afraid to step onto it. Finally he walked out several yards and then bent down and touched the ground as if to see whether it was real. He pinched the substance between his fingers and rubbed the white grain back and forth, feeling the texture. If he could have seen himself smile, he would have been embarrassed at the childish wonder of it. He stood, wiped his fingertips on his dark trousers and moved farther out toward the sea. The foam of small breaking waves was sluicing up onto the sand and leaving it a shade or two darker, but still the whiteness caused the water to look so clear and pure he could not help himself, and he removed his brogans and socks, rolled his pants legs up over the sheath of his knife and stepped out into the water. The slickness of wet sand tickled the soles of his feet, as if he'd stepped onto clay. The water was also warm, and he instantly thought of the heat that had smothered him when he first encountered it this morning but had forgotten once the ocean came into sight. The breeze that came off the sea had cooled his sweat and taken the flush off his face. He looked down into a foot of crystal water, cleaner than anything that came from the spigots of the city, and without hesitation he bent and cupped a handful, tossed it into his face, then brought up another handful and started to drink. The gulp was halfway down his throat when he gagged; the raw taste caused him to spit the offending swallow out in a spray and sent him into a coughing jag.

"Jaysus!" he spat, and it was as if the smell he'd been puzzled by earlier was now in his mouth.

"Ha," came a bark of laughter from behind him, and Byrne spun about to see Faustus standing just above the tide mark in dry sand. "First time at the ocean, Mr. Byrne?" he called. "Oh, she does look glorious and pure, doesn't she? Enough clear blue water to slake the thirst of an army. Especially inlanders who have never known a clear stream or lake they couldn't drink from."

Byrne was backing away from that water, licking his lips and spitting every three steps, trying to clear the taste from his mouth.

"Salt, my friend. Wonderful sea salt. Never been in salt water, have you, landlubber?"

Byrne had not seen Faustus on the excursion train. How he'd made the journey over the river from the rail station was a mystery, but there he was, dressed in a cream-colored suit and wearing a straw boater. He had his cane in his hand and was teasing the sand in front of him with the tip. Byrne made his way back to his socks and shoes, still within earshot of Faustus.

"Our boys from western Georgia and the mountains of Carolina had the same experience when the first regiments were driven to the sea. They were exhausted and scared, and that first sight of clear, clean water made some of them so damned giddy they tossed themselves right in and started gulping to relieve their thirst," Faustus continued.

Byrne redressed his feet and remained quietly embarrassed.

"A belly full of salt water will give you the trots, though, son."

"I will take your word for it, sir," Byrne said, and there was an amusement in his voice now that came from self-deprecation. "Though I do remember my mother using a dose of it to wash out my mouth after losing a tooth or two."

Byrne stood and rolled down his pant legs, only to find that the surf had gotten to the last four inches, leaving his cuffs wet and his knife sheath dark.

"So, Mr. Faustus, I didn't see you on the train. How did you come to find me here?"

"Believe me, young Pinkerton, there are more ways to get around this state than just on Mr. Flagler's trains. It is in fact one of the beauties of the place, that freedom of movement."

"I did notice that not everyone is free," Byrne said, nodding toward the loading docks and the convict labor group.

"Ah, of course you, being such an astute observer, would have seen the work crews in their highly distinctive prison garb," Faustus said. "Hard to believe that a generation ago those Confederate uniforms were being worn by brave young men trying to save the South from just this kind of future.

"Yet I believe the Union armies had secured several large shipments of the clothing near the end of the war, and finding it hard to sell them in that present market, they simply doled them out to the states for convicts and beggars, neither of which group can be choosy."

"To the winners the spoils," Byrne said. It was a facetious statement—in Byrne's world it was smart-assed—but Faustus picked up on it.

"Like your employer, the winner," he said. Byrne stayed quiet. He did not argue matters of fact.

"Mr. Flagler obtains generous contracts with the state of Florida to lease the labor of convicts for the muscle it takes to build a railway. Those are just a few you saw. He employs them for one dollar and twenty-five cents a month. When he has to hire the few locals in these parts or culls laborers from your part of the country, Mr. Byrne, they are paid that much per day. It works out quite nicely for him, even though he does pay for their room and board, of course, along with the salary of the guards. The man isn't some slave Satan."

If the information was meant to influence Byrne's perception of Flagler, it was wasted on his ears. His mother had made less than a dollar and a quarter a month sewing piecework back home in their tenement apartment. He had seen rag pickers, the dregs of the dregs in New York, standing knee deep in refuse at dumpsites along the East River and reaching in to find anything they could to salvage and resell on the streets. Convicts sweating through a day or a month's hard labor if only for food did not stir his compassion. No, his first thought was of the sometimes nefarious leanings of his brother. The fact that he didn't have to scour the group of criminals for a glimpse of Danny was a blessing, confirmed by the telegram in his pocket. His second thought was of the possible threat to his boss, and that pulled his attention from the ocean and sand to the pier and the sound of the train engine beginning to rumble and throttle up.

Byrne took one last look at the sea to the south.

"It is quite a sight," he said aloud but mostly to himself.

"There will be many more surprises along the way, young Pinkerton," Faustus said.

Byrne took a step in the direction of the pier. "You catching the train back, sir?"

"No. You go along, Mr. Byrne. Each man to his master."

Byrne continued up the slight rise, thinking of a rejoinder, but when he turned again to Faustus, the man was simply gone.

When all returned to the rail depot and Mr. Flagler was securely returned to his private car, Byrne marched quickly to the caboose, hoping not to run into Harris. Flagler had said nothing of his Pinkerton detective rejoining his group wearing trousers that were wet to midcalf. There was no doubt in Byrne's mind that the observant rail baron had not missed the sight. But then Byrne was hired help. Now he just looked the part. He was climbing the steps of the car when Harris came around the corner. The sergeant met the discoloration of his new charge's pants legs at eye level.

"Ah, lad. Took a bit of a dip in the deep blue sea, did we?"

Byrne said nothing but could feel the heat rise in his face.

"Can't blame you, son. Hell of a sight for a tenement kid, eh? Didn't know such color existed on the planet myself when I took my first trip down here. We arrived late at night and the crew chief needed help with some security problem down at the oceanfront, and I had to rub my eyes twice to believe what I was seeing.

"I'll tell you, boy. With a full moon shining on that beach, what with all that whiteness, I thought it had snowed."

"It's a strange place, Mr. Harris," was all Byrne could think to say.

"That it is, son. So get yourself changed. There's a whiff in the air that Mr. Flagler's needed in Palm Beach as soon as we can get there." Harris waved what appeared to be a sheet of teletype in his hand. Whatever the message was, the sergeant did not share it and hustled away.

After he'd dressed, in the only other pair of pants he owned, Byrne went out onto the depot siding and found a patch of shade over a bench. There was a discarded newspaper on an unused luggage cart and he picked it up. The *Jacksonville Times Union.*

On the front page was news from Washington of which he had no interest or knowledge. Something about trouble in Cuba, wherever that was. A piece about emerging conflict in Germany. On the inside pages there was a testimonial for Herbine, described as "the most perfect liver medicine and the greatest blood purifier."

Byrne had seen or heard the equal in New York City from corner criers or on store window announcements since he was a boy. But as he skimmed the pages, a clump of unfamiliar words caught his eye:

> *Jacksonville is scheduled to have a triple hanging on Friday, August 7th.*

He reread the first sentence and then worked out the rest.

> *Governor Jennings has signed death warrants fixing that date for the execution of three murderers convicted in the circuit court for Duval County, and they have been forwarded to Sheriff John Price, of that county. The men are Frank Carter, convicted of the murder of Charlie Phillips on November 2; Frank Roberson, convicted of the murder of James Smith on October 26. All of the murders, of course, were committed in Duval County.*

Byrne read the item again, counted the names and wondered what had happened to the name of the third man. He was also taken aback by the governmental announcement. The punishment of hanging for convicted murderers or traitors had long been replaced by the use of the electric chair in the state of New York. Now, Byrne was no stranger to brutality. Three times as a police officer he'd been called to the scene of suicides in the city. But one glimpse of a hanging by the neck from a staircase or plumbing fixture, the body loose and discolored, was enough to sour any thoughts of such an end's being condoned by a civilized state. He laid the paper down on the bench next to him and conjured the scene of turquoise water and white sand beach. The juxtaposition of such an Eden with three hanging men was difficult to fathom. But a whistle jarred his thoughts: "All aboard, Mr. Byrne," Harris shouted. "Next stop Palm Beach."

Byrne was on the rear apron of the caboose when they started, a perch he favored when they were leaving a place, and he watched Jacksonville disappear. The landscape quickly returned to that of hot, spare pine tree forests and low, prickly-looking scrub vegetation. The train was still gaining speed when Harris joined him.

"Since you've the knack for reading, lad, here's a clipping from early in the week," he said, handing Byrne a folded sheet of newsprint:

> *Jacksonville, Fla., Feb. 16 – Specials from Titusville, Fla., indicate an alarming state of affairs in the Indian River Country. H.M. Flagler, owner of the Royal Poinciana Hotel on Lake Worth, is building a railroad to the hotel. This road cuts through many of he prettiest places on the Indian River, and thirty of the property owners, it is said, have combined and placed dynamite along the route of the said railway through their lands. These bombs are placed so that they will explode at the stroke of a spade. Signs warning all engineers have been posted, and the property owners have notified the railroad officials of the steps taken. James Holmes, a banker of Jansen, Fla., and J.V. Westen, Tax Collector of Brevard County, have been arrested for complicity in the dynamite plot. Mr. Holmes's lawyer has advised him to remove the dynamite, and it is reported that he has agreed to do so.*

Harris watched while the younger man's lips moved. When they stopped, Byrne was still staring at the page.

"You know anything about dynamite?" Harris said.

"Blows the hell out of stuff."

"Aye."

"We watched 'em use it when they were building the foundations of the Washington Avenue Bridge," Byrne said. "But not up close."

"How close?"

"Close enough to hear someone yell 'Fire in the hole!' and then feel the ground move under your feet."

Harris shook his head. "My father, rest his soul, was a miner in the Old World," he said. "Explosions every day. While he and his mates ate lunch. Blow the hell out of the ground and turn coal into a chokin' dust."

"Then I seen the results of a stick or two goin' up in the loo of a tavern in Derry. Turned the bar into dust as well."

"Bloody anarchist, were ya?" Byrne said, turning on an accent for the first time and cracking a grin.

"Motivation to leave the mother country," Harris answered. "But these farmers don't know nothin' from dynamite if what it says there is true, and mind you I don't for a minute believe a pinch of what newspapers say. But you can't set it off with the whack of a spade."

"Electric," Byrne said. "From a box."

Harris looked at Byrne for a moment. "You were closer to the Washington Avenue Bridge than you made out to be."

"Sometimes."

"Well, just in case, I'll want you up with the conductor and engineer. Keep those all-seein' eyes of yours out front, and let 'em know if you spot any thing that looks suspicious. I already told them to hold down the speed. We're taking the threat seriously, especially when Mr. Flagler is aboard. These folks down here take their land being snaked away from them personally."

Byrne stood and looked into the eyes of his fellow Irishman: "Where don't they take it personally?"

Byrne had not yet ridden in the locomotive and found himself up front on an outrigger step, watching the rails spin out ahead, listening to the pound of engine cylinder and slide of metal, smelling hot grease and burning coal. The engineer and boiler man were rough dressed in canvas dungarees, their clothing stained with soot and coal dust, their brows speckled with sweat. Unlike in the passenger cars, Byrne felt at home, except for the landscape that unfolded one flat mile after the next.

Mile upon mile of pine forests ran to the horizon on the west, with occasional open acres that were stripped of lumber and spread out in tall grasses. On closer inspection, the dark dot-like objects on the distant plain turned out to be cattle, which he'd never seen anywhere but in the stockyards where the beasts had been penned awaiting slaughter. Recalling the smell and blood of that place caused him to refocus on the tracks in time to pick out a new structure. He called out to the engineer to slow, but the response came as a sneer.

"It's just a siding, boy. For local ranchers and grove owners to use when they're loading," the engineer said. When they came close, Byrne could see that the dock-like platform was bare. The weathered wood of the foundation was old work with newer lumber used on top. The new wood brought the ramps up to the level of the train car carriage.

"Used to be a small-gauge railroad here till Mr. Flagler bought up the old line and put down standard tracks," the engineer said as Byrne stared at the siding.

"Suppose someone hid underneath and jammed a pipe out into the wheel gear?" Byrne said.

"Ha! She'd shear any piece of metal clean off," said the boiler man. "This engine's pushing two hundred pounds per square inch in a cylinder bigger'n two square feet with each stroke, son. Nobody's goin' to trip her like that."

Byrne nodded, not knowing what the hell the old man meant, but started looking for something more formidable that might be a danger to Mr. Flagler's train. Eight miles east of the small town of Palatka, he found it.

Near the end of a wide, yawning curve in the tracks, Byrne again picked up a squared-off blemish in the sameness of the trees and scrub grass lining the way. In the distance he recognized an upcoming siding, but as they came close, he could tell that this time there were a number of people on the platform. Closer still, he made them out to be not just field or farmhands but also women and children. The engineer squinted at the sight himself, an unusual situation that made him pull back on the throttle, taking away the speed that he had already been ordered to cut back on. Less than a quarter mile away, someone on the tracks began waving a red flag. The engineer applied the brakes and coasted to a stop at the siding.

"You'd best go fetch Mr. Harris," he said to Byrne and then set his jaw. "This ain't right."

Harris was working his way along the walkway alongside the fuel tender with a storm cloud forming in his face.

"No goddamn unscheduled stops," he shouted, but his eyes were looking out on the dozen or so people standing on and about the siding rather than at the train crew.

"You want I should just run over the man and hack 'im into pieces," the engineer said and pointed out through his observation window. Several yards away an older man, perhaps in his late fifties, his hair as white as Mr. Flagler's, was standing between the rails, feet spread wide, arms akimbo.

"Christ on a cross!" Harris spat and then said to Byrne as he started down the iron stair, "You're with me."

Byrne scanned the crowd on the platform, level with the train: four men, thin and of average height. The rest were women in worn dresses with defiant looks on their faces and either holding protectively onto small children or standing next to boys whose eyes were wide and dancing over the enormity and close metallurgy of the locomotive.

When Harris's feet touched the ground and started moving out toward the man who stood ten yards farther up the tracks, three of the men on the platform started down the platform stairs. Byrne felt the metal wand at his hip but did not touch it. He scanned the men's clothing again, could detect no weapons and moved to a spot halfway between the crowd and where Harris was now confronting the flag bearer.

"I demand to see Mr. Flagler," the man was saying. "I know that his personal car is attached and since he and his railway company have ignored our continued entreaties to end his unfair and despicable takeover of our land and our access to market, I demand to confront him in person."

The man was dressed in a worn gray suit, shirt buttoned to the neck despite the heat, and he set his newly shaved chin a few degrees at an upward cant.

Harris folded his huge arms, gripping each elbow and widening his stance. Was he containing his anger or just building steam to knock the man off the rail bed, Byrne wondered.

"I'm sure you're a fine country lawyer, what with your command of the King's English," Harris finally said. "But Mr. Flagler does not meet with anyone without an appointment, and he does not answer to demands.

"That said, I'll be pleased to ask you to move yer arse, sir, or I'll have that train plow you under like a bushel of yer own tomatoes."

The lawyer or farmer, or whatever he was, widened his own stance and crossed his own arms in defiance or in imitation of Harris, and the smell of confrontation blew into the crowd, causing it to begin coming down the platform steps. Byrne again assessed them. These were obviously farmers, the boots under their cuffs stained by the soil, their weathered faces creased by the sun and their forearms cabled with work-hardened muscle. Still, they were nothing like the vicious gang members or violent dock workers he'd dealt with in the city. Nevertheless, he found the handle of his wand with the tips of his fingers.

"I surmised that you would be unconvinced," the man said to Harris, his tone unchanged in the face of thousands of pounds of steel and a big Irish tough. "Behind me, sir, is a charge of explosive that upon my signal will be detonated to make these tracks impassible until Mr. Flagler answers to our grievances."

The words caused both Harris and Byrne to slide to the side and peer down the tracks with intense scrutiny. Some thirty yards down the line they could make out some form of package that appeared to be wedged beneath the westside rail.

"We have men in control of a device, a plunger if you will, who will not hesitate to blow this train to kingdom come if you attempt to pass."

Byrne watched Harris's back and could see the muscle in the big man's neck start to bulge and his skin grow redder. Harris seemed to take a deep breath and looked down at the ground. After an anxious moment he turned and began walking back toward the train, his eyes scanning the group of farm families, who had now all gathered at the base of the platform.

When he reached Byrne's side, Harris winked. The look was not one of resignation or defeat and only made Byrne get a better grip on his baton. The three forward men in the crowd began nodding, muttering their victory, thinking perhaps that Harris was on his way to fetch Flagler. But Byrne had seen Irish like Harris before, men who would never in their lives be trumped on the street by any lawyer, dandy, pimp or bureaucrat.

Turning as the sergeant passed, he watched as Harris shouldered between the three men and then with a quickness that belied his size, he shifted. His hand darted out and snatched the back collar of a boy who had been looking down as Harris walked by, as in deference to an embarrassed adult. Harris then whirled back toward Byrne with the gangly child of some eight years, who was now flailing like a rag doll plucked from a toy chest.

Harris had taken three steps back before the crowd could even react, but with one of their own in peril the three front men began to move to block him. The first man reached out to grab the child, but the whoosh and snap of hard thin metal on his forearm stopped all three in their tracks. The stunned man yelped, bent with the pain and doubled over at the waist, his now useless arm cradled to his stomach. When Byrne spun the baton a second time, the vibrating sound of air, like the buzz of a giant insect, caused the others to stare at him, seeing the flash of metal for the first time. With the boy screeching now as Harris dragged him toward the lawyer, another man gathered himself and took a step but was instantly caught by another stroke of Byrne's weapon, this time across the back of the hamstring, which dropped him to his knee. Byrne stepped back, squared himself, let them all see the baton in his hand and spun it wide with a speed that made a few of them gasp.

"You'd best stand where you are, folks. I believe it would be in your interest," Byrne said, not knowing himself whether that was good advice.

He saw that Harris had already pushed the lawyer aside and was heading down the track, dragging the boy behind him, the child's toes tripping on every rail tie. He'd already covered half the distance and called back with a warning that the crowd was only now realizing: "You want to blow one of your children to that kingdom with us, counselor, you'd best get to it."

No one moved except Byrne, who began backing his way down the tracks. The crowd stood mesmerized until a woman, likely the boy's mother, tried to break away but was restrained by the lawyer. On the streets and in the filthy tenements of New York, Byrne had witnessed a dozen acts of self-preservation and utter despair that led hopeless people to sacrifice their children. But these were not those kind of people.

Byrne caught up to Harris's side and looked ahead. Several sticks of dynamite were bound together and wedged under the western rail. A line of sheathed cord ran from the explosives down the embankment and off into a stand of saw palmetto.

"Seen one of these before, lad?" Harris said. The boy he had by the scruff was still wriggling his skinny arms and legs like a pinched snake. But he stopped his squealing when the question was asked, perhaps thinking it had been directed to him, perhaps listening for the answer.

"Yeah. It's a charge that gets blown when whoever's at the end of this cord sends an electric charge through the wire," Byrne said, recalling what he'd seen during the bridge building next to his neighborhood.

All three of them, including the boy, followed the offending cord into the bushes. Harris raised his voice: "And if they wish to blow this little tyke to pieces, they can send that current now."

Byrne winced at the bravado. But Harris was right. If they were going to explode their makeshift bomb, they'd have done it by now, or simply waited until Flagler's car was directly over it and taken out the train, the track and a dozen passengers.

"They're only here to make a point," Harris said softly. "Which doesn't mean they won't just blow it when we give the kid back."

The boy had been silent till then.

"Maaaawww!" he cried out.

"Couldn't'a said it better myself, boy," Harris said. Then to Byrne: "Do you know how to disarm the damned thing?"

Byrne looked down.

"Best guess, I'd just yank the wire. No electric current, no trigger, like snappin' off the firing pin on your pistol," he said in a voice that made it sound more like a theory than an absolute.

"Fuck then," Harris said. "I'll bring the boy over between you and the bushes and you yank the wire."

Without being able to tell what the men were doing, the farmers and families became restless and started to move up the tracks. Byrne got to his knees, found the charge into which the insulated wire was crammed and pulled it loose, digging the dynamite out from the rail and tucking it under his arm.

"OK. Let's go." He took a step back toward the train. Harris stood still, looking from the explosive pinned next to Byrne's ribs then up into his eyes.

"It's safe?"

"I've seen 'em do it all the time at the bridge," Byrne said.

Harris hesitated for one more beat, then yanked at the boy and followed. When they approached the lawyer, his mouth was loose and hanging slightly open. Nothing came out. Those in the crowd were staring at the package under Byrne's arm. When Byrne climbed up onto the engine rigging, the engineer and fireman aimed their eyes at the same thing and were equally quiet. Harris didn't let go of the boy until he had one foot up on the iron stair, and then he shoved the child to the ground toward his crying mother. He raised a thick finger and pointed at the lawyer: "Don't make threats unless you're willing to carry them out, counselor. This ain't no war, sir. It's business."

With that he signaled the engineer to continue forward. As the train began to crawl, Byrne saw two men emerging from the palmetto bushes, their faces up but defeated, their big hands at their sides.

"No more stops," Harris ordered. "We need to get to Palm Beach."

Byrne climbed back over the rigging of the coal car and into the traveling compartments, still a bit dazed by the entire episode. He was working his way toward the back of the train when he realized the sudden gasps of air from some of the passengers and their quick movements to get out of his path were based on the fact that he was still carrying a load of dynamite. When a young mother grabbed her two children and pulled them close, covering their heads with her arms, he looked down at the dark red sticks in his possession: "It won't blow up unless you light it, ma'am."

Still, he took off his jacket and covered the offending package before entering the club car. There were already several men up against the bar, taking some comfort from short glasses of bourbon, and he determined to keep his face down and scuttle on through before anyone asked any questions. But when he looked up to eyeball the rear door, he saw that Mr. Faustus was in a corner and was involved in an intense conversation with Mr. McAdams, whom Byrne had not seen out of his own coach car since the beginning of the trip. It appeared an intense discussion because Byrne could see the muscles of the old man's jaws flexing, grinding his teeth in some effort of restraint, and the skin of his scalp had turned a shade of red not unlike the color of the dynamite Byrne held in his arm.

McAdams, on the other hand, was as cool as if he were at a summer social, raising his drink to his lips with profound grace and smoothness while whispering something to Faustus that had struck the older man silent.

Chapter 8

Marjory McAdams left the Royal Poinciana and walked the distance back to the Breakers alone. The heat of midday reached only into the high seventies with the ocean breeze rising. She strode briskly. Those who nodded and smiled their greetings as they passed would have turned their eyes away instead if they could have seen the visions she was conjuring in her head: the fire-seared trousers of a dead man, his shirt melted into his charred skin, his body lumped onto the crude lean-to floor like a roll of soft dough settling flaccid without the shape of formed muscle and air-filled lung, and the flame-scarred face with the obscenity of rolled bills protruding from the mouth and that one single eye that had turned a milky white as if the fluid inside had actually boiled. Marjory shivered in the heat, breathed deeply, and extended her stride. She tried again to reconstruct the face as it appeared when the man was alive. And what of the watch? Had Pearson or any of the others noticed that exquisite silver pocket watch the dead man was wearing on a chain attached to his vest? She had seen it. Certainly Pearson would not have missed it.

She spoke only briefly to staff at the Breakers and made her way to her suite, which was oceanfront and on the third floor and which she preferred despite the stairs. The maid was finishing with the bed and gathering linens. Marjory searched the young woman's face as she had the other workers, looking for pain or some sign of loss.

"Hello, Armie, are you all right?" Marjory said.

"Ma'am?" the girl said.

"I'm sorry, your name is Armie, yes?"

"Yes, ma'am."

"Are you. Excuse me, were you, living in the Styx, Armie, and how did your family fare in the fire?"

"Uh, yes ma'am, I was in the Styx, ma'am, but I ain't got family with me, ma'am."

The girl was younger than Marjory, but many of the locals and even women from other parts of the state and beyond followed the work that the trains and resorts had created for them.

"Do you have someplace to stay, Armie? Someone to stay with?"

"Oh, yes ma'am. Mizz Fluery, she say she already found us a roomin' house on the other side of the lake, ma'am. We gone stay in a big place over near the church on Mr. Flagler's order hisself," the girl said, her chin and voice rising with the use of the man's name as if she was talking of a proud uncle. "Mizz Fluery say Mr. Flagler gone build us our own places in West Palm an ride us to the island ever day for work."

"How nice," Marjory said, but the tone of her voice set the girl to lower her eyes and turn to gather the linens and leave. Marjory did not doubt the rumor. Flagler was noted for innumerable projects he had built along his burgeoning railway. But she had been around wealthy, powerful and paternal men enough to know that there was always a price for their philanthropy. When the girl offered to bring in fresh water for her basin, Marjory declined and let her leave.

Alone in the suite, Marjory again washed the grit and salt sheen of humidity and sweat off her face and then removed her blouse and bathed her arms with a sea sponge her father had given her as a present from a place in Florida called Key West. She removed her skirt and sat on the edge of the bed and washed down her legs, as well. When she was finished, she pulled a sitting room chair over to the double French doors to the balcony and then opened them to the beach and ocean. A salt breeze was blowing in, sweeping back the sheer curtains. She sat and crossed her ankles on a European ottoman, and with the wind brushing the silk of her camisole and her bared legs, she dreamed she was flying.

She was a child in a tree, most likely one of the huge oaks at the family's vacation home in Connecticut. She'd been allowed to climb there, the rules for young ladies and societal appearances be damned in the summertime, said her mother. In the dream she was high in the upper branches, and a mist floated under her, obscuring the ground below. She felt frightened and glorious at the same time, the wind in her face, the gauze below and an odd smell of salt in the air though she knew they were nowhere near Nantucket, which was the only place she'd been to smell the sea. She stepped out farther on the limb, standing up but keeping her balance by grasping the thin branches just above. The exhilarating feeling of simply stepping off, spreading her arms and soaring over the familiar grounds of their summer getaway was glowing in her head. But that glimmer of ultimate danger kept her feet in place. She raised her nose to the wind and closed her eyes. The freedom of soaring, or the fear of death? Decide, my dear. You could fly for seconds or for miles. You could fall screaming for fifty feet, or soar forever. She stepped off. The air in her lungs caught in her throat as she went out and down. She was falling but at the same time hearing a knock at the door, someone assaulting the wood, the noise snapping her awake in midflight.

Marjory's eyes shot open and her hand went immediately to her chest. The knocking was real and shook her awake, and she lurched forward, seeing the empty blue sky before her at first and then the horizon, the ocean, the beach, the railing, and finally the floor beneath her.

"My Lord!" she said and caught her breath, closed her eyes and touched her face. Now she distinctly heard the knocking at the door, stood and realized her state of undress. In reaction she brought her spread palms up in a butterfly pattern to cover her exposed breasts.

"Uh, coming!" she called out. "One moment please, I'm not decent!"

When she had wrapped herself in a housecoat and slipped her shoes back on, she finally went to the front door of the suite and opened it. Before her stood a tall black man, his hat in his hands, the brim pinched between the tips of extremely long and strong fingers. There was a sheen of sweat on his face, and he was dressed in the manner of a bellman.

"Yes?" Marjory said, still out of sorts from her dream but her head clearing by the second.

"Excuse me, Miss McAdams. I'm very sorry, ma'am, to disturb you, ma'am. My name is Santos, Carlos Santos. I come to fetch you for Mizz Fluery, ma'am. She needs you to come meet her, please and it's in a hurry, ma'am."

His voice was urgent, his eyes also. Marjory stepped back and took a second accounting. He was a muscular man, one could tell by the squared shoulders, the stretch of fabric over his arms and the V-shape of his chest tapering down into thin hips. Marjory recognized the look and then studied the face, clean shaven and with astonishing green eyes.

"You're the ball player, yes?" she said.

"Uh, yes ma'am."

"I've seen you during the games, the ones with the Cuban Giants that Mr. Flagler displayed out back."

"Yes ma'am," he said again, with no less humility at being recognized.

"If I'm not mistaken, you played third base, yes?"

"Yes ma'am."

"And pitched one game?"

"Yes ma'am."

The baseball games, always played by Negro teams, were organized by the hotel during the winter months and were a favorite among the guests. Marjory had become quite enraptured during the first season that the Royal Poinciana was open. The Cuban Giants were an especially entertaining team with a group of athletically talented men who seemed unbeatable. Most of the hotel guests knew of course that relatively none of the players were actually from Cuba but played under assumed names so they would be allowed to participate in venues where Negroes were not allowed.

"I believe I saw you hit a home run against a Mr. Satchel Paige," she said, recalling a game from one of those earlier seasons.

"Yes ma'am. Uh, but Mizz Fluery, ma'am, she really needs to see you ma'am," he said, taking a step back as if to draw her out of the room by creating a vacuum.

"Oh, of course," Marjory said, gathering herself. "Right away, Mr. Santos. If you could wait in the lobby, sir, I will be right there."

Marjory dressed in her most conservative black skirt and a ruffled blouse that buttoned high on her neck. She supposed the clothes she selected were in response to the fact that she had been in such a mode of undress when Mr. Santos was just outside her apartment door. She rolled her hair and tucked it up under a straw hat and went downstairs.

Santos was just near the entryway. She went directly to him, and again he drew her outside by backing his large, muscular body away. Not seeing Miss Fluery, she looked questioningly into the black man's eyes.

"She's in the laundry, ma'am," he answered the unasked question. "She's holding someone there and can't come herself, but she needs you."

There was no panic in the man's voice but an urgency that started Marjory's own blood to step up its pace in her chest. This Santos was obviously keeping his voice low and out of earshot of others, and the conspiratorial feel made her even more excited.

"Where?" she simply said.

"The laundry, ma'am."

"Let's go then."

Santos motioned to the Afromobile parked at the base of the stairs. Before Santos had the chance to help, she climbed up into the seat. He swung his leg up over the saddle and with powerful strokes set the vehicle moving quickly north down the raked stone path in the direction of the electric plant.

Santos got them to the laundry in minutes and came to a stop at the front door of the long wooden structure. Marjory had been to the building before because she'd been intrigued that, unlike the hotels she was familiar with in the North, the laundries at the hotels in Florida were not located in the basement. There were no basements in Florida. The water table was simply too high, and one could not dig down far before striking water, her father had explained. The next best location was near the electric plant, where the commercial-style steam laundry machines and the huge, flat mangles for pressing the sheets and table cloths could be easily powered and still kept out of sight of the guests.

Marjory hopped out of the carriage before Santos could assist, but she did allow him to open the door to the laundry for her to pass. When she stepped into the building, she was hit by a wave of heated, wet air and a cacophony of noise that had been only a low rumble from the outside. Here in the midst of the machinery, hissing steam pipes, rotating rolling pins, and the snap of fabric being shaken and folded, it was an assault on the ear.

Marjory adjusted her eyes to the darkness, there being only a dull wash of sunlight leaking through the windows near the roofline. Before her were a dozen or more Negro women moving as if to a complicated dance from washing to drying to pressing to stacking the innumerable loads of laundry. Santos finally led her to the back of the open workroom to a small office with a door, where they could talk without shouting. Inside was Miss Ida, standing uncharacteristically still when there was work all around her. Her left arm was crooked at her waist, her right elbow was settled in one palm and her other hand wedged into her brow, a sign of worry or of deep thought, or of defeat. It was difficult to judge. Sitting in a straight-backed chair in the corner was the woman called Shantice, who had found the body of the white man behind her shack. The young woman's feet where pulled up so that her heels rested on the edge of the seat and her skirt was wrapped around her legs. She was bent at the waist, her head rested on her knees, and she was weeping.

Marjory looked first at Miss Ida and then at the childlike figure in the corner and said nothing. The muffled noise from the big room settled like a cocoon around them.

"They's word out that Sheriff Cox gone arrest this poor girl for the killing of that white man," Miss Ida said, breaking the silence. Her voice was more tired than Marjory had ever heard it, as if it held a century of hard and weary trouble.

"The sheriff went out to her house and inspected the body. The boys out there who was trying to salvage some of they own possessions watched after him. They said he walked around a bit and done kicked some burnt up trash around Mizz Shantice's place and dug around with a stick where her eating place used to be. They say he poked into some ash and found a ol' carvin' knife that was black from the fire and held it up and stared at it like it was Jesus' golden chalice itself and then put it in a bag of his.

"Lanie Booker's boy said the sheriff done smiled an said, 'We got ourselves a murder weapon' an then told the rest of 'em to wrap up the body and put it in the wagon. Then he asked the boys where Mizz Shantice was at an' they said she was workin' at the hotel. While the sheriff was loadin' that man, one of the boys come runnin' to me."

When Ida May was finished with her report, she looked up into Marjory's eyes, and the expression may have been, although it was foreign to the woman's nature, a plea. "It ain't right, Miss McAdams," she said. "You know this ain't right."

"Right?" Marjory said, gathering herself. "Why it's … it's quite unacceptable." She looked around at Santos as if he would join her and therefore embolden her reaction of astonishment and disbelief.

"Why … why we were all standing there ourselves. This slip of a girl could no more kill and drag a man of that size across this room. And with a knife? Good Lord! She would have had to be standing on a chair to put a knife into such a man's throat, and you saw the wound yourself, Mizz Ida."

The girl called Shantice started to rock on the chair, a keening sound coming from her throat.

"Oh, I am so very sorry," Marjory said moving over to put her hip against the young woman and pressing the girl's head into her own skirts. "You weren't there at all, were you?"

"I was at the fair, ma'am," the girl said, avoiding Marjory's inquisitive gaze. "Mizz Ida. I swear I was at the fair and I ain't never seen that man before I seen him a layin' there all burnt up."

Marjory looked to Miss Ida with a "see there" look on her face.

"Surely there are witnesses to that," she said. "Folks who accompanied her to the fair?"

Miss Fluery dropped her hand to her lonely elbow, crossing both arms.

"Logic nor witnesses don't make no difference in this, Miss McAdams," she said. "The only thing we need is a way to get this girl off the island and headed back to Georgia country before the sheriff comes an' finds her or I'm afraid there'll be a hangin'.

"A white man has been found dead in nigger town and that's the only truth they gone need. That's the way it's always been and that's the way this will be too.

"If you can help us get Mizz Shantice here across the lake without being seen, ma'am, that's all I'm askin'. If you can't, then I am truly sorry for bringin' you into it."

This time it was Marjory's turn to be taken aback by the housekeeper's graphic language. She yawped once, her mouth opening in a circle, and then closing with a perceptible pop. She was not naïve about matters of discrimination and race. Her father had been open about discussing the

Reconstructed South and the advent and demise of slavery whenever she had asked. Her penchant for crossing societal boundaries and neighborhoods in New York City had given her a firsthand look at how different classes were used and often abused at the hands of power. She was also familiar with the sheriff's heavy-handedness and the tacit approval given him by Mr. Flagler and his lieutenants, including her father. The small town of West Palm Beach on the inland side of Lake Worth was booming, with the train bringing in supplies and in return hauling out thousands of pounds of tomatoes and pineapples and a dozen other warm-weather vegetables and fruit up to the cold Northeast. As the rail workers moved south down the line, they were soon followed by carpenters and masons and construction workers from the North and even the Southern states, searching for opportunity. And not just to work at Flagler's huge hotel projects but to lay the foundations for towns like Juno, Lemon City and Miami itself. With so many people in so short a time, carrying so many dreams to fulfill, it was inevitable that tempers would flair, jealousy and greed would hitch a ride, and something would break. Why, an item in *The Gazetteer* last June reported that the first train-car load of keg beer had arrived in town, and it wasn't but two months later that Sam S. Lewis—who was awaiting trial for killing the tax collectors J. F. Highsmith and George Davis in Lemon City—was broken out of the jail in Juno by a lynch mob and then hung from a telegraph pole, his body riddled with bullets. The jailer himself was killed by the mob when he was mistaken for the colored deputy sheriff come to stop them. Marjory couldn't say for certain, but she often considered that the arrival of copious amounts of beer and men behaving in animalistic ways were somehow connected.

At the behest of Mr. Flagler, Sheriff Cox had begun to clamp down on the lawlessness of not just the inevitable drifters but also the workers, railroad men out for a night or carpenters out to relax after a day of swinging hammers. There would be no such bad behavior for Mr. Flagler's rich guests to witness or even hear of in his Eden. The idea of making an arrest and bringing to a quick and quiet close an actual homicide on the island itself would be of paramount interest, and the quicker it was done, the quicker would come the praise and reward.

Miss Fluery's request for help might pit Marjory against the sheriff, a challenge she rather warmed to, but would also give her opportunity to ask young Shantice questions in a more, one might say, conducive surrounding.

"Can you keep her someplace in hiding, Mizz Ida?" Marjory said, looking into the eyes of housekeeper and then to Mr. Santos, who was still standing at the door as if at guard.

"Yes, ma'am," Fluery said, "We do know how to hide our own. For a time anyways. Can't say how long though. That would depend on how hard Sheriff Cox gets to lookin' an how mad he get when he can't find her."

Again Marjory took a few minutes to chart a course of action in her head.

"I frankly don't think it would do well to keep her on the island overnight," she said. "The sheriff will surely have someone watching the walking bridge to the mainland, and at some point he will begin threatening or simply paying off anyone he can for information as to her whereabouts.

"Can you row a boat, Mr. Santos?"

"Yes, ma'am."

"Well, sir, I can secure one. If we meet up near the old dredge wharf north of the golf course at say, nine o'clock this evening, I believe you and Mizz Shantice may row across the lake unseen.

"Can you alert someone on the other side to meet them and take Mizz Shantice in for a couple of days, Mizz Ida? At least long enough for me to consult my father and find a way to calm and control the sheriff?"

"We know folks on the mainland, ma'am. Folks who we can trust, yes."

"All right then, dear," Marjory said to Shantice in an odd sing-song voice, as if she were talking to a child and not a young woman and a noted prostitute.

"Don't you worry a bit, we'll see that you'll be safe, dear, and that the truth will be told. You may indeed be back working by the weekend. Now wouldn't that be fine?"

Shantice had stopped her tears and keening during the discussion but had yet to raise her face to the others. She looked up now to Miss Ida, perhaps wondering which of her professions she might again be working, but the baleful expression on the housekeeper's face gave her a defining clue.

"I will find her some clothing for traveling," Miss Ida finally said, speaking perhaps to herself as much as to the others in the room. "Some young men's clothes. We do not want to bring no trouble to our town friends."

She turned specifically to Marjory. "We often dressed girls on the old underground railway in men's clothes so's not to draw attention to them."

"Fine then," Marjory said. "It's settled. If you will take me back to the hotel, Mr. Santos, I will prepare to meet you tonight at the wharf."

Santos opened the office door and allowed Marjory to pass out into the heat and steam and noise of the work room. A large Negro athlete and a young, high-society white woman moved through a place where neither of them belonged, and not a single face lifted to note their passage.

Chapter 9

On the pathway back, Marjory redirected Mr. Santos to the Royal Poinciana instead of the Breakers. A plan was forming in her head, and she would need accomplices if it had any chance of succeeding. Not that any of those whom she pulled in on the enterprise would have any idea of their involvement. It would be best that way. A bit cruel perhaps, but best.

When Santos cycled up to the rear entrance of the hotel, this time Marjory allowed him to help her out of the carriage seat and then paid him a dollar for appearances. "Nine o'clock," she whispered. "The boat shall be there, pulled up into the brush just north of the wharf."

Santos accepted the money, held her eyes for a moment and said: "Thank you, Miss McAdams. And I do believe that Mizz Ida thanks you too, just in case you didn't hear her say so."

Inside the hotel Marjory strolled across the ornate lobby with the air of a girl with nothing but leisure to direct her. She nodded to a familiar couple, spoke a greeting to a passing valet and found the nearest powder room, where she fixed her hair, her cheeks and her mouth and became presentable to the society that would now surround her. She thought of her dead mother, the lessons passed down at an early age and the decisions she had made on her own: which lessons to follow, which to disregard and which to simply give the illusion of following, depending on what company one was in. She had loved her mother dearly, but since her death Marjory had in many ways defied her strict views of comportment in a young ladies' world. She saw it as payback for leaving her all alone to fend for herself. What she was about to do would have made her dearly departed mother blanch in front of proper company. But Marjory liked to think that in private she would have said, "Atta girl, M," using the nickname that was employed only when they were alone together.

"Live one life, M," her mother had rasped as she lay on her death bed. "And make it yours."

Marjory returned to the lobby and wrote a note at the front desk, then folded it into an envelope. On the front she wrote in a fine, boarding school script "Mrs. Roseann Birch" and found her way to the Birches' fifth-floor corner suite. Her knock at the door was answered by a maid.

"Good afternoon, Abby," McAdams said, recognizing the young woman who always traveled with the family. "Is Mrs. Birch in?"

"Why yes, Miss McAdams. Ma'am is taking her refreshment on the side portico," Abby said with a raised "if you know what I mean" eyebrow that she would have used only with someone like Marjory, who had become close to her employer in the time since Marjory had lost her own mother. "I will find out if she's taking visitors, Miss McAdams."

Marjory was used to the exquisite appointments that her friend always made to the living space when she arrived from New York at the beginning of the season. Despite her sometimes boisterous character in public and displays of athletic prowess before her male counterparts, the woman had a delicate eye for artwork, and her husband was rich enough to accede to her passions.

McAdams was drawn as always to a framed mass of gold, reds and purples titled "Japanese Bridge, Water Lily Pond," by a French impressionist whose name Marjory could never recall. She started slightly when Abby returned and called her name.

"Ma'am would like very much to see you, Miss McAdams," she said, indicating the way with an open palm.

Roseann Birch was stretched out on an odd-looking wooden chair, the seat and backrest of which were angled in the rear to such a degree as to make the buxom woman look as though she were tipping backward.

"You can't believe how comfortable it is till you sit in it, honey, which might be a while," Birch said with an amiable gruffness unusual to any other woman of her station. "My husband got it as a present from a friend in Westport, New York, up in the Adirondacks. Hell of an ugly thing, but my, when you lean back and get your feet up, it's a wonder."

Birch's feet were indeed up, ankles crossed on the cover of a thick leather-bound book which was itself placed atop an expensive-looking ottoman. The crystal goblet in her hand was half-filled with what Marjory guessed was a chardonnay, and she looked over the rim with a satisfied but still sharp glint in her eyes.

"Sit down, sweet Marjory, and we shall swap some gossip, and though I will not stoop to adding to the delinquency of a minor, I can get Abby to bring you an apple juice or even a small sherry if you like?"

Marjory pulled a wrought iron patio chair over the slate patio decking and sat at Birch's right hand.

"Nothing for me, ma'am," she said. "I really wasn't planning to stay long but did want to see if I could join you at your table for dinner tonight. My father is not due until tomorrow, and I'm quite tired of dining alone."

Birch looked over the rim of her glass again, studying Marjory as she assessed the request. She took a deep draught of the wine. "Bullshit."

Even Marjory, who had known this undoubtedly frank and spicy woman for some time, felt her eyes go wide at the profanity.

"OK. OK. I apologize dear. That may have been uncalled for, but we'll see," Birch said, setting her glass aside. "And what else are you requesting, sweetheart, knowing that you are always, always, always welcome at our table and that you don't have to ask. Hmm? Any other guests you think might make the evening interesting? Like maybe the fire inspector? Or maybe that cast-iron kettle of a sheriff from the other side of the lake?"

Marjory was caught unawares. She knew Roseann Birch was more plugged in to the workings of the island than any of the other guests and, in some cases, more than management itself. Her advantage was a woman's amiability to chatter while carrying on through the day and her understanding that such talk was not limited only to upper-class women. Abby, and every housekeeper, maid, laundress, kitchen sweep and handmaiden, were her allies in word-of-mouth communication. She was as open to them as to any member of her high-class sisterhood, and during her time in the hotel, she had turned them from wary to willing in sharing with her the stories of their world. At first they did it for her generous tips, then for her entertainment and finally for their own hunger to know more about the other side, a woman's place in a society far different from their own. Birch had won over all except Ida May Fluery, who respectfully maintained the wall of separation between the whites who hired and the Negroes who did the work.

"Oh come now, dear," Birch said in reaction to the look of surprise on Marjory's face. "Word has been spreading like chicken feed all day about the fire in the Styx, and now that bowling ball of a man Sheriff Cox is strutting around the coop like the mad hatter himself."

She took a sip of wine and leaned over and said in a conspiratorial whisper that was totally unnecessary on her own patio, "I've even heard there might have been a dead body involved."

Marjory took a moment, knowing that she had to stoke her friend's curiosity without revealing too much. She would have to protect herself and her plan as much as protect Birch from some embarrassing questions should the effort go awry.

"I smelled the smoke myself, Mrs. Birch. It raised me out of my bed, and I've heard talk that the entire community where the workers lived was consumed by the blaze."

She let that soak in but could tell by Birch's face that it was too little news.

"I've also heard tell, like you, that there was a death involved. Word at the Breakers is that it was the body of a white man that was found."

It was like finding a new aperitif. Birch's face lit, her eyes widened, and she may have actually licked her lips with the tip of her tongue.

"Oh, my," she said, not alarmed but intrigued. "No wonder that disgusting keg of a man is running around the island as if he had even a scintilla of power here."

Birch moistened the tip of her index finger and began circling the crystal rim of her now empty wine glass. The crystal began to vibrate, and the glass began to sing at a high, clear pitch. Marjory had seen Birch pull her parlor trick before, but this time it seemed a rote performance.

"Any speculation on who this dead man is?" she finally said, looking directly into Marjory's eyes. "Local? Or one of us?"

"Oh, no. Not a guest, I wouldn't dare think," Marjory said, pressing her fingers to her heart as though the possibility would be devastating. "Certainly someone would have come forward by now, don't you think?"

"I wouldn't know what to think at this point, dear," Birch said, but the look in her eye meant she soon would know as much as it was humanly possible to find out.

With her line of inquiry now set into the most extensive system of gossip and rumor on the island, Marjory moved on to equally important pursuits.

"On the subject of dinner guests," Marjory now said, as though the chitchat about a dead man and a snooping sheriff were simply diversions from the important parts of life at the Poinciana. It was her turn to give the matron a coy look. "Could you invite Mr. Foster from the steamship family to join us?"

Graham Foster was a young man in his early twenties who fit most perfectly into the Royal Poinciana's growing clientele of moneyed society. He was the son of a steamship magnate who had become fast friends with the Flaglers. The railroad baron had been a prime customer of the elder Foster for the delivery of his building supplies and the transportation for his advance work crews. For the far-seeing Flagler, it was an investment in a future that he himself would control. Once his rail lines were laid, Flagler would be the main transportation for all things moving up and down the Florida east coast, instead of the steam shippers. If Foster couldn't see he was cutting his own throat, let the instant gratification of money now be his bandage.

As for the son, Graham, he was also more interested in spending his father's wealth than in looking ahead at a dying company that he would inherit. In many ways he was quite dense. Marjory McAdams liked that in a man.

Her request that Graham Foster join them for dinner may have caught Mrs. Birch off guard, but Mrs. Birch was the kind of woman who could see her own traits when they showed up in other women.

"Why, Marjory, you loathe that young man. What could you possibly want to use him for?"

McAdams professed to pout. "I think *loathe* is a bit too strong," she said. "He is a bit of a showboat, but he is also only a handful of years older than I am, and unless you can find me another dinner companion less than three decades my elder, I will simply have to make do."

Birch watched her young charge's eyes, sure there was something mischievous behind them.

"Very well, then. I shall invite young Mr. Foster and then deny all culpability if I am asked." Birch brushed Marjory away with a flutter of her fingertips. "Run along, dear. And do ask Abby to come pour me another of this delicious French nectar."

She had planned it all on the run, and she was amazed that so far it had gone swimmingly.

Mrs. Birch had held up her end of the bargain. When Marjory arrived for dinner that evening, the Birches' table was occupied by Mr. Birch and Marian and Robert Rothschild, he of the Manhattan real estate Rothschilds. Marjory nodded to Mrs. Rothschild as the men rose to greet her.

"You are stunning, my dear," Robert Rothschild said, and meant it.

"Why thank you, sir," she said with a light curtsy.

Marjory was dressed in a pale blue dress that was long and slim at the waistline and included the newly popular leg-o'-mutton sleeves that billowed out and accentuated the thinness of her youthful figure. She was naturally a slip of a girl, but tonight she had gone to the trouble of lacing up her corset a few extra notches, which, in addition to accenting her waspish waistline, added a bit more umph to her breasts. Though most of the older women, including Mrs. Birch, wore a high-necked style, it was not inappropriate as evening wear to include a low-cut bodice.

"I would concur," said Mr. Birch, who, despite his reputation as a careful and circumspect banker, was a jovial man in social company and was known by most for having an appreciative but careful eye for the younger ladies, careful indeed considering his wife's strength and demeanor.

Marjory then turned to the still standing Graham Foster. He took her fingers in his and raised them to his lips but did not touch. At least he had been taught some manners in his upbringing.

"What a pleasant surprise, Graham," she said with enthusiasm. "I wasn't aware that you'd returned to the island. How wonderful to see you."

"It is an absolute pleasure, Marjory. And you do look incredibly fashionable."

As they all sat, Marjory could feel Foster's glance of appreciation into her cleavage. He was dressed in a dark waistcoat and trousers made of a carefully striped fabric. The dress was formal, as was expected for dinner at the Poinciana, but Marjory figured she knew him well enough that his concern for this clothing wouldn't cause him to hesitate when the time came.

He was a thin and angular man, sharp at the knees, elbows, shoulders and nose. He was clean-shaven but wore the standard mustache that had become popular as of late, and it partially covered his unnaturally pink, thin and almost girlish lips. His eyes were a puppyish brown, at least when she was in his company, and there never seemed to be anything behind them other than an obsequiousness to please her. She smiled at him and felt a slight trickle of shame.

The dinner was of typical fare for the Royal Poinciana, exquisite in every respect. The table linen was impeccably white at the hands of the laundresses Marjory had visited that very afternoon. The silver and crystal were of the finest European style.

The six diners went luxuriously through the courses: green turtle soup, heart of palm salads, oven-baked salmon, a potpourri of shrimp, scallops and clams casino from the Bahamian islands, a sampling of cheeses and apple wedges and—for all at the table—a serving of a strange and succulent fruit called kiwi. Mrs. Birch maintained a steady diet of red wines, and the rest also imbibed a variety from the Poinciana's well-stocked collection.

The conversation ran from a discussion of summer plays they had all missed in the city, a room-by-room recitation tour by Mrs. Rothschild of her sister's opulent home in Hyde Park, a highly political debate by the two elder men over the Spanish-American conflict and its effect on the U.S. economy, which was put to an end by a then-braying Mrs. Birch that "no country that produces such lousy wine is worth conquering," and finally an agreeable assessment of this year's hotel baseball team and a promise by all to attend this Friday's game against the visiting team from Asheville, North Carolina.

Throughout the evening, Marjory listened with forced interest to Graham Foster's descriptions of his family's plan to offer steamship service to Cuba from the terminus of Flagler's train in Miami, his braggadocio over a new type of steam engine he himself was building for use on a single-passenger personal vehicle, and his plan to break a land speed record in such a contraption.

All the while she smiled coyly, feigned great concern for his safety, looked adoringly into his too-close-set eyes and ate a half-dozen oysters with such slow, deliberate and sensuous care that even Mrs. Birch (who'd been watching the couple closely) was forced to clear her throat in either admonition or glee.

It had taken only one after-dinner dance to the hotel orchestra's rendition of "And the Band Played On" for Marjory to convince Foster to walk with her in the gardens. With her fingers on his forearm and the smell of night-blooming jasmine in the air, it was hardly fair how easily it was for her to talk Foster into taking her on a ride on the lake in his company's rowboat.

"It is such a beautiful evening and you do know how I love to float, Graham."

The young man was bewildered.

"I thought you hated the last time we went out in that tiny boat," he said. "In fact, if I recall, Marjory, you said you'd rather be swimming."

"Yes, well, I do enjoy the swimming. But then I would have to remove this lovely dress," she said, again employing the coy smile and using her off hand to gesture down along her delicate waist and long skirts. He went silent. Perhaps he was envisioning it.

"I believe the boat is up on the ramp at the company dockage," he said. "It may indeed be under guard by the watchman, but it shouldn't take any time at all to fetch it."

So now they were out on the water, the oar locks creaking gently as Foster rowed without haste onto Lake Worth. Marjory had situated herself in the bow at a half turn, looking out at the lights of the Poinciana, keeping track of their progress north so she would know when to guide her "beau" to shore and a rendezvous near the old dredge wharf by nine o'clock.

"The stars are so beautiful tonight," she said. "Perhaps if we get farther north out of the glare of the hotel, they will be even brighter."

Foster quickened his pace.

"They are beautiful but much colder than the sparkle in your eyes, Marjory."

Demurely, she turned her cheek away with a smile. Where did he come up with these lines? Was there a cheap magazine like the *Farmer's Almanac* of trite phrases men studied to impress the women they hoped to woo?

Foster waited a few beats, letting the work of his silver tongue do its duty. Surely she was enjoying his company. Hadn't she touched his arm just so? Hadn't she had a grand time dancing in his grasp? Her suggestion of the boat ride was certainly proof that her feelings had changed toward him.

"Frankly, Marjory, if I may, I wasn't sure that after our last meeting, I would have the pleasure of seeing you again."

"I do apologize if you took my attitude in the wrong way," she said, recalling that the last time they'd been tossed together by a lady friend of her father's, it had been a disaster. She had taken umbrage at Foster's arguement that men were superior to women in any field of outdoor pursuits, such as game hunting or fishing. Her father did not have the time to deflect young Foster's perilous line before Marjory had challenged him to a fishing contest aboard Captain Connelly's deep-sea yacht. The next day, Marjory pulled in the largest swordfish of the outing, and then she added insult to injury on the return by announcing at about the one-mile marker from Palm Beach Island that she was overheated and was going to swim the rest of the way to the beach. Infuriated by Foster's smiling dismissal, she stared him directly in the eye and then stunned three of the four men aboard by removing one layer of her overclothing, mounting the rail and then diving like a true professional into the aqua water. It took several minutes for her father to convince the captain that Marjory was an excellent swimmer and would probably be back in their hotel suite long before they made dockage.

She had not seen Graham Foster since. But she knew he had access to a rowboat.

As they moved easily to the north, Marjory now listened with half an ear to her companion's monologue about the subject he was most familiar with—himself—and kept the other half on the night sounds along the lakefront. An owl called its kaweek, kaweek from a hunting perch somewhere in the water oaks on the island shore. A splash off to the west, but not more than thirty yards away, gave truth to the fishermen's tales that large tarpon did indeed feed in the nighttime waters of the lake. Marjory turned away from Foster to check on their progress to the dredge dock, and as they drew near, turned on her charm once more.

"Might we just drift a bit, Graham? I so love the quiet here, and the stars truly are a wonder."

Foster stopped rowing and talking. He had been facing back toward the receding lights of the Poinciana. Now he turned and saw her view of the blackness to the north and was, at least for a moment, transfixed by the sight of the constellation Virgo hanging low in the sky and the star field around it dipping down to the horizon.

"You do have the constant touch of the dramatic that follows you," he said. It was perhaps the first statement of truth she'd heard from him, and she felt a twinge of regret at what she was about to do. But the feeling did not stop her. She slid forward to the edge of her seat, moving closer to him. He reacted as she knew he would to the subtle invitation, shipped his oars and matched her movement until their lips met.

When he pressed, she retreated.

"Oh, my, Graham," she said, feigning breathlessness. She reached out to clutch both sides of the boat as if to steady herself. "I, I … oh, my."

Now her right hand went to her throat, and she she knew that in the darkness he would not detect the lack of any sort of blush to her skin.

"I do believe I'm becoming quite dizzy. You have taken me by surprise." She looked at him with that learned woman's technique of peering up with the eyes while keeping her chin low. Foster did not move; he was still leaning forward, frozen in an awkward pose.

"Not unpleasantly," Marjory added. She then looked about, as if unfamiliar with where exactly they were. "Could we possibly go ashore here? The lack of solid ground beneath my feet is quite, umm, unsettling."

Foster settled back in his seat as if commanded and reached for the oars.

"Absolutely," he said, scanning the shoreline and picking up the obvious dark outline of the dredge dock. "I apologize, my dear. My intentions were honorable and I did not mean to cause you to swoon."

The slightest touch of bravado was in his voice. A man taking responsibility for his manliness, thought Marjory. Ha! All her previous guilt disappeared.

"Just there." She pointed to the dock. "Could we go ashore there?"

Foster pulled the last few strokes and beached the bow onto the rim of wet marsh that served as the shore. Without hesitation he removed his shoes, rolled up his pants cuffs and got out to push the rowboat higher onto solid ground so that Marjory could get out without soiling too much of her gown. He took her arm, and they walked up to high ground while she breathed deeply and appeared to be gathering herself.

"My," she said again, using a word she rarely uttered when she was not in the company of people she wished to socially impress or to con into thinking she was weak. "I'm not sure what came over me. But I'm certainly better now."

"Are you sure?" Foster said, looking into her eyes but again injecting that touch of overconfidence and double meaning into his voice.

McAdams noted the question was lacking in true concern, and she showed her confusion with a questioning face.

"I mean are you sure that you don't know what came over you?"

Now he was smiling. Did he really think his kiss had caused her to swoon? She turned her face away, hoping it was taken as a blushing moment instead of mild chagrin. Men, she thought, and then without looking up, she took his arm and turned south toward the hotel.

"There is a path made by the workers. Can we walk together back to the hotel?

Foster looked back once at the rowboat, and she read his hesitation.

"Surely everyone knows whose boat it is and will not dare to move it." She squeezed his arm just so. "And it has been such a wonderful night. Let's not let it end so soon."

As they walked arm-in-arm through the brush along the lakeshore, McAdams knew that she would not see the baseball player and the young woman even if they were close by. But she did hear the unfamiliar trill of a bird she knew was not native to the island, the whistle low and sounding too much like a pigeon from Brooklyn to be real. Foster made no reaction to the sound; he was again listening to himself. As McAdams moved more quickly down the path and away from the dredge dock, he was again expounding.

"Mr. Flagler has certainly done a marvelous job with the hotel and the beginnings of the town on shore. Business has doubled since his arrival, and that means at the very least a doubling of my own trade."

McAdams was perplexed at where he was going with such conversation and afraid she was losing his focus. He was looking out on the lights of the Poinciana and the approaching paths of the manicured lawns and golf course. He stopped and turned to her.

"I will be a rich man," he said, the statement full of what was not being said. He grasped her other arm and pulled her closer.

Damn, she thought. I've gone too far. He's actually going to propose to me.

"I will inherit my father's steamship business and be set for life. The more people who hear about the beauty and climate of this place, the more we'll ferry them and their necessities for building and living here. There are plans to widen and deepen an intracoastal waterway that for the next one hundred years will be the major transportation line to the very tip of Florida. People will forever flock to our boats."

Foster turned his head just so, waiting for her to raise her face to his. "You can be part of all that, Marjory."

"Why, Graham Foster," she said, much louder than his romantic whisper. She freed her arms, planted all ten fingertips into Foster's chest and pressed him back. "Aren't you just the forward thinking one? And a bit too forward in other ways, I might add."

She stepped back, turned toward the hotel and began to walk.

"By the way, if you intend to inherit Florida's transportation world with your steamships, you should have a conversation with my father when he arrives on the island tomorrow. I do recall on his last trip he talked of some fellow named Ransom Olds, who was interested in coming to Daytona Beach, where he said people were sure to go absolutely ga-ga over his new motor car."

Chapter 10

Look at yourself, lad!"

Harris had come forward to the train engine landing, where Byrne had stationed himself ever since the dynamite fiasco some three hours before. Byrne followed the order, looked down at himself and noted that he was indeed covered with soot and coal oils, even though he thought he'd positioned himself out of the stream of smoke and ash.

"We'll be pullin' into West Palm soon enough, and before we cross over to the island, you'd best be lookin' smart, son.

"Go on back and change into something clean, if you've got any. Mr. Flagler is entering his domain, and I promise you you're going to be damned embarrassed to be in the company of such opulence lookin' like a coal peddler."

Byrne headed for the caboose. Harris cut his eyes at the engineer and fireman, who were equally soiled, and gave them a shrug. "No offense, men."

Within the hour Byrne was stationed at his place on the rear platform. He'd brushed his coat, inspected his shirts, picked the one with the least dirt around the collar and polished his brogans with Harris's boot black. By now he was used to the movement of the train and could feel it slowing as they eased into the populated area of West Palm Beach, if you wanted to call it populated. Byrne had poked his head around the corner to look forward several times, thinking that at some point he'd be able to see a skyline of the city, but was disappointed each time by the continued flatness of brush and scrub pine and the seemingly endless tangle of green. Soon, off to the east he picked up the reflection of water, a lake that Harris would later call Lake Worth. To the west they passed several acres of cleared land and rows of crops that his mentor would tell him were pineapple plants. Byrne had seen the fruit once in New York when a street merchant had somehow gotten a load of the oblong, prickly-looking things and made a show of whacking at the individual husks with a machete while guaranteeing "such sweetness and juicy flavor like you've never imagined in your lives." Byrne noted there was a crude sort of sprinkler system spewing water over the crops, which led him to believe there would be plumbing in the city. He would be proved wrong.

A dirt road began to parallel the tracks, starting as little more than a two-rut wagon trail and then turning into a hard, flat roadbed and then improving, if you could say that, into a surface tamped down with a strange, shell-like crust. As they entered the town proper, a few two- and three-story wooden buildings sprouted on the side streets with signs for O.W. Weybrecht, the Pioneer Hardware Store and E.H. Dimmick, Druggist. But many of the businesses were in tents or carts not unlike old Mrs. McReady's outside his New York tenement.

The train slowed and with the familiar hiss of the steam brakes, came to a full stop. Byrne was about to hop down to take position on the ground outside Flagler's car when Harris appeared at the door.

"Not yet, lad. They're switchin us onto the island spur. Just the hotel guests in the last two cars, the parlor car and Mr. Flagler's number 90. The rest of the lot'll stop at the station in town and then be headin' south to Miami.

"We'll take you down that route in the future, Mr. Byrne. For now the boss needs us here," Harris aimed his exaggerated nod off to the east. When Harris disappeared inside, Byrne stepped over to the other side of the platform and looked toward the lake. In the hard sun he could see an enormous, gleaming-white structure rising up alone on the opposite shore. He determined it at least seven stories, with huge mansard roofs at either end and a broad cupola at the middle. It was no doubt the Royal Poinciana, but it looked out of place along the flat horizon of blue lake water and low green shrub. Byrne hadn't seen anything since Washington, D.C., to compare, and as he looked down the side of the train cars, he spotted several of the upscale passengers leaning out of their windows and pointing. They were apparently joining in his simple astonishment. The train began to move again, this time curving along a spur and then up onto a bridge that was taking them across the lake, the grand hotel growing larger and more impressive with each turn of the wheels.

Even from the slight elevation of ten feet above sea level, the greenness of the place washed over Byrne. The coastal shrubs, the hotel's manicured lawns in the distance, all ringed by aqua colored water that itself seemed to take on a tinge of green. He could smell the salt again, the air filling by the minute with that tang, the bite that was no longer the fish monger's scent but one all its own, simmering in the heat and carried by fresh wind.

Byrne watched what from a distance had looked like rag-topped stakes become sentries with plumed hats and then morph into impossibly straight-trunked and smooth-skinned royal palm trees with filigreed blades sprouting like fans at their heads. As the train eased off the bridge at the island end and slowed next to the hotel's southern entryway, Byrne picked up the strains of music. It was a joyful, welcoming tune he could not name, but it had the same effect of making him grin and did the same to those people gathering to greet the new arrivals. When the cars came to a hissing stop, he could see an eight-piece band tucked under a garden trellis. He jumped down off the iron stairs and smartly gained his position at the door to Flagler's car, as instructed.

There were some thirty people in the crowd. Byrne swept his eyes over them and assessed them: moneyed was the first impression, men in clean summer suits, most of light hues, all wearing banded boaters or white fedoras. The women were all draped in long dresses of white that were nearly blinding in the bright sun, and they too were in hats of wide brim and varying shapes. Byrne's second impression was that despite seeking this extraordinary Florida sun, they had all gauzed their skin from its touch: the hats, the long sleeves, the veils.

He saw no darkness, no slouch or averted look, no movement at the edges of the group that hinted of predation. Despite the hats, the men were all openly showing their faces; smiles and grins abounded. The music stopped, spontaneous clapping began, and Byrne turned to see Harris at the foot of the steps to number 90 and Mrs. Flagler standing for a second of adoration at the top. She was dressed in the same manner as the women awaiting her, and Harris offered his meaty hand as balance as she stepped into the graces and greetings of her own admiring flock. The respectful ovation continued as Flagler appeared, he too in a straw boater, but now in an impeccable light-woolen suit that seemed far too business-like for the occasion. He had already donned the darkened eyeglasses that shielded his eyes from the bright light, and he stepped down unaided after graciously tipping his hat to the gathering.

Byrne followed as unobtrusively as possible to the inner circle. Harris had done the same. And so too had Mr. McAdams, Flagler's second-in-command. He took up a position immediately to Flagler's left—bathing in his boss's greetings and adoration, or protecting him? Byrne watched the hands of those who reached out to shake hands with the patrician, tracked anyone whose fingers might go to the inside of a jacket as Flagler approached, anyone whose eyes were down first and rose only at the last minute. The music started again as the group moved toward the hotel, the entourage stopping only long enough for a kiss to Mrs. Flagler's cheek by another white-draped woman or a pleasant bow by an apparent friend or business acquaintance of her husband. Harris was just giving Byrne an eye-rolling high sign when both of them snapped their heads forward at the completely unexpected yelping of a dog. The shoulders ahead seemed to turn at odd angles, and hat brims tipped downward. Byrne picked up the movement at ground level of a white object that was coming quickly through the forest of legs in a more or less direct line to the man he was supposed to protect. Byrne's wand was already out in his hand, and he flicked it out to its length as in his peripheral vision he sensed Flagler begin to bend at the waist as if doubling over. Byrne began to step into the void that seemed to be naturally forming in front of the old man before he got his first full view of the white dog and heard Flagler say in his loudest and most emotional statement since Byrne had met the man: "Delos!" The white dog leaped into his master's waiting arms, licked the old man's chin and engendered the only smile that Byrne would ever see on Flagler's face. Byrne retracted the baton and tried to slip it back into his coat unnoticed.

The procession continued up the steps and into the south portico of the hotel, but Harris stopped at some unseen boundary and turned to his protégé, giving Byrne the sign again that their responsibility was finished. Byrne nearly banged shoulders with Mr. McAdams.

"Interesting walking stick," McAdams said, looking into Byrne's eyes with a mixture of interest and mirth and then down to the coat pocket where the baton was now secreted. "But I assure you, young Pinkerton, that if you had broken the neck of Mr. Flagler's favorite living thing, it would have been the last act of protection you would have performed on this island."

Byrne looked unblinking into McAdams's face. The man was twenty years his elder, nearly his height, had flecks of gray in his hair, and the scent of eau de toilette rose from his collar in the heat. But there were also sharp creases at the corners of his eyes. The lines made him look distinguished, or perhaps deeply tired. His words had not come off as an attempt to put Byrne in his place. That would have been a tone with which Byrne had long ago become familiar when in the company of the higher class. He considered a rejoinder, perhaps a comment that if his reflexes were so poor that he couldn't check his first reaction, he truly wouldn't deserve the position of protector. But he simply said, "Yes sir."

He took a step backward, then two more when a flurry of soft white fabric and a high-pitched song of "Father! Father!" seemed to push him out of the way.

Later, Byrne's sense of it would be as a cloud of bright chiffon and a waft of gardenia, a glance of tumbling auburn and a glimpse of porcelain skin. The enveloping hug between McAdams and this sudden woman was equal parts strong, athletic, loving and dear.

"Oh, father. I did miss you so."

Byrne saw the thin waist, outlined by the pull of her dress under her father's arms. He saw the hard knot of muscled calf as she stood on tiptoe. He saw the kiss she blessed to her father's cheek, and he saw the eye, green as an emerald, which caught and seemed to both notice and acknowledge him over her father's shoulder.

"Eyes right, boy!"

Harris was at Byrne's sleeve, pulling him back toward the train.

"Out of your league, lad. Out of your class. And out of your head if you think for a second more of the daughter of Mr. McAdams."

Byrne blinked and turned his attention to the hands before him as Harris flipped through a roll of money, counting out twenty dollars and then placing it in Byrne's palm.

"That's a week's pay, Mr. Byrne, for services rendered and more expected," Harris said. "Get your things out of the train car. It'll cost you a nickel to walk the bridge back to the other side. Over in town I would recommend the Seminole Hotel, corner of Banyan and Narcissus. Can't miss it. It's the biggest damn building on the mainland. I'll come and get you there when you're needed.

"And I'd warn you of spendin' time on saloon alley if it would make any difference. They're a tough bunch of rail workers out there on a weekend night. But I'll figure you know how to comport yourself in such an environment."

Within minutes Byrne had his duffel containing everything he owned in hand and was walking back along the rails toward the bridge to the mainland—walking not exactly with purpose. For some reason he kept looking back at the grand hotel, over his shoulder at first, then in an almost sidestepping crab-walk, unable to stop staring at the glow of the place, the unusual set and rustle of the long-bodied palm trees. Was he looking for another glimpse of the girl in the brilliant white dress? Or trying to set this new fairyland in the proper context of his new life? It had always been his way to assess a place—a neighborhood, a row of residences, a beer hall, a tenement alleyway. Who belonged there and who didn't. Where was the danger mostly likely to lie? Where were the escape routes? There was something here that made him wary other than its setting and smell and air of opulence. He'd known the feeling from being in the moneyed center of New York City, the feeling of not belonging and always watching it as an outsider. But this was different, and his sense was that he was both fascinated by the island and too suspicious to turn his back on it. The other thought was that this was the kind of place his brother, Danny, would see as an opportunity, a target and a mark.

"Pardon, sir! Pardon!"

Byrne spun at the call and was met by the sight of a contraption that was half bicycle and half wickered lounge chair rolling toward him. A black man was up on the seat, calling out for his attention, while an elderly white couple sat in the settee, looking out in blissful comfort. The gentleman tipped his hat to Byrne, and he returned the greeting. The driver's face was as unreadable as a pewter plate. Byrne stepped aside to let them pass and then watched the back of the skinny black man's shoulders and the sway of his hips as he peddled the carriage away toward the hotel at a pace and rhythm he might be able to keep up for the rest of his life.

At the lake a swing gate on the bridge was mounted by a boy not more than ten years of age who was collecting five cents to use the pedestrian walkway to the mainland. Byrne flipped the boy a nickel and started the six-hundred-foot trek across water. Again the transparent quality of the water captured him, but he also found himself using the handrail more often than his natural athleticism would usually need. He was an urban lad, not used to being on or above water, and a new experience was throwing him off his game. He would need to master it, he thought, especially if he was going to spend time in this place where water was such a dominant feature. Nearing the end of the bridge, he slowed his pace. A knot of people had stopped, perhaps a dozen men, women and a couple of children, waiting on the walkway while some form of inspection went on. He noted they were all Negros, dressed cleanly in the way of domestic workers and carrying a variety of satchels and bags and duffels not unlike his own. The impression was that they were a group traveling or moving, but from where? The island? He stopped and took a place next to the last man, who nodded quickly up the line as if indicating Byrne should pass them by. Byrne stayed where he was. He watched the process and noted that some official was taking little time in dismissing the men and children but more thoroughly questioning the women. The man was tall and lanky and scarecrow looking, with bony shoulders and a gaunt face. At one point he reached out a long finger and lifted the chin of a woman who had seemed not to want to look into his eyes.

"Your name, woman?" Byrne heard the official say.

"Lila Jane Struthers," the woman replied in a voice, not defiant, but proud of the words spoken.

"Mizz Struthers. Do you know the woman called Shantice Carver? And don't lie to me now 'cause I been lied to too many times today."

"I know her, sir, yes sir," the woman said. "But she work the maids' side, sir, an' I work the laundry."

"Have you seen this Shantice today?"

"No, sir. Lots of days go by I don't see her."

"When was the last time you did see her?"

"I believe I seen her over here, sir, on the night of the carnival," the woman said, and this time Byrne did pick up the taste of defiance in her voice.

"I guess ya'll following the party line today, eh Mizz Struthers? What? You all got together and decided what to tell the sheriff's office before you even got asked?"

"I don't know nothin' about no party, sir," the woman said. "An this the only line I been in today."

The inspector made a dismissive sound in the back of his throat and moved his attention to an elderly man. Byrne took a new assessment of the scarecrow, concentrated on the man's eyes, the line of his nose, the set of his feet for balance and another, longer look at the man's hands to determine their strength. Was his thin build deceiving? How quick would he be to deliver a blow, or avoid one? Did all the sheriff's men wear such black coats? And what exactly did the insignia on his lapel badge say? The official dismissed the old man and moved down to Byrne, taking in the length of him from eyes to feet.

"No reason for you to wait, sir. Move on."

Byrne didn't move. From this close distance he could read the letters stamped into the man's badge: "Deputy Sheriff."

"Do I gather that there is some kind of search being performed?" Byrne said, turning his language level up a notch for the fellow. "A woman, I presume?"

The deputy's assessment of Byrne stopped for an additional second at his feet.

"Not to be concerned, sir. Strictly a local matter."

"Would that be local as on the island, deputy?" Byrne said. "And would the matter have anything to do with the train?"

The deputy stepped in close to Byrne, turning his head away from the workers.

"It's a matter of a Negro prostitute shankin' some poor bastard over in the island backwoods, sir," the deputy said. "Not something that the Pinkertons need be bothered with."

Byrne stepped back, thinking: I've got to do something about these shoes. It's like wearing a bloody sign across my forehead.

The first stop he made was at the telegraph office located in the town's new railroad depot. The office consisted of a single planked window where the dispatcher, ticket seller, weigh master, and telegraph operator where all embodied in the same man, a large and surprisingly friendly man with eyes as bright as blue marbles, eager to help anyone in line, which, when Byrne arrived, numbered zero.

"Uh, yes sir, Mr. Byrne. I can check on that right away, sir. Only take a second, sir, if you don't mind, sir," the clerk said after collecting the worn telegram Byrne had offered him in the way of introduction. The man spun to collect a shoebox from the wooden table behind him. Byrne could see the wired teletype machine sitting lonely and motionless.

"Any correspondence to this office is kept here and in confidence, sir, as required by the government and reiterated in the training of each and every operator within the system, sir, which in this case would only be me, of course," the clerk said breathlessly, with a smile on his face that had not a hint of cynicism. His fat fingers were flipping through the box in search of a message that Byrne's telegram had been retrieved, but when the man finally pulled out a sheet and handed it to him, it was only the copy of the message he had originally sent.

coming to meet you in three days... ma is dead...

"No, sir," the clerk answered to Byrne's question. "No one has came to collect it, sir, and it was received as you can see right there on the date, sir, on the very same day, or close to it anyways, that it was sent from New York City."

Byrne pinched the paper between his fingers. "Would you know this man, Daniel Byrne, the one to whom the telegram was sent?"

The clerk looked down at the paper as if there might be a photograph there. "Uh, no sir. I don't believe so. Though they is a lot of folks who come through here, sir," the clerk said while letting his gaze focus behind Byrne. The juxtaposition of his statement and the empty room seemed to have no ironic effect on the man. "But then I am not required by regulations, nor am I trained, sir, to know on sight each and every person who sends or receives messages, sir."

Byrne pointed again at his brother's worn telegram.

"The man I'm speaking of sent that message from your office four weeks ago, according to the date."

The clerk again studied the paper.

"Yes, sir. That would be from here, sir, according to the identifying numbers, sir."

"But you don't recall the man who sent it?"

The clerk shook his head.

"Very well, then," Byrne said, refolding the telegram.

"Was it your daddy?" the clerk said as Byrne turned to leave.

"Excuse me?"

The clerk pointed his finger at the pocket where Byrne had tucked the telegram.

"Ya'll got the same name."

"No, it's my brother," Byrne answered. He walked away. In strict confidence my ass, he was thinking as he made his way back onto the street.

Harris of course had been right about the Seminole Hotel, named, Byrne soon found out, after the Indian tribe that now occupied southern areas of the Florida peninsula. It was a four-story structure that towered above the rest of the wooden shops and tents and pole barns that created a wobbly-legged colt of a downtown. Byrne could smell the fresh-sawed lumber, hear the hammering of nails nearby and practically taste the sun-heated flavor of newness. It was the frontier town he'd read about and heard stories of in those Wild West reenactments along Tin Pan Alley in New York. But this was not the West. This place was called Florida.

"Yes, that's right, Michael Byrne, with a Y after the B and an E at the end," he said to the hotel clerk at the check-in desk at the Seminole. "No. No specific length of stay. Might be a day. Might be a week. I'm with Mr. Flagler's security team. A Pinkerton."

What the hell, he thought. Since everyone could guess his occupation by looking at his shoes, he may as well use the status and that threat of authority that he and his boys exuded to gain advantage on the streets of New York City.

"Certainly, Mr. Byrne. We do have a fine room available fronting the lake on the fourth floor with a wondrous view of your employer's island," the clerk said with a new smile.

"Something on the second floor, if you will," Byrne said, his tenement background speaking without consideration of his new surroundings.

"Yes, sir. Of course, sir."

The room was spare. The furniture was fine and sturdy and quite possibly newly hewn in hardwood. The floor was of a dark, close-grained pine he didn't recognize. There was a throw rug in the middle that was brand new. The single bed had a chenille coverlet, and he tossed his duffel onto it and went to the window. Even from the second floor, the Royal Poinciana stood monolithic across the lake. He raised the double-hung casement window, felt the breeze blow in off the water and again took a deep breath of the wondrously new scent of sun-warmed salt air.

He stripped off his coat and shirt and filled the dresser-top wash basin. The china bowl was polished and had a gold leaf band around the rim. It was free of any chips or scratches. He cupped the water in his hands and splashed it up into his eyes and rubbed his face, repeating the gesture three times before picking up a hand towel and wiping himself dry. While dabbing his neck and shoulders, he looked up into a face that had a slight stubble of beard and a new sheen of red sunburn on its nose and cheekbones, and in his father's Irish tone, the face whispered: "Jaysus. What the hell are ye doin' here, Mikey?"

When he returned to the front desk, he used his already established authority to ask a question: "I'm looking for a man who left word he was awaiting me in town. His name is Daniel Byrne. Has he ever registered here?"

The clerk looked up into Byrne's face.

"A relative?"

"Yes."

"With the same spelling then?"

"Obviously."

"I believe I would have recognized it then, sir. I don't recall anyone using that particular name before. But I've only been employed here for the past few months."

Byrne asked for the names of other hotels in the city; the clerk gave him a list of three.

"Unless of course your relative is on the island, sir."

"That I can check myself, thank you," Byrne said. From what he had seen so far of the island, Danny would have indeed had to strike it rich to be ensconced across the lake. Inquiring for dinner, he was told that the Midway Plaisance saloon and restaurant on Banyan Street had just received a new brew that had become quite the rage and that they could serve up a fine fresh catch of the day that would provide a taste Mr. Byrne had most likely never encountered in his previous life. He'd tipped his cap to the clerk, thanked him, and covered a brief smile. They might have a sun and smell and heat that could not be encountered in New York, he thought, but certainly nothing that couldn't be presented on a table. The restaurants of the city were unmatched in any corner of the world if, of course, you had the money. He would see about this catch of the day and this supposed new brew.

Byrne rolled up the sleeves of his white shirt two turns to the middle of his forearms and stepped down from the hotel porch to the street. His telescoping wand was in the deep pocket of his trousers, and now he had a mighty ache for a beer. The walk to the saloon took him less than ten minutes, during which he was offered the finest hot bath and shave, the foremost in leather boots, the most affordable and profitable piece of real estate left in the Palm Beach area, and a "trip upstairs mister that will be your slice of heaven on earth." The blatant bray of merchants and hookers brought on the first fit of nostalgia for his native city he'd felt since arriving. His reaction was the same as if he were home. He ignored the hype and kept his wallet in his front pocket with a light chain attaching it to one of his belt loops. He also registered every face he saw. Danny could not have changed too much in three years' time. Michael would know him from a hundred paces. But he had seen enough to surprise him in the last few days that he was taking no chances.

It was past four in the afternoon when he stepped into the wooden saloon of the Midway. It being the dinner hour, the place was near full of men in both work clothes and respectable suits. The smell of fried fish was in the air and that unmistakable scent of fresh hops and barley and yeast that conjured a liquid that would cut the dust from your throat and take the pout off your face.

Byrne shouldered his way to the bar and bought a pint of Anheiser beer that he would later find out was part of the first load of keg beer delivered to the town of West Palm Beach. He took a deep draught, closed his eyes in appreciation, and then worked his way out to the canvas-covered porch area of outside tables. He scanned the gathering, memorizing faces and modes of dress, as well as anything sinister attached to belts or stuck down into boots, and listened intently to the sound of voices and accents. He heard a familiar tone from one corner and moved to a huge wooden cable spool that was making do as a table top. His three binder boy acquaintances from the train were sitting at the nine, twelve and three o'clock positions of the round top. Byrne picked up one of many wooden crates being used as chairs and took the six o'clock spot.

"Top o' the day to you, Pinkerton," the man from the Tenderloin said. He waited until Byrne was settled in his seat. "Please, join us."

The cynicism was cast as a joke, made even more so by the creamy foam he left dripping from his mustache.

"What brings you slumming here on the west side, Pinkerton?" said the Italian. "Figured you to be settling in the island castle near the boss man."

"No, I'm just a junior lifeguard, Pauley," Byrne said, watching the street boys' eyes for a reaction to the fact that Byrne had gone out of his way to check the train's passenger manifest and had figured out who was who among the small group. Gerald Haney had used the same name on the manifest. The German was Henry, a common Americanization for the name Hienrick. The Italian from Cherry Hill was probably Paulo originally. Pauley's face went blank, trying not to react to Byrne's correct guess, which was a reaction in itself.

"Besides, I don't think they serve good beer to the champagne crowd over there." Byrne raised his glass to the group and took another long swallow, gaining his own foam line above his lip.

The group joined him in the toast, and that common thread of young men and drink gained him another tenuous link.

"So, I thought you boyos were on your way to Miami," Byrne said. "It must be something more than the arrival of keg beer to keep you from your date with fortune."

Gerald Haney smiled to his mates, and they grinned in return. It seemed a learned response to deflect questions of their questionable business.

"Aye, Pinkerton. Fortune is where you find it," he said. "And when you hear tell of it on the street, only a fool ignores the call."

"And the call is?"

Haney drained his glass before answering.

"No more free courses in real estate business, Irish. You'll have to be buying."

Byrne acceded to that logic and bought the next two rounds while Haney, with an occasional word from Paul and Henry, told him the word on the street was that Flagler had been buying up even more property on the west side than he already owned. They'd heard that the entire hotel working class was transferring to the west side of the lake.

"They all got up in mass and moved?" Byrne said, thinking of the stoic face of the black man driving the bicycle carriage. "Sounds like a bit of a phenomenon."

"Word is that they were burned out," Paul said. "Accordin' to those that know, their little village over there called the Styx was set fire in the night and the entire place gutted." Paul's chin came out with the statement, proud that he had gleaned information off the street so soon after his arrival. For his trouble he got an immediate glare from Haney.

"The real word is that prices on the island are going to skyrocket," Haney said quickly. "But the hard part is getting hold of the sellers. They're already being wined and dined by the gentry. To get ahold of any of those land titles, the speculators are going to have to be connected and sharp. Might be worth stickin' round for a bit, though. Never know when the trickle down might start. Some guy tradin' up wants to dump what he already has on the mainland so he can qualify for something on the island."

He leaned in conspiratorially to Byrne.

"Knowledge is money, boyo, and since your ear is closer to the rich than ours, keep us in mind should ya hear somethin' juicy, eh?"

Byrne did not dismiss the possibility. Being noncommittal, he'd learned, kept doors open. Haney was right about one thing, information is what the world ran on, be it business or law enforcement. It was a lesson he'd learned firsthand from Danny. He'd have to build a network if he was going to find his brother and survive in this land of sun and heat and haves and have-nots. Eventually the binder boys all rose and bid him farewell. A waiter arrived and asked if he was going to use the table for more than drinking, and Byrne asked for a lunch recommendation. In minutes was served the finest-tasting fish—called yellowtail snapper—that he'd ever put to fork. He stayed for another forty-five minutes, eating and drinking and recording the faces around him. If he were a smoking man, he'd have lit a cigar. Fine fish and fine beer. What more could a man want while sitting in the sun with money in his pocket? The answer surprised him when it came sidelong out of his head. It was the memory of bright chiffon and a waft of gardenia, a glance of tumbling auburn, a glimpse of porcelain skin and the shine of an emerald eye.

Chapter 11

"All right, Marjory. I'm listening. Tell me what you know."

The McAdamses had retired to their quarters in the Poinciana, a suite of rooms that were not the equal of the Birches', but the tiffany, Ming, fine leather and dark mahogany were still extraordinary for an employee. Mr. McAdams had loosened his collar, kicked off his shoes and made himself a heavy glass of scotch. He was exhausted from the New York trip but took his favorite place in a high-backed wing chair with a view of the golf course and asked again.

"Tell me what this urgent matter is all about."

Mr. McAdams was always accommodating to his daughter. Since his wife's death he had been more lenient than perhaps he should have been. He recognized that he had somehow transferred from his wife to his daughter the need to listen and to some degree share his confidences. He saw it as a way of gaining insight into himself, having the feedback from those who loved and knew him best. They wouldn't bullshit him. They wouldn't be sycophantic, sucking up to gain favor or advantage. And he knew they wouldn't use what they learned to knife him in the back. The conversations were frank—Marjory had inherited that characteristic from her mother. But in certain cases, like this one, he would withhold some truths, just as he had with his wife. Truths that might hurt her. Truths that might hurt his standing in her eyes. But it didn't stop him from being blunt.

"What is it with this fire that has so intrigued you? What do you know of this dead man found in the ashes?"

Marjory had to calm herself. Her telegraphs to her father had been vague of necessity. And she knew how he reacted to hyperbole and emotion in these retellings of her experiences and concerns. She adopted the style of her mother, serious and businesslike, when she could.

"On Monday, Papa, the servant's village, the Styx, was burned to the ground. I was out on the porch at the Breakers that night with a friend. A female friend," she added. This was, after all, her father.

"We smelled the smoke and then saw the glow of flames in the trees and went to investigate."

"Yes." McAdams had already been advised of these facts. He already knew who the friend was, the senior housekeeper in whose company his daughter had often been seen. He had decided not to fight that battle, his daughter's penchant for fraternizing with the staff. He had never wanted to stifle her inquisitiveness or shield her from knowing the ways of people, especially those outside her class. Such associations had served him well as Flagler's front man, his forward scout, so to speak. "You learn the truth by listening" had been his own private motto, and he would not hamstring his own daughter by denying her that knowledge. In this situation, though, he was concerned that his broadmindedness would come back to haunt him.

"Go on, dear."

"So I went out to the fire site," she said. "To help if I could."

McAdams raised one questioning eyebrow. The look was not unfamiliar to Marjory. It was disapproval of her actions, of her logic, but her father would never say a word, just give the eyebrow, point made.

"We watched the fire, while it ate everything up. It was hor …"

Marjory stopped herself short of stepping across the emotional line she knew her father disliked.

"It destroyed nearly everything. The homes and that wooden dance hall and most of their belongings. They were left with nothing."

"I know you're concerned. And Mr. Flagler has already taken steps to build accommodations for his workers across the lake. I do believe they will in fact be an improvement over the housing those people had thrown together in the Styx," McAdams said.

Marjory now abandoned the rule against displaying emotion. "Yes, I know. But it will be no benefit to the poor woman whom that abominable blob of a sheriff has accused of killing that man."

McAdams held up his hand, lowered his head, showing her his acquiescence to the fierceness his daughter owned.

"I know about the body. But please tell me that you did not also witness this."

"I'm sorry, but yes, a few of us did see the body. It was not so bad as when Mama and I saw that dead little boy in the Bowery that day."

The memory tightened the skin around Mr. McAdams's eyes. It was one of the few times in their marriage that he had admonished his wife. Her penchant for social work in the city had led her numerous times into undesirable neighborhoods in the lower bowels of Manhattan, but she had always reassured him with explanations that these were group trips with other like-minded women and they never traveled without escort, often off-duty police officers hand-picked by trusted commanders close to prominent members of their society.

But the idea that his wife would take ten-year-old Marjory along with her crossed all bounds of acceptance. While the entire group was walking near Chatham Square, ostensibly scouting out a location for some cockamamy poorhouse for unwed mothers, a child half Marjory's age fell, or was pushed or simply thrown, from the window of a six-story building they were passing. In relating the story his wife had been unable to determine whether she'd heard the gasps before the thud of the body or the other way round. She said she'd tried to shield Marjory's eyes from the crumpled body that lay before them. But Marjory later had dreams of birds losing flight in midair and reacted with a twitching shock whenever she heard a thump from some innocent occurrence out of sight. She had actually taken one of her dolls and positioned its arms and legs in a horrific tableau that his wife said was a remarkable reconstruction of the dead child's position on the sidewalk. In time Marjory seemed to have forgotten the incident, but obviously not altogether.

Mr. McAdams, in his dry manner, stated only the facts as he knew them.

"And I understand, Marjory, that the sheriff—and I do wish you would be more circumspect in your descriptions of the man—has conducted an investigation."

"Which is the entire problem. This so-called investigation has led to a ludicrous assumption that a poor Negro housemaid put a knife into the man and then tried to burn his body to cover the crime and led to the destruction of her own home and entire village."

Mr. McAdams put his chin in the space between the forefinger and thumb of his right hand and tilted his head just so. It was a sign Marjory recognized as the point at which the conversation had turned from an exercise in listening to one bordering on argument.

"And this accused woman, did you know her, dear?"

"No."

"Had not Mizz Fluery introduced you to her?"

"No, Papa." She hated lying to her father.

"So you did not know that she was a known, shall we say, escort of sorts with a rather tawdry reputation?"

"I did not know she was a prostitute, no," Marjory said, rising to the debate that was now growing into the kind of lecture from her father she always railed against.

Mr. McAdams closed his eyes at the sound of the word *prostitute*, as if it were a glob of spittle that sullied both Marjory's upbringing and her beauty.

Marjory recognized her limits and knew from her father's look that she may have stepped over them. Logic had always been his game. She retreated to it quickly.

"There were several people at the fair on the mainland who saw the woman there. She wasn't even on the island at the time of the fire." This of course was speculation and was in fact Marjory's entire motivation. Had Shantice Carver actually seen something she was never intended to see or not?

McAdams took a sip from his glass and remained stoically silent, but listening.

"And it is quite possible that Mr. Pearson himself recognized the dead man," Marjory added, letting her ace come out of her hand in an effort to gain favor. "You can ask his opinion. I know he'll speak to you with candor."

Mr. McAdams remained quiet in the face of his daughter's salvo. It was not the effect she was looking for. He finished his scotch with a slight flourish, a signal that the conversation was over.

"I shall speak with Mr. Pearson. And I will also attempt a meeting with the sheriff. Those things I can do under my limited authority," he said. McAdams lowered his chin, dipping his forehead just so, and looked up at his daughter with his eyebrows raised. It was his conciliatory look, the one that asked for her patience, her discretion and her obedience.

"But please, my dear. Go no further with this until we talk again. I promise I'll share with you what I can. But please, Marjory, leave this alone for now."

The look and the slightly pleading tone always cut to her heart, made her feel guilty for adding burden to her father's life.

"I will," she said, standing and stepping to his chair. He would get to the truth, to what was known by whom. And then he would share that knowledge with her. That she was sure of. She bent to kiss his cheek. "It is wonderful to have you here."

Chapter 12

When Byrne emerged from the Seminole Hotel the next morning, he made sure not to step directly into the light. He'd learned that the sunrise in Florida was not the same event as in New York. Unfiltered by smoke and ash and undiffused by a hundred tall buildings and their cast of shadows, the sun here had the power to create temporary blindness in a Yankee whose immediate response was to squint and shade his eyes with a raised hand.

Today the lesson paid off. Byrne stayed back under the shadow of an awning. He spotted Mr. Faustus, leaning against a hitching post in front of shop baring the sign "L.A. Willson, Fine Boot and Shoemaker. Perfect Fits and Most Approved Styles Assured. No Cheap Work."

Faustus was dressed in dark trousers and a white long-sleeved shirt buttoned tight to the neck and at the wrists. He had apparently left his tailed coat and his vest at home but still wore his high hat. Despite the early hour, he had a lit cigar in his mouth, the scent of which Byrne caught in the mild breeze. Since Faustus's boots were shined, perfectly sound and in no need of repair, Byrne assumed Faustus was waiting for him.

"Good morning, young Mr. Byrne," Faustus said, coming off one haunch.

Byrne, his eyes adjusted, stepped down off the porch and joined the man.

"Good day to you, sir."

"A fine day in paradise, Mr. Byrne," Faustus said with a flourish of the cigar. "With this mild wind blowing in from the north, the ocean will assuredly be as a child's soft blanket, and it is a perfect morning for fishing."

"Fishing, sir?"

"Why yes, young Pinkerton. Have you never been fishing on the deep blue sea?"

What Byrne knew of fish was the odor of the docks on Canal Street in the Lower forties, the mongers wheeling their carts up Broadway, the chopped-away fish heads washing in the slush of the gutters. But his memory of last night's dinner, combined with Faustus's use of the description of this fabulous water, caused a spark of interest to flash in his mind. He looked into Faustus's eyes, where there was a certain liveliness that he'd not seen before: no business, no cunning, no historical lesson, just an inkling of adventure.

"Fishing?" he repeated. Faustus raised his immense eyebrows in invitation. Byrne thought of the bait-and-switch of the Bowery but knew he was too smart if that was the man's ploy. Besides, Faustus was turning into someone who seemed quite connected in this new town. Perhaps connected enough to know where to find someone named Danny Byrne even if his brother had changed his name. Byrne felt as if Faustus was investigating him as much as he was investigating Faustus. As a result, the man intrigued him. Why not come right out and ask if he knew of Danny and get it over with? Surely he'd been blunt with everyone else. But bluntness did not seem to be Faustus's style, a trait that Byrne recognized as his own in the past. Could Faustus be an ally, or nemesis? And if Byrne was being subtly recruited, to what end?

Within an hour they were aboard a twenty-six-foot sailing launch, pushing off onto the lake from the docks of A.T. Rose, Boat Builder, on the southern boundary of the city.

When Byrne had agreed to Faustus's excursion, he'd first asked if he would require anything special: clothing, equipment, food.

"Not a thing, young Pinkerton. Just your curiosity," Faustus had said and winked.

Within short walking distance of the hotel they passed through a boatyard of sorts with hulls in partial repair or stages of construction. The smell of fresh-cut wood mixed with that of thick lacquer and paint. Faustus tipped his hat to a craftsman who was at the task of shaving what looked like a pole of fine ash wood into what Byrne assumed would eventually be a mast. Other workers were scraping the dried scales and what appeared to be barnacles from the bottom of a launch that had been pulled with ropes and pulleys from the water up and onto a cradle of sorts. The equipment and docks and the wood itself looked new and fresh and hardened in the sun instead of the dank and rotted pilings and the stench of fish and oils and filth Byrne had experienced on the wharves of New York.

At a dock jutting out into the lake was a waiting vessel. Faustus called to the man coiling lines on the bow and introduced him to Byrne as Captain Abbott.

"All loaded with rigging and lunch for two as requested, Mr. Faustus," the captain said, taking the older man's elbow and guiding him onto the deck. Byrne waved off the offer of help and stepped down onto the gunwale and then to the deck boards while trying to lock his eyes onto Faustus's. The fact that the old Mason had anticipated that Byrne would automatically agree to the fishing offer bothered him. But his irritation at being manipulated was soon overwhelmed by his fascination with this new enterprise.

After pushing off from the dock, Captain Abbott yanked on a line that unfurled a fabric sail. "Watch your head, boy!"

A heavy wooden beam swung by just as Byrne ducked, and the sail filled with a woof. The forward movement underfoot almost felled him, but he caught his balance and stood with his feet apart as the captain cleated the line and then skittered past him to gain control of the tiller handle. Byrne's head and eyes swung in three directions trying to keep up with the mariner's actions, the swing of the boat, and its relation to the land.

"Ha!" yelped Mr. Faustus. "That beam that nearly took your head off is called a boom, young Pinkerton. That's the one to watch when Captain Abbott starts yelling 'Coming about!' or it will certainly boom you upside the noggin.'"

"I see," Byrne said, trying to be cynical but unable to keep a smile from starting at the corners of his mouth.

When Abbott yanked on yet another line and the boom pulled in, the boat heeled a bit to one side, and Byrne moved to the other and sat on the raised gunwale, now looking ahead to see where they might be going and feeling the pleasant rush of wind in his ears. The only times he'd been on the water in New York were in a stolen rowboat on the East River with Danny and on the ferry to New Jersey. The wobbling rowboat and the crowded ferry were nothing like this. As the canvas stretched and the lines tightened, he could feel the craft's speed increase and took the chance of leaning out to watch the pointed bow slice through the lake, sending out the V-shaped lines of disturbed water. The lack of motor noise and the pure physical pull of the sail were intoxicating. It was almost what he imagined flying to be like.

Off to the northeast he could see the diminishing view of the upper floors of the Poinciana. For the next half hour Byrne remained quiet, studying the movements of the captain and inspecting the craft: the sturdy brass of the cleats and fittings, the polish of the teak decking and the weaving in the rope lines. He finally relaxed after deeming the whole operation seaworthy despite his lack of experience to tell him any different. While the captain continued to make small adjustments to the sail and the tension of the lines, Mr. Faustus was now pulling out what Byrne assumed to be the fishing poles and equipment and what must be the bait they were to use in catching fish.

"Step on down here, Mr. Byrne, and let me show you what we've got," Faustus said.

What he had were four long rods from six to eight feet in length. Faustus explained that they were made from split Tonkin bamboo and Calcutta reed. He picked one up at the base and wiggled it, causing the pliable fiber to bend and whip at the end.

"A little more give in the shaft than you're used to," Faustus said, without looking up. "But it gives you much more control of the fish once he's got the hook in his mouth."

Byrne said nothing. He knew Faustus had seen him use his telescoping rod to manage the crowd of farmers during the train ride. Even now the weapon was in the deep pocket of his pants.

"I'm sure you'll get the feel of it," Faustus said, handing one of the poles to Byrne.

It was light in his fingers. The base appeared to be made of maple, and there were simple wire loops attached at equidistant points along its length. He took his own turn flexing the pole, snapping its end and creating a whipping noise not unlike the sound his own metal rod made when he was using it with a fury. Next Faustus brought out a box and removed two large brass reels each about the size of a small child's head. Byrne could tell they were heavy by the strain that showed in the old man's forearms and tendons when he lifted them and set them on the deck. He showed Byrne the iron gears and brass casings and the cork handle that spun the device. On an interior spool was wound some sort of linen line. Faustus pinched a loose end and pulled off a length of the line.

"Twenty-four threads spun together," he said. "Maxiumum strength when it's dry is about sixty-six pounds. But that won't matter out here. We won't be picking them up out the sea like some hangman. The idea is to hook them and then outguess them. Let them pull the line through the water until they wear out their hearts, but keep them from breaking free just the same.

"Oh, you'll see, my friend. It's a glorious thing."

The captain sniggered behind them, not in derision of the words but in a shared recognition of another man's addiction. Byrne himself was surprised by the old Mason's excitement and by the fact that every minute closer to the fishing grounds seemed to peel another year off his aged face.

Captain Abbott yanked in a length of what Byrne had now learned was the mainsail sheet line and hollered out a word of advice: "Hold onto somethin', fellas, the inlet's a bit choppy today."

Byrne saw a rise and fall of ocean swells he'd never witnessed before. Ditches and troughs, was his instant thought. Mounds and hollows to split any axle. He held fast to the edge of the gunwale and felt the bow rise on the first wave and then braced himself as it plunged down into the following trough. He expected impact. But the boat's bow knifed through the water, and the landing was not nearly what he'd expected. The next forward plunge sent a spray of sea out from either side of the bow like sheets of snow from a plow blade. By the fourth such rise and fall, Byrne was studying the angles the captain was taking, admiring his expertise at controlling the boat's pitch and roll with the tiller. By the sixth swell, Byrne was humbled.

Within minutes they were through the inlet and onto the smoother, rolling ocean. Captain Abbott let out the boom and took a more southerly course. Faustus stepped up onto the gunwale with a handhold on one of the mast stays and stared out onto open water. Byrne followed suit on his side of the cockpit, worried now that he would miss another new experience. The sky was cloudless and blue, and the sea borrowed its color and then bent it into greens and turquoise, depending on the depths.

"Your employer loves these waters and this coastline as much as anyone with an appreciation of such beauty," Faustus said without turning. The statement took Byrne by surprise, but since there didn't seem to be a question involved, he let it stand without comment. Captain Abbott, on the other hand, responded with a derisive snort.

"Did you know that Mr. Flagler's first forays into this part of Florida were by sailboat? No one who rides this sea could miss its Edenic pull."

Byrne let the old man's words stand alone. There will be a point in them, he thought. Faustus, he'd already determined, was not a man without a point.

"But I fear Flagler's island is not just a single jewel to delight his friends and rejuvenate their spirits for the business of business in the North," Faustus continued, finally turning to look Byrne in the eye. "There will be trouble in that paradise, young Pinkerton. And in your position, it will be trouble you won't be able to avoid."

"I appreciate your concern, sir," Byrne said, deciding whether he should rise to what he was already perceiving to be bait. "And from what I've heard on the street, trouble is already there."

Faustus stepped back down onto the cockpit deck.

"I'm glad I did not underestimate your abilities at intelligence gathering. Would you be speaking of the death of a white man in the Negro quarters on the island?"

"There was talk of it on the street," Byrne said.

"And did the speakers have any idea who the unfortunate fellow was or what his business might have been there?" Faustus said, carefully watching for reaction.

"I don't recall any talk of business, no. Did you understand him to be a businessman?" Byrne asked, playing the game, giving what he could to get what he might.

Faustus moved on, but Byrne had seen a twinge of pain in the old man's eyes.

"At this point in this virgin land, everyone is in business. There are people buying, people selling. Be it the labor of their hands, the guile of their intellect, the dreams they lust after or the lust itself."

"And your business, Mr. Faustus? What exactly is it that you do?" Byrne kept his tone as innocent as possible although he perceived he'd made a fine move in their little chess game.

Faustus sat on the starboard gunwale and began the process of attaching the reel to the heavy end of one of the poles.

"I've been involved in a wide variety of enterprise in life, my friend. I've used my hands as a shipwright in Biloxi, my intellect as a student of medicine in New Orleans, my tongue as a merchant of everything from ladies' plumed hats in Savannah to gunpowder in Charleston.

"I served as a field surgeon in the Civil War and afterward worked as a surveyor of the broken land of the South."

Faustus turned his face up to the sun with a look that showed neither pride nor regret.

"I have been blessed and cursed in the activities of commerce and men for many years, my young fisherman," he said, handing Byrne the completed pole. "And either way, it can be a befuddling thing to see.

"Presently, I admit I'm in search of good men. Men with honesty and moral fiber in their souls. Men who believe in the goodness of others and are adept at bringing that quality out. Men who, instead of taking advantage for their own gain, recognize that gain can and should be shared."

Ah, the pitch, Byrne thought.

"And have you met such men, Mr. Faustus?" he said.

"Oh, yes," Faustus said. "But I have also been fooled by those with the look and intelligence and talent for such things, only to be disappointed."

The old Mason was now looking into Byrne's face as if it was familiar to him, as if he were speaking to Byrne himself in this obviously heartfelt sense of disappointment. Such accusation had no basis as far as Byrne's actions were concerned, but still he had a nagging sense of responsibilty. It was Faustus who broke the spell.

"For now, young Pinkerton, let us lure the beasts from the deep and see what challenge they may afford us."

Byrne shook off his apprehension and watched while the man opened the hatch of a wooden barrel lashed into one corner of the cockpit and came out with a small, silver-sided fish, which he proceeded to carefully skewer with the finger-sized hook he'd tied to the linen line.

"First we'll do a little trolling on our way to the stream, eh, Captain Abbott?" Faustus.

Abbott was a man whose eyes seemed nearly colorless and thus able to reflect the intense shimmering light off the water rather than absorb it. His skin was dark and seamed. His lips formed a taught line and were the color and consitency of red onion skin. Perhaps they would split and bleed if he used them to excess, Byrne thought. Maybe that's why he so rarely spoke.

"As you will, sir," he said, and although Byrne saw the man's Adam's apple move, his lips did not. Byrne thought instantly of a ventriloquist he'd seen in the Bowery.

Faustus baited his own hook and showed Byrne how simple it was to cast the fish into the bubbling wake behind them and let the line spin off his reel. He'd put a canvas glove on one hand and used his thumb to occasionally slow down the rate of the linen leaving the reel. In less than five minutes, the old man suddenly jerked the tip of the rod up, like Byrne might have done with his own baton, and then began to turn the handle of the spinning reel. Without hesitation, Capt. Abbott turned the boat into the wind to slow it. The boom swung to the middle of the cockpit and almost smashed into Byrne's head. He was captivated by the sudden tightening of Faustus's line and the deft way the old man reeled and then stopped, apparently feeling the direction of the pull on the other end and then reeling again. There was a small sweat and an obvious joy on Faustus's face.

"It appears we've got ourselves a nice dolphin," Faustus yelled over the popping of canvas as the sail went loose in the wind. "Grab that gaff over there so you can hook him when I bring him along the starboard side!"

Byrne searched in the direction Faustus had indicated but had no inkling what a "gaff" might be. Without taking his pale eyes off the battle, Captain Abbott reached out a leg, put his foot on a cork-handled hook like Byrne had seen ice deliverymen use to handle their blocks, and kicked it over to him. Byrne picked it up and, thus armed, stared back at the sea, following Faustus's line into blue water. Minutes passed as Faustus coaxed and manuvered, reeled and stopped. The flexible tip of the rod bent and swung like a willow in the wind. Finally Byrne saw a flash of silver light below, then the body of the fish, slowing in its struggle, and soon he could see the dark circle of its eye.

"Alongside, son," Faustus said, now pulling the defeated catch to starboard. "Hook her in the gills if you would."

Byrne bent and reached overboard. He was talented with a piece of metal in his hand and gaffed the fish and pulled it up out of the water, surprised by its heft, forty pounds at least. He flopped it down into the foot of the cockpit and withdrew the gaff while Faustus pressed his polished shoe across its broad side.

"Comin' about!" Capt. Abbott called out, and this time Byrne reacted to the words and ducked. He felt the jolt as wind filled the sail and the boat was again under way. Faustus bent to remove his hook from the fish's mouth. "She'll make a fine meal, this one," he said.

Byrne continued watching the fish, its tail still waving as if it could propel itself to escape in the air as it had always done in water. But it was a different world up here, and old defenses didn't work. Finally Faustus grasped the dolphin and slid it into a shuttered bin filled with chopped ice.

"All right, Mr. Byrne. Time for your own lesson on the finest fishing grounds in the world."

Faustus baited the hook on Byrne's rod and tossed his line overboard. During the next hour the men pulled in a dozen fish: several pompano, two more dolphin of equal size to the first, three of what Faustus called redfish, and a four-foot-long shark the face of which Byrne openly compared to that of a Tammany police sergeant.

Byrne snapped only one line when a dolphin dove unexpectedly and he yanked back to stop it instead of letting it run. His observations of Faustus's moves and technique were so thorough that several times Byrne would make the correction just before the words came out of the old man's mouth.

"You're a quick study," Faustus said while removing the hook from yet another fish's mouth. "As I knew you would be.

"But we've a much bigger challenge ahead, and it's in water you still have never imagined in your deepest dreams."

The look in the old man's eyes was disconcerting in its almost religious anticipation. Byrne found his skin tingling with the excitement to come after already being flabbergasted by the experience of fighting the running, instinctual muscle of big fish with a simple bending length of wood and a spool of linen thread. What could the old Mason now have up his sleeve?

"Into the stream, sir!" Capt. Abbott called out, and when Byrne followed Faustus's gaze, he had an answer.

"Jesus, Mary and Joseph," he whispered, looking out and then down into an translucent blue water that was like no color he'd ever witnessed or thought possible.

Byrne felt the shift of current below them, the boat being pushed against its will to the north. He looked first to Faustus, but the man's face had taken on a look of one witnessing a deity. Even the craggy Abbott appeared to have a glint of a smile on his slash of a mouth.

"It's the Gulf Stream, son," Faustus said. "She's nothing less than a magical river that circles the Gulf of Mexico and then comes surging round the tip of Florida off Key West and runs like a fire hose northbound to New York and on to Nova Scotia.

"Ships have been using her muscle to take a free ride north for centuries. If you just sat on her in a rowboat, you'd float your way to shores of Europe herself without taking a single stroke. There's a whole troop of Norwegians who pluck tiny sea hearts off their beaches that were once washed off the shores of the Caribbean and simply got lost in the stream and took the ride for thousands of miles."

Byrne had no doubt of Faustus's geography lesson, but it was the color of the water that hypnotized him. He laid his chest across the starboard gunwale and reached down to actually touch the water, convinced that if he scooped up a handful, he would have a puddle of blue in his palm.

"This is where the finest of the breed work their own fishing grounds, Mr. Byrne. Where they can run as fast as lightning and strike at will, then flash away into their own deep universe."

Faustus was working again at the rigging. Byrne looked over and saw that he was attaching an odd-looking piece of metal to the end of his line. Oblong in shape, like a teardrop, the thin leaf of shiny tin had a hook protruding from the fat end, and unlike Faustus's other lures, there was a strange barb at the very tip akin to whaling harpoons Byrne had seen at the city docks. It was obvious by its design that such a hook was not going to slip easily out once it speared through the mouth flesh of a fish.

"I had this spoon custom-made by a friend in Philadelphia name of Samuel H. Jones," Faustus said, tying the pointed end of the teardrop to his line and clamping a series of split lead weights the size of peas to the line to pull it deep. "Sam claims he caught the most beautiful fish he'd ever seen in Florida on a spoon like this up on the Indian River inlet. A tarpon, he called it, as big as a man."

The old man dropped the lure into the blue, and Byrne watched it glitter in the deep light as it sunk deeper and deeper, maybe thirty yards, maybe forty before he could no longer track it. He looked up into Faustus's eyes and saw a mixture of anticipation, lust and competition that unsettled him at first and then stirred a tingle in his own hands that he recognized as the energy that came only when he had his metal baton in his palm and the threat of violence in his veins.

"Let's drag her south a bit, Captain," Faustus called out, and Abbott swung the boat about and set a wide sail. Since nothing was said about casting Byrne's line, he settled a haunch on the gunwale and was content to stare into the water, the depths somehow haunting, as if calling him to fall in and glide down into its warmth. The sun was high now, the reflection causing Byrne to shade his eyes whenever he looked out to follow Faustus's line into the sea. Despite the breeze he could feel a light sweat under his shirt and also the sting of sunburn on the back of his neck.

"She'll take it if she wants to," Faustus said once, though the statement seemed to be directed at no one in the boat. "That's the power she holds, to do what she wants in a sea of possibilities."

The words caused Byrne to conjure a glimpse of the white of fabric and green eyes of McAdams's daughter, a recollection that despite his surroundings and the thrill of the day had not left him.

"Ever had a woman like that, young Pinkerton?" Faustus said, and Byrne looked up to see the old man looking at him instead of the water. "One with the power to snatch and hold you?"

If the old man was performing some Masonic magic trick, reading his mind, Byrne would not have been more taken aback.

"No, sir. Never."

Faustus chuckled.

"Well if you do, young man, hold on just as tight as she does and enjoy the hell out of the adventure."

The pole in the old man's hand yanked forward, and the linen line started spinning off the reel like a strike of heat lightning. He instinctively pulled back on the rod. It bent in a U shape, and Byrne was sure the laminate would splinter in Faustus's hands. He could have sworn he heard the sound of cracking wood, but it may have been line zinging off the sides of the cast metal.

"My god!" Faustus pointed the tip of the rod toward the water and let the line and the fish run. When he felt the beast turn, Faustus raised the rod, took in a few turns of the reel, and felt just a bit of the weight of muscle that was at its end. Now the surprise had left his face and been replaced by a startled joy.

"Oh my, lad, what have we got?"

Byrne was staring after the line, watching it rip through the water like a sharp knife through satin and creating a similar sound. Then before his eyes, it went slack.

Snapped, he thought. But Faustus didn't move.

"Wait, wait, just you wait now," he said.

The moment Faustus had hooked the fish, Captain Abbott had again swung into the wind, and even he could not keep his eyes from the sea where the linen line now lay like a string of spittle.

"Wait, wait." The captain repeated Faustus's words, and Byrne felt the hairs on the back of his neck tingle.

The explosion erupted less than thirty yards off the starboard stern. Byrne swore he saw it coming, a sun glint in the depths, a flurry of silver bubbles rising. It then let loose like a fire hose just below the surface, a burst of water sprayed into the air, a fountain that contained in its middle the body of a silver fish like some scaled angel.

Byrne could not have been more stunned if he'd witnessed a rogue firework explode from a Lower East Side manhole cover.

In midair the beast bent its back to match the arc of Faustus's fishing rod and then twisted its body in a violent shake and plunged back into the sea.

"Christ on a cross!" said Captain Abbott, the first nonnautical utterance that had come out of the old sea dog during the entire trip. The boat had come to a standstill, rocking in the long waves. Byrne looked at Faustus for a clue. Both old men watched the water and the tip of the rod. Again like a rip of lightning through a cloud, the fish burst the surface, flying higher still while shaking its huge body like a dog trying to dry itself with a shiver and twist.

"She's a hundert an twenty if she's a pound, sir," Abbott said, still in reverence.

"And bound to run, Captain."

"Yes, sir. Coming about, sir."

Abbott swung the boat by pumping the tiller until the sail could catch wind. Faustus made his way forward in the cockpit, keeping the fish on the port side. Again the line went taut as a guitar string, and Faustus let it spool out.

"The line will put a drag on her," he said. "She'll have to swim against it. All we can do is follow and hope she's not strong enough to break it." For the next hour the men worked the line and the boat, Faustus trying to anticipate the moves of the fish, Abbott following his called-out directions.

Byrne could already tell from the beads of sweat rolling off the old man's face and the bend in his back and bow of his shoulders that he was tiring. The joy had drained from his face, along with a certain degree of grit.

"Damn, she's strong," he said in admiration. He took his eyes off the ocean for a second to look at Byrne, who could do nothing but wipe the old man's face with a cloth dipped in fresh water. "She'll run for a while, but at some point she's going to buck again, son. And truth be known, I don't think I'm strong enough anymore to match her."

Byrne turned to look at the captain.

"No. You, son," Faustus said. "First, get my holster out of the bin there."

Byrne was used to taking orders and conceded that Faustus was the one in charge. He went directly to the bin and realized what the man had asked for. Holster? He glanced back at the old man, who was back to the business of horsing the fish.

Byrne began pawing through the bin, searching for and finally finding a dark leather holster wrapped tightly and pressed into one corner. He pulled it out and stood with a .36 caliber Griswold revolver in his hands. What the hell was he planning to do, shoot the damn fish?

"Strap it on, lad," said Abbott without looking. "Loose like."

Byrne uncoiled the belt, buckled it around his waist and notched it so the old leather settled on his hips, the gun handle at his right side, all the while wondering what the hell.

"OK," he said.

Faustus grinned at the gunslinger pose.

"Get rid of the gun, young Pinkerton, though I do not doubt your proficiency with such a mechanism.

"And slide the holster round to the front. Next time she gives us a lull, we're going to stick the butt of the pole right into that pocket. That way you'll be able to use that back of yours, son."

Byrne got the picture, pulled the gun and held it for a second in his hand, the familiar weight of it and the warm metal against his palm. He laid it in the bin and then twisted the holster so that it was positioned between his legs and moved to Faustus's side. On the old man's command, he grabbed the pole with both hands, and they jammed the butt down into the holster. For the first time Byrne felt the power of the fish below.

"Jaysus."

"You got that right, Irish," he heard the captain say behind him.

"Now, son. Visualize the line below. It's working in a long curve. The beast pulling it this way and then changing course and pulling it the other," Faustus waved his hand in a wide motion to describe the movement. "When you feel the pressure ease, you know she's changed course and you've got to move the tip to make sure the line doesn't snap when it catches up to the turn."

For the next hour Byrne felt and listened, watched the line, leaned back with the holster digging into his crotch but glad for the leverage it afforded him. His own young muscles began to ache, and each long minute he gained respect for Faustus and the fish. While he worked, Faustus talked, giving him what knowledge he had. The old man also fed him fresh water so he wouldn't have to take his hands off the pole. At one point Abbott removed his own captain's hat, doused it in the drinking water and then without a word unceremoniously flopped it on top of Byrne's head and left it there, the shaded coolness running down his face and neck.

All three men could feel the fish slowly turning its easterly course more and more to the north to follow the current of the Gulf Stream.

"Path of least resistance," Faustus said. "Just like all living things when we tire.

"But beware of the heart in this one, she'll give it one last try to escape."

The Florida sun was now in the western sky. Byrne could feel the tightness on the skin of his neck like it had shrunk as it sizzled under the direct heat. They were into the third hour, but he had refused to ask how long this could go on. His back felt like one giant muscle, bunched and aching. At Faustus's instructions he'd let his arms extend, giving up on flexing them except to reel a small amount of line when he felt the need. The wind continued to blow but mercifully did not increase. Their ride on the swells had become so rhythmic there was almost a music to it.

Byrne was about to turn the rod again when the line went slack.

"No pressure," he said, alarm in his voice. He let the tip go down toward the water and looked at Faustus. "Did it break? Has she broken it?"

"No!" Faustus reached out to push the rod back in high position. "She's turning on us. Reel the line, son. Reel the line."

Byrne spun the handle. Abbott stalled the boat into the wind. All three stared out to the northwest, waiting.

Sun glanced off the wave fronts and tossed deep blue shadows on the backsides. Each glimmer on the sea's surface caught the men's attention. Byrne's knuckles were white on the sweat-stained wood of the rod, his fingers nearly numb as they worked the reel.

The captain saw it first, his sea-trained eyes, despite their age, picking up the silver below the surface.

"There!"

A finger jutted out due north.

Again came the rise of silver and the rip of water. The fish was closer this time, as if she needed to see who had beaten her. The long body cleared the ocean but not nearly as high as the first times. The twist was not as violent. The buck was almost listless. But the shine of scaled flesh was even more spectacular in the glancing sun.

After the splash no one said a word. Byrne felt the tension return to the line, but it was decidedly feeble.

"Keep reeling," Faustus said.

In another thirty minutes they pulled the fish up from the blue and alongside. Faustus leaned over and grabbed the line, twisting it once around his palm, and drew the tarpon near. But when Byrne went to fetch the gaff, the old man said, "No. Just hand me those pliers, son."

Abbott had left the tiller. "I was wrong, sir," he said, looking over the gunwale. "It's a hundert and fifty easy."

The mouth of the fish was huge and gasping, its boney structures stretching the tough skin.

"Reach down and grab a gill," he said to Byrne while he probed the inside of the fish's mouth with the pliers to find the hook. In a second he twisted his wrist and Byrne heard the pop of gristle being torn. The hook was removed. When Byrne started to lift, Faustus again said no, traded handholds and grasped the gill himself and lowered the fish's mouth back into the blueness. Then he let go and they watched six feet of silver float down behind them and, with a mere twitch of the tail, turn and disappear.

Faustus stood for a long minute, watching. His starched white shirt was soaked with sea water and sweat. A streak of fish blood tracked across the front. His polished shoes squished in the puddle of scum, guts, water and fish oil on the cockpit floor. His look was at once both humble and majestic.

"Time to go home, captain," Faustus said. Abbott pulled in a sheet line and called "Comin' about," and the sail popped in the wind, heading southwest.

Byrne said nothing, partly stunned, partly exhausted, partly understanding. He unlatched the holster and gave it to Faustus. He handed Abbott's hat back to the captain, who shook it once and then pulled it tight over his grey head.

"Might have been a record, sir," Abbott said, yanking down the brim to shield whatever look there might have been in his eyes.

"Aye," said Faustus, who reached into the bin and took out the handgun, replaced it in the holster and rewound the belt. He looked up with that grin of his on a now tired face.

"But would that have made it any more glorious?"

Even Abbott smiled. No need to answer.

"As for you, young Pinkerton, it was a job well done. A lesser man would have given in. And an even lesser man would have screamed bloody murder at the thought of letting that one go."

Byrne remained quiet.

"I do not think that I misjudged you, despite my inclinations from influences past," Faustus said, and now their eyes were locked.

"Did you think that I was like my brother?" Byrne said, guessing what he now felt in his bones.

"The family resemblance is unequivocal," Faustus said.

"Do you know where he is?"

"Yes," Faustus said. "I believe I do."

Chapter 13

He did not want to move from his bed the next morning, but the pounding on the door demanded it. Faustus had refused to elaborate on his comment that he might know where Danny was and would only say that he would make his inquiries and update Byrne when he could. But Faustus was not the kind of man who came bashing at your door.

Byrne rolled to one shoulder, feeling first the sting of crisp skin on his neck fairly scraping across the pillowcase and second the ache of muscle in his back. He made it up onto one haunch, his ass the only place he didn't feel pain.

The fist on the door continued.

"Rise and shine, lad. I know yer in there," Harris's voice boomed from the hallway. "Shake the hangover out of yer head, you've work to do."

Byrne got to his feet. The heat in the room went straight to his face. He ran his tongue over his lips and discovered the cracked layer of blister that had formed there.

"Coming," he said with a rasp, and even the inside of his throat felt sunburned. He crossed the room with his cotton boxers on and opened the door. Harris was at first taken aback at the sight and then let an infrequent smile show up on his big pie-shaped face.

"Well, well, Michael. It wasn't the devil of drink at all that struck you, lad. 'Twas your introduction to the great Florida sun, eh?"

"I went fishing," Byrne said, moving back to let Harris enter.

"Indeed you did, lad. And caught more than you bargained for, eh?"

Byrne thought of the tarpon in flight, the twisting, beautiful look of the thing.

"Yes," he said. "Much more."

"Well, you're not the first white-skinned New Yorker turned crispy red, and you won't be the last. But that won't excuse you from your duties.

"Here's another dole of spending money." Harris peeled off bills from a wad that had materialized in his big fist. "You'll have to go over to Buholtz's on Banyan and buy yourself a proper suit. We've been asked to be present at Mrs. Flagler's society ball this evening, and we'll both have to be in costume, like nobody's going to recognize a couple of Irish mugs like us bumpin' round in a mix of them.

"Still, we'll make an attempt to watch over the old man. Be at the grand ballroom at six. I'll be honest with you, it's a first for me. We've never gone off and away from the train before, so I'm not sure what they might be expecting. But someone's nervous these days."

Byrne thought of the rumors that someone had been killed on the island during a fire in the servant's quarters. Should he share this intelligence with Harris? He wasn't sure he should but couldn't say why. Did he not trust his own sergeant? That wouldn't be a first considering the lessons learned doing his corruption work as a New York police officer. He'd be surprised, of course, if Harris wasn't already aware of the rumor, but since he'd not mentioned it, Byrne decided to hold his own cards for now.

Harris had tightened his Irish mug during his giving of orders, but couldn't hold it when once again he looked at Byrne's ruby red nose and cheeks.

"Ask the desk clerk where you can find some aloe, lad," he said with a look of empathy on his face. "It's a plant they use here to give you some relief. You cut the leaf and squeeze out the gel inside and rub it on that sunburn. You'll survive."

Byrne went to the mirror after Harris left. His eyes were swollen. His nose looked like one of the old regulars at McSorely's, red and wrinkled, his cheekbones like they'd been rouged in one of the Tin Pan Alley follies. He'd have laughed if not for the pain. Harris was right, he'd live. But he sure as hell wasn't going to shave until he had to.

Byrne pulled a shirt over his burned shoulders and neck and gathered his dirty clothes in one of the hotel pillow cases. At the front desk he asked the clerk for both a laundry and someplace where he might obtain some of Harris's mysterious aloe plant. The answer to both queries was the same. On Banyan to the north was Joe Cheong's laundry in the back of Jones's cigar factory.

Byrne was able to locate Cheong's, which was little more than a wooden lean-to with tubs of fresh water and an old steam press. Under the awning was a covey of small, bird-like women fluttering about. He was reminded of similar businesses in corners of the Lower East Side. The needs of men—and the commerce that went with it—had quickly been transplanted from the established streets of New York to the new Florida. After negotiating a price for the laundry, Byrne spent several moments of awkward pantomime and pidgin English asking for the aloe. The head woman, a diminutive Chinese with gray hair and an abrupt air, simply stared at his odd gestures and finally took up a sharp-bladed knife from under the counter and signaled for him to follow her. She led him to a small private garden of sorts. Several plants he did not recognize had been hand planted and carefully tended. The woman went directly to a dark green, crown-shaped bush that Byrne took for a cactus of some kind. The woman hacked off three of the stiff leaves with her knife and held them out to him. When he hesitated to take them, she singled one out, scored it across its three-inch width, snapped it in half and then with her fingers kneaded the middle of the leaf, milking out a yellowish gel. Without touching his face, she showed how Byrne should dab the gel onto the tips of his fingers and then smear it on his own skin.

He followed her instructions and immediately felt relief. The woman accepted a dollar as payment. When she returned to the laundry, Byrne took off his shirt and applied the gel to his neck and shoulders, ears, and forehead. Whether the juice from the plant truly had any medicinal value was of no consequence to him. It diminished the pain of his sunburn and was thus well worth the money.

With his spirits buoyed, Byrne made his way through the streets. The walking loosened the muscles in his back and legs. Near Narcissus he began to walk past the shop of Hawthorn & Dorsey, which had a small, almost toylike red and white barber pole out front. He remembered the crowd he'd seen in front of the Royal Poinciana, their clothes and their fine ways, and he hesitated. He thought of the young Miss McAdams and did a U-turn, put his hands in his pockets and walked into the shop. It was impossible to be unobtrusive. One man, be it Hawthorn or Dorsey, was sitting in a high wooden chair reading a copy of *The Gazetteer*. There was a single chest of drawers against the wall, scissors and razors, brushes and wash bowls on its top. A mirror was mounted behind.

"Good morning, young sir," the man said, hopping to his feet and folding the newspaper. "Shave and a haircut?"

Byrne had never had anyone but his mother cut his hair and had never had a calm man come close to his throat with a razor.

"The cost?" Byrne said.

"Twenty cents," the barber answered and added, "each."

"Very well," Byrne said, giving the barber a look that was meant to say "I know the bait and switch trick but will give you the business regardless."

The man smiled and reached out a hand: "D. H. Hawthorn. A pleasure to serve you, sir."

The barber helped Byrne remove his coat and set him on the stool. He snapped open a folded sheet with a flourish and wrapped it round Byrne's neck.

"New to these parts, sir?"

"Yes," Byrne said. "Just in."

"Nasty business the sun down here. I shall be extra careful of the sunburn."

"Thank you."

"Care for the newspaper while we work, sir? I'll do the haircut first."

"Fine," Byrne said, and Mr. Hawthorn not only unfolded the small paper and laid it across Byrne's lap but proceeded to tell him everything that the journal had printed that day and then some. By the time the haircut was done, Byrne knew all about the feud between the liberal newspaper editor and the sheriff, which had come to the point of the editor being arrested, that J. T. Berry and J. B. Thomas had killed a bear on the west side of Cedar Lake Tuesday morning, that a lighthouse at the preposterous cost of $90,000 had been recommended for the mouth of the Hillsboro River well south of the city, and that a young man such as himself would do well—if he had a mind and the means—to attend a land auction along the East Coast Railway tracks just up the line next week "which very few folks know about and could result in a fine and profitable acquisition if you get my meaning, sir."

When asked what kind of business he was in, Byrne answered only that he was in "security" and then tapped the heels of his brogans. From that point on the barber was quiet and seemed particularly careful with the razor when it came time for Byrne's shave. Pleased with the clean look he saw in the mirror, Byrne tipped Mr. Hawthorn a dime and proceeded down the street to Buholtz's.

While the New York shopping districts, even along Bowery, had increasingly featured specialty shops with specific goods for specific needs, Buholtz's was a general merchandise store that, despite its small size, overwhelmed customers with its variety of dry goods stacked and hung and pigeon-holed into every conceivable place: hats and caps, boots and shoes, bolts of multicolored and multitextured cloth, racks of dishes and cutlery, cooking utensils and pots, and stacks of baskets, blankets and ladies' bloomers.

Byrne stood, feeling as out of place as a young man could, until a salesman came up and asked if he could help. Byrne chose to state his predicament rather than try to hide his social ignorance.

"I need a proper suit for one of Mrs. Flagler's formal dinners at the Poinciana tonight," he said.

The salesman began to look him over, no doubt for size. But Byrne took it as an assessment.

"As a guest," he added.

"Certainly, sir. My name is Bob Campbell and I will be pleased to assist. This way please."

He was led to a deep corner of the store, behind piles of boxes and crates that created a semiprivate area with several jackets and trousers and vests hung against a wall and a full length mirror on another wall.

"My, you are certainly tall and broad shouldered," the salesman said. "And it is very short notice. But our specialty, Mr. uh?"

"Byrne."

"Our specialty, Mr. Byrne, is our line of ready-made clothing," Campbell said, again taking a step back and eyeing him. Byrne thought of the time Harvey Cannon measured him up at the Rockaway Pub before asking him outside for a fight. He'd whipped Harvey's ass without once taking out his baton.

"I'd say a thirty-eight long might do," Campbell said and began going through the racks.

In less than forty minutes, Byrne had been outfitted with a dark suit of tails with a finely brocaded vest and a monumentally stiff white shirt that made him wince when it was buttoned against his sunburn. Though Bob Campbell pushed, Byrne declined new shoes, much to Campbell's chagrin. When the total bill came to forty-two dollars and change, he swallowed hard, decided against the hat that was suggested, and paid. Alterations to take in the waist of the pants and to accommodate Byrne's unusual request to lengthen the right-hand pocket and add a leather sheath to its interior would be completed in an hour. With the remains of Harris's fifty dollars, Byrne went down to the corner of Banyan and Olive and had two beers and a fillet of yellow tail at J.C. Lauther's Saloon and Restaurant.

After lunch Byrne picked up his packages and returned to his hotel room. He stripped to his underwear, split open the aloe leaves as the Chinese woman had shown him and used the rest of the balm to again cover his face and neck. Then he raised his window, let the ocean breeze flow in and lay down. Within minutes his dreams came with jumping fish and gang members swinging heavy clubs, of the clean smell of salt air and the stench of running sewage, of the feel of squinting into bright sunlight and doing the same in an effort to see down dark alleys, of the vision of a young prostitute outside Harry Hill's concert saloon in the Bowery and that of a woman in dazzling white chiffon and bright green eyes who seemed to be watching him through it all. He awoke with a start, positive that he'd overslept. But when he checked his watch, it read four fifteen. He lay for a few minutes more, staring at the ceiling, recalling his half-dream visits and jumbled recollections. For years his mother had a strange addiction to the palmists and so-called seers who haunted the neighborhoods of the poor in New York. His father called them shysters and purveyors of a fool's hope and forbade her from spending money on them. She did anyway. She once told Michael that dreams were the windows to the future and that she took her dreams to the seers for interpretation. She saw great things for both him and Danny.

"It's a world here of democracy, boys," she would tell them. "No grand marquesses or lords keepin' ya down. Your work and your brains is what you need, and you both have plenty of that."

At the time Danny was all bravado and spunk, yelping about becoming the "king of the Bowery." All Byrne could do was answer "Yes, Mama." He thought of her now and his own disparate dreams and what they might mean. Where the hell was Danny? And did Faustus really know the answer to that question?

In twenty minutes he was washed and dressed and polished. The man he saw in the mirror was a version that should have made him uncomfortable but instead let him straighten his shoulders and give himself an uncharacteristic wink. When he passed the clerk downstairs, he saw the man's face brighten, though when he recognized Byrne, the look turned sober. As Byrne approached the bridge to the island, he actually looked forward to greeting the deputy who'd been scrutinizing the pedestrians the two days previous. But he noted that although the boy collecting a nickel for passing was in place, the lawman was absent.

"What, no one here to go through everyone's pockets today?" he said to the boy.

"They all went south on a fugitive hunt, sir."

"A fugitive hunt?" Byrne recalled Harris's anxiety over unknown threats to Flagler on this night. "What kind of fugitive?"

The boy gave him a look that insinuated there was no way he was giving up valuable information without remuneration. Byrne dug into his pocket for change, dropped the nickel fare in the boy's hand, but pinched a half-dollar piece between his fingers and let it speak for itself.

"That one they been lookin' for. The niggra lady. The one that killed the man on the island. They done found her in Key West," the boy said, whispering conspiratorially and holding out his palm. "They say she was dressed in men's clothes and tried to get aboard a northbound ship."

"They plan to bring her back here?"

"Damn straight. An if they ever find out who that dead man is, they just might be a lynchin'."

The boy's demeanor and language reminded Byrne of young Screechy back in Tompkins Square. He dropped the half dollar in the boy's palm. When it comes to the young and wise, the streets are the streets.

A lynching, Byrne thought, moving on across the bridge. His newfound friends, the binder boys, had spoken of one only days before, and he had no reason to doubt the veracity of their story. How did a place with the architectural splendor and rich sophistication that he was walking to put up with something as crude as a lynching? He'd heard the stories told by the old ones from Dublin of the beheadings and such by the English, but Jaysus, that was ancient times. Public hangings! Across the lake from Mr. Flagler's golf course!

Halfway across the bridge he gave up the ruminations and took off his new coat and unbuttoned his collar. It may have been early evening, but there was still a heat in the air, and he was sweating. He would readjust his wardrobe once he got to the other side. Once more he took in the view of Palm Beach Island, measuring her, memorizing her coastline and the movement of the water beneath him. His attention fell on a dockside gathering of boats and people. A half-dozen men were moving about a centerpiece that he still could not make out. Something large was being raised on some form of block and tackle. The huge object spun and caught the low sun. Thirty steps closer and Byrne recognized the thing as a fish! It was roped at its scythe-like tail and was being raised to hang upside down. The thing was at least ten feet long, a fantastic-looking beast with a long pointed bill that seemed impossibly fragile, as at one point in the hoisting the entire body, at least four hundred pounds, appeared to balance on that sword-like tip. Men gathered as a gang around the suspended fish, and it became obvious that a photographer had set up his tripod and was capturing the moment. Closer still, Byrne could see that the men, with the exception of the bandy-legged one dressed in light-colored dungarees and a black-brimmed captain's hat, were no doubt guests of the hotel with their florid faces and estimable paunches. After the flash of the photography powder, they all shook hands and moved up from the dock, back-slapping and nodding in their accomplishment. The captain and what was later identified to Byrne as a blue marlin were left behind, the fish slowly spinning in the breeze, its color draining in the failing light. Byrne thought of the tarpon, silvered and flashing as Faustus had removed his hook and let it go and the old man's words: "But would that have made it any more glorious?"

As he approached the Poinciana's grand ballroom, Byrne was already convinced that he was a poseur and was equally sure that he didn't give a shit. He knew the minute he walked up the steps to the hotel entrance and caught the same changing smile from the tuxedoed greeter that he got from the clerk at the Seminole. You might pass at a distance, but never up close. The greeter stepped forward. Upon inspection, the employee's suit was at least two cuts above the forty-dollar variety Byrne felt so proud in: the fabric finer, the lapels silk, the tailoring perfect. But even the high polish he'd given his brogans did not cover their street look. Still, he held a higher power and used it.

"Michael Byrne," he answered to the greeter's request for an invitation. "Mr. Flagler's Pinkerton." The man made a sour face but passed him through. Security breach, Byrne thought. Anyone could say they were Pinkerton and the boy at the door would wave them in.

He passed through the lobby, purposely not looking up at the grand ceiling like some tourist, and then scanned the crowd to find Harris standing near the doors to the ballroom. When Byrne joined him, Harris's mouth held that grin at the corner of his mouth. He'd read Byrne's expression.

"I tol ya to lose the shoes, lad. Didn't I?"

"I'm not one of them and don't want to be," Byrne said through his teeth. "Fuck 'em."

"Aye, now that's the spirit," Harris said. "And it's also the idea of havin' us here. Nobody who might want to start trouble is going to mistake us for busboys either. And that might be enough deterrent on its own.

"You just use that photographic memory of yours. Mr. Flagler's true friends and relatives will be near him at the front of the ballroom. I've confidence you'll have them down pat early enough. After that you can spot any strangers."

"What kind of threat are we talking about, sergeant?" Byrne asked, puzzled. "A bloody assassination?"

Harris chuckled deep in his throat, the sound of an echo in a big wooden barrel.

"No, lad. It's the pissed off ones we're watching tonight. Mr. Flagler's land acquisitions can make him enemies, even those of the higher society and not just those hick farmers at the train sidings.

"In this rarefied air, boy, the more money you have, the less you like to lose it."

Christ, the rich, Byrne sneered.

"Stay on the edges, lad. Use the walls and keep your eyes open. Don't get caught up in the finery, if you know what I mean." A trio of middle-aged women floated by in gowns that were low-cut and dragging trains behind.

"Watch for the angry faces. We'll be fine."

Harris led the way into the grand ballroom, and once again Byrne had to consciously remember to keep his mouth from gaping open.

The hall was some two hundred feet in length, with a soaring ceiling lined around its edges with electric bulbs that highlighted the frescoed painting that adorned it. Romanesque white columns lined the walls for the first fifteen feet up, and then large scalloped arches framed a dozen high windows.

The dance floor was a polished parquet wood of the kind Byrne had never seen even though he'd witnessed the ballroom at the Astoria Hotel from the kitchen doors. A cop friend of his had smuggled him into the newly built hotel on Thirty-fourth and Fifth Avenue to meet a girl selling perfume at a boutique inside, and they couldn't help but poke around. But New York's finest had nothing on this place. The orchestra was at the far end of the hall, playing something classic and staid, and though most in attendance were sitting in the straight-backed chairs that lined the dance floor, a few couples were out moving with grace. Byrne could hear the swooshing of the fine dress fabric brushing the elegant wood. He and Harris split up, and Byrne moved behind the arched columns to "work the walls." He was watching the men, most of whom were dressed in black tailcoats with vests made of white piqué. Byrne did not have to be reminded that he had been talked into spending extra on the dark brocaded vest he wore and did not look down.

As he moved closer to the front, he could see a subtle change in both the finery and the distinct smell of money. The chains on pocket watches became more delicate, the gold metal taking on a shine of higher carat. Stick pins appeared in ascots and four-in-hand ties. An elderly man whom Byrne had seen dancing with aplomb was now carrying a walking stick with an ostentatious silver lion's head. Finally, at a table nearest the orchestra, he spotted Flagler's shock of white hair. The railway baron was standing in a circle of men who were listening closely to his every utterance. Byrne focused on their faces. Not an angry look in the crowd, although he quickly determined that all of them would be acquiescent to the man's words even if he were mumbling horse shit. Byrne widened his view of the circle about Flagler, eyeing the corners and the space behind the columns that he himself was using for cover.

His gaze landed on Mr. McAdams, who was also entertaining a gathering of men of means who had found a quieter place far to the left of the orchestra. McAdams was, as seemed to be his practice, leaning into the man beside him, talking directly into the listener's ear as if the words were only for him. Byrne watched long enough to memorize the listener's face and then went directly to the nearby seats. If the father was here, where was the daughter?

He scanned the crowd, first the women sitting nearby. Their hands, many in gloves matching their gowns, were in their laps or holding small beaded purses. Most of them were wearing hats ornamented with feathers and ribbon that partially obscured their faces. Byrne was convinced that Miss McAdams would not be wearing a hat. He concentrated next on the dance floor, which was now filling up with couples, the more graceful turning figures and stylish poses to the waltz music, but even the less adventurous moved in soft, reaching, confident steps. He checked the younger women, those with waspish waists and athletic movements, but did not see her. For nearly an hour he moved among the crowd, nodding at those who nodded at him.

He was watching a demonstrative gent with a bulbous nose and a voice like shoveled gravel rattling on about some soldier unit called "Roosevelt's Rough Riders" he'd seen in Tampa, across the state, on their way to Cuba. As if on cue the orchestra struck up a quick tempo to drown the man out, and the careful dancers began to leave the floor.

With a clearer view across the room Byrne caught sight of a flash of white fabric and a glimpse of red curl and shifted from behind a pillar to see Miss McAdams in the arms of a tall man, both moving fluidly to the new beat. The gent was in a tuxedo that stood out from the rest, with a sharp center crease in the pants and cuffs dusting the tops of a pair of patent leather shoes covered with cream-colored spats. The tune carried the same one, two, three count of the previous waltzes, but at a pace that seemed to energize Miss McAdams while keeping her partner on his toes. Hers was a driving, aggressive and reaching step that seemed utterly confident, while the man worked at keeping up. Others on the dance floor moved from the middle and let the couple take over, and Byrne began to lose his unobstructed view. Still he watched, catching a blur and a smile, mostly the man's, due to his height or his showmanship, until the final strains, when McAdams struck an ending pose that was pure rhapsody. It was the first time in Byrne's life that he wished his feet had rhythm.

Before the next song began, the couple exited the floor, several men complimenting McAdams. Her partner trailed behind her and shook every hand offered. They seemed to be coming directly at Byrne, who decided to simply stand his ground. From several feet away he couldn't tell whether McAdams's cheeks were colored from cosmetics, the blush of unsolicited compliments, or exertion. Just before she reached him, she spun on the heel of one slipper, the train of her dress swishing up onto his own brogans. "Graham," she said, "could you fetch me something to drink, you dear? I am absolutely parched."

"Delighted, Marjory," the one called Graham said and moved away.

Without hesitation McAdams continued a full rotation and looked directly into Byrne's eyes.

"And delighted to meet you, sir," she said, offering her hand. "I am Marjory McAdams."

Byrne took her fingers and bowed but wouldn't pretend to kiss them. He'd seen a hundred such scenes during special event details and thought it prissy at best.

"Of that I am fully aware, Miss McAdams," he said, and then added, "Nice dancing."

She tilted her head just so and hesitated. The silence made him uncomfortable. There was a heat coming off her, and she smelled of newly planted oleander, sweet flowers and musk. Up close, her complexion was unblemished. Byrne was fighting a losing battle to keep his eyes from hers.

"So, do I call you Mr. Pinkerton, sir, as my father does?"

"I would hope not," he said, and then realized he still had not dropped her fingers. She slipped the rest of her hand into his without looking down and shook it slightly before letting go.

"Michael Byrne," he said.

"A pleasure, Mr. Byrne. And do you like the waltz?"

"Very much."

"And do you dance?"

"No."

A pout formed on her lips, and even though it was an obvious tease, Byrne couldn't keep the look from tripping his heart.

"I am simply an observer," he said, trying to recover.

She smiled. "I'm told that Pinkertons do quite a bit more than observe."

"I've heard that too, Miss McAdams," he said, enjoying the sparring if it could hold her before him for even a minute more.

"And from the look of your sunburn, your observations have mostly been from outside, Mr. Byrne."

His hand started to go to his face but he stopped it.

"Boating," he said, "on the sea."

He picked up on the instant brightening of her eyes, the green almost magically taking on a bit of blue at the edges of the iris, as if his own recollection of the Gulf Stream's color were reflecting there.

"The ocean is one of my favorite things about being here," she said. "Obviously you are wasting no time enjoying the uniqueness of Florida."

"Like I said, I'm an observer."

Now she smiled without teasing, a natural smile, one that he had brought out.

"So you are a boatman. Are you a swimmer as well? An ocean swimmer?"

He thought of the blue again, how he had wanted to simply fall in and let it take him, but he also thought of the taste of the salt when he had seen the ocean for the first time, what, two days ago, three?

"I have managed the East River," he said, without elaborating that on that single occasion he had fallen in while trying to steal an armload of oysters and was pulled back spitting and gasping by the hand of his brother.

Marjory raised an eyebrow, whether surprised by his audacity to swim in that putrid river or his stupidity in doing so, he could not tell.

"Well, perhaps you may join me for a more pleasant bathing hour in the ocean some time, Mr. Byrne. The beach off the Breakers is quite lovely this time of year, and the water temperature should be much more to your liking than the rivers around Manhattan."

Byrne was trying to find another word of wit to make the conversation last when the dandy she'd called Graham returned, holding a crystal goblet of clear liquid.

"Water, Marjory," he said, though his eyes were on Byrne rather than McAdams.

"Good evening, sir. I don't believe we've met," the man said, offering his hand to Byrne.

"Oh, do forgive me. Mr. Michael Byrne, this is Mr. Graham Foster," Marjory said.

Byrne did not like Foster's shoes. He did not like the crease in Foster's pants or the silk brocade of his vest. He did not like the smart handshake Foster gave or the glisten of some kind of pomade in his hair. And over the man's shoulder, Byrne did not like the look of a hurried and sober conversation between a messenger boy and an older gentleman whom he'd spotted earlier and took for a hotelman, noting that although he greeted the guests and seemed to be well known, he did not participate in their conversations and was not necessarily anxious to have Flagler's ear like the others.

"Since you are both boatmen," Marjory was saying, without a hint of fun or sarcasm, "you may have tales to share."

Byrne may have let an unconscious grin twitch at the corner of his mouth, but he was no longer paying attention. He watched as the hotelman moved unhurried, but with a purpose, to the other side of the room and pulled Mr. McAdams aside, turning him away from his group and whispering something into his ear. The stoic expression on the men's faces was what alerted Byrne. They did not crinkle their eyes in even customary pleasure. They did not tighten their jaws in consternation or masked alarm. Their faces simply went blank, passive, and reflexively internal. Something was up.

He shifted his eyes back to Foster and Marjory McAdams.

"A pleasure to meet you, sir," he said, with a slight bow but no handshake.

"Miss McAdams." He took her fingers, looking at the lines of question forming at her brow. "As you know too well, I'm working. Excuse me," he said and moved away without another word.

Byrne moved to the nearest wall and watched Mr. McAdams across the room. The man was extremely cool, carefully holding his new knowledge, working it in his head, looking around as if unhurried and unbothered. He shook a guest's hand, touched an elderly woman's forearm just so. And then he moved ever so gentlemanly toward Flagler's table. Byrne slid to the other side of the column and followed with his eyes. McAdams approached Flagler but moved behind the white and regal head, and then slipped past. He continued down the line, beyond the seated Cornelius Vanderbilt and his wife and then to a man whom Byrne almost immediately recognized from New York. A businessman, Byrne thought, and then began his own internal way of finding the face inside his mental collection. Uptown? No. During some special occasion when Byrne was a guard? No. It was during a police action, he was sure. The businessman rose, excused himself, and moved off with McAdams to a corner, where they were joined by the hotelman. The way the businessman dipped his head in acquiescence was the tip-off. Such a man of power was not used to subservience, and thus when he showed it to McAdams, the moment glared. Byrne was now sure that he had seen him before. It was at a prostitution bust at the Haymarket Dance Hall on Sixth Avenue just south of Thirtieth Street. Byrne had been a simple cop at the time, called in to provide manpower and muscle for the raids that were done for show when the press shook up city hall and the pols needed to look like they were doing something to control the sex trade in the city. The businessman was one of the society types that got caught up in the dragnet one night. Byrne had seen the man take the commanding lieutenant aside and peel off a number of bills into his palm, enabling himself to simply walk out onto the street. Since the man was never booked, Byrne did not know his name, but he also never forgot a face.

Harris was still on the other side of the dance floor.

"There's news running round the room," Byrne said quietly when he got to his sergeant's side.

"Indeed," Harris said, without alarm or question. "It's not a matter of concern to us, lad."

"Care to fill me in? It seems to be of interest to a few in power, including the man sitting next to Mr. Vanderbilt," Byrne said, nodding toward the Flagler table, where the businessman was now resuming his seat.

"That's Birch, a Manhattan real estate man and a banker friend of the lot of them," Harris said.

"And the one in the tailless coat on his way out of the room," Byrne asked, directing Harris's attention to the hotelman who had first sought out McAdams.

"That's Pearson. He's the hotel manager. Deals with every crisis, big or small."

"OK, what's the crisis?"

"Not our concern, Mr. Byrne. We are here solely to protect Mr. Flagler."

Byrne coughed into his hand and then looked into Harris's face with a grin meant to match the old Irishman's now famous tic.

"And since when did good intelligence and an ear to rumor not serve that cause, Mr. Harris?" Byrne said.

The sergeant looked pointedly into Byrne's face, any sign of playfulness on his own completely gone.

"Go back to work," he said and then walked away.

Chapter 14

Byrne watched Harris disappear into the crowd before he looped around a column and made for the exit. Go back to work indeed, he thought. He'd heard the expression too many times as a cop when he'd noticed the graft of the captains, the politicians on Bowery and the shakedowns by the Tammany crowd. He had no taste for turning his back.

He went through the lobby and out onto the wide porch entrance, walking at a slow pace, acting unhurried, like a guest seeking a bit of fresh air. If he smoked, he would have taken a cigarette out and lit it. Rather he put his hands in his trouser pockets, one touching the baton, the other pinching his fold of money, and made his way down the steps to the driveway apron. When the livery boy looked up, Byrne engaged him.

"Stunning evening," he said. The boy was dark eyed and impossibly skinny. He cut his eyes left and right, making sure the man in the evening clothes was talking to him.

"Yes, sir," the boy said, keeping his face forward.

"Hard to believe anything could ruin the peacefulness of such a night." Byrne shifted his own gaze toward the boy, making sure he knew to whom the conversation was being directed.

"Yes, sir," was again the answer.

Byrne took his left hand out of his pocket, the fold of bills held loosely within sight.

"If there were something happening, something unusual being talked about on such a night as this, how much would you think that information might be worth?" he said.

Now the boy shifted his own gaze, first to the money, then up, furtively, to Byrne's face.

"Might be somethin' like two dollars," he said, starting at a bit of a higher figure than he might realistically make, leaving room for negotiation, just like any street-smart kid in New York.

Byrne didn't have time for negotiation. He peeled off two dollars and put the rest back in his pocket.

"Word is they bringin' that whore back to town," the boy said, looking at the money. "The housewoman that kilt that white man in the Styx. Sheriff Cox done caught her runnin' and is draggin' her back to jail."

Byrne let the idea settle on him and then handed the boy his money.

"Tonight?" he said.

"Boy comin' in from West Palm says right about now."

Byrne looked out on the dark water and could make out a few lights from his own hotel and a few sprinkled north in the city. He thought about the lynching he'd read about in the Jacksonville newspaper and the hanging of the accused killer of the tax assessor. Harris was probably right. The information was the kind of gossip that would spread fast, even to the group of men inside. Byrne decided he would tuck the knowledge away. It had no relevance to his work. He went back up the stairs and was moving toward the entrance when he saw Marjory McAdams hurrying across the lobby toward him. He fixed his face, trying to look more charming than he was, trying to find something sophisticated to say. She blew past him without recognition. He couldn't gauge whether the look on her face was a hard anxiety or angry fire, but he watched her pass through the doors and then followed. She skipped down the steps with her dress trailing. There was one of those odd bicycle contraptions waiting. A large black man, athletic and handsome, helped her into the carriage and then moved like silk up onto the seat, stepped on the pedals and started to roll. He looked up once as Byrne hurried down the steps and caught his eyes, held them for an instant with a look that said "Don't even try to stop her" and then sped off toward the ferry dock.

Byrne stood frozen for a minute, heard the engine of the ferry grind and pop in the distance, and marched inside to find Harris. His sergeant was now near the front of the room, behind the orchestra, watching Flagler's table. Byrne went to his side, took his elbow and whispered into his ear.

"I have to leave."

Harris turned only his head, looked into his charges' eyes and said: "Give me a reason."

"Intelligence gathering and a bit of protection."

"Protection for who?"

"The daughter of Mr. Flagler's acquisitions engineer, his right-hand man, McAdams. I believe she's gone to the mainland to get involved in a prisoner being brought to the jail, a hotel worker, a Flagler employee if you will."

"It's a rumor," Harris said. "I've already told you it isn't our business."

"It's a rumor flying all over, including to the management of our boss's hotel," Byrne said.

Harris turned away, perhaps assessing all he knew about Byrne, his abilities, his talents and his seriousness.

"Make sure she's safe, but bloody damn stay out of the rest of it," Harris said. "The sheriff is a shite, but we don't need to antagonize the bastard." Harris might have perceived only the nod of agreement because when he turned, there was nothing but air where Byrne had been.

Byrne went down the front stairs in two gliding jumps. He had the coat off and the top button of his shirt loosed before he reached the pedestrian bridge. He scanned the lake on the south side for a glimpse of the ferry and saw the lamp it carried far ahead, swinging already into the docks on the other side. His brogans had long been broken in for running the city streets, and he lengthened his stride. The moon was still down, the sky above black velvet and sprinkled with stars that afforded little light. Still he ran with a purpose, remembering the feel of the bridge from his walks, aware of keeping his step high to avoid tripping on a raised wooden slat. He focused on a light at the end of the walkway where the boy should still be standing and made his path straight and unwavering.

He was breathing hard when he got to where the bridge tender was standing. The boy looked him up and down, the sweat-soaked evening shirt, the face red and chest heaving.

"Someone chase you out, then, sir?"

Byrne was looking south at the ferry dock. The boat was empty. The passengers, McAdams and the big Negro, were nowhere in sight. He reached into his pocket and brought out a dollar.

"Take me to the jail," he said, thrusting the money at the boy.

The kid looked at the money.

"You're kidding," he said, his tone skeptical to an offer to get paid to go where he'd wanted to be all night. Byrne brought out another two dollars and pushed all of it into the boy's hand.

"Right. This way," the kid said, grabbing the cash and leaving his post behind.

They went west on Clematis, crossed Narcissus where the shops and restaurants were darkened and the street nearly empty. But Byrne could hear music and laughter coming from a block north on Banyan, where most of the saloons would still be open and evening drinkers would do what they ultimately did late into the night. The boy seemed more anxious than he was and skipped a few steps ahead. They crossed Olive Street, and before they were halfway up the block, Byrne could see the flickering glow of torches being held high at the next corner. Closer still he counted nearly a dozen people gathered in the street, keeping their distance from an enclosed, boxlike wagon with barred windows high on the sides and a small square in the door to the back.

"It's the prison wagon," the boy said over his shoulder. "They ain't took her out yet."

The jailhouse was a two-story, wood-framed structure with four small windows set high in the first floor and flanking a slated door. There were three standard windows on the second floor, their panes flickering with reflected firelight. An outside staircase led up along one side. Byrne scanned the crowd. The first person demanding attention was a black-suited man the size of a finely fatted heifer who was planted near the jailhouse door. His hat was clamped on his head like the cover on a teapot. Byrne could not see his eyes, but the man was digging between his thin lips with a toothpick like there was something worthwhile in there. There was an aura about him; perhaps it was the distance that everyone else kept from him or the nonchalance he showed at what was clearly a tense event. Byrne pegged him as the sheriff. At the other side of the door stood the skinny armed deputy who had questioned Byrne at the bridge two days ago. His eyes were down and he was in low conversation with the bulging man. The shadows were such that

Byrne could not see his bobbing Adam's apple. Another man dressed in the same dark utilitarian suit as the others appeared at the top of the staircase. He hurried down, his heels banging on the steps, the sound of gangling keys in his hands. At the plank door he twisted a key in the lock and pushed it open, the entrance now like a black maw in the firelight. Though the wagon could have been stopped just outside the jail door so that the prisoner would endure barely seconds of exposure to the gathering crowd, the sheriff had obviously set the stage for a bit of drama. He got more than he bargained for.

The key man crossed to the wagon, stepped up to the rear door and unlocked it. When he swung open the hinges and climbed inside, people turned and whispered to one another. An obvious drunk from Banyan Street openly blurted, "They ought to hang the nigger bitch right now." There was a short silence, and then Byrne heard an almost imperceptible thud, something hard against something soft, but when he turned he could see nothing in the shadows. The low sound of violence escaped everyone else's attention except for the fat sheriff, who cocked his head and also looked briefly out into the darkness but then seemed to disregard it.

After a few moments the key man backed out of the wagon. At the end of his extended arm came the shackled thin wrists of a smallish Negro woman. Byrne could see that in addition to the handcuffs, she was wearing leg irons. There was a white kerchief tying up her hair, and she was wearing a man's shirt and the same style of pants with the single stripe on the leg that Byrne had seen on the prison work crew at Jacksonville Beach. The key man yanked her toward the jail, and she stumbled and went down. The cry that escaped her was small and birdlike and made up of both pain and fear. The key man did not turn his head but continued to drag her across the hard pack.

"Dear God in heaven," came an exclamation of anger from the crowd, and for the first time Byrne caught sight of Marjory McAdams marching in from the shadows, her Negro companion rubbing his knuckles and trailing behind her.

"Must you treat this woman like some kind of animal?" Marjory shouted.

The key man stopped in his tracks at the sound of an authoritative female voice. Marjory stomped directly to the jailer's side, gave him a frozen stare and then bent to the woman, touching her hands and then her face and mewing consolations that Byrne could not hear. No one moved at first. The sight of a young woman dressed in high fashion, her flowing ball gown dragging in the dirt, coming to the aid of a Negro working girl being hauled into the calaboose on a murder charge stunned them. The heavy man at the jail door seemed the only one not affected. He tipped his hat up as if to better absorb the scene and then motioned to the deputy to intervene, saying something that Byrne could hear only as a low rumble.

The deputy crossed the distance in three elongated steps and said: "Ma'am, ya'll gonna have to step back now. This is a official transfer of a prisoner and they ain't no time for your whinin'."

When the deputy grabbed McAdams's shoulder, Byrne wasn't sure whether it was his touch or his statement that lit her fuse, but Marjory came bolt upright, the crown of her head barely missing the deputy's chin, and then stared into his face.

"If you touch me again, sir, I will abandon my duty as a civilized woman and scratch your eyes out."

The deputy tucked his chin and pulled back as if he'd been slapped. The entire gathering went quiet for a full beat, and then someone at the edge of the darkness guffawed.

"Ha!"

The deputy blinked, gathered himself, and raised his free hand over his shoulder while uttering "Why you prissy, high-fallutin' bitch I'll …"

Three men moved—Byrne and the Negro chauffer with incredibly similar speed and fluidity, and the sheriff with a single step and the forming of the word "STOP!" at the edges of his mouth. Everyone else sucked in their breath.

The deputy's face was no more than a foot from Marjory's, and his hand had not yet begun its forward motion when the whooshing sound of a steel whip split the space between their noses. Both sets of eyes went large with the feeling of cut air. The baton instantly retraced its path between them but this time stopped like an immovable girder across the deputy's raised wrist. His hand would be going no farther.

The deputy first looked to the Negro, guessing wrongly that he must be responsible. But the chauffeur was staring at Byrne, not believing someone could have been so fast and accurate. Marjory's eyes followed the gleaming steel shaft from the deputy's hand to Byrne's fist and then to his face.

"STOP RIGHT THERE!" The sheriff's voice finally escaped his mouth, and the resonance was nearly as arresting as Byrne's baton had been.

"Morgan, back off!" he said to the deputy and strode across the street, bringing more than just his girth to bear on the scene. It was as if his huge presence itself forced the deputy and the Negro and Marjory to move simultaneously apart. Only Byrne seemed unaffected. He'd been in the company of large, powerful men before. Still, he was so focused that his baton was still raised to the level of the deputy's hand, which the lawman had already pulled back.

The sheriff waded in.

"Miss McAdams, I believe," he said, his lowered voice now dripping with courtesy. "Surely this is no place for a lady like yourself. Such an unseemly event."

Marjory squared her shoulders. "Unseemly, indeed, Mr. Cox," she said. "The idea that you would be dragging this poor woman through the streets like some animal carcass from a hunting party of yours certainly qualifies for the term."

Sheriff Cox did not avert his eyes. "This Negress is a killer, Miss McAdams. I believe that disqualifies her from your description, ma'am."

"As I expected, Sheriff, you have a failed understanding of the law of civilized countries, including this one, that anyone accused of a crime is presumed to be innocent until declared guilty by a court," Marjory said. "She is not a killer until a judge and jury say she is."

The fat man's eyes narrowed, and his thin lips went tight.

"In fact, Sheriff, I doubt that you even have a sworn warrant for this woman's arrest," Marjory said. The sheriff stayed silent, searching, it appeared, for some kind of rejoinder. But the deputy called Morgan couldn't stand it.

"Now just a goddamn minute, you little smart ass. This nigger bitch don't have no rights and she done shanked a white man in the belly an' that's enough law for us." He pointed a long finger at Marjory and then took a step toward Shantice, who still lay curled on the ground. Byrne saw or felt a dark shadow move beside him. The big Negro had appeared like a wall between the deputy and the tiny woman. The deputy came up short, astounded either by the man's fluid speed or his audacity.

"Why you…" His face was flushing while he reached into his coat. A long-barreled revolver came out with his hand. The flash of Byrne's baton swept the air and snapped the deputy's wrist like a limb cracking in the wind. The man yelped, and the gun fell to the ground.

Now it was the sheriff whose movements were quick and sudden. He stepped forward and with an amazing strength grabbed a handful of his own deputy's jacket and pulled him back as if he were weightless.

"Now just hold on, by God," he boomed, his voice reverberating off the storefronts of Clematis Street. He put his palm up to Byrne as if it were the hand of the deity he'd just invoked. "Ya'll just calm down, boys."

The Negro chauffeur seemed to shrink in the face of an authority he knew almost by instinct to obey. Byrne lowered his baton to his side.

"Pinkerton, this ain't none of your affair," Sheriff Cox said. "I'm the law here, even if Miss McAdams believes she's the lawyer. And I am lawfully taking this prisoner into custody."

Byrne was only slightly surprised that the sheriff would know of him and his Pinkerton affiliation. He stepped back.

The sheriff motioned for his key man to help Shantice Carver to her feet.

"If you wish to attend the woman's arraignment by the judge on Friday afternoon, Miss McAdams," he said, matching her diction and turning to face her, "then you are, as a citizen of these United States, fully within your right. The charge will be murder.

"Now folks, clear the damn streets," he commanded, and all involved began to move away.

Byrne looked over his shoulder once to see the deputy scuttle back across the yard, holding his wrist to his belly.

The trio of Byrne, Marjory and her chauffeur moved up the street to where the bicycle carriage was parked. Marjory was still flushed with anger. The two men were uncomfortable and independently decided to let her cool.

Byrne held his hand out first.

"Michael Byrne," he said.

"My name is Santos," the man said, shaking Byrne's hand. "Carlos Santos."

Santos's big hands and strength reminded Byrne of his friend Jack. His voice and look reminded Byrne of the westside neighborhood called Little Africa in Greenwich Village, where the Italians and blacks had been razor fighting for years. Byrne couldn't see a lick of Spanish in the man, but his protection of Marjory McAdams stood Santos well as far as Byrne cared. The handshake was a bond.

"My apologies, gentlemen, for not introducing you," Marjory finally said, her fists still clenched in knots. "But that fat bastard, pardonnez-moi."

"Pardon which, Miss McAdams, your French, or your manners?" Byrne said. Santos looked at him and started to smile. Marjory lost an edge off her anger.

"That man is infuriating and dangerous," she said, civilizing her tone.

"He's a lawman with power," Byrne said. "They get that way."

Now Marjory was concentrating on his face.

"And why is it, Mr. Byrne, that you are here in the first place. This, as the sheriff said, is not your concern. Your only duty would be the protection of Mr. Flagler and his trains, if I recall correctly."

"Yes, well, protection can take many forms," Byrne said, trying out the explanation he'd have to give Sergeant Harris. "The fact that a wanted killer was being returned to the jail was too close to ignore."

"I see. And your reason for stepping in with that, that… metal whippet of yours?"

Byrne could see no better answer than the truth.

"It seemed like the right thing to do."

Marjory continued to assess him. "Very well, then, Mr. Byrne. If you are of a mind to do the right thing, come with us." She turned to Santos. "We need to visit those who had taken responsibility for Miss Carver's safety and find out what happened."

The big man held out his hands in a questioning gesture.

"But ma'am, that's a three mile journey north, and this carriage isn't going to make it past the city streets." He was looking to Byrne for help, but none was forthcoming.

"Then we will walk the final two miles," Marjory said and swung herself up into the seat. "Mr. Byrne tells me he is a fine swimmer and boatman, so I'm sure he has the physical abilities to stride alongside."

Byrne shrugged at the challenge. Santos looked back and forth between the two of them, climbed aboard the bicycle seat and turned up the kerosene lantern that hung on his handlebars. He swung the rig north and quietly said, "More like two and a half final miles," under his breath.

While Santos peddled, Byrne kept even alongside by half jogging as Marjory exercised only her vocal cords, filling Byrne in on her version of events. She told him about the island's workers all being asked to celebrate on the West Palm Beach side of the lake, enticed by free food and carnival rides and music. She described the late night fire in their compound, how only she and Miss Fluery had responded and how the dry wood had simply flashed into flames and destroyed nearly everything.

She told him of the aftermath, the rummaging through the ashes in the morning light and the shocking discovery by Miss Carver of the body of a white man in a lean-to behind her burned-out home. At that point she looked carefully at Byrne, searching for reaction to that piece of news.

"And no one recognized this man, this white man who you say was dressed in fine clothing?" Byrne said, thinking only marginally of his own new clothes and the way they had made him feel as if he were in costume, pretending to be something he was not. "Are you sure that he wasn't a customer of Mizz Carver? I mean, you did say she was a lady of the evening."

In the lamplight he could see Marjory's eyes. It was the same look he got from Faustus, the assessing one, the unsure one, almost as if they were trying to catch him in a lie. But she relaxed.

"Yes, Mr. Byrne, she may be a prostitute. But if you had been there to hear the poor woman's anguish, you would know she was truly shocked."

"Yes, sir," piped in Santos, who was taking it all in from his seat above. "Mizz Shantice was damned scared. Too scared to be makin' it up, sir."

"And she described the dead man as having a roll of money stuffed into his mouth," Marjory said. "And surely everyone who looked could see it plain and simple when we got to the place where his body lay burned."

They were near the edge of town now, and the darkness was so complete Byrne could see only parts of Marjory's face in the flicker of the lamp.

"Now, in your experience, Mr. Byrne," she said, "could you imagine a prostitute who would kill a customer, leave a substantial amount of money in his mouth and then proceed to scream his location to all within earshot?"

Byrne spoke in the direction of her voice. "No, Miss McAdams. In my experience, no."

A second later the wheels hit a series of ruts that nearly tossed her from her seat.

"Walkin' time," Santos said, unable to peddle hard enough to get the contraption going again. "But ma'am, it's still a couple of miles and I don't know how you going to manage in that dress."

He and Byrne heard the extended sound of fabric ripping. Then came the distinct whoosh and fop of a large bundle of cloth being tossed out behind the carriage and landing in the two-track rut of a roadway. There was enough light for them to see Marjory's white figure jump out of the wicker seat and land lightly on her feet in the dirt. The train to her dress had been removed, and her petticoat was hanging just above her dancing slippers.

"Let us walk, gentlemen," she said as if she'd simply disposed of a hat. "You may lead, Mr. Santos."

Santos carried the lantern, but it was of little use out here. The circle of light it tossed was like a bubble in the deep black. Byrne had long since sweated through his shirt, and he could swear that the combination of perspiration and Santos's light was drawing the clouds of mosquitoes that feasted on them. On occasion they would hear the call of owls hunting in the night or the rustle of brush that could have been any wild animal from opossum to fox to the well-regarded panthers that roamed the area. Byrne had already heard tales of hunting from men at the restaurant bar and wished he'd picked up the deputy's damn pistol when he'd had the chance.

Marjory kept pace and continued to talk, maybe covering for her nerves at being in such a dark and insect-infested place. She told Byrne about the efforts of the hotel staff to secrete Miss Carver off the island once they'd heard that the sheriff was accusing her of stabbing the dead man. She told him of the way Santos had taken Carver across the lake at night, though she did not go into detail as to how a rowboat had become available.

"And Mr. Santos assured me that he had found people up the way who could keep her safe," she said, with an edge of accusation in her voice.

"I swear they are good people, Miss McAdams," Santos said, not afraid to defend himself. "They were with the Underground Railroad up in North Carolina. They got people from Georgia all the ways to New York, ma'am."

Marjory went silent for several moments.

"We'll just have to see what happened, Carlos. I apologize for judging you or them."

They continued on for more than an hour, the lamplight thrown out ahead of them. The palmetto and scrub pines thickened on either side, as did the insect cloud. More than once Byrne had to use the back of his hand to wipe mosquitoes from his lips, and he heard Marjory cough sharply at one point and then spit with disgust. But she never stopped and never complained. He was impressed by the pace she kept and wondered at her motivation. She was a rich young woman with a fancy ballroom and a feast fit for royalty awaiting her back at the Poinciana. Was this naïve sense of justice for a Negro chambermaid really strong enough on its own to drag her out into the steaming wilderness? He'd spent most of his life studying people and anticipating their moves based on hunger, lust or greed. None of those were driving her. The most devout who prayed aloud for compassion had their priorities, even if it was to smooth their way to heaven. But McAdams didn't appear to be one for religion. So what the hell was driving her?

You're a cynical bastard, Michael, he said to himself. Marjory kept up until the trail ran into a clearing that opened out in front of them.

"Windella Plantation's pineapple fields," Santos said. "The Wilsons' place is just the other side."

Coming out of the bush, the trio was met by a freshening breeze off the lake, and with the horizon now in sight, Byrne could see the glow of the Poinciana far in the distance like a lighthouse beacon on the sea. A memory of waltz music played in his head and the smell of women's perfume and clink of fine crystal.

"What was the name of that tune you danced to tonight?" he said to Marjory, whose face was lit only on one side by the lantern. She turned and looked at him as if he'd spoken in tongues.

"The 'Voice of the Waves,'" she said. "A John Hill Hewitt song, but why in God's name would you bring up such a question, Mr. Byrne? We are as far from that silly moment as we are from the moon."

"That's what I was thinking," Byrne said and moved on.

Crossing several acres of pineapple plants, as yet in the shape of small cabbage heads, Santos led them into the trees. In a few minutes all three could detect the low yellow glow of a light. Closer yet they could make out a squared window in a small clapboard house. When they were within calling range, Santos cupped his hand and yelled: "Mr. Claude! Mr. Claude Augusta Wilson! It's me, Mr. Claude, Third Base Santos. We comin' in, sir!"

Before their circle of light could hit the front steps, a thin black man with wide shoulders, dressed only in a pair of bib overalls, stepped out of the door. His head was peppered in tufts of white hair, which also sprouted from his chest. In one hand he raised a lantern of his own, and in the other hung a shotgun the length of his own leg. He returned the call.

"Third Base? That really you, son? God in heaven, boy. What are you doin' visitin' in the middle of the night?"

The man called Mr. Claude never raised the gun barrel, even when it became obvious that Santos was not alone. But he stood his ground as strangers—a white woman in a torn-away ball gown and a white man in a sweat-soaked tuxedo—stepped onto his raised porch. Santos began explaining and Mr. Claude listened, all the time casting his eyes at Marjory, surveying the damp and drooping hairstyle, the expensive necklace, the dirt-speckled dancing slippers. He also checked Byrne, the formal getup, the straight and athletic posture, and the fact that the white man kept his right hand in his deep trouser pocket despite the sweat and heat.

"And now the sheriff done brought Mizz Shantice back to the jailhouse and says she's gone to be charged a killer," Santos said, finishing up.

The statement snapped the man's head around. "I'm truly sorry to hear that, son. Really I am. We been workin' sunup to sundown here what with the dry weather an' all tryin' to keep them apples watered an' alive an' we didn't hear nothin' 'bout it," Mr. Claude said.

Marjory stepped forward, brushing back a strand of hair from her face and smoothing what was left of her skirts in an attempt to be presentable.

"Sir, can you tell us what happened? It was our understanding that Mizz Carver would be safe here out of the hands of the sheriff, who is simply looking to blame and punish her for a killing she obviously had nothing to do with."

He looked up with his eyes only. "You Miss McAdams? The one Third Base here tol' us about?"

"Yes. Forgive me," she said, adjusting her voice. "Yes, I am Marjory McAdams and this is an, an associate of ours who has offered to help, Mr. Michael Byrne."

The man reached out to take Marjory's offered fingers, and when Byrne leaned in, Mr. Claude met him halfway, watching to see what the stranger might draw from his pocket. When Byrne offered only an empty hand, Mr. Claude made note of the fact that the pocket did not pull heavy as it would have if a handgun had been left there.

"Claude Augusta Wilson," he said as introduction. "Please, ya'll come inside before the insects done carry us all away."

Inside was a single room divided by a curtain that hung at an angle from the middle of one wall to the middle of the wall adjacent, ostensibly creating privacy for one triangular corner of the square. The room was smoky from a dark smudge pot that sputtered in one corner and kept the mosquitoes at bay. Mr. Claude set his lantern in the middle of a long wooden table, pulled out a chair and motioned the others to sit. In the glow Byrne could see a rough cabinet of dishes against one wall, a shelf loaded down with books along another. A spinning wheel and what appeared to be a loom dominated one corner and was surrounded by wicker baskets of cloth. Another door, he figured, must lead to a kitchen of sorts, and when he looked up, he realized that the ceiling was open to the high palmetto fronds that thatched the roof. Byrne was used to the meager furnishings of his own Lower East Side dwellings and did not judge. But he noted that a carefully made area rug covering one part of the wood slat floor came alive with color when the light spilled onto it. Thus the loom made sense. He recalled his own mother's piecework.

"Tina," Mr. Claude called out toward the curtain. "It's OK, Tina. It's Third Base and some of his friends come lookin' for Mizz Shantice. Ya'll come out and make some coffee now. An the rest of ya'll stay in bed, hear?"

A tiny black woman emerged from behind the curtain in a simple housedress that she smoothed with her hands, just as Marjory had done before on the porch. Mr. Claude introduced her as his wife, and she curtsied, said "Evenin'" and went through the side door. No noise came from behind the curtain, leaving Byrne to guess how many children might have been told to stay in bed behind it.

Mr. Claude sat at the head of the table and took a deep breath as though clearing his mind.

"That was one scared woman you brought us, Third Base," he said. "An' I swear she done curled up on one of the chillin's beds and was up to nightmares that wouldn't let her close her eyes.

"Tina and I thought we could get the word out to folks up the line in Titusville an' then to Georgia and get her movin' in a few days, but then Thomas and the boys heard the sheriff an' his deputies were slap askin' every Negro in town if they seen her."

"An' I ain't tell 'em nothin' daddy!" came a shout in a child's voice from behind the curtain. "If they smack me all day I ain't tell 'em nothin'."

"Ya'll hush up, Thomas, an' go to sleep," Mr. Claude said, raising his voice though his anger was only half there.

"Now you know we ain't scared off by such," he continued. "We been through it before. When a brother of mine come by and offered to get Mizz Shantice down to Miami on the train and then on a boat to New York City, I was certain he had the connections to get it done.

"We dressed her up in men's clothing for some disguise. The brother give her a wad a' money an' off she went. First I heard of her being caught was you just now tellin' me."

Mr. Claude had been succinct in his explanation, leaving few questions to be asked. The table went quiet. His wife came into the room with a coffee pot and four cups and poured. Byrne sat back in his chair and sipped the coffee but was alarmed by the taste and had to control his face not to show displeasure. But Mr. Claude noticed.

"I apologize we don't have no real coffee. That's just made up of parched corn, sir. But you can add you some sugar and it's all right."

His wife set a small china bowl of sugar in the middle of the table, and Byrne allowed himself a pinch. As they all drank, he was again drawn by the colors of the rug and then spotted an insect the size of a man's finger that he'd already been told was called a Palmetto bug. The thing sneaked in from some dark corner, perhaps drawn by the smell of sugar in the air. Byrne watched it scuttle across the floor toward the table. And he noticed for the first time that all four table legs were set down into open tin cans. The bug climbed up the side of the can and then down inside. Byrne waited for it to emerge on the wooden leg and continue its way up, but the thing never came out.

"It's the kerosene, sir," Tina Wilson said. She too had been watching the bug and the strange white man in her home at the same time. "The cans are half-filled with kerosene and it kills 'em dead 'fo' they can get up to the table. Onliest way to stop the insects in Florida they eat you out of house and home."

Marjory gathered her skirts around her. All the rest in the room returned to the discussion.

"Did Mizz Carver describe for you what occurred on the night of the fire?" Marjory said, keeping her voice neutral. "That is, who she saw, if anyone at all?"

"Like I said, she was awful scared," Mr. Claude reiterated. "Said only that she found a dead white man and just repeatin' it made her even more scared."

"You say you know this brother and trusted him," Santos said. "Do I know him?"

"I don't suppose you do, Third Base," Mr. Claude said. "He's a white man, a Mason like me." Claude raised his left hand to show the Masonic ring on his finger. The emblem was too small for Byrne to see, but he knew what it looked like.

"You know this brother's name?" Santos said.

Mr. Claude hesitated and looked at his wife.

Byrne cut in: "Is he an older man, white hair and goatee, tends toward frock coats and polished boots and a show-off hat?"

"You know him," Mr. Claude said, a statement, not a question.

"Yes. Amadeus Faustus. I was fishing with him yesterday."

"Yeah, he do like goin' out on the sea an catchin' them big fish," Mr. Claude said. "But he don't never bring none back to eat. I never did understand it."

Byrne turned to the others.

"I can talk with Faustus. I'm due to meet with him tomorrow."

They all got up to leave. Marjory had left her coffee barely touched. Mr. Claude was in despair as he stood on his porch. In his experience, little good could come of the situation unless someone intervened, and that meant someone of standing and wealth and very white skin.

"Will you be able to help her, Miss McAdams?" he said, the tone almost pleading, which was something that did not come easily to the man's voice.

"We will try," Marjory said. She stepped closer and touched her cheek to the old black man's. "Thank you," she whispered.

The three of them walked again in the glow of the lantern. They crossed the field, keeping their own counsel.

Byrne finally broke the silence.

"Interesting fellow," he said to no one in particular, but then to Santos: "What was that Third Base all about?"

"Baseball," Santos said.

"Ah." Byrne was familiar with the game. He'd heard stories of the New York Giants but had seen only the Italians play near Old St. Patrick's Cathedral near Mott and Prince Streets. He'd never seen a Negro man play.

"Mr. Santos is the best player on the hotel's seasonal baseball team and is most likely the finest third baseman in the world," Marjory said, an actual touch of pride in her voice.

"Some of the fans like Mr. Claude just call me Third Base," Santos said. "They know we have to use Cuban names to play on the team an' it's like slave names to them. They know it ain't real, so they give us a nickname."

Where each of their thoughts went from there was a secret. No one spoke until they reached the carriage. Marjory climbed up into the seat. "I'm not sure we accomplished a damned thing."

"Did you expect to? Other than relieving your anger?" Byrne answered and was immediately sorry he'd spoken his mind.

Marjory held her tongue for a long moment. "No, I suppose not," she finally said. "Though it's never a bad tactic to do some intelligence gathering."

"Touché," Byrne said, thinking of his conversation with Sergeant Harris.

"Ah, French, Mr. Byrne?" Marjory said. "Shall we now pardon you?"

"Hell no," he said, his smile matching hers in the flicker of flame.

Chapter 15

THE image floated up in his dreams all night: Marjory, her white dress dusted with dirt and torn to the calf but still swirling in the ocean breeze as she stood outside the Poinciana. Her hair was damp from sweat, tendrils pasted against her neck. Her eyes, the greenness now visible in the light of the hotel, tired from the journey but still holding a glow that told you her passion was part of her, awaiting a challenge.

She had sent Santos away after they arrived back at the ball, which had long since wound down. They were at the south entrance and stood away from the porches, she being wary of being seen in such disarray. Byrne offered to walk her to the Breakers, but she declined with that hint of stubbornness in her voice that kept him from insisting. He repeated that he would find Faustus in the morning but first had to explain himself to his Pinkerton sergeant.

"You made a selfless sacrifice tonight, Michael Byrne," she'd said. "Interesting."

She'd stepped forward and put her cheek next to his just as she had done with Mr. Claude, but Byrne could not imagine the old man having the same reaction as his. Despite the evening's trials he could smell the warm lavender rising up from her skin, and her cheek felt as smooth as a whisper.

"Thank you, sir." She turned and walked east toward the ocean. Maybe he'd closed his eyes at that instant, but the same image had come to him every time he woke during the night and was with him now.

He rose from his bed in the Seminole Hotel and washed in the basin. He'd hung his new clothes from last night on the closet door, dirt halfway up the legs of the trousers, which were also peppered with tiny brambles that were spiked and painful to pick away. The shirt was no longer white, though he hadn't lost a button during the entire adventure. His coat, which he'd draped across his arm or tossed in the carriage, was the only part of his forty-dollar purchase that had somewhat survived. After being chewed out by Harris last night for leaving his post and chasing "your bloody intelligence," he'd wished he'd kept the money he'd spent as he might need it when he became unemployed. Harris had only calmed a bit when Byrne described how he'd escorted Mr. McAdams's daughter and had indeed been forced to step in and prevent a physical altercation between her and the sheriff.

"With your magic wand?" Harris said, that twitch of a grin at the corner of his mouth.

"Aye."

"Oh, what I'd of paid to see that fat bastard's eyes when that came out."

Byrne was gruffly dismissed and warned to be available in the morning.

The recollection now caused him to dress quickly and head downstairs to breakfast. Having tasted, with admiration and appetite, scrambled turtle eggs and ham with cornbread, Byrne headed out on to the street in search of Faustus. The old man had nearly promised to find Danny, hadn't he? Last night's shenanigans aside, it was time to find his brother.

The air was dead still outside, not even a breeze from the ocean. Byrne started for the docks first, walking south along the lakefront; the water was silent, stretching out like a hot pane of glass. In the distance he could see a sharpie, its sails hanging limp and useless, the boat seemingly stuck in the calm a hundred feet from shore like a tired wagon with its wheels plunged solid into mud.

When he got to the docks, he spotted Captain Abbott sitting on a crate mending a net.

"Ain't seen 'im," was his answer. "It's no day for fishin' less you want to shore cast, and hell, it ain't worth it anymore. Hell, the fishin' here has all but dried up what with all these tourists. We'll be lucky to have a fish in Florida in another ten years."

Grumpy old man, Byrne thought.

"Where might I find Mr. Faustus on a day such as this, then?"

"Two places." Captain Abbott did not look up. "Watchin' 'em dig holes on that plot of land of his on Clematis, or drinkin' beer at the tavern 'cross the street. Course why a man would drink that swill instead of God's own elixir of rum from the islands is beyond me."

Byrne left Abbott to his grumbling. The captain was correct on where best to find Faustus. As Byrne approached Olive Street along Clematis, he spotted the man standing in front of a cleared piece of land watching brick masons working a line of about fifty feet. Survey string mapped out the rest of the foundation that ran some sixty feet deep into the plot. Faustus was leaning on his cane and dressed as if he'd attended his own shabby ball the night before: his top hat was tipped to shade his eyes and his tailed jacket and trousers were again of a fine but faded cloth.

"Mr. Faustus, good morning, sir," Byrne said.

"Ahh, Mr. Byrne. I trust a fine evening was had by all at the Flaglers' welcome home ball in the palace?"

Byrne let the greeting sit, considered his tactics, then decided to hell with being polite or patient.

"Have you obtained the whereabouts of my brother, Mr. Faustus? I am anxious to find him."

Faustus stared ahead at the work before him. The fact that the old man would not meet his eyes sent a shiver of dread through Byrne. It was well-known body language on the street—a man who will not look you in the eye is either hiding bad news or lying to you.

"In due time, young man. In due time," Faustus finally said. "First tell me of your exploits of last night. Rumor is abounding."

Byrne fought back an anger that was rising in him. Was Faustus playing him for some reason? Maybe he had no information about Danny. Maybe he was just keeping Byrne on the hook like one of his fish, enjoying some game.

Well, if he wanted games, "All had a good night, I'm sure, with the exception of Shantice Carver and of course Mr. Claude Augustus Wilson, who probably did not enjoy being awakened in the middle of the night."

Byrne watched the names register on Faustus's profile. The old man seemed to work the angles in his own head.

"Yes, well. We did try with Mizz Carver. Unfortunately, despite our efforts to sneak her aboard a ship going north, she was obviously apprehended.

"But also obvious is your knowledge of the occurrence," he added, "which does surprise me. I've not yet heard from my dear friend Mr. Claude, but you have done some diligence. Congratulations."

It was now Byrne who watched the bricklayers, slapping and tapping the stones into place in front of them.

"Masons building a Masonic Temple?" Byrne said, and this time the statement turned Faustus's head around.

"You are indeed an extraordinarily informed and perceptive young man, Mr. Byrne. You continue to impress. Yes, this will be the location of the first temple to be built in this region of Florida. And we will need men of strong moral fiber and dignity to fill her, sir.

"They will be men who voluntarily ask to join, and they will be accepted because they are good men who believe in God and hold high ethical and moral ideals. It will be a place to learn and to teach what friendship, morality, and truth really involve, and to practice on a small scale the reality of brotherhood."

If it was an invitation to join Faustus's group, Byrne ignored it. He knew nothing of the organization and had more pressing concerns.

"Do you know where my brother is or do you not?"

Faustus seemed to think about the question for a moment.

"Floridians do not stand out in the sun for nothing, Mr. Byrne. May I buy you a chilled beer?"

It was nine o'clock when they walked into the Midway Plaisance, and before Faustus made the distance between the door and the bar rail, a pint of beer was standing and waiting.

"Morning, Mr. Faustus," said the woman behind the bar. "Hot already, eh sir?"

"Indeed, Miss Graham. A draft for my friend here if you please." It was unusual to see a woman tending bar, but considering the hour, Byrne dismissed the propriety and motioned for a beer of his own.

Whatever the beliefs of Faustus's brotherhood of Masons, Byrne was glad they didn't include abstinence. The draft was as excellent as the first time he'd drunk it here with the binder boys. After taking a few swallows,

Byrne decided that his approach with Faustus on the street had perhaps been too disingenuous. He changed it.

"I'm no lawyer, sir, but it seems to me that there are some inquiries to be made about this incident of the man killed during a fire on the island. I mean, there are folks who say this Carver woman was not even there at the time of the man's death."

Faustus took a drink and made perhaps the same decision on candor as Byrne had.

"And you come across this information from which folks, Mr. Byrne? Miss McAdams from the hotel?"

Byrne gave up trying to plumb the breadth of Faustus' connections to information.

"Yes. And some of the hotel workers who are in a position to know."

"And therein lies the problem, Mr. Byrne," Faustus said. "As a Northerner, you may not understand the ancient mores that still hold this land and the law that still governs it. The sheriff is not a forward-thinking Southern man. If a Negro woman has been accused of killing a white man, it would be a foregone conclusion that she is not only guilty but should in all practicality be hanged for such offense."

Byrne had seen enough on the streets of New York to know that neighborhoods of Greeks, Italians, Poles and Jews operated on their own laws and precepts, just like anywhere else. The "we deal with our own" attitude was one that the police had always worked both with and against to keep a lid on crime and to protect the moneyed civilians of the city. But even in a frontier like this, he believed logic could still prevail.

"So let's prove she didn't do it. Certainly that doesn't get ignored in a place that's trying to become civilized."

Faustus took another silent drink. He wiped away the residual foam.

"Let us?" he said. "Did you use the contraction 'let's' as in you and I, Mr. Byrne?"

Byrne took a breath. "From my understanding, you are a lawyer, sir. And from your mouth to my ear you have admitted a medical background. And from my observation, you also know most of the prominent people in this small town. So unless I'm a fool, I'd bet you know the coroner and you know how to do a basic autopsy and there is no better way to find out how a man was killed than to look for yourself."

If he'd read Faustus correctly, the old man was avoiding some knowledge of his brother. An uncomfortable knowledge. Maybe a terrible knowledge. Maybe a knowledge that now lay in the coroner's office.

Faustus absorbed the young man's challenge. "A fine presentation, Mr. Byrne," he said, draining his glass and spilling a few coins on the bar. He stood up and with cane in hand motioned to the front door. "Let us."

The undertaker's was on Clematis in a low-slung wooden building with a tin roof and double-wide doors in the front. There were sawed-out places in the front wall for windows, but any view was blocked by paper hung from the inside. Wagon tracks led from the street to the back.

Faustus knocked at the door and, without waiting for an answer, walked in as if it were a storefront, which in effect it was. George Maltby made his living by burying local folks, preparing the bodies of nonlocals for transportation north to their hometowns, and on occasion doing contract work for the county government, including holding the unclaimed bodies of victims of crime until given the order to move them either into the ground or to a family claimant.

When Byrne stepped into the building, he noted that it was unnaturally cool. He was to learn later that the undertaker's building was directly behind the G.G. Springer's Ice Making Factory. Maltby had talked Springer into running a duct into the back of his place. The decision pleased both men as it kept the odor of Maltby's particular business from passersby as well as from Springer's customers, who came to load their own ice blocks from his factory's back door. But when he first walked in, Byrne took the chill as a sign of death, and it unnerved him. The room was, like many of its day, a single square structure. But this one was halved by a plush purple curtain like that of a Broadway stage. When Faustus called out Maltby's name, a plump and unusually jovial man swept away the corner of the curtain and stepped out like some master of ceremonies for the Herald Square Theater in the Bowery.

"Well hello, hello, Mr. Faustus and friend," said Maltby, recognizing Faustus at once and making Byrne wonder how often the old man had occasion to visit the undertaker.

"To what do I owe the honor, sir? I hope most sincerely that it is not a personal matter, meaning not a personal friend who may have fallen to an early departure from this grand and glorious world."

Though the undertaker's girth reminded Byrne of the sheriff, his face was in direct opposition: florid and fat with pumped up cheeks that resembled a clown's, eyes that seemed perpetually large and wide open, and lips that seemed unnaturally red.

"Thank you, George, for your concern," said Faustus, tapping his cane. "But no, we've come on a bit of unofficial business and mean to inquire if you have taken possession of a body brought the other day from a fire on the island?

"My understanding is that the victim has not yet been identified, and for medical inquiry, it is my hope that I may spend a few moments in examination of the remains."

Maltby's expression fell immediately from the laughing clown to that of the down-turned smile of its forlorn opposite.

"Well, um, gosh, Mr. Faustus. You know, Doc Lansing already did that for the sheriff. I mean, he came in and took a look and said he was going to file a report with the sheriff's office on the cause of death and all."

"I was aware of that," Faustus lied, and he did it well, Byrne thought. "But my inquiry is of a different nature, George. And as I said, it will take only a few minutes. I require no extensive cutting or probing or further altering of the body from what you may have already accomplished."

Maltby was still wary. He may not have been under specific instructions from the sheriff to shield the body, but it was a criminal case. And even though Faustus was a well-respected, if not always present, member of the community and a man known for his broad knowledge and a true Southerner like himself … Oh, what the hell.

"Well, I don't see any harm in that, Mr. Faustus. I mean, it is science and all, eh?" Maltby extended his hand to show the way.

Behind the heavy curtain three waist-high tables were lined up in the middle of the space, and all were occupied and carefully shrouded except for the middle one, where Maltby had obviously been working before he was interrupted. Next to that corpse a table sat upon which rested a tray of tools, a leather box of what looked like rolls of hair samples in a variety of colors, and a collection of jars and bottles of makeup, lipstick and moisturizing creams. There was also some kind of hand pump that brought to Byrne's mind a plunger the likes of which the reluctant railway bombers might have used only a few days ago. Byrne was struck by the odor of chemicals that suffused the air, not so unpleasant that he had to cover his nose but enough to warn him that worse might be yet to come.

"I was just now preparing to do a formaldehyde transfer for this poor soul," Maltby said when he noticed Byrne's gaze. "He's going home on the train to New York tomorrow, and the family very much wants him to look as if he has a tan when he arrives."

Faustus paid no attention and moved directly to the far table, where a corpse was wrapped in a simple wool blanket.

"I, uh, was reluctant, sir, to begin the process of embalming on this gentleman, though," Maltby said, quickening his own pace to catch up with Faustus before he began uncovering the body. "I mean, since no relative or representative has claimed the deceased ..."

"Yes, why waste the expensive arsenic or formaldehyde if you're only going to dump him into a pauper's grave," Faustus said abruptly. "I understand, George."

Faustus stood at the head of the corpse and waited for Byrne to come alongside. There was a long pause, both men anticipating the possibilities they had both been dancing around for days.

"Are you prepared for this, Mr. Byrne?" Faustus said quietly.

"Yes."

Faustus pulled back the blanket and looked down at the burned and partially decomposed face of the corpse. Despite its condition, the look of the body confirmed the rumors of not only the fire but the identity of the dead.

Byrne's face was stoic, unwavering. His eyes went first to the head and stayed there, studying, it seemed, the contours of nose and cheekbone and then chin. His brother could lose many things in death—color and flesh and dancing eyes and muscle mass—but not that chin. It had always been out there, up and defiant when he had to be, turned just so to the right when he was pretending to ponder a trade or study a situation, tucked and careful when he was in a fight. Danny's eyes were closed, whether by death or by the coroner, and Byrne was relieved not to have to see their blueness, or the opposite, an unseeing lack of color and light.

Faustus watched as Byrne's own hand carefully reached out to place just his fingertips on the corpse's wrist. On Byrne's face, a single tear rolled down his left cheek.

After allowing the moment to pass, Faustus leaned in to the body and carefully examined it from the face down. He was careful not to touch anything, in deference to Byrne, whose reaction had confirmed what Faustus had been surmising all along. When it seemed obvious that Byrne would hold back any more show of emotion, Faustus shifted into professional mode.

"You have done some work here, George," Faustus said, and Maltby stepped closer.

"No sir, not really. I did tap the internal organs to keep them from bloating, but certainly no cosmetic work and an extensive work it certainly would be if his family did indeed contact me and request some form of restoration ..."

"Ah, but George," Faustus said. "Here at the throat it appears you've done some stitching and a bit of cover with, what is that, clay?"

There was silence from the mortician. Faustus turned and picked up a steel probe from the tray behind him and then pointed at a circular area of the corpse's throat that was obviously a different color from the pale flesh. Faustus poked at the area and in so doing uncovered a series of white stitches that had been used to close a hole.

"Oh, yes. Well, it was a nasty-looking wound and seemed quite inappropriate to leave open," Maltby started, but Faustus looked up and held the undertaker's eyes. "Getting squeamish in your old age, George? I somehow find that hard to believe."

Faustus turned the body's head to the side with some difficulty against the rigor and examined the back of the neck.

"I see no one had to repair an exit wound. Does that mean, George, that you found the bullet that entered this man's throat? Lodged perhaps in the cervical vertebra of the spinal column?"

"Well, certainly not, Mr. Faustus. That would not be of my purview," said Maltby, who was now sweating despite the coolness of the room. "If such a thing was discovered it would have been by Dr. Lansing, who was, as I said, contacted by the sheriff to do an autopsy of the victim."

Faustus ignored the undertaker and was examining the body's torso.

"And as for the knife wound that was originally given as cause of death," he said, now to no one in particular, "I see no indications here of such a wound nor an attempt to cover it up if there had been one. Can you help me out with that, sir?"

Maltby had obviously had enough. He stepped to the table, took hold of the blanket and pulled it up over the corpse. Despite his profession—and one would think an innate sense for such things—the undertaker had not picked up on the slight show of grief and emotion on Byrne's face.

"Mr. Faustus," he said. "I don't see how this serves a scientific purpose and really I must ask that this line of questioning be directed to the sheriff or Dr. Lansing as I do not find it appropriate here, sir, with all due respect."

The undertaker had taken a defensive stance, arms now folded over his chest, and stood in front of the corpse as if now he was willing to defend it.

"That's fine, George. Really," said Faustus, gathering his cane and hat. "I certainly didn't mean to upset you, sir. We'll be on our way."

Byrne showed no unwillingness to follow, but as they were making their way through the curtain and out of the shop, the undertaker shuffled behind them. "And excuse me, sir," he said to Byrne. "I didn't get your name or title, sir?"

Byrne was about to answer when Faustus cut him off.

"He didn't give it, George."

Outside, the heat and humidity wrapped about Byrne's face. He stood staring out into the brightness of the sun, wondering why he had come to this place called Florida. Why had he not just left it alone? Let his constant admonishment over the last few years stand—Danny had left and was simply never coming back. At least there would have been that tiny sliver of hope that his brother was still alive. He took a deep breath and turned to Faustus, who stood silent beside him.

"You knew it was him, my brother?"

"I could certainly see the family resemblance," Faustus said. "The locale of your own origins and the sound of your heritage were in both of your voices. I surmised it to be a distinct possibility."

"You talked to Danny?"

Faustus seemed to study the head of his cane. "I had met him, but under a different name," he said. "He had introduced himself as a Mr. Bingham. Robert Bingham.

"This is a land where people are often reluctant to use their given names, especially the sort who are in the business that Mr. Bingham was in."

"Which was?"

"He introduced himself as a lawyer, an entrepreneur, a real estate broker and a representative of Northern interests," Faustus said, his voice flattened so as not to show emotion. "He was extremely bright, like you, Mr. Byrne. He had your talent for observation and recollection. I rather liked him at first."

"And then?" Byrne said.

Faustus cleared his throat. "At our introduction he was wearing a Mason's ring. At first, I tried not to pry, but after a few days of friendly conversation I made him out to be a fraud. He was using the symbol as a way to meet those he might take advantage of."

"A big sin among the brotherhood, I suppose?"

"Yes. A big sin. No more though, I suppose, than a man who wears a cross of Christ around his neck while coveting his neighbor's wife."

Byrne had never been one for religion, and he'd learned in the city bars that the discussion of same was better avoided.

"Is that why you were testing me? To see if I was like my brother?" Byrne said.

"Precisely. Your attributes are admirable. And as I said, your brother shared many of them. I couldn't be sure that a sibling might have the same powers of deception as well. Trick me once, shame on you. But trick me twice, shame on me."

"So the coin, the fishing trip, even the beer this morning were all part of your litmus test?" Byrne let a slice of sarcasm slip into his voice.

"Yes. Had you bitten my coin, taken advantage of my largesse, or shot me and Captain Abbott dead on the sea and taken off with our boat, I would have judged you differently, even in the afterlife."

"But I didn't."

"No sir, you didn't. And now, with the possibility that a young woman is being railroaded into a murder charge, you have come to see if WE can find the truth of the matter."

Byrne did not have to state the obvious. His purpose may have been selfless last night. Now he had a distinct reason for finding out the truth. Now he was looking for the killer of his brother.

"So where's the bullet?" he said without hesitation. It would be the first question any good investigator would now ask, the logical question.

"I believe we will have to inquire of Dr. Lansing to answer that, my young friend."

Faustus turned on his heel and began walking back to Olive Street. Byrne had to lengthen his stride to keep up. The old man had taken on a fired energy, and this time it was neither by the lure of fighting fish or deep blue water. Byrne could see a pursuit of something in Faustus's eyes that was being pushed by an anger that he hadn't shown before. The old Mason doesn't like being lied to, he thought.

When they got to a small storefront with a druggist's symbol and the title "Dr. Lansing" painted above the wooden door, Faustus turned. "I will only be a minute. Could you please wait outside, Mr. Byrne?"

Byrne started to object but second-guessed his reaction and instead took up a place in the shade of the tin awning as a group of raggedy farm workers trudged north toward the fields. A mule-drawn wagon, loaded with green tomatoes, passed on its way to the rail station. Behind Byrne's eyes was a vision: he and Danny as boys, scouring the streets of their East Side neighborhood, watching like small animals but considering it a game, a race for some piece of food that fell from the back of a wagon. They'd skitter out into the traffic and snatch the gift from the cobblestone. Danny with that laugh of his that went gleeful at the thought of winning some prize, even if it was actually no prize at all but a morsel to add to their empty stomachs. Danny, always with that pride that he'd somehow gotten over on someone else. Danny with his dreams of finagling his way to "land and money" for a family whose members were now almost all dead.

Byrne's head turned at the sound of a man's angry voice coming from inside the pharmacy, but he was unsure whose since he had never heard Faustus raise his voice except in joy of hooking a tarpon, and this was not a note of joy. He moved in front of the door and put his back to it, hearing the sharp smack of wood against wood, like the sound a cane might make when it is rapped flat and hard against a countertop. A woman in a long day dress and carrying her purse stepped toward Byrne, meaning to enter the shop. He tipped his hat: "I'm sorry, ma'am, but the doc is presently treating a difficult patient. It would be best if you came back in a few minutes." He did not move from blocking the door, and she gave him her back and continued down the street. Moments later Faustus stepped out into the sunlight. He seemed unusually calm, but there was color in his cheeks that was just beginning to subside.

"A single .38-calibre round," he said. "Lodged in the vertebra as suspected. The bullet was removed and presented along with the findings of the autopsy to Sheriff Cox."

Faustus started off in the direction of the saloon. "Pity," he said, disappointment in his voice, and when Byrne, following, looked over his shoulder, there was a small, thin man in suit pants and suspenders standing in the doorway of the doctor's office looking much chagrined and defeated.

Chapter 16

Marjory McAdams awoke that day with a determination that can only be held in its unflinching doggedness by the young. It was not unlike the ocean swimming that spurred her furiously to stroke for miles out of sight of land, or the late-night trudging that she'd done last evening through the dark brambles of West Palm Beach farmlands. But today it was knowledge she was after, and her first stop would be at the knee of the "motherly" Mrs. Birch. If she then had to bring Mr. Birch into it, so be it.

"Good morning, Abby," Marjory said when she was greeted at the door of the Birch suite by the maid.

"And to you, Miss McAdams."

"Is Mrs. Birch available?" Marjory walked in and glanced about the room without the normal invitation.

"No, ma'am. She is out taking her mornin' golf. She is s'pose to be back for lunch though."

Marjory moved deeper into the room.

"And Mr. Birch?" she said. "Is he available?"

The maid moved around Marjory, cutting her off from looking further through the rooms but doing so in a subservient way so as not to appear authoritative or defensive.

"No, ma'am. They is playin' together this morning. Mr. Birch plays with her most all the time now."

Marjory raised her chin. "Ah. I've heard that the men on the links have brought Mrs. Birch's displays of gumption to the manager," Marjory said. "Perhaps Mr. Birch has been asked to accompany her in order to keep her on the leash."

The statement may have been too gossipy to share with a maid, but Marjory took the chance. Whether she would continue to probe would be determined by the answer. The stoic face of the maid cracked only slightly.

"Ain't nobody put no leash on Ma'am," she said. "Not even Mister."

Marjory turned in a small circle, pretending to look at the objects of art. "You've been with them a long time, Abby, yes?"

"Only when they come to Florida, ma'am. But that's three winters now."

"And you plan to stay with them? I mean full-time? I've heard that Mr. Birch may be acquiring property here on the island, which sounds like you might be needed year round."

There was worry in the Negro woman's eyes. She was trying to study her own words ahead of time, before they left her mouth.

"They talk about buyin' land all the time, ma'am. Mrs. Birch, she love that real state stuff. But they ain't said nothin' to me about winter time other than about me goin' to New York City an' I ain't much for that cold weather, ma'am."

The revelation that Mrs. Birch was more of a partner and consultant with her husband in matters of real estate than she'd ever let on caused McAdams to go silent for so long the maid became nervous.

"Like I say, Miss McAdams. Ma'am s'pose to be back for lunch."

"Oh, yes," Marjory caught herself lost in thought and now started back toward the door. "Just tell her I stopped by to talk to her about the Carver woman."

A small gasp came from Abby and snapped Marjory back to the present.

"Mizz Shantice? Is she all right, ma'am?" Abby almost begged for an answer.

"Why, yes, I suppose. If you can call being in jail under the heel of the sheriff being all right," Marjory said. She looked into the now expressive face of the maid. "I didn't know that the two of you were friends."

"Yes, ma'am. Well, we knowed each other for a long time. Course we all knowin' each other here," Abby said. "Did ya'll talk with her, ma'am? I mean in private?"

"No. Not really Abby. Why? Do you think she has something to say to me in private?" Marjory's eyes were now intent but unable to keep the maid's own eyes from going to the floor.

"Uh, no, ma'am. I'm just worried on her, that's all."

"Well, several people are trying to help her, Abby. So hope for the best and be strong, dear." The hair was up on the back of her neck, and Marjory knew from experience that the new information was pushing her even harder. She stepped out onto the hotel veranda, where only a few couples and women strolled arm in arm on their morning constitutional.

If the Birches were actively looking to buy property on the island, which she already knew from the binders she'd obtained, if "Ma'am" was truly as deep into her husband's land acquisitions as Abby seemed to indicate, that is why Marjory had seen Mrs. Birch walking, with that aggressive and manly gait of hers, from the direction of the Styx only half and hour before Ida May Fluery smelled fire in the air.

When she got back to the Breakers, the first maid she talked to knew exactly where Ida May Fluery was: "Why, it's a baseball game on today, Miss McAdams. I spect Mizz Ida down there sneakin' a look at her boy."

Whether Henry Flagler was a baseball fan or not, he knew many of his upscale New York vacationers were. Watching a quality game in the middle of winter was a luxury he knew they would brag about to their equally upscale friends, who were still reluctant to travel south. It was little trouble for his engineers to lay out a baseball diamond on the open land within walking distance of the hotel. Grass was cheap in Palm Beach. So were players.

By the time Marjory reached the field, the stands that were erected only a few feet from the base paths were nearly full. Vacationing men were in the majority of those sitting in the sun, giving hearty ovations for each well-executed play. But several women were also in attendance, sitting with their husbands or in groups, their wide-brimmed hats or open parasols providing shade. The men were too polite to say a word, standing or stretching around any obstructed view. The women clapped softly with gloved hands when it seemed appropriate.

Marjory had been to the games before. She admired the athletic skill, the quickness and exactness of the players, the act and react of muscle memory honed by years of repetition. The fact that the athletes spent most of their days pushing carts, carrying baggage, cooking or washing, or peddling carriages only made the game more fascinating. They did this out of pure love. A game that gained them only a few extra hours off their daily work still drove them to a glorious pursuit of perfection. The field was as meticulously manicured as any of Flagler's gardens and was probably cut and trimmed and raked by the very men who played on it. In the hard sunlight the green glowed and the white chalk lines were as bright as the women's clothing.

Marjory paid scant attention to those in the stands, instead looking down the third baseline where a few black workers gathered to watch their own. Marjory knew that if Ida May was here, she would be watching Santos. Marjory walked behind the stands, smiling and nodding to hotel patrons as she glided by. As she passed behind home plate, she stopped for a moment to watch the giant black man out on the pitcher's mound. He was tall and easily over two hundred pounds. She'd seen him before, amusing the crowd with his bear-like movements and wily, smiling presence. He knew that the game was as much entertainment for the upper class as it was a competition. Yet when it was time, his arm was ferocious. At that moment he delivered a fastball. The hard slap of the leather ball in the catcher's glove was like a rifle report, and Marjory blinked hard at the sound.

"Steeeeeriiiik," called out the umpire, an equally large but soft white man who ran the games with an authority he would doubtfully own anywhere else on the island.

Marjory moved on.

At the end of the bleachers she spotted Miss Fluery in the shade of a black umbrella, accompanied by three other housemaids Marjory recognized. She tried to catch the woman's attention but in vain. Fluery's eyes were only for Santos, who was out on the field, not thirty feet away, just inside the third base line. Santos was coiled, awaiting the next pitch, his back curved like an iron awl, his hands out in front of him, the cabled muscle in his bared forearms flexing, and his eyes staring with an intensity she had not seen in the dark of last night. Marjory heard the crack of the bat, almost felt it, and hardly had time to blink when she saw Santos launch himself, glove hand stretched high into the sun, where it snatched the ball out of the air, the sheer force of the drive bending his torso back. Still he landed on his toes. It was the third out, and he flipped the ball out of his glove, caught it with his bare hand and rolled it to the pitcher's mound before jogging off the field.

From the crowd behind and to her right, Marjory heard a hotel guest exclaim "Did you see that nigger jump! Wonderful!" Santos passed the bleachers and another said, "Nice job, boy," as the rest applauded.

Only then did Ida May Fluery turn and recognize Marjory standing nearby.

"May we speak, Mizz Fluery?" Marjory said, stepping forward. The other servants discretely faded away, leaving the two women, who moved together down the white foul line.

"Have you heard?" Marjory spoke first. "That Mizz Carver has been arrested and jailed?"

"Every worker on the island knew by sunup, ma'am," Fluery said, a statement, not as caustic as it could have been.

"Yes, of course," Marjory said, instantly losing her faux motive for coming to see her. "We, umm, Mr. Santos and I, that is, went across to try to speak for her last evening. She did not seem to have been abused. I mean, beaten or physically punished."

"Then the Lord have mercy," the housewoman said.

"But I fear that it will be difficult to convince the sheriff or the court, if it should go so far, that Shantice is not the one who killed the man in the Styx unless we can find someone to speak out for her."

Ida May stood silent, looking out onto the greenness of the outfield, not at Marjory. She knew she was being led.

"Do you mean someone to speak for her good name, 'cause there isn't a person on this island who didn't know Shantice was a whore," Fluery said.

"No. No, I didn't mean that," Marjory said, as if that fact actually embarrassed her. "I meant that you had said there were others with Shantice when she was across the lake at the carnival. Perhaps they would be willing to say they were with her and where exactly they were when the fire began.

"Do you know who, exactly, was with her that night?"

Again Fluery hesitated. Bringing in others' names in white men's situations was never wise. Guilt by association was something to be avoided in her world. Yet she could see no hidden agenda in McAdams's question.

"I believe Abby Campbell say she was with Shantice," she finally said. "They been close a while, though I cain't say why."

"Abby Campbell? The girl who works for Mrs. Birch?"

"That's the one."

"Do you believe her?" Marjory said, then caught herself. "I mean, is she believable, if she had to speak, say, in front of the sheriff or an attorney?"

"She be believed as much as any Negro woman might be to folks like that."

One of the opposing outfielders ran out to his position. Marjory did not see him doff his hat in their direction, so did not register whether it had been to her or to the head house woman. She was rerunning her previous conversation with Abby in her mind. Why didn't the girl say she was with Shantice the night of the fire? Why not offer her help once Marjory had told her that her friend was in dire need? Had they indeed been together that night? And where? And what had they witnessed? She would need to talk with Abby again, this time with a stronger sense of authority.

"I believe we'll need to employ an attorney for Miss Carver," Marjory finally said, turning to Fluery and delivering the statement that had motivated her to come there in the first place.

"No one has money to pay no lawyer for that girl. An' it won't make no difference if they did," Fluery said with the same tone she used when McAdams first asked if she knew of Carver's arrest. She had no tolerance for white people who disavowed the obvious. The game had resumed, and Fluery began walking back toward third base, Marjory alongside.

"I shall provide the money," Marjory said, as if working it out in her own mind. She needed a way to question Shantice Carver, to find out whether she had been on the island that night, to find out what she had seen. Marjory needed to know why and where Mrs. Birch had been when Marjory had seen her coming out of the woods that night. Since the Carver woman was obviously reluctant to talk, as Marjory had been in the laundry, maybe a lawyer in pursuit of her defense could glean some answers.

As they moved closer to the stands, Marjory spotted a man, wandering, looking out of place, a bit disheveled for the paying customer, so to speak.

"And I shall also provide the attorney," she said to Ida May before taking the old woman's hands and bidding her good-bye. "Don't you worry."

Byrne had come to the ball game with one intent: to find Marjory and arrange a time for her to meet with him and Faustus, to share with her the information from the morgue and the doctor's hesitant report. In return he would get back from her anything—anything—she knew about the killing and the Styx. He would be circumspect. He would not show the anger burning in his gut. He would not go off half-cocked. He would ask questions, watch reactions, intuit meaning, just as he had always done. But he would find the person who shot his brother.

"Well, Mr. Byrne. I see you actually took up my offer." Marjory's voice came from behind him, causing Byrne to spin round.

"I, uh, well, I wouldn't have missed it," he said, raising his palms to indicate the scene around him. "It's ... unexpected."

"Oh, not for them." Marjory pointed relaxed fingers to the bleachers and chairs. "They have come to expect it. After all, what is summer weather without baseball, especially now in the middle of winter, when they can brag about attending a game while their friends in New York are all huddled by the fireplace?"

Was that cynicism he heard in her voice, or braggadocio? Byrne was arrested by the sight of the man now coming to home plate with a bat in his hands. Santos actually looked bigger than he had in the dark, trudging with them in the fields, sitting at a small wooden table, even peddling a carriage while perched on a raised seat. When Santos reached the plate, took his wide stance and swung the bat in an exaggerated, slow-motion practice swing, he looked like something carved and regal, overlooking its domain.

"Your friend?" he asked. Santos was cocked and took the first pitch, a ball off the plate. The umpire bawled, "Baaawwwwl."

"In a sense," said Marjory, who was also watching the batter. "More of an acquaintance."

The second pitch was delivered from the thin, rope-muscled Negro on the mound. Again, the batter barely flinched. "Baaawwwwl."

"A protector, then?" Byrne said.

"I, Mr. Byrne? What would possibly make you think that I would need protection?" Marjory turned to study the side of Byrne's face, wondering whether by some impossible means the Pinkerton knew more than he should.

"Someone of your charm and beauty might need someone to ward off the suitors," Byrne said, only slightly embarrassed by what had come out of his mouth. He watched the next pitch come in low and hard. Santos turned on in a flashing instant. The sound of snapping oak exploded in the air, and heads turned as one to watch the ball sail up, up, up and out over the tree line. Byrne, though, kept his eyes on Santos, who also, when the outcome was obvious, turned his attention to the bat as he jogged toward the first base, studying its splinters and now angled shaft and then tossing it aside. The big man jogged around the base paths to the applause of the crowd, and Byrne unconsciously reached into his pocket to feel the thin metal baton. It would stand no chance in a face-off.

"If you did need that protection, he would certainly be my choice," Byrne said. Marjory had a curious look on her face, amused yet studious.

"I shall consider it, Mr. Byrne, if the need should arise," she said. "But you didn't come out here to watch baseball or to banter."

"Not really," he said, stepping back from the crowd in small, nonchalant steps so as not to draw attention. Marjory followed. When they were out of earshot, he tipped he head to her ear. "I have located Mr. Faustus. He is a Mason and a lawyer on the mainland and has made some curious findings at the undertaker's and at the doctor's where the autopsy was done."

Now it was Marjory's turn to not to flinch, the news coming in low and hard, but she held her stance.

"Really?"

"Mr. Faustus was able to examine the body himself and obtained the paperwork submitted to the sheriff," Byrne said, trying to please her, uncharacteristic territory for him. "The doctor removed a bullet from Mr. Bingham's throat."

Marjory plucked a hanky from somewhere in the folds of her skirts and pretended a speck of something was in her eye, a tactic to gain a second from her surprise.

"I'm sorry, did you say Bingham? Was that the poor man's name?"

"It's the name Mr. Faustus knew him by. He apparently had a reputation as a con man. Underhanded, bit of a thief," Byrne said. He had already decided to keep secret his brother's true identity—and his connection.

"Well no wonder he was a stranger to us then. I know most of the people on the island, but in the streets on the mainland, I would be quite lost—as you could tell last night, Mr. Byrne. But such news is certainly helpful to Mizz Carver, and if your Mr. Faustus is willing, I would be delighted to employ him to speak out in her defense before the judge at her hearing on Friday."

Byrne was pleased with himself, seeing her intensity, obviously energized by his news.

"Then if I may, Miss McAdams, you could have the opportunity to ask him yourself if you would accept an invitation to dinner tonight," he said. She in turn seemed to be picking out a response, but quickly a smile came to her face.

"It would be a pleasure, Mr. Byrne."

Chapter 17

THE sun was hot on his shoulders, sweat running down the middle of his back, and lye soapsuds flowing down his arms. A long-handled scrub brush, a pail of water and an entire railcar had met Byrne when he got back to the mainland.

Harris was waiting for him on the front porch of his hotel with a cigar stuck in the side of his face and a look of worry pushing his thick eyebrows together.

"Michael, me boy. Michael, me boy," he said in a disappointed tone that reminded Byrne of his childhood years when he was about to get the strap. A vision of his father snapped on in full color inside of his head. The old man's sunken cheek bones, eyes trying to look angry but only showing how it was going to hurt him to mete out the punishment his Old World upbringing demanded. Byrne would take that strap in a second to see his father's face again.

"Too much time on yer hands, eh, Michael?" Harris continued. "Didn't yer mum tell you it was the Devil's work, those idle hands, boy?"

The sergeant failed to elaborate and simply gave him his orders: "Get yer arse down to the rail station and take the soap and brush to number 90. Mr. Flagler will be taking a trip to Miami, and the car is expected to be spotless and shining like a new coin by tomorrow."

Byrne could tell by the delivery that there could be no argument and that the reasons such duty was being foisted on a security man were not going to be given. He'd had several hours on the rail side to dwell on it. After scrubbing another section of the side boards, he gathered a different pail of fresh water and tossed it up against the car, washing down the suds. He repeated the act and then went to the nearby water pump to fill the buckets again.

Had Harris finally gotten sick of Byrne's "intelligence gathering" excuse and decided to come down on him? Had he heard about the confrontation in front of the jail and been told by the sheriff to keep his new boy in check? Had he been seen in the company of Faustus, a man Harris had once warned him to stay away from, and had that information been passed along? Or had Byrne simply been caught sticking his nose into something that the powers that be would just as soon see left alone?

"The hell with you all," he said to himself. He'd long decided that he didn't have enough trust in Harris to tell him that the only reason he'd signed on for this job was to find his brother. He wasn't changing tactics now just to keep from washing a train car.

He picked up the brush, sloshed it in the soap bucket and returned to scrubbing the last panel of Flagler's car. Then he'd have to tackle the bright work on the steps and door frames and then polish the brass railings and handles.

"Now there's an enterprising Pinkerton, lads," came a voice from over Byrne's shoulder. He turned to see the binder boys lined up behind him in their scruffy suits, all with shit-eating grins on their faces. Byrne turned back to the work, hiding a grin of his own.

"So the old man is headin' out again, eh?" said the voice again: Haney, the talker, as usual. "Where's he goin,' Michael? Miami?"

"Can't say for sure," Byrne lied.

"Might give us a leg up, my friend. Money goes where Flagler goes, ya know. Might be some property he's been scoutin' down the tip of the peninsula. Some say the old coot's thinking about takin' the train down the islands to Key West."

The outlandish statement brought a guffaw of incredulity from Haney's mates. Byrne picked up a bucket of fresh water and splashed the side of the train.

"Isn't that a bit daft, even for Flagler?" Byrne said, picking up the second bucket. "No one takes a train across the ocean, Haney. Even him."

"Aye, the man has a vision, Pinkerton," Haney said.

"Aye, the man would have to be drunk," Byrne said.

"Excellent invitation," Haney laughed and clapped Byrne on the shoulder. "Don't mind if we do, aye, boyos. Past lunchtime anyway."

While Byrne wrung out his sleeves and tucked in his shirttails, the four of them walked down to J.C. Lauther's Saloon.

The saloon was barely a tent with a few hand-hewn wooden tables about. But there was construction in progress on the lot, and the beer was cold.

"So you're going to Miami hunting property, eh, boyos?" Michael said after draining half a bottle. The keg beer at the restaurant had been tastier, but Byrne wasn't going to argue.

"Word is, some rich woman from Ohio name of Tuttle talked Flagler into building the train down to her place, and he's going to build another hotel," Haney said. "The Tuttle woman has the south side of the river to herself, but we all know how that works, eh, boyos?"

"Brooklyn as soon as they built the first bridge over the East River," said Paul.

"And bets are that bridge in Miami goes up in a month after Flagler gets there," Henry said.

They were all so damned sure of themselves, Byrne thought. Like they had some secret no else had. Like no one was as smart as New Yorkers when it came to finding the angle. They were just like Danny.

"Well, good luck, gents. Just don't end up like your friend Bingham," Byrne said, dropping the name his brother had adopted and waiting for the response.

There was silence at the table as the trio absorbed the statement. As usual, it was Haney who finally spoke.

"Bobby Bingham was the fellow stabbed and burned then?"

"Word is," Byrne said, using Haney's favorite attribution for information, "he was a binder boy like the rest of you. But he was working the island."

Byrne had no knowledge of Danny's intention the night he was shot, but he figured these boys, who had always been locked out of the property grab on the island, might respond if challenged.

"Fucking Bingham!" Paul said. "He wasn't a businessman. He was a shite thief and a ripper who'd do anything to steal a dollar and your good name along with it."

The boys let that one settle, no one speaking up to refute it.

"So Bobby the con man got it stuck to 'im, eh?" Haney said, watching Byrne's eyes carefully.

"Not exactly." Byrne leaned in and the boys followed suit. Nothing like a good bit of inside information to bring heads together. "Word is he wasn't stabbed at all. Shot in the throat was the reason for Mr. Bingham's passing."

"And let me guess," said Haney. "Not by the niggra they've got locked up in the jailhouse unless she was dealin' opium or another bit of nastiness that darlin' Bobby wanted and wasn't willing to pay for."

Byrne felt a twitch at the corner of his face on that one. Danny might have been many things, but he'd never dealt in the opium and morphine game.

"Well, whatever the negotiation was about was lost on the dead man's lips," Byrne said.

Again the table went quiet. Bottles were tipped. Questions were formed and unsaid. Byrne waited them out.

"Did anyone claim Mr. Bingham's body?" Haney finally asked. "Or his things?"

"Not as of yet," Byrne answered.

"Figures for that son of a whore," Paul said.

Byrne's face tightened this time. The slur was too close to his heart. He'd been able to disguise his reaction to the words against his brother, but he couldn't hold it together when someone cursed their mother. Everyone at the table could see Byrne's reaction.

"I'd of told you before, Pinkerton," Haney finally said. "But you've a family resemblance to the now departed."

Haney's mates looked at Byrne's face like a magic shroud had suddenly been lifted, their eyes widening at what their leader now knew was true.

"He was my brother," Byrne said, looking hard into the face of the one who called Danny a son of a whore.

"Jaysus. Sorry, mate," Paul said. "I wouldn't of … you know."

Byrne waved off the apology.

Again the table went quiet, a moment of silence, so to speak. But no one sitting there could put off business for long.

"Did you see his things then, Mr. Byrne, if that's the real name?" Haney asked.

"It's our real name, yes," Byrne said. "And yeah, I was at the undertaker's." The curiosity hook was out, and Haney was biting.

"Bingham's, uh, I mean, your brother's valise? Was it with his effects?"

"I may have seen a leather pouch, sort of like the ones you fellows have," Byrne lied. "Why? What would have been in his valise if it was found with him?"

"Ha! Everything, man. His papers, his identification, his money, promissory notes and any binders he was still holding," Haney said.

"He was loose like the rest of us. Stayed in different places, moved from hotel to shack to tent just like everyone else. You don't leave anything anywhere. You carry everything you have with you just in case you might have to leave on the double, get me?"

"Got you," Byrne said. "Perhaps I'll have to revisit the undertaker and recanvas possessions."

"Aye, you'd do better in the sheriff's office, Mr. Byrne. Just like the roll of money word says was in your poor brother's mouth. Cox has anything of value that was found over there."

Not a man at the table, including Byrne, doubted the statement. He got up, spilled some coins out on the table and prepared to leave.

"Good luck in Miami, boyos. I've got some polishing to do."

Byrne showed up at the appointed hour for dinner with Marjory McAdams and Faustus before the others. Faustus had instructed him to meet at the Dellmore Cottage on the island, where "I will speak to Mrs. Moore, the proprietress there and have a suitable meal prepared."

There had been no time to have his fancy new suit cleaned and repaired, so Byrne made do with the jacket and tried, perhaps in vain, to match it with a clean pair of trousers. He hoped the lighting would be dim.

Faustus arrived ten minutes past the hour, impeccably dressed. Byrne noticed that his garb was relatively new, versus the frayed version he had seen before. Faustus's long-tailed coat with a brocaded vest was of a fine fabric, and he wore shined and pointed shoes that surely could be used as weapons if aimed toward another man's lower regions. The two men met on the porch of the Dellmore with the Poinciana in full view and stood in polite silence in a cooling ocean breeze. Mrs. Moore greeted them and offered drinks, which both declined with a sense that clear-headedness might be required for the evening. After several minutes, Byrne decided to let Faustus in on his friends' concern over a valise that may have been in his brother's possession at the time of his killing.

"They were certainly honest with you, Mr. Byrne," Faustus said. "The binder boys are notorious for keeping their paperwork nearby. I'm afraid I was too focused on your brother's wounds and should have asked the undertaker what if any personal effects he may have collected. The fact that his clothing was nearly burned away might have led to that unfortunate dismissal on my part."

Byrne wondered whether Faustus was nervous about presenting himself as a lawyer to someone of Marjory's high station. That conjecture was quickly abandoned when she arrived fashionably late.

"Absolutely charmed, my dear," Faustus said, with a show of the hat and a bow. Byrne was surprised Marjory hadn't curtsied, the pleasantries were so thick.

Byrne could not find fault with Faustus's impression. Marjory had worn a dress of the lightest shade of green that had a remarkable effect with her eye color and at the same time set off the highlights in her auburn hair. When she turned, the flow of air around her carried a whiff of flowers so delicate that Byrne thought he'd imagined it, and the fading light from the west seemed to catch in the folds of her garments and accentuate the delicacy of her figure. He, too, was charmed.

Once they were seated at a table in the small hotel's parlor, Marjory also declined an offer of wine, and a consommé printanier was served.

"I am quite impressed, Mr. Faustus," Marjory said. "I was aware of Mrs. Moore's reputation as a fine cook, but not that she entertained private parties here."

"Ah, she is an old friend, Miss McAdams, and it was quite wonderful of her to do this on such short notice. But my understanding from Mr. Byrne is that time is of the essence."

Byrne took the first spoonful of soup. Faustus was done with the pleasantries.

"I have heard bits and pieces so far, but if I am to represent this woman in a legal hearing, I really need as much information as possible," Faustus said. "So, could you start from the beginning, Miss McAdams?"

Marjory's fingers were entwined, her wrists resting carefully on the table's edge, her eyes focused, ever so carefully, on Faustus. The old man did not flinch or avert his own look. as polite custom might demand. Two strong personalities were assessing, were making instant determinations, and were, perhaps, making plans.

Marjory's eyes broke first. She picked up her soup spoon and delicately took three small tastes of the consommé. "Very well, sir. On Friday of last week, I was on the southern porch of the Breakers when the maid smelled fire."

They talked through the soup and through the croquettes of shrimp, Marjory recalling the trip to the Styx as it blazed, the morning when Shantice Carver came crying out of the woods after her discovery of the body, the accusation by the sheriff and Marjory's own decision to secrete the woman off the island. She made no mention of seeing the banker's wife coming out of the woods before the fire. They were into the main course of broiled plover when Faustus reminded Marjory that she had committed a crime.

"Aiding and abetting a fugitive is a punishable act," he said. "Certainly you know this, and I would have to say it was either foolish or highly commendable on your part."

"I believe the girl to be innocent, Mr. Faustus. I also know the reputation of the sheriff," she said. "He is a racist and a pig."

Faustus choked only slightly on a spoon of currant jelly. He dabbed his mouth with a napkin.

"Well, that said, can you provide me with the names of those persons who will swear that Miss Carver was at the fair at the time that our Mr. Bingham was shot to death?"

Byrne snuck a look at Faustus. They had not spoken of whether to use Danny's real name or whether to reveal his sibling relationship. Faustus had made the decision alone. Byrne was not opposed.

Marjory took the opportunity to dab at the corners of her own mouth before answering.

"Yes, I believe I can," she said without immediately offering up the name of Abby.

"And these persons would have been attending the fair themselves?"

"Yes."

"And why not you, Miss McAdams?"

"Pardon me?"

"Why were you not at the fair? My understanding is that you were active in arranging the event in the first place. In fact, I've been told that you convinced your father to talk Mr. Flagler into financing the affair. I would think you'd have attended to see how well it was carried off."

Byrne, who'd been relegated to the role of observer, one he was quite adept at, listened carefully. Faustus's voice had not changed in timbre or enunciation. In another man's mouth, the question could have come off as an accusation. In his it was merely a professional inquiry.

Marjory blushed slightly. "You are correct. It was something my father and I spoke about several times, giving the workers a sort of holiday, something to lift their spirits.

"As for attending, I thought it would be an intrusion, akin to the lordly master overseeing the dance of his slaves. It was supposed to be an event for them, not for us."

"I see," Faustus said, dipping his head as if begging her pardon. But his next question had no ring of begging in it.

"And, if I may, did you know Mr. Bingham? I mean through your travels or when you may have been visiting in West Palm?"

"The name wasn't familiar. And I certainly didn't recognize the man I saw that night."

Marjory turned her head away as if she were seeing the grisly sight again.

"Do forgive me, Miss," Faustus said in reaction.

Byrne found the crack in Marjory's usual hardened core curious, but said nothing. Seeing his own brother burned and dead had put a vise around his heart that nearly squeezed him to unconsciousness.

"I would like to employ your help, Mr. Faustus, as representation for Mizz Carver. I will gladly pay the going rate for a criminal attorney.

I believe there is expected to be an arraignment on Friday. Would you be willing?"

Coffee had arrived, real coffee, and Faustus took a long, luxurious sip before answering.

"It has been several years, but my licensing in the state of Florida is up to date and I shall be willing to aid in Miss Carver's defense. In fact, if we are allowed to present our findings to the judge on Friday, it is quite possible that the charges will be dropped altogether.

"I would, however, have to visit with the woman tomorrow, gain her approval, and hear her side of the story."

"I'll be more than pleased to introduce you," Marjory said, her instant smile lightening the otherwise dark and moody room. "I will of course ask to sit in during your discussions. I mean, I would suppose someone other than a stranger, someone with a woman's touch, might reassure Miss Carver of our intentions."

Faustus again seemed to hold Marjory's eyes for an extra few seconds. "We'll have to see what the sheriff's policy is on that matter. It is not usual for such discussions to be witnessed by anyone other than a client and the client's attorney. Privilege, of course. But certainly it is a possibility."

With all manners and pleasantries to the host concluded, the dinner broke up. On the porch outside, Faustus bid good evening and walked quickly into the night, headed for the bridge to West Palm Beach. Byrne lingered for an uncomfortable minute and was rewarded for his hesitation. Marjory was staring up at the sky, her head tilted, her pinned-up hair in danger of unraveling and falling in cascades down her back.

"Oh, look at the stars, Michael. Isn't it a gorgeous night?"

The sound of his first name in her voice struck Byrne mute.

"Or do you not like the stars?" she said to his silence.

"Uh, no. I mean absolutely," he mumbled.

She took a step toward him and hooked her arm through the crook of his elbow. "Then you will walk me back to my hotel?"

He knew she was out there, deeper in the water, though her teasing and laughter had abated. Somewhere she was floating, perhaps lying on her back in the motion of the swells, tingling in the warm ocean water while she held that curious smile on her face.

She was enticing him, luring. He knew this to be true. But he also knew that his reaction to seeing her inexplicably disappear into the beachside bushes and then come running out stark naked and sprint into the ocean was going to override any question of her motives.

On the walk back from dinner she'd used his first name three times, each one sounding like a wonderful note of music. But they'd walked mostly in silence, she lightly holding his arm and he trying not to show his enthusiasm or nervousness. When they reached the turnoff to the Breakers, she'd pulled him in the opposite direction.

"It's much too lovely a night to go in," she said. "And the beach is beautiful in the moonlight."

The moonlit sand made Byrne recall Harris's tale of once mistaking it for snow. Marjory removed her shoes and they walked near the tide mark, she pointing out the sprinkling lights of phosphorescence being washed up on the shore, he being too thrilled by both the sight of the living organisms' glow and the fact that she had taken his hand in hers as they moved south.

Then she'd stopped and stared out at the ocean and the beam of moonlight that appeared as a silver arrow to the horizon. "I have to swim. It's too gorgeous not to swim," she said and made a break for the bushes. He was still puzzled by her actions when she came bolting from cover, her long legs and torso flashing white in the light and her flowing hair catching and throwing glimmers of red.

"Come on then, Byrne! Where's the Irish in you!" she called out, launching herself like a spear into the sea. He watched the hole into which she'd disappeared, no doubt his mouth agape, and then five feet farther out her head appeared, and then her arms like an amphibious butterfly's wing swooped up from her sides, reformed into a point, and without losing forward motion she again speared into the water. She repeated her dolphin-like move three or four more times, growing smaller with each distance gained, and then was gone into the darkness.

It took him more time than he cared to remove all his clothes and dump them in a stack and then run in after her. He shivered only once, when the water, perhaps seventy-eight degrees but still well below body temperature, reached his groin, but he copied Marjory's motion and dove forward. He was not nearly as graceful as she, and after a couple of attempts he stopped and gained his feet on the sandy bottom. Now he knew she was out here, but where? A collection of clouds had moved in front of the moon, and the path of light had diminished. He waited until the gauzy gray passed and then spotted her, breast-stroking toward him.

"My God, isn't it marvelous," she said, stopping an arm's length away. Her auburn hair was slicked back on her head, her face pale on the side where the moonlight struck it. Droplets of water clung to her eyelashes.

"Yes. I should say it is," Byrne said, amazed that his voice even worked.

She spun and jumped high into the air, her arms going up as if trying to slap the moon itself, and exposing herself to where her hips widened slightly from her tiny waist. She disappeared again when she came down and Byrne was left looking around again until she surfaced, directly in front of him, this time closer than an arm's length. He could feel the wavelets. Both of them were holding their breaths when she moved up against him and her hard nipples brushed his skin. Then her breasts flattened against him as he pulled her close and wrapped his arms around her. He moved his lips to hers, and when they touched, they were cold and salty until he felt the warmth of air come from inside her mouth. He felt the tip of her tongue flirt at the seam of his own lips, but when he opened them he got a mouthful of salt water and she laughed in her throat and bent back her head to look in his eyes. He felt himself hard against her hips.

"You are absolutely unpredictable," Byrne whispered, still quite flustered.

She laughed. "You, though, are highly predictable," she said and moved again against him.

"I won't deny that."

"Ha! Not that you could." She rolled her hip against his hardness and then broke from his embrace. She floated there for a moment, her chin just in the water, her eyes dancing a bit above it.

"Are you sure you can swim? I'd hate to leave you floundering out here."

"Well, I just might need some help," Byrne said, sensing in her words that she was either going to leave or challenge him to a race and wanting neither one. "And to be completely honest, no, I can't swim."

The look on Marjory's face suddenly turned from impish to something thoughtful, like a decision was being made.

"Neither could your brother," she said, averting her eyes. "But neither could Daniel be completely honest."

At that she quickly performed another of her dolphinlike plunges and was heading out to sea, to deeper water. After a second, Byrne recovered his voice and called several times for her. But he heard her strokes diminish as they faded in the distance.

"Christ!" he said, growing instantly flaccid and colder than when he first walked into this idiot sea. Harris was right. Out of your league. Not a chance in hell for immigrants like us. He made it back to the beach, to his clothes, dressed and sat on the sand in a direct line between Marjory's footsteps and the bushes where she'd stashed her own clothes. He sat an hour, until nine o'clock, and then gave up. If she knew Danny, then she'd have recognized his body the night she saw him dead in the Styx. If she knew they were brothers, then why the ruse? Why the game? What the hell makes sense in Florida, he thought, and put on his brogans, took one last look out to sea and walked away.

Chapter 18

The next morning he was up, standing ready at the rail station next to Flagler's newly washed car long before Harris made an appearance.

"Morning, sir," he said when the big man approached. Harris was in his standard working attire. But his reluctance to make eye contact alerted Byrne that something was up.

"Mornin'."

"She's looking good, eh?" Byrne said and instantly felt like a stable boy asking for a compliment.

"Aye, a fine job."

"Will we be hooking up here and going across the bridge to pick up Mr. Flagler then?"

"Aye, we will. But not you, Mr. Byrne."

The use of Byrne's proper name was a step back from Harris's now familiar "lad." Byrne said nothing and let his silence force whatever it was out of Harris's mouth.

"I'll be accompanying Mr. Flagler to Miami. But we've another job for you," he said. "We need you to go with a group of gentlemen from the hotel on a bit of an expedition this morning."

Byrne let the query in his face do the asking.

"Mr. McAdams and some regular guests are taking in a round of hunting in the Everglades, and they'd like you as some kind of security, I suppose. You'll be taking a rail dingy down south a ways."

"Security?"

"Yeah, security."

"For how many?

"Three. Plus a guide."

"Hunting?"

"Yeah. Deer and wild hogs and such. Maybe even a panther, which would be a sight, eh?"

"Four armed men who need security?" Byrne said, his voice cynical.

"Look, Byrne," Harris said, finally letting the frustration and a touch of anger slip into his own voice. "This is a request by the powers that be. Mr. McAdams works directly for our boss. If he asks for one of us to go out on the road with him, we go."

"So this is a direct request from Mr. Flagler?" Byrne said. He'd played this game with the Tammany group in New York. You ask where the orders came from, ask how high up the line the responsibility lies and hope you know when to stop asking before you cross that line and become a liability.

"Mr. McAdams came to me and asked for you," Harris said, looking Byrne in the eye. "When I balked and went straight to Mr. Flagler, he didn't object. That's what I know and that's all I know. You wait here until they fetch you."

For a moment, the two men studied each other. Harris was not going to offer more, even though more was running around in his head, Byrne knew. Harris had taken on the role of the sergeants in New York, unsatisfied with their own superiors but unwilling to challenge them. Yet the big Irishman still couldn't help himself. He stepped forward to Byrne's side and whispered conspiratorially: "There's a stink in the air, lad. The high and mighty are talking about the fire in the Styx, askin' each other who set the damn thing. Everybody knows the land value was shootin' too high on the island to have a bunch of Negro workers livin' on it. Now they're all watchin' each other to see who comes up with the title to the piece. Somebody knows somthin' and somebody's gonna get rich."

Harris backed away. "It ain't a game a tenement kid wants to get in on, lad."

Byrne climbed up onto the railroad platform, took a seat in one of the wooden straight-backed chairs and watched the rising sun. The red orb had cleared the palms and gumbo limbo trees of the island to the east, and he could feel the heat build by degrees. The pores of his skin opened, and the inevitable moisture of sweat sought a cooling breeze. He thought of the chill of the ocean water last night and then the heat between Marjory McAdams's thighs, and he closed his eyes and forced his head to logic.

Danny the arsonist? He thought about the possibility. Could his brother have gotten in so deep through his schemes and maneuvering as to be involved in burning down a community for some sort of payoff? Byrne couldn't believe it. He'd never seen his brother as someone who could maliciously hurt innocents. Yes, he'd shyster some rube on the streets, trick a man out of his pocket money, steal a piece of food from a merchant, sweet-talk someone into paying for his drinks, even run a land scam like the one the binder boys described. But deliberately burn down people's homes? Impossible. Maybe his brother was involved in the deal, or maybe he blanched at someone else's plan to burn the Styx and got a bullet in the throat for his refusal.

And where did Marjory fit in all of this? She knew Danny and had kept that from Michael. What did she know about his killing in her own back yard? And why was she so set on defending this Negro maid?

He looked up when he heard the train whistle from the bridge from Palm Beach Island and watched its trail of smoke crawl across the stubby townscape. He did not stand when it neared but observed the manipulations to the siding as the engineer and crew latched on to Flagler's gleaming private car. Moments later he saw Flagler and his wife pass between the cars, entering their own. The old man attended to the careful steps of his wife and then looked up at the sun-touched wall of the station where Byrne sat. Their eyes met for a brief second. Byrne swore there was a momentary look of question on Flagler's face just before he stepped into his car.

With a blast of the whistle and a huff of steam, the completed linkage of train shivered and clanked and groaned into motion. Byrne could feel the foundation of the station platform vibrate as thousands of pounds of steel moved southward toward Miami. Whatever you thought about the rich old coot, you had to admit it was a hell of an accomplishment bringing such things to this sleepy seashore world. Byrne watched for the rear platform and saw Harris there, staring out. He could not tell whether it was a look of sadness or warning.

Chapter 19

Byrne took his coat off, pulled the bill of his cap down to shade his eyes and rolled up his shirtsleeves. But he remained seated at the train station, as he had been instructed. He nodded at those who greeted him, trying to look nonchalant while the questions of reason and motive roiled in his stomach.

Why the hell was he here? Why was Flagler dismissing him from his personal guard duty? Why would anyone ask him to go out with a group of the hotel elite on a hunting excursion? Hell, he knew it wasn't his storied proficiency as a game hunter that prompted it … a tenement kid who'd rarely even seen a rifle. And Harris said there would be a guide. So what was the danger there? The party would also include Mr. McAdams, whose young daughter had just last night been swimming naked in the ocean with him and then disappeared. So what? Do they take young men who besmirch a lady's reputation out into the swamp and shoot him? Ha! You're stinking paranoid, he said to himself. Faustus was trying to get in to interview the Carver woman this day. Marjory was going to join him. Byrne would have to wait until he got back from this charade in the glades to find out what the Negro woman would tell them. There was too much happening to endure this shite. Yet, an hour after Flagler's train pulled out, he sat there watching to the north as a hand-pumped rail cart creaked toward him. It wasn't until he recognized Mr. McAdams that he stood, dumbstruck, at the site of the transportation he and the four others were obviously taking on this impromptu hunting trip.

"Hallo, Mr. Byrne!" called out Mr. McAdams as the flat-bed cart coasted to a stop. "I see our request was successfully passed on to you."

Byrne hopped down next to the track, eyeing the cart, the men, the supplies and the stacked rifle barrels arranged on the small space. When McAdams offered a hand up, Byrne took it, stepped up on the hub of one wheel and was pulled aboard. At the center of the cart deck was a two-handled seesaw contraption, which Byrne recognized as the power behind the vehicle. And just to the front of the cart was a stiff and sturdy eight-foot-tall pole with fabric wrapped around it with sail line.

"Mr. Byrne, this is Mr. Birch and Mr. Pearson from the hotel and Mr. Ashton, a magnificent guide of the Everglades region."

Byrne touched the brim of his cap in greeting and shook hands all around. Birch was the man Byrne had recognized at Flagler's table the night of the ball, the man from New York who'd paid off Byrne's commander during the prostitution raid. He shook Byrne's hand with a simple politeness, his eyes holding no recognition.

Pearson, the general manager, had been pointed out to him before by Harris. "Tight assed and shifty" was the sergeant's assessment. Byrne studied them all, as always, making note of each man's facial hair, eye color, mode of dress. If they were nervous or uneasy with his presence, none showed it. Birch and Pearson gave nothing away. Ashton was the local. His eyes were pale and reminded Byrne of Captain Abbott's in their stoic nonchalance. He had the look of a man simply performing a job.

"We're going to go south a bit, Mr. Byrne," Mr. McAdams said, looking, with a white bandana knotted around his neck, the part of some explorer. "Down at the Hillsboro inlet, Cypress Creek goes west into the great swamp. You will be amazed at the wild boar, the deer, wild turkey, honestly." There was a friendly enthusiasm in the man's voice, as if he were selling a new homestead to a customer. If he knew of Byrne's assignation the night before, he wasn't acting like a put-out father. Byrne relaxed, but only a bit.

"You may even get a shot at a snowy egret, Mr. Birch," he said to the banker. "The kind with the wonderful feathers your wife loves to adorn her hats with. Treat them with a bit of arsenic for preservative and she can take them back to New York to her milliner."

Birch gave McAdams a nod but did not seem to be in the mood for jovial repartee. The guide moved to the hand pump, and with elbows locked, he put all his weight on the fore handle. The cart began to crawl southward. When the handle reached its lowest level, he quickly jumped to the now raised side and did the same. The cart gained momentum. Byrne assessed the mechanics, and when he realized none of the others intended to assist the guide, he took up position at one handle and copied Ashton's labors. If Byrne expected a sign of appreciation for his assistance, he would be disappointed. Ashton simply kept pushing down at his turn and stared out at the passing landscape, his eyes seemingly searching the brush and tree copse for some movement or sign. On occasion he would turn his nose up into the air. Yeah, right, like you can smell the boar or deer or whatever the hell this group is supposed to be hunting, Byrne thought. Nice touch for the city swells. But after half an hour of steady and not overly strenuous pumping, the guide's nose did indeed work to advantage.

"Wind switch," he said, mostly to himself, and stepped away from the pump handle. The dense vegetation had cleared somewhat, and Byrne too could feel the breeze catching them from behind. While the handles continued to move up and down, Byrne kept pushing his end and the cart continued to roll. Meanwhile, Ashton unfurled the cloth from the tall pole and extended what Byrne now recognized as a boom, and voila! A sail puffed out and the cart became a land boat. The pump handle in Byrne's hands started moving on its own, and he let go. The ingenuity made him smile and the feeling was infectious, for the other men, with the exception of Ashton, also began to grin.

"Hard work often inspires ingenuity, Mr. Byrne," Mr. McAdams said, noticing the smile. "Even in as rough a place as this." Since the statement was not a question, Byrne felt no obligation to respond. He instead looked out on what he now recognized as cleared land, not unlike that of the vegetable farmers farther north, where he and Harris had encountered the would-be dynamiters.

"This area will someday be a massive grove of pineapples," McAdams said. "A young Japanese man with dreams of a plantation has approached Mr. Flagler. Imagine, sweet pineapples by the crate going north to Manhattan. Some men know the possibilities of land, Mr. Byrne. That it is the foundation for everything else."

Again, Byrne did not answer. If the guy was going to pontificate in vague phrases, so be it. Byrne knew a babbling man in the Bowery who stood on a wooden box and spewed verse and quotations all day for the sake of nothing more than the sound of his own voice. If Mr. McAdams thought he was imparting knowledge with his statements, it was going over Byrne's head. The others simply nodded, as if they understood. Ashton adjusted the sail, ignoring or not caring.

Past the clearing, the wild growth filled back in, and within two hours Ashton's focus shifted to the south. When he spotted some landmark, he pulled in the sail and relashed it to the mast. Minutes later Byrne spotted a rail switch and a siding ahead. They rolled to a stop, and in the resulting quiet Byrne could hear the sound of moving water. Ashton jumped down, walked the rail to the switch and, after fiddling with a lock, shoved the mechanism, which swung a diverting set of rails to the siding. He motioned for Byrne to pump the cart forward, then used the switch to realign the rails. The men began to unload. Once armed and strapped with rifles and canteens and satchels of lunch, the group moved south along the rail bed that cut through a wall of pond apple trees and small cypress and then opened to the sandy shore of a narrow river.

"Mr. Ashton will lead us up the creek," McAdams said. "But keep alert, fellows. The game is numerous and, might I say, diverse."

Byrne singled out McAdams and finally asked: "If I may, Mr. McAdams. But what exactly am I supposed to do here?"

"Why, you're to watch our backs, Mr. Byrne," McAdams replied as though the task was obvious. "You're the Pinkerton. Security, young man, security."

The creek narrowed, the palmetto thickened, and an uneven ground cover of sedge grasses, strangler fig and cypress roots caused all but Ashton to stumble and slog. Byrne found himself stepping into unexpected troughs of standing water, the thick mud at the bottom sucking at his now ruined brogans. He had to keep his eyes on the ground before him and take circuitous routes around obstacles. The air seemed to grow heavier and wetter, and he found it increasingly difficult to breathe. Spanish moss hung from the trees like dark tattered rags, filtering the sun. This was the great swamp they talked about. Faustus had told him that it ran west to the horizon, a glade of enormous size, as mysterious as any deep forest. Less than an hour in, Byrne stopped to take a drink. When he looked up, there was no one in sight. The blue shirt covering Ashton's back was gone. McAdams, with the white bandana around his throat, had disappeared into the green.

"Christ!" he said, moving off in the direction he thought they'd gone. He could make his way through a maze of backstreets and alleys in the dark, but there was nothing familiar here. He would suddenly step into a hole and feel water up to his knees, the smell of it like a ripe whiff of old Mrs. McReady's vegetable cart. Each craggy cypress looked just like the one before. His landmarks were useless. He was moving around the hump of a root ball from a downed tree when he looked into a boil of grasses and swore he saw a huge log of marled wood with a row of teeth. He stopped stock still when the log's eyes came into view and stared into his own. Byrne swore he could hear the beast breathing.

They were in a stare off, an eight-foot alligator and a tenement kid from the Lower East Side. Then, as if the gator heard or somehow presaged what was to come, it lunged. Its wicked movement caused Byrne to dive in the opposite direction, away from the maw of teeth. A rifle's report sounded, and at the same instant, Byrne felt his left side pull at him as if a whip had slapped his hip.

The sting came after he'd spilled to the ground, and a burning heat followed. He watched the alligator practically crawl over him on its way to a nearby hole. Byrne saw the tail disappear, looked down for the hot spot at his side and saw a stain of blood on his shirt growing just above his hip and under his left rib. He swung his head around in the direction of the rifle shot and went decidedly quiet.

Whoever had fired did not call out. There was in fact no noise at first as he lay there. Then he heard a careful step, the snap of a twig, a slow slosh of water. If one of the hunters had taken a shot at the gator and had hit Byrne by accident, wouldn't the man shout? But if Byrne was the target, would that gunman now move in to finish the task? Byrne sat perfectly still and listened. Another slosh. The sound of fabric brushed by a tree limb. Byrne looked for cover. The hole where the alligator had taken refuge was an arm's length away. Another tick of sound, this time the light scratch of metal on wood. Byrne chose the gator over the rifle barrel and rolled quietly into the mouth of the hole. Again he listened, but the sound was muffled by the covering of muck and root and tangle of leaves. He closed his eyes and concentrated. Was that the sound of his own breathing or that of the reptile behind him? Was the animal cowering in the back of the hole, rattled by the explosion of the gun and this human chasing it into its hole?

This time, Byrne felt the footstep as much as heard it. The water and mud around him seemed to move with the nearby compression. Byrne reached into his pocket with his right hand and withdrew the baton. He found purchase against a root and dared to peek around the edge of the opening of the hole in time to see the barrel of a rifle slide into view, then a hand on the stock, then a booted foot stepping forward.

Byrne's swing was as pure and strong as an axman's. The baton extended with a snap from its own momentum, and the hard metal struck solid on the man's kneecap, shattering bone and causing an ungodly scream. Byrne watched the man pitch forward, burying the barrel of his rifle deep into the muck in front of him. The gator behind him burrowed deeper into the hole at the sound of another species in horrific agony.

Byrne scrambled out with a fierceness that defied the bullet wound in his side and was quickly on Ashton's blue-shirted back, riding the man with a knee on his spine and slipping the baton across his throat in a choke hold. Byrne took a deep breath and blew the anger out, then shifted the baton up under Ashton's chin and pulled his face up.

"You may be the best guide they have in these parts, sir. But you aren't much of a shot," Byrne said, letting the words seep through his clenched teeth.

Ashton gurgled.

"At any rate, you aren't going to be doing much wilderness work with that split kneecap for a while, so how about telling me who it was that hired you to kill me?"

Ashton still didn't attempt an answer. Byrne moved his knee between the man's shoulder blades and forced his face down into the standing water. After a good count to twenty he let him back up for air.

"You might as well tell me, Ashton. The money won't do you any good dead. Tell me and you might crawl out of here to spend your fee on a good hickory cane."

Ashton blew out his breath, drooling water and phlegm.

"It was them," Ashton said. "McAdams and them. They wanted a huntin' accident."

"Why? What the hell threat am I to them? I'm a Pinkerton. Did they tell you I was a Pinkerton?"

"Didn't tell me shit. Just said you was gettin' too nosey."

"Nosey about what? The Negro woman?"

Ashton took another breath, wheezing through the pinched throat space Byrne was allowing him.

"Hell no. Nobody in these parts cares about some Negro. It's the real estate. That's all they ever care about is the land."

Byrne withdrew his baton and flipped the man over. He pulled the rifle out of the muck and ejected the load, then searched Ashton's belt and pockets and collected the ammunition.

"Wouldn't want you trying to shoot me in the back again," he said. He did a sweep of the jungle around him. The others might show up any minute, reacting to the single shot Ashton had taken or even the man's scream when his kneecap exploded. Or maybe they'd just hide like the gator and wait until they figured it was safe to come out. At any rate, Byrne wasn't staying around to discover whether any of them had the balls to shoot him themselves. He knew there was a rock road near the coast similar to the one that he, Marjory and Santos had walked two nights previous that was used by carriages and wagons traveling between West Palm and the new town of Miami. If he could get to that road, help might run into him. While Ashton lay on his back holding his knee, Byrne examined his own wound. It was a through and through. The bullet had gone in just below his ribcage and he found the exit wound when his index finger slipped into the hole in his back. He took his shirt off, spun it into a rope and tied it around his waist, pulling the knot tight at the point of entry near his gut. He was bleeding heavily. He picked up Ashton's canteen, took a drink for good measure and began moving carefully to the east. The guide did not beg not to be left alone. All he managed was to get up on one elbow, spit once in Byrne's direction and then watch the Pinkerton disappear.

Chapter 20

Amadeus Faustus was not unknown to the sheriff. Although the lawman had been distrustful when word began to travel that there was a sharply dressed Mason in town who appeared to be of wealth and Southern breeding, he simply watched Faustus carefully at first, and then dismissed him. The man did speak a highfalutin' English, which made Cox nervous. But the rich men of the island did the same, and Cox had learned to put away his initial feelings of inadequacy. Instead he dealt with them identically: he would be deferential to a point, bend to their wishes if there was something in it for him, and always be suspicious of their motivations. He knew they were all after the same thing: more. More land, more money, more champagne, more unearned respect.

His allegiance, if one could call it that, could be only to Flagler and by proxy some of his lieutenants. Flagler and his railroad were vehicles for money, and Cox did not even try to conceal that he too was lustful for large gobs of the stuff. Thus, this man Faustus got only the most basic from Cox: a building permit for his church or whatever it was to be, an occasional word of warning when the rail workers where due to invade his favorite tavern on Clematis, and a tip of the hat and a greeting when they passed on the street.

So on Friday morning when Faustus showed up at the jail on Poinsettia Street announcing that he was there to represent the Negro prostitute in the matter of killing the vagabond hustler, Cox was taken aback.

"Is that right, Mr. Faustus?" Cox said when the old man, in the company of that mouthy little bitch daughter of McAdams, met him in his upstairs office and asked to interview the prisoner. The bulbous sheriff took his time answering. His eyes worked deep inside his thick face, the pupils rolling across the swollen lids like twin black marbles, first at Faustus, then over to the McAdams woman. It was, after all, the girl's father who had telegraphed him about the killing of that scumbag Bingham and asked him to take care of it with as little impact on the island as possible. The fact that the dead man was found in the back yard of the whore made it simple. She shived him. End of story.

So why was McAdams's daughter showing up now? He'd been pondering the question since the night she'd confronted his deputies outside the jail. Playing the soft-hearted slave lover. Did her old man know about that episode as well? There was something going on, and Cox came to the conclusion that he'd watch it play out and decide as things went along whether there was something in it for him.

"Well, Mr. Faustus, sir. If you are the negra's legal attorney, you know that you are by law afforded an opportunity to speak with your client," the sheriff said, standing up behind his desk and making a show of searching for the keys.

"I thank you, sir," Faustus said. "And I would like Miss McAdams to accompany me as she is, as one says, footing the bill."

Cox smiled his greasiest smile, the one meant to charm all the gussied up rich bitches over on the island.

"Why of course, anything to accommodate the McAdams family."

It wasn't much of a jail. When the sheriff unlocked the door and pushed it open, dank, sour air rolled into their faces. The tiny woman was curled up against the far wall, shielding her eyes from the brightness of the sun. Faustus had seen worse prison cells in the war and even in the modern cities of Atlanta and Memphis and New York. It was actually no more than a bare wood room with four slots for windows on each side. No iron bars, no cages, no chains. There was a simple wooden chair in one corner, a stained mattress on the floor in another, a chamber pot in a third. Marjory followed him in and hurried to the woman's side.

"Oh you poor dear thing," she said, going down on one knee and placing her palms on either side of Shantice Carver's face. The woman's eyes looked nervous and confused to Faustus, but he hesitated to put any meaning to the observation. Two well-dressed white people had just entered her jail room, and the sheriff who had arrested her closed the door behind them. If I were a young Negro housemaid with a murder charge hanging over my head, he thought, I too would be confused.

"Hello, Mizz Carver. Please don't be afraid, ma'am," Faustus said, with the kindliest voice he could muster. "My name is Amadeus Faustus. I am a lawyer and have been asked by Miss McAdams, whom you know, to try and get you out of this mess."

The woman got to her feet and looked from one to the other, completely lost.

"Where's Mizz Ida?" she asked Marjory. "She got to help me, ma'am. Ya'll know she the only one can help me."

Marjory looked up at Faustus. "Miss Ida May Fluery is the head housekeeper at the Breakers, where Shantice worked. She's kind of the stepmother to all the girls."

"An' where is Mizz Abby? You got to talk to Mizz Abby, ma'am. We was together when that man got hisself kilt," Shantice said, the rush of words coming at a high, desperate pitch. "We seen him down the Styx, but when we hightailed it out of there, he was standin' straight up and healthy like a high-steppin' mule and wasn't no more dead than this fella here."

Faustus raised his eyebrows at the sudden flow of information.

"OK, OK, now Shantice. It's all right," Marjory said. "You know Mizz Ida and I tried our best to get you to safety? Right? You know that? So we'll do our best to help you now. OK? We are here to help you.

"Mr. Faustus here knows the law. He needs to ask you some questions so he can take care of this business with the sheriff and with the judge when he gets here. So just calm down now."

"Please, young lady," Faustus said, pulling the lone chair to her side. "Please sit down and take a few breaths."

Carver sat before Faustus as if a child before the schoolmaster.

"Miss McAdams," he said, and the authoritarian in his voice was obvious. "I will have to ask you to leave us alone at this point, ma'am. It is simply against all legal convention for a second party to be witness to an attorney–client discussion. There are things this woman may say only to me as her legal representative, things that are privileged between us."

Marjory reacted as if she had been slapped. This was not the way she had intended, not the plan, not the play she needed to make. Yet here they were. Information that she desperately needed was at hand. and an outsider was telling her only he would be privy to it. She could squelch the entire situation right now, tell Faustus the deal was off. Would such an action bring her more scrutiny? Would the Carver woman tell him who and what she saw that night, even as Marjory stood outside the door? And what would Faustus do with that information if indeed this woman had seen everything? She had employed him; wouldn't he be beholden to her as well, with his attorney–client argument? Marjory saw no immediate way out. She had gone too far to turn back now.

"Very well, Mr. Faustus. I leave it to your professional wisdom," she simply said and turned and slipped out the door.

The housemaid had not changed her demeanor, an underling, awaiting some form of scolding or punishment.

Faustus started in a comforting tone: "I need only for you to tell me your story, ma'am. Tell me your story, as clearly and honestly as you can. Start where you think all of this business with the dead man and the night of his undoing, the night of the carnival, began."

Carver took the few breaths as directed and balled her hands into fists in her lap as if a decision had been made. The truth was coming and damned be those whom the light would not be kind to.

"It was all Mizz Abby's idea," she began. "I ain't sayin' I didn't go along with it, but it wasn't me that come up with it."

"And who, exactly, is this Mizz Abby?" Faustus said.

"She Mizz Birch's housemaid. We been knowin' each other for a long time, since we was girls growin' up and workin' and such. She's my friend and don't pass no judgment on me because of what I do to get along."

"You mean the prostitution?"

"Tha's right," Carver said, her chin high. It was not pride, but any shame or need for justification had long been reconciled in her.

"We is friends an' we talk a lot together cause she on the inside of the hotel and I mostly worked outside, at the laundry and cleaning the kitchens and such. She mostly is with the rich folks and she knows things."

"OK," Faustus said, only needing to prime the pump at this point, keep the woman talking, and she would tell the story in her own way.

"Well, I got customers, you know, men from the hotel that come out to my place for their needs. Sometimes Mizz Abby would tell them 'bout me if they asked, you know."

Faustus simply waited.

"So at the beginnin' of this season, it was her own boss that did the askin' and Mr. Birch himself come out for my company," she continued.

"You saw this Mr. Birch regularly?" he said.

"Couple times a week."

"And what changed?"

"Well, I done tol' Abby and she and me, we laughed about it and all. But then a while ago Abby said that the Birches was thinkin' on gettin' rid of her. She been workin' for them for three seasons and they treated her good and she was mad.

"Abby knowed that Mizz Birch would rip the roof off if she knew her husband was off the porch with some nigger girl like me, so she come up with this plan to get her share of money offen' him by sayin' she gonna tell the missus."

"Blackmail?"

"If'n that's what you call it."

"So did this Miss Abby confront Mr. Birch?"

"No, she too damn scairt to do it her own self so she asked me to do it an' I say uh uh. I ain't gone mess up my business on doin' somethin' like that."

Faustus broke one of his own rules by skipping ahead.

"So you needed a go-between, someone to handle the negotiations?"

Carver stared at him for a moment, deciphering the words.

"We needed a man to do the threat, yeah. So's I knew this white man who was, uh, well, I know he did things like that with white folks ,and we done set it up. He was going to tell Mr. Birch that he knew what was what and that he would tell Mizz Birch unless Mr. Birch paid him not to. Then this white man was going to give the money to Abby."

"And the man was Mr. Bingham?"

"I ain't knowed his real name, but he the one dead for sure."

Faustus began to pace, an unconscious habit he undertook when trying to formulate questions or weigh information. The idea that a prostitute and a housemaid might concoct such a scheme was not inconceivable, but his experience with such folks in the past made him doubt that the women would shoot the man dead, and for what?

"On the night that this Mr. Bingham was killed, the night of the fire, my understanding is that you were not on the island."

The woman bowed her head.

"No, sir. That's not exactly right."

"No?"

"We was at the fair over this side, but then we went back cause Abby didn't want that man cheatin' us out our money."

"You knew when Mr. Bingham was to meet with Mr. Birch?"

"Yeah. An' we was there. Only hidin' round by Mr. Pott's boardin' house in the dark just watchin'."

"And what, pray tell, did you see?" Faustus' voice ratcheted up.

"The man, what you call Bingham, was at my place, back by the wood pile where Abby had tole' him."

"He was alone?"

"Yes, sir. All dressed up like some swell. Like some bidness man an all."

"And did Mr. Birch arrive while you were watching?"

"No, sir." Shantice said, but the quivering in her hands told Faustus there was more so he stood silently, waiting.

"But Mizz Birch did," she said.

"Mrs. Birch?" Faustus said, giving away his surprise.

"Yes, sir. We done heard someone walkin' up the road and walkin'hard. Then we seen Mizz Birch astridin' like a mad bull."

"And did she meet with Mr. Bingham?" Faustus asked.

"If'n she did, sir, we didn't see it. When we seen Mizz Birch come up, we was scared and hid ourselves back in the bushes behind the boardin' house and then hightailed it back to the lake, sir."

"Before the fire?

"Yes, sir."

"And you never heard a gunshot?"

"No, sir."

Faustus took a second, assessing and processing the information and how it skewed his original hypothesis. Simplicity, he reminded himself. Rules of human behavior.

"Did you see anyone else there that night who might vouch for you, Mizz Carver, anyone at all?"

"No, sir. Wasn't anybody else. They was all over at the carnival."

Faustus had stopped his pacing. He had no reason not to believe her account, was in fact duty sworn to accept it as her attorney. At that point he went to the door and summoned Marjory. Marjory hesitated at first, searching the attorney's eyes for some clue. Now she had taken on the look of the student before the headmaster.

"I thank you for your candor, Miss Carver," Faustus said, turning to the house woman. "And we shall be in touch before the magistrate arrives."

"You gone get me free?" Carver asked in a voice touched with only the smallest tinge of hope.

"I will do my best, young lady," Faustus said, moving to leave. A thought, a recollection of a piece of information that Byrne had shared from his friends the binder boys, entered his head. He turned back to Carver.

"One more question," he said, and she looked up. "When you were watching this man, this Mr. Bingham, you said he was dressed like a business man. What made you believe that?"

"He was in fancy clothes. Not like some party or somethin'. But not like he was comin' to the Styx to do somethin' shady like. An' he was carryin' a bidness case. Like a leather case that would hold papers and such."

Faustus dwelt on the answer for a moment and went out the door.

Chapter 21

When Byrne awoke, he was freezing. The hard light of midday was in his eyes. His back was either on fire or frostbitten. He turned his head to the right and saw a wet wooden sideboard next to his face. He turned to the left and looked a dead fish in the eye. When he began to regain his sense of smell, he closed his eyes again and hoped this was not hell.

The last thing he recalled was finding the road, a trail of crushed rock barely wide enough for a wagon. He'd been limping, holding his knotted shirt to his side for two hours. When one entire side of the shirt and one loosed sleeve became soaked in blood, he'd quit looking at the wound. On the road he'd meant to turn north, but his brain was too blurred and spinning to be sure he'd made the right selection. The sun suffered an eclipse, its center gone black, and when the rim of light around it came down over his head, he'd passed out.

"Michael! Michael Byrne. Can you hear me?"

Called by the devil, Byrne thought, hearing the words and expecting Lucifer himself. A face started coming into focus. Danny? Had he joined his brother in hell?

"Come on, son. Put some effort into it now," a familiar voice said. The intent eyes of Amadeus Faustus looked down on him.

"OK, boys. Let's get him down out of there and into the back of the bar," Faustus said. "Watch that wound on his side, now."

With that, four men slid Byrne down out of a fish wagon loaded with red snapper and ice, carried him into the tavern, and laid him out on a table in back.

Faustus went to work without a word: soothing, questioning, or otherwise. He used a razor-sharp knife to cut away pieces of the shirt still tied around Byrne's waist. He loosened the pants and stripped them off as well, probing with careful fingers around Byrne's rib cage and then his hip. A boy came in carrying a large wooden case.

"Put it just here, Adam, and get some water for this man if you please." Byrne looked at the case, trying to determine what might be coming. The box was labeled with a distinctive cursive lettering spelling Johnson and a red cross.

Faustus opened it and withdrew a bottle of liquid. He'd left the knot of Byrne's shirt in place, fastened there with both dried and sticky blood, and thus staunched some of the flow. Now Faustus pulled at it, pouring antiseptic over the area.

"Sssssss," Byrne hissed between his teeth.

"Easier to work with wounds on a corpse," Faustus said. "But I still prefer working on the living. Don't you, Mr. Byrne?"

"In this case, yes," Byrne said, his head coming more alert with the pain. His voice was raw and foreign to his ears.

With the wound exposed, Faustus took a dressing from the case and began dabbing at its edges.

"Fairly large caliber. Smaller than a musket ball but bigger than a handgun, although you've had a few hours to pucker a bit."

"Rifle of some kind," Byrne managed.

Adam returned with a beer mug full of water. Faustus directed the lad to pour some into Byrne's mouth. "Not too much now," he said without looking, concentrating instead on the entry wound.

The feeling in Byrne's throat was cool.

"Loss of blood and dehydrated," Faustus said. "You were lucky the fish wagon came along when it did. The driver said you were in an unconscious pile when he spotted you under a cabbage palm. Not quite like the gutters of your Lower East Side but still an ignominious spot to die. Can you roll onto your side, please?"

Again Byrne hissed at the pain when Faustus poked the corner of the antiseptic-soaked swab into the hole in his back.

"I trust you know what you're doing, Faustus," Byrne said. "This isn't Appomattox."

"Ha! You're not in the hands of an amateur, my friend. And in fact I've twice read *Johnson & Johnson's Modern Methods of Antiseptic Wound Treatment*. I believe a copy came with the first aid kit."

When Faustus was done with the wounds, he and the boy helped

Byrne off the table and into a back room of the tavern. A cot was pushed against one wall, and they laid him down on the old stained mattress. When he tried to close his eyes, the walls began to spin. The room was dark and dry and the temperature high. Byrne could feel the tingle of blood coming back into his skin.

"The wagon driver was smart enough to cover your side with the ice he had aboard. It probably kept you from bleeding out more than you did," Faustus said, sitting nearby in a straight-back chair.

"The bastards tried to kill me," Byrne said, looking at the old Mason but seeing the faces of Ashton, McAdams, Pearson and Birch.

Faustus sat quiet for a moment, letting Byrne's anger seep out of the way.

"Who, exactly, are they?" he finally said. "And what do you think their motivation to kill a Pinkerton employed by the most powerful man in the state would be?"

When Byrne listed the men on the hunting trip, Faustus seemed unable to let the names of Flagler's right-hand man, as well as the manager of the Poinciana and a banker of high esteem, sit under the title of attempted murderers in his head.

"The guide, Ashton, did the dirty work, and I smashed his kneecap to pieces for his trouble," Byrne said.

"I heard he was brought into Dr. Lansing's early today," Faustus agreed. "The three others you've named brought him in on one of the pump carts. Some of the boys said it was quite a sight, a banker and a hotel big shot working the pump and perspiring like pigs, I believe they said."

Byrne wryly smiled at the vision.

"They described it as a hunting accident," Faustus said. "You've reason to believe differently?"

"He would have blown my head off if the damned alligator hadn't scared hell out of me first. The lizard was eight feet in front of me. No way Ashton was aiming at it and not me."

"Did you question Mr. Ashton as to his actions?"

"He was, what you might call, forthcoming, considering there was a steel baton across his throat," Byrne said. "According to him, it was real estate. Said I was getting too nosey about some deal. What the hell would that mean? I haven't so much as considered buying a piece of land even if I had the money."

"But what are you getting your nose into?" Faustus said. "The shooting death of your own brother, a man, and excuse my bluntness here, who was known as a swindler and not just in the real estate field. Then there's your defense of a poor Negro prostitute arrested for said killing. And let's not forget your wooing of a prominent young woman. Don't deny it, sir, I long ago learned to read the eyes of incipient love and the sprinklings of lust."

"She knew my brother."

Faustus raised his eyebrows.

"She admitted she knew him. And she's admitted being there when they found his body." The ache in his side was perhaps the lesser of two pains. "So what the hell else does she know about this whole affair, including who killed Danny?"

For several moments, Faustus sat mute. Then he leaned forward, putting his elbows on his knees and speaking in measured, clear statements of fact.

For the next hour he recounted verbatim his interview with Shantice Carver, her admission of the blackmail scheme, her coconspirator Abby, and her observation of Mrs. Birch approaching Byrne's brother in the dark near the place his body was found.

"Whoa, whoa, whoa," Byrne interrupted. "Birch, did you say? Birch was the name of one of the Poinciana men on the hunt this morning. He was introduced as some kind of banker. And I recall his face from the city, a man who paid his way out of a prostitution raid at the Haymarket Dance Hall."

Faustus simply stared at Byrne out of the shadows.

"I don't believe in coincidence, my young friend. And I doubt that you, as a good investigator, do either."

"I'm not an investigator," Byrne said. "I'm a Pinkerton guard, as you and everyone else reminds me."

"Ha!"

"What ha?"

"I do have contacts in the north, despite my Southern disposition. And my inquiries have resulted in an interesting description of a man with your name and physical appearance who was involved in some investigation of the most dangerous sort.

"You at one time took on the role of tracking the misdeeds of your own superiors and their political bosses. Highly placed and dangerous politicians at that."

Silence from the bed.

"In fact, rumor has it that a compromise was made. Your life may have been spared if and only if you left the city and never came back."

"Never was not a word that was used," Byrne said quietly.

"Nonetheless, I don't believe you when you say you're not a born investigator. And I don't believe that you can observe a moral and ethical misdeed without being pulled to make it right."

"What is this, the code of the Masons or something?" Byrne said, his voice sounding more cynical than he wanted.

"It is not just a code of Masons. It is a code of true men in a civilized society."

"You call this civilized?" Byrne said, sweeping his hand across the dingy room.

Faustus laughed. "Ah, the voice of a true New Yorker. Nothing exists outside of Kings County."

Byrne thought back to his friend Jack Brennan and his squad of young Pinkertons who'd never stepped outside the city, and he had to admit to Faustus's portrayal. He decided to change the subject.

"What else did Carver say she witnessed that night?"

"She denied seeing anyone else at the scene of the crime and swears she did not hear a gunshot nor did she see the fire begin."

"Did Marjory say anything? I'd sure as hell be surprised if she didn't know this Birch woman, if they're as prominent as they appear."

"She said she knew of her," Faustus said, but his voice betrayed him.

"And you think she's lying?"

"It's a very close society on the island. The separation between the daughter of Flagler's right-hand man and the wife of a prominent banker would be thin at best.

"But I plan to speak with Mrs. Birch tomorrow to see if she has any of her own insights into the events described by Mizz Carver. And in addition, your information about your brother's new affinity for carrying his binder case was also confirmed by our client. She saw him with it on the night in question. So I shall also be visiting the mortician for another round of questions about its disappearance." Faustus stood. "For now I suggest you get some rest. A bullet wound can be quite debilitating if not given the time to heal and fight off infection."

With that the old Mason left the room, and Byrne soon fell into a fitful sleep, with the images of gators and Tammany and a naked Marjory McAdams swimming through his head.

Chapter 22

This time Byrne woke with the sound of clinking glass in his ears, the smell of stale beer and cigar smoke and hot cooking oil. A sudden anxiety came into his head—was he in New York, in the trash alley behind McSorely's? When he felt for the curb, he heard a moan. He was back in his mother's apartment, she was dying in pain, her face ashen, a tear glistening down a grayed cheek. He forced his eyes open, determined to help her. The wound at his side bit him hard, and the moan came again, from his own mouth.

Reality. I was shot yesterday. I'm in Florida, in the back room of a tavern, and there are slats of sunshine coming in low through the window, which means its morning. Faustus is supposed to be here. We need to find out what Mrs. Birch knows. And shit, I was shot yesterday.

He swung his feet off the cot, sat upright and probed at the bandage Faustus had applied the night before. It was in place and not spotted on the outside, a good sign even though it still hurt like hell when he moved. Carefully, he pulled on a pair of clean pants and a cotton shirt that had been placed at the foot of the cot, his own ruined clothing gone from sight. When he felt he could stand, he did, while a bright light pulsed behind his eyes, causing a bit of a swoon. He refused to go down. A minute, maybe two, and the dizziness passed. He moved to the door that opened to the barroom and went on through.

"Well, top o' the day, Mr. Byrne," said the woman at the bar, who was busy stocking beer mugs and bottles and any other thing that could create noises meant to penetrate a man's brain.

"Many a man has stumbled through that door in the mornin,' sir, but you'd rank right up with the best of them for lookin' like an overrun dog."

"Aye, and to you," Byrne said, making his way to a stool at the rail and finding purchase with one haunch to steady himself.

Without comment the barkeep poured him an ale from a tapped keg and placed the mug and a hard-boiled egg in front him.

"Patti Graham's the name," she said, extending her hand. "This here works for hangovers, sir, so it can't be any harm to a gunshot wound neither."

Byrne shook the woman's fingers and then sipped at the beer, a blessing in his throat. He took another.

"Heaven," he whispered.

"That's what they all say," the bartender said, pushing a lock of her blonde hair out of the way. "Hell, I bet Mr. Faustus last night that a bullet through the gizzard wouldn't put a good man down any more than a feisty night on the town.

"He said, Mr. Faustus that is, that he would be in this mornin' so take yer time, sir. That egg'll start you back to healin', guaranteed."

With the help of a fingerbowl full of shaved salt, Byrne had finished the first egg and was onto another by the time Faustus arrived.

"Now isn't that a fine sight to see? Belly up to the bar the very day after cheating the dark angel of death," he said.

"Maybe there's just magic in that Johnson & Johnson," Byrne said, feeling better with his second mug of beer.

"I see the clean clothes fit," Faustus said. "You can wash up out back next to the privy where there's a barrel of clean rain water. And since you're in such good shape, taking refreshment and all, I believe I'll be off to the undertaker's and a possible visit with one Mrs. Birch on the island."

Byrne slipped off the stool, keeping the look of pain out of his face.

"Give me ten minutes, then, and I'll be right with you."

Faustus exchanged glances with the bartender, who only shrugged her shoulders.

"Your call, son," he said, slipping up onto Byrne's empty stool and ordering a morning beer for himself.

Faustus and a limping Byrne were making their way down Clematis Street when they saw Maltby the mortician heading toward them.

"Well fancy that, I was just now heading to see you, Mr. Maltby," Faustus said. Maltby was less enthusiastic than when they'd first visited him and pointed out the discrepancies in Danny Byrne's autopsy.

"Yes, well, gentlemen, I am on my way to the island on an urgent matter."

"Oh my," Faustus said. "I do hope one of our guests has not met an untimely death."

"No, sir. There's been an accident, and I'm told a housemaid has fallen to her death down an elevator shaft."

"Really?" Faustus said. "And did they inform you of this woman's name?"

"Abigail Morrisette was the name they gave," Maltby said, information that, considering the station of the victim, seemed irrelevant. "She was a Negro woman who was employed there."

At the sound of the name, Byrne turned to look out over the lake to the Poinciana. Abby, he thought. Another witness dead? Had she too known his brother?

"Well then, in that case," Faustus said, "I do believe we're heading in the same direction. May we accompany you, sir?"

The undertaker was too flummoxed to object. All three men walked down to the nearby docks and boarded the ferry boat to the hotel. The group remained relatively silent on the short trip across the lake. Maltby was no doubt trying to figure out the angles; why would Faustus be interested in yet another death on the island? And would he again be asked to quash any questions over the matter? These things were best taken care of quietly.

Faustus and Byrne were turning questions of their own. What had Abby seen the night of the fire, and what did she see transpire between Danny Byrne and Mrs. Birch? Was it something that would have been worth killing her for?

When the ferry tied up at the dock on Palm Beach, Faustus and Maltby were the first ones off. Byrne lagged behind, leaning into his wound.

"Please, you two go ahead. There is a ride here for me," Byrne said, nodding to the so-called Afromobile parked at the side and its stoic driver. "I'll follow when I catch my breath."

Faustus gave him a silent look: I know where you're going and be damned careful, it said.

At the concierge desk of the Royal Poinciana, Maltby's papers, written on Dade County Sheriff's stationary and authorizing him to remove the body of the victim, got them an escort to the basement of the northern wing of the hotel. Along the way Faustus, with an air of officialdom, asked questions of the concierge.

"Can you tell us, sir, when this unfortunate accident occurred?"

"Very early this morning, I'm afraid. Perhaps five or six."

"You're not sure of the exact time?"

"There were few people up at that hour other than early staff members, and as far as we know there were no reports of any sort of, well, screaming."

"Then who discovered the body?"

"I believe it came to our attention through one of the wait staff. He had encountered difficulty in getting the freight elevator to work for a delivery on the fifth floor, and when one of our maintenance men arrived to rectify the problem, well, there she was."

"I see," said Faustus. Maltby remained silent. "And who, may I inquire, identified the unfortunate woman?"

"There was some difficulty at first," the concierge said. "There are so many housemaids and linen staff and such, and they all look the same."

Faustus raised an eyebrow in disdain, but the look was lost on the concierge. "I believe the original waiter was brought into the shaft and recognized her as a Miss Abigail Morrisette. Her records indicated that she was assigned to the Birch family, one of our more prominent seasonal guests. Mrs. Birch is quite upset."

It was the first time that the concierge gave any indication of empathy over the situation.

The men followed the concierge to the basement.

In the tight space, Faustus noted the presence of electrical wiring running under the floorboard above his head. The availability of electrical service inside homes and structures was inconceivable even five years ago in the South, he knew, and would have been only a dream in frontier Florida before the arrival of Mr. Flagler. The group moved to a now open service door that led to the very bottom of the elevator shaft.

On the bare floor lay the crumpled body of a young Negro woman, perhaps in her early twenties, dressed in the typical maid's uniform of the day. Her face was covered with what appeared to be a dinner table napkin. She could have been sleeping there but for the impossible angle of her right leg, which was folded like a hanger, the knee bent in the opposite direction from what would be normal. Her left forearm was similarly broken, snapped between the wrist and the elbow, forming a grotesque third bend in the arm.

Faustus crouched at the woman's head and removed the napkin. Abigail Morrisette's neck was obviously broken, and a certain amount of rigor mortis had already set in. Pulled by gravity, the blood had drained from her face, already seeking the lowest parts of her body.

"That's enough for me." Maltby was watching over Faustus's shoulder. He turned to the concierge, who was looking up into the rising shaft, avoiding the two men's inspection. "I will require a thick blanket and two men with strong backs to remove the body to the mainland."

The concierge nodded. "Certainly. The sooner the better. We must get the elevator back in service before the luncheon rush."

But Faustus did not stand. Instead he took Abigail Morrisette's head in his hands and moved his fingers over her scalp, finding flat contusions from blunt trauma but no unusual shapes such as the use of a blade or an obvious dent in the bone that some handheld object might cause.

"Satisfied, Mr. Faustus?" Maltby asked.

Faustus raised one finger to him and took the woman's right hand in his own, straightened her frozen fingers and inspected her fingernails. On more than one occasion during the war he had been witness to the aftermath of rapes and other degradations visited on women of the South by Yankee soldiers. And although proof was rarely used to any legal remedy, there were times when a family took some comfort when Faustus was able to tell them that their daughter fought and scratched against such attacks. Removing a pen knife from his pocket, Faustus scraped under the dead woman's nails and looked closely at what he could only speculate might be a trace of powdered flesh.

He asked Maltby to assist him in turning the body over. The undertaker gave Faustus an angry look but bent to help. Faustus carefully looked for obvious wounds or blood on the woman's clothing but found nothing. But gripped in her left hand he discovered a matted and crushed wad of feather. Faustus was a student of the unique birds of Florida and was thus an opponent of the fashion of using their plumes to decorate women's hats. The wad of this feather held the pinkish tinge of the plume of a roseate spoonbill, one of the most uniquely colored wading birds of the state. How a maid would have one held tightly in her dead hand would be a question for another woman.

He stood. "I, sir, will require an introduction to Mrs. Birch."

The concierge knitted his brow and looked from Maltby to Faustus and then back to Maltby. The undertaker remained unambiguously silent.

"Very well," the bureaucrat said and then extended his palm toward the service door. "Shall we retreat?"

While Maltby attended to the removal of Abby Morrisette's body, Faustus was taken to the Birch apartment on the fourth floor. There would be a different excavation here, entailing a bit more tact and a lot less muscle.

With the concierge as his introduction, Faustus was greeted at the door by a young black woman, dressed just as the corpse downstairs. She was a replacement from the housemaid pool, and despite her age, which Faustus guessed was twelve or thirteen, she was already adept at greeting important white folk with deference and stoic servitude. Not once did she look up at the visitors.

"Yes, sir. Mizz Birch be out on the porch. I will tell her you are here."

The girl left them at the threshold. Faustus looked about the vestibule, sneaking glances around the corner at the collections of art pieces, cut glass objects and hand-carved furniture. A lot to lose, he thought to himself.

After a suitable five minutes, a woman with the carriage of a tired old lioness approached, her hands folded in front of her large breasts and stomach. She was dressed in a dark conservative skirt that reached to the floor and a pristine white blouse with a high embroidered collar that rose up under her chin. Her face was inquisitive. Not unusual for a person being greeted by the coroner, yet her eyes were intent and steely and on full alert. If she had been grieving, it had not been with tears.

"Mrs. Birch, if I may," started the concierge. "This is Mr. Amadeus Faustus. He is working with the undertaker's office with our, uh, situation."

"Mrs. Birch," Faustus said, "My deepest condolences, madam. I understand that Miss Morrisette was a longtime employee, and I hate to bother you at such a tragic time."

Faustus extended his hand and Mrs. Birch took it, just by the fingers, nearly touching the Masonic ring with her own thumb but never taking her eyes off his face.

"Have we met before, Mr. Faustus? In New York perhaps?"

"I don't believe so, ma'am. I certainly would have remembered."

"How is it, sir, that you know of my longtime employ and personal admiration of Miss Abigail?"

Faustus had his hat in his hand, and they had not yet been offered a chance to step inside.

"I've had the opportunity to speak extensively with one of Miss Morrisettes' close friends, one Shantice Carver, who elucidated on her, Miss Morrisette's that is, close relationship to you and your husband."

Faustus saw the muscles in the woman's jaw tighten. "Mr. Conlon, unless you have any specific inquiries of your own, would you please leave us alone? I believe Mr. Faustus and I need to speak alone."

Not only was the concierge nonplussed by the request, he fairly bolted from the apartment with as much politeness as would not slow him down.

"Will you join me on the patio, sir?" Mrs. Birch said.

Faustus followed the woman through her expansive parlor and out through the French doors into the sunlight. When she sat in the big Adirondack chair, Faustus noted there was a half-filled goblet of wine nearby. Mrs. Birch took a substantial draught from the glass before asking Faustus if he would join her.

"I will have a brandy if there's any available."

Birch rang an annoying silver bell, and the young maid appeared.

"Bring us the bottle of brandy from the parlor bar and a glass for Mr. Faustus. And do bring more of my chateau, dear."

Faustus stood at the railing looking out on the deep green of the fairways beyond.

"Was Mr. Birch as fond of Abby as you?" he asked.

"Other than his use of her in procuring a whore for himself, no," Mrs. Birch said. "I doubt that he even noticed the girl in the three years she was with us. Though his obvious taste for Negro women leaves me to wonder if I was misled in that also."

Faustus blinked at the woman's bluntness. If she was drunk, it did not show. If she'd somehow obtained the news of her husband's philandering and was simply angered, he would use that to advantage.

"May I assume, then, madam, that you are aware of your husband's, uh, dealings with the Carver woman?"

"Dealings? Is that the way you Southern Masons refer to whoring and prostitution? Dealings?"

The maid returned, bringing the brandy and wine and bearing a look of embarrassment on her cheeks. She put the liquor down on the table and, forgetting to pour, started backing through the doors.

"Close the doors behind you, dear, if the conversation makes you uncomfortable," Mrs. Birch said with a chuckle.

Faustus filled her glass with wine and poured a substantial tumbler of brandy for himself. They both drank. Now it was his turn to be blunt.

"My understanding, Mrs. Birch, is that you were here on the island the night of the fire in the Styx. It has come to my attention that you were in fact in the woods that evening, seen in the company of a man known as Mr. Bingham, now deceased. If you will, madam, could you tell me about that meeting?"

Mrs. Birch took yet another draught of wine. "Would you like me to start before or after I shot the bastard in the throat and stuffed his bribery money into his offensive mouth?" she asked.

Byrne had a bicycle carriage driver take him to the northern entrance of the Royal Poinciana, where he could enter through the side door. The night of the ball, Harris had given him a quick tour of the first floor, where the executive suites were located, and it didn't take Byrne long to find the office of Mr. McAdams. Byrne hesitated at the door, taking a deep breath against the pain in his side, then went into McAdams's rooms without knocking. Byrne knew the art of busting down doors of gambling and whore houses as a cop. You usually had to watch for the scrambling customers and employees scurrying out before they got caught in a lineup, but rarely did you have to be concerned that someone was going to take a shot at you or draw a blade. Byrne figured his confrontation with McAdams would be even more business like. Yet McAdams and his colleagues had tried to kill him yesterday, so when Byrne entered, his steel baton was out.

McAdams was caught sitting behind a large walnut desk on the other side of the room. The look on the man's face was probably quite foreign to him: surprise and fluster passed through his eyes and a dumbfounded O formed on his mouth. Byrne grabbed a wooden straight chair, swung it to the door and jammed its top rail under the knob. Flagler's architects had not yet adopted the habit of hanging office doors to open out instead of in, and the chair would provide a lock that couldn't easily be broken.

"Well, my God, Mr. Byrne. How wonderful to see you, alive and well!"

Byrne took two long strides across the room and finished his approach with a whip of the baton. The whoosh ended with a crack across McAdams's desk top, shattering a porcelain figurine and sending a metal-tipped ink pen flipping through the air until it stuck point first into the wallpaper to the left.

"Don't start, McAdams," Byrne said, his voice hard but in control. "Your plan to shut me up with a bullet in the Glades leaves you in a poor position to backpeddle now."

The rip of the baton had frozen McAdams with his knees flexed, hands still on either of the chair armrests, defenseless.

"Well," he said. "Obviously our Mr. Ashton overestimated the accuracy of his firearms skills. You were supposed to have bled out before we even got back to town."

"Hunting accident, eh?" Byrne said. McAdams was giving it up far too early for his liking.

"Something like that, yes," McAdams said. "But you weren't supposed to still be walking around asking questions."

McAdams had straightened his legs, maybe gaining confidence, and Byrne knew better than to allow it. He poked the man in the chest with the baton, forcing enough pressure to McAdams's sternum to make it hurt, enough to make him stumble and sit back in his chair. A flash of fear came into McAdams's eye. He was not a man accustomed to physical violence.

"Are you admitting that you tried to kill me?" he said, trying to show enough anger to jack up the fear factor. "Just because I know about this whole real estate swindle you guys have going?"

Byrne had no idea what Ashton had been talking about when he'd explained the motive for killing him out in the glades. He was bluffing. But you use the little you have to get more. It was one of Danny's old tricks and a detective's tactic. Turn their words back on them.

"We knew you were poking around in affairs that were none of your business," McAdams said, an air of control returning to his voice, the one he'd used on the handcar out to the glades. "It was our business, a quiet business, a quiet affair until other parties got involved. There is a way to do such things in a civilized manner."

"Like killing the messenger of bad news, sticking a wad of money in his mouth and then setting up some poor Negro housemaid to take the blame. That's civilized?"

"That was never supposed to happen," McAdams said. "Mr. Bingham was supposed to conduct himself in a straightforward manner. Sell the land documentation for the price agreed and walk away. It was a business proposition, nothing more."

Byrne was winging it now. He took the baton from McAdams's chest and began using the tip to flip over papers on the man's desk.

"You wanted the land. Bingham wanted the money. It should have been simple. Why kill him?"

"He was dead before we got there," McAdams said in a way that sounded as if he was actually disappointed.

"We, Mr. McAdams?" Byrne said. "You mean Birch and Pearson? You must be talking about your coconspirators because you were still on the train out of New York with me when he was killed."

"None of us killed him, Mr. Byrne. He was dead before any of us got there. The meeting was set up in the Styx because it was considered a safe place on that particular night when it was supposed to be empty. But when they arrived, Bingham had already been shot."

Byrne tapped the shaft of the baton again on the desk top, the armrests of the chair, the head rest only inches behind McAdams's skull.

"And why not you, Mr. McAdams? If you were the one to put this all together, why didn't you make the payoff yourself?"

"As you said, I was on the train. My duties are not easily discarded. And there was a deadline. The property had to be cleared and the paperwork signed or the deal was off. Bingham was the bearer of the deed, and he'd been pushing the price higher and higher, trying to use the time constraint to make us barter."

"Sounds like a sharp businessman to me."

"He was a cheat and a bastard," McAdams said.

Byrne's baton crashed down on the desk, this time splitting a piece of the hardened walnut on the edge nearest to McAdams. He was not going to tell this man that it was his brother who was killed.

"But you still sent a woman to deal with him instead of doing it yourselves," Byrne said.

"I had no idea Marjory was going to take on the task herself," McAdams said. "I thought she was going to get Birch to do it."

Byrne froze at the admission. It was his turn for shock. He'd pieced together an assumption that Birch had sent his wife to make the land deal and that the prostitute and Abby Morrisette had gotten it all wrong. He was even entertaining the possibility that Danny had seen a chance to kill two birds with one meeting, a real estate swindle and a blackmailing at the same time.

The possibility that Marjory McAdams had anything to do with it was a blow.

"Marjory? You sent your own daughter to pull this off?"

"I already said I didn't send her," McAdams said. "But you underestimate my daughter if you think she lacks the wherewithal to carry out such a task. She is quite capable. And she proved so by acquiring the deed as expected."

"She has the land deed? This document you bought from Bingham that gives you title to the land that the Styx was built on?"

"Marjory and I kept in touch via the telegraph. She passed on business messages to me, so she was aware of the timetable we were working against. She elected to take the matter into her own hands and paid Mr. Bingham for the deed. The fire was a fortunate accident that cleared the land."

Jaysus, Byrne thought. The man is actually proud of what he and his daughter had done, like it was some brilliant accomplishment, acquiring valuable land where a man lay dead. Again he let anger rule his hand and the baton whooshed down again with a ripping blow.

"A man has been killed, McAdams," Byrne snapped, raising his voice for the first time. "People's homes and possessions burned. For a real estate deal?"

McAdams went quiet. Byrne could tell by the man's breathing that he was consciously trying to calm himself, like he might do in a boardroom during hard negotiations.

"You don't understand the ramifications," McAdams said, his voice under control. "This island, in fact this state, is about to turn a corner. And the new avenues that open will make many men rich beyond their dreams."

"Wrong, McAdams. You don't understand the ramifications of a conspiracy to murder. It's a charge that will put you all in jail, where riches don't spend well."

"Murder? My God, man, there was no forethought of murder. That's not the way we do business."

"Right, you hire others to do that," Byrne said, swallowing the pain in his side rather than let McAdams see him wince.

"There is no proof of any such thing," McAdams said. "And besides, I believe someone is already in custody for the murder of Mr. Bingham. As for your unfortunate hunting accident, Mr. Ashton is deeply sorry."

Byrne folded up the baton and slid it into his pocket. He would not need intimidation any longer. McAdams had said enough.

"We'll see what a judge has to say about that when Miss Carver's hearing is held tomorrow. I believe your cover-up of the crimes you have committed will be exposed."

McAdams folded his hands across his stomach in a classic pose of deep thought and let Byrne turn toward the door, but when the Pinkerton was halfway across the room he spoke again, this time in a voice of paternalism.

"We have many powerful friends and connections in New York, Mr. Byrne. In the tapestry of money and business and politics are found many crossovers, the reaches of which are myriad and deep."

Byrne turned.

"I have no use for your money, sir. So I'm not interested in your bribery, or anything else you or your conniving family might offer."

He started toward the door. McAdams let him take two more steps.

"But do you have an interest in the whereabouts of your father, Mr. Byrne?" he said, his voice sounding self-assured, confident, and not a little greasy.

Chapter 23

The arraignment of one Shantice Carver on the charge of murder was to be held in the stuffy second-floor room of the jailhouse. Faustus was there early, standing at the foot the outside staircase, smoking a Cuban cigar and watching the procession of attendees climb the stairs.

The traveling judge, John E. Born, had ridden in his carriage from the town of Juno, where the Dade County seat was established. Faustus knew that Born had been newly appointed as the third county judge in the area by Gov. William Bloxham. He also knew that Bloxham was a staunch backer of Flagler and considered the railroad baron a land developer who would save the state from its present financial ruin. In Bloxham's first term as governor he'd sold four million acres of state land in the Everglades for twenty-five cents an acre to bolster state coffers, a real estate move only a true swampland-for-money entrepreneur could love. Faustus wondered about the new judge's integrity, whether he would owe his allegiance to the governor, and thus the Flagler powers on the island.

The night before, Byrne and Faustus shared what they'd each discovered. Mrs. Birch's admission to Faustus of firing the shot that killed Danny was hearsay. But Faustus put it out there first, unadorned, and had watched carefully as the muscles in Byrne's jaws tightened.

Byrne had put on his characteristic internal and stoic face, and Faustus had waited an appropriate time in silence. "It was my duty to request that the woman turn herself in to the sheriff," he said at last.

"And?" Byrne said.

"If I can recall her words correctly, she simply stated 'My dear sir, we do not turn ourselves in. We hire the likes of you to avoid such messiness.'"

Byrne recounted his meeting with Mr. McAdams, explaining the real estate deal that Danny had somehow become involved with and the fact that Marjory McAdams had been involved all along. Faustus stored all his newfound knowledge away. Today his goal was to have the charges against Miss Carver dropped, repercussions be damned.

Next up the staircase were the sheriff and his cadre of deputies. The fat man wore a tight but not unfriendly look on his face.

"Good day, counselor," he said to Faustus as he tipped his hat and climbed the stairs, his huge legs pumping like mechanical pile drivers. Faustus could nearly feel the shivering of the wooden structure beside him. Trailing behind the sheriff, almost as an afterthought, was a man Faustus knew to be the attorney Marcus Willings, a real estate lawyer who had been appointed as the temporary prosecutor for the district. He was a civilized and studious man, given to bookish language and also given to bend to the sheriff's wishes in all matters. His was simply to be Cox's puppet.

Next to arrive was a thin, bespectacled man that Faustus recognized immediately as the editor of the local *Gazetteer* newspaper, whose nickname was "Town."

"Glad that you could come, Mr. Cryer," Faustus said.

"Not a problem, Mr. Faustus. It just so happens that I too am to face the judge this morning in a civil matter."

"A civil matter, sir?"

"The sheriff has filed suit against me and the newspaper for slander," Cryer said. "You do recall the crusade we led last year against the rampant crime threatening the city and Sheriff Cox's inability to handle the situation?"

"Yes, certainly," said Faustus. "I believe that at one point the man threatened to hickory whip you."

Cryer chuckled at the recollection. "But I am rather more intrigued by your message on the murder charge and your investigation, Mr. Faustus."

"Then my effort was not in vain, sir. Though I admit my motive for inviting you was to have the proceeding recorded by someone outside of the parties involved."

"Again, a role I take as a matter of duty. It is what we do."

At nine o'clock the first-floor door to the jail was opened, and Shantice Carver was led out by a single deputy. She was dressed in the same clothing she'd worn when they arrested her days ago. With her head bent low and feet shuffling, she looked like a lost soul heading for the gallows. Faustus stepped out. "Miss Carver. Pick your head up, my dear, you will be walking from this place in a short time as a free woman or my name is not Amadeus Faustus."

The woman's eyes met his, and their redness, their utter deadness, took Faustus back to a place on a battlefield in North Carolina in 1865 where he did not want to go, to faces that he had struggled mightily to forget.

"Please, my dear," he said. "Despite our circumstances in life, hope is not a dirty word."

The guard snorted and pushed Carver forward up the staircase. Faustus turned and looked across the street before heading up himself. Leaning against the rough-hewn wall of a new dry goods store, Byrne was watching. He tipped his head to the old Mason. It was a sign to Faustus that steps had been taken to guarantee certain evidence had been secured as they had discussed the night before.

The sheriff's sparsely appointed office had been reorganized as an impromptu courtroom. A dozen cane chairs were arranged on the open floor facing Cox's desk. Faustus knew this to be a ploy, done only for show. Citizens of the area were openly restricted by the sheriff from attending court proceedings ever since the lynching two years ago of the alleged killer of the property appraiser. In the past, when traveling judges came to conduct business, they said they merely assumed that the place was empty because no one in the community gave a damn about the cases they oversaw, or such would be their excuse if questioned. Sheriff Cox ran his shop the way he deemed appropriate. Yet there was a twinge of consternation trying to hide in his fat face this morning as he straddled one of the now overburdened chairs and watched as the new judge sat behind the sheriff's personal desk.

"All right, gentlemen, let's get on with the matters at hand before the damnable sun begins to cook us like steamed vegetables," Judge Born announced, eschewing the typical "all rise" and all other formalities of courtroom decorum that Faustus was used to in his city experiences with the law.

"I am Judge John E. Born, the new circuit court representative. And for those of you who may find yourselves here on a regular basis, you should know that I don't take kindly to the use of my time for listening to manure shoveling, and I am not, and I reiterate, am not beholden to any proprietor, owner, county politician or railroad baron as the case may be in my rulings or interpretations of fact."

The judge looked up only once from his sheaf of papers during the pronouncement and that was when he'd used the phrase "railroad baron," as if to challenge anyone who might not interpret his meaning.

"I owe my allegiance only to the law, gentlemen," he then said. "And while I sit here, it is the law and justice that will be served."

Faustus heard the sheriff shift his weight, the cracking and groaning of the wooden legs of his chair rising in complaint.

"In the matter of Miss Shantice Carver, who is being arraigned this morning on the charge of murder in the first degree," the judge said, looking at Carver.

"I assume, ma'am, that since you are the only female present, you are Miss Carver, and I ask you to rise."

Both Carver and Faustus stood.

"You honor," Faustus said. "My name is Amadeus Faustus, and I will be representing Miss Carver in this matter, sir."

The judge lowered his reading glasses, peering over the top of the lenses for an uncomfortable length of time. If he was surprised that a Southern lawyer would be representing a raggedy-looking Negro woman in a capital crime, or was taken aback by the sight of the well-dressed attorney towering over the small black prostitute, it did not show in his face.

"Excuse me for digressing, sir," he said instead. "But are you the same Amadeus Faustus of the 39th Regiment of the North Carolina Confederacy at Murfreesboro in the year of 1862?"

Faustus took in the judge's northern accent, his similar age, and the obvious scrutiny in his eye, but did not falter.

"The very same, your honor. I was an officer with the medical corps during the battle of Stone River."

The judge let time pass again.

"I sir, was with the Union Army under General William Rosecrans at the time," he said. "Your name and your actions during battle are legend, Mr. Faustus. For treating and saving the lives not only of your fellow soldiers, but those of wounded Union troops as well. I commend you, sir, to your face."

This time the wood of the sheriff's chair stayed silent.

"Now then," the judge said, returning to his papers. "According to this document prepared by the sheriff's office, Miss Carver, who is employed by the Poinciana Hotel, is charged with the stabbing death of one Robert Bingham during an altercation on the island of Palm Beach.

"Said crime is alleged to have occurred on property next to Miss Carver's domicile where later was found a murder weapon, that being a knife.

"Further stated is the fact that Miss Carver is known to also be in the business of prostitution and that Mr. Bingham was a known customer, this being offered as motivation for the killing after an alleged argument over a transaction consummated by the individuals involved."

The judge looked up from his reading, his eyes this time focused on Sheriff Cox.

"This is your report, Sheriff, and included is a finding by the local acting medical examiner as to the death of Mr. Bingham by stabbing, is that correct, sir?"

"It is, your honor," Cox said.

The judge looked down at the papers again, offering nothing but a studied silence before looking up at Faustus.

"By your presence, sir, I assume you have a rebuttal of these facts, or is your client prepared to plead guilty to the charge?"

"I am prepared to present only the real facts, your honor," Faustus said, knowing he was overstepping his bounds but hoping that the informality of the country court would give him leeway. "As the document before you is filled, sir, with lies."

The legs of the sheriff did not fail him. The big man came out of his chair as if he'd been goosed, and he drew in a breath with which to power his indignation. But the judge beat him to the bark.

"Sit down, Sheriff Cox! You will have your turn," Judge Born snapped. "And Mr., uh, Prosecutor, Conlon. Be it understood that you represent the state at this hearing, not the sheriff." Conlon nodded.

The judge turned to Faustus.

"I do hope you have something of substance to back up such a statement, Mr. Faustus."

"I do, your honor."

"Be succinct, sir."

Faustus clasped his hands in front of him and with a voice devoid of emotion but unwavering in conviction, began to enumerate.

"First, your honor, after a close examination of the body of said Mr. Bingham, which I myself conducted in the presence of witnesses, the deceased did not die of a stab wound but of a bullet, sir. And as is proven by the powder burns that still mark his throat, said bullet was fired at close range. Thus, the bullet entered the front of the neck at an upward angle and lodged in the third thoracic vertebra."

Faustus then turned, ever so slightly, toward the sheriff.

"These facts, your honor, have been covered up by the sheriff's office in conspiracy with the appointed medical examiner. I submit, sir, that an independent examination by an expert of the court's choice will in fact come to the same conclusion that I have, your honor. As you well know, sir, from your own aforementioned military service, bullet wounds do not lie."

The judge remained impassive. Faustus continued.

"Secondly, sir, I have eye witnesses, including a manager of the Royal Poinciana, his assistant, a daughter of Mr. Flagler's vice president, a handful of residents of the community, and Mizz Carver herself, who will testify that when the body of the deceased was discovered, he had a roll of cash money stuffed, sir, into his mouth. That money, your honor, is neither included in the victim's effects, nor is it in the sheriff's report. I bring it to your attention only to dispel the sheriff's convenient theory that the motive for Mizz Carver's so-called actions where monetary in nature."

The judge was now staring at the sheriff, his glare itself daring the man to stand again and refute Faustus's words.

"And thirdly, your honor, I have personally obtained a confession by the actual killer of the victim, who, to my face and in her own words, admitted that she shot said victim in the throat after confronting him over a blackmail attempt, she being the wife of a well-regarded Palm Beach banker who was a frequent patron of my client's, uh, services, sir."

Despite the explosive nature of the statements, the judge remained stoic, more thoughtful than was comfortable for either Faustus or the sheriff. But behind him, Faustus could hear the frantic scratching of a pen on paper and imagined the excitement that a journalist such as Mr. Cryer must be feeling.

"What say you, Mr. Conlon?" the judge finally said.

"Bullshit!" the sheriff bawled, yet he remained in his seat.

"I, I, I don't know, your honor," Conlon babbled. "I was just recently, your honor, apprised of the ..."

"I see," said the judge, cutting the man off. "Although I do not doubt Mr. Faustus's abilities to medically assess a true bullet wound when he sees one, it should not be too difficult to find a coroner of ability and state sanction to confirm the manner of death of Mr. Bingham."

"Already buried," grunted the sheriff.

"Under whose authority?" said the judge.

"Seven-day rule, your honor," replied the sheriff. "It's a city ordinance. A hedge against disease when we can't find next of kin."

"Another statement that is patently false, your honor," interrupted Faustus. "An associate of mine, a Pinkerton by standing, has secured the body of the victim despite attempts made last night by some unfashionably late and previously unemployed grave diggers to carry out orders to remove said body from Mr. Maltby's funeral parlor."

Despite himself, Sheriff Cox twisted his head to take in the visages of his deputies sitting in the back row of chairs. They in turn looked at one another, stupidly shrugging their shoulders.

"And, your honor, said Pinkerton is in fact the true brother of the deceased, whose real name is Daniel Byrne," Faustus said, again in a clear and unemotional statement. "Being the only surviving relative of the deceased, Mr. Michael Byrne is outside at this moment, and he has rightfully claimed his brother's body. He will agree to an independent autopsy."

This time Sheriff Cox stood, staring at Faustus, his mouth open, a look of complete astonishment pulling down at the flesh of his face. "Pinkerton," he whispered.

Judge Born scratched a note for himself and again took a few moments. The temperature in the room was rising rapidly. The judge took a handkerchief from his coat pocket and mopped his brow. Almost as if he'd given permission, the sheriff followed in form.

"Right." The judge turned to Faustus. "And as to this confession, counselor, may I assume that you do not have said confession as a signed document, or are you going to surprise us all even more?"

"No, your honor. Following the conversation with the suspect, I was dismissed from the room where the admission of guilt was made. And I believe, sir, that perhaps a statewide prosecutor may need to be empowered to delve into the matter as said suspect is an out-of-state resident."

"If I may ask a basic question, Mr. Faustus, in view of such incredible statements that you have made before this court. Have you any witnesses, sir, to vouch for your client at the time of Mr. Bingham's, uh, Byrne's demise?"

"At this point, your honor, I do not. As it stands, the only witness, a seasonal maid at the hotel and a friend of my client, has also been murdered. And I have reason to believe she was killed by the same hand that took the victim's life in this case."

Carver, who until that point seemed not to have been listening, looked up at Faustus and pleaded with a single cry: "Abby?"

The room had gone silent but for the frantic scratching of the newspaper editor's pencil.

"By God, man, I must say you strain your own credibility with such statements, Mr. Faustus," said the judge. "Are you aware of this occurrence, Sheriff Cox?"

Cox was staring straight ahead, gathering himself, or perhaps simply burning.

"We were informed of an accidental death at the hotel this morning, your honor," the sheriff said with an emphasis on the word *accidental.* "I sent the coroner, uh, acting coroner, to retrieve the body, yes sir."

"And in the interest of the sheriff's upcoming investigation of said death," the judge said, looking from one man to the other, "would you be willing, Mr. Faustus, to aid in that inquiry with whatever knowledge you have of the situation?"

"Quite simply, your honor, the deceased, Miss Abigail Morrisette, was a coconspirator with my client in the blackmailing scheme. After the aggrieved woman confronted and killed Mr. Bingham, she discovered that her maid was involved, and in an attempt to silence her, pushed her down an elevator shaft."

"If the sheriff would inspect the suspect woman this day, I believe he will find a set of scratch marks on the left side of her neck. If he takes traces of the skin matter from under the murdered woman's fingernails, he will find skin and face powder consistent with the suspected woman's wounds. There seemed to be a bit of a cat fight, your honor."

At this point Faustus stepped toward the sheriff, removing an envelope from his inside coat and placing it on the table before him.

"And this, sir, is a bird feather found in the hand of the dead girl. I believe you can easily match it to feathers missing from the suspect woman's hat."

"May we know the name of this out-of-state woman?" Cox asked, reaching out for the envelope.

"Do you plan to investigate her in this matter?"

Cox turned to the judge. "Considering what you have brought before this court, it would seem now that I must," Cox said, and Faustus could see the wheels turning in the man's head: the opportunity of holding power over one of the Flagler's guests, the use of such power to demean their haughty ways, or perhaps to be paid off for not doing the same.

"Then I should say, your honor, her name is Mrs. Roseann Birch," Faustus said, turning to the judge. "And now, your honor, since there is another viable suspect identified in the murder for which she is charged, I request that my client be released on bail, sir."

Judge Born watched the two men, bemused perhaps by Faustus's chess playing and Cox's transparencies.

"Bail will be set in the amount of ten dollars," he replied.

"Now hold on one damned second there, yer honor," Cox blathered, letting his street language slip through. "That cain't be right!"

The judge had endured enough, and in the absence of a gavel, banged his fist on the wooden table.

"Not only is it right, sir. It is just," he barked. "And it will also be just for me to summon a special prosecutor from Tallahassee to look into the whereabouts of the money Mr. Faustus has spoken of, the discrepancies of the medical report on the victim's death, and the attempts to withhold that information from this court and the legal system.

"You will find that a new day is dawning in the state of Florida, sheriff. Things will no longer be done as usual. Welcome to the twentieth century, sir."

Cox stared at the judge, his back teeth grinding, the muscles in his jaw flexing, but he was silenced by his chastisement.

"And as for you," the judge said, turning to Faustus. "You with your bevy of bombshells, I would ask one question that may seem basic, but must be entered in the record just the same. Motivation, sir? For a woman of social standing to engage in such heinous crimes?"

Faustus simply raised his eyebrows in that way of his.

"We may be entering a new century, your honor, but as the playwright says, and it has ever been, 'Heaven has no rage like love to hatred turned, nor hell a fury like a woman scorned.'"

With the arraignment abruptly ended, Judge Born was quick to toss out the only other business of the day, the motion of a civil suit by the sheriff filed against the local newspaper editor. It would be, under the circumstances, superfluous at this point, the judge said. With that, he seemed to say a silent prayer and called an adjournment.

The parties involved all exited the room and descended the steps, led by Faustus, who, after paying Shantice Carver's ten dollar bail, was at his client's elbow, trying to explain to the woman what had just transpired. The judge followed, trailed by the sheriff, who was whining vociferously about a miscarriage of justice. He in turn was being harangued by the newspaper editor, who was asking questions about what the sheriff intended to do about accusations of a double homicide on Palm Beach Island. Bringing up the rear was the sheriff's now-shy deputies and bailiff, who were in no hurry to incur their boss's wrath.

At the base of the staircase, Michael Byrne waited, cap in his hand despite the strong sun. When Faustus saw him, he tried to catch his eyes, to indicate that all had gone well. Faustus was worried about the steel baton he feared was concealed under Byrne's hat. To help deflect the possibility of violence, Faustus quickly turned to the judge behind him.

"If I may, your honor," he said. "I would like to introduce you to Mr. Michael Byrne, brother of the deceased victim. He has recently taken possession of the corpse in question and will both verify his identity and give permission for the new autopsy."

The judge nodded at Byrne but did not extend his hand.

"My sympathies for your loss, Mr. Byrne. It is my hope that this extraordinary affair can be sorted out, and be assured, sir, that an investigation into the miscarriage of justice will be overseen."

Byrne bowed his head just enough to show respect, but not enough to lose sight of Sheriff Cox, who was glowering at him from the final step of the staircase.

"If there is anything else, Mr. Byrne, that needs to be brought to my attention, as if enough has not already been elucidated this morning, then do not hesitate to call on my office," the judge said.

"There is one thing, your honor," Byrne said, stepping in front of Sheriff Cox before the man could take his final step off the staircase. "I would like my father's watch returned."

The metal baton flicked out from Byrne's hand like a stinger. Its tip caught the chain on Sheriff Cox's vest and froze there. The motion was too fast for the fat man, or perhaps he was already too stunned from the day's explosions to react.

"By God ..." Byrne cut him off. "It is a Swiss-made silver fob watch with blue-steel hands and my father's initials, CHB, engraved on the back."

The judge looked at the sputtering sheriff and held out his hand. Byrne lifted the watch out of the vest pocket with the tip of his baton. After the judge inspected the piece, front and back, he unfastened the chain and placed the watch in Byrne's hand. The Judge winced, as if a terrible odor had just invaded his nostrils, spun on his heel, and walked away.

"By God, Byrne," Faustus said, uncharacteristically awed. "You never cease to amaze, my young friend."

"Nor do you, Mr. Faustus," Byrne said. "I trust that since Miss Carver has shed her leg irons, things went well upstairs?"

"As well as could be expected. Whether there will be any follow-through is yet to be ascertained. I doubt, though, that Sheriff Cox will be in authority for long. I do not think this particular judge is one to look the other way. But there is little we can do now except to wait, I am afraid, for justice to come around."

Shantice Carver was still standing at Faustus's side, trying to decipher perhaps from their faces and words just what the hell had just occurred. They, however, were both looking out across the lake, taking in the white shine of the Royal Poinciana glowing in sunlight.

"I suppose you are, by necessity, going to leave us now," Faustus said. "You are in possession of your brother's body; you can take him home. That was your purpose, was it not?"

Byrne kept looking out on the water.

"This state will need men like you, Mr. Byrne, to succeed."

Byrne still did not look at the elderly man. "You mean to build grand edifices to my ego?" he said. "To plunder and devour? To shift a natural beauty to a man-made one in our own concrete and glass image?"

Byrne closed his lips, realizing he was proselytizing in a manner that was foreign to him.

"Don't mock yourself, Michael," Faustus said. "You are a man of ethics and morality, and in your heart is a sense of justice that a society cannot exist without. The Flaglers and Birches and McAdamses of the world can build sanctuaries unto themselves, but it takes men like you to build a civilization."

Shantice Carver stood next to the men, drawing a pattern in the sand with the worn toe of her work shoe, and they both seemed to recognize the piety that was being splashed around on all parts.

"I may take on your challenges someday, Mr. Faustus," Byrne finally said. "But for now, there is one final thing I do have to do."

"Yes," Faustus agreed, reaching out to shake Byrne's extended hand. "I suppose there is."

Chapter 24

On Tuesday morning Michael Byrne stood on the rail platform at the southern entrance to the Poinciana. He was dressed in his Pinkerton clothes, the trousers still a bit salt stained but the brogans cleaned and polished. He was there on Harris's orders to help Mr. Flagler board the train to New York.

It would be his final day of work. He had already tendered a resignation and would be accompanying his brother's body on a train later in the week. He watched the McAdamses, Birches, and the rest boarding for their trip back home.

If a warrant had ever been issued for the arrest of Mrs. Birch, there was no one available or willing to present it. Rumor had it that Sheriff Cox had not been seen since Judge Born left him stammering in the street after the recovery of Byrne's watch.

Yet Mr. Flagler, accompanied as always by his entourage, walked imperiously from the hotel. At exactly nine fifteen, after assisting his wife, he climbed aboard number 90. If he took note of Byrne, he did not let on. Byrne had no doubt that such a man would have been fully informed of the accusations against his inner circle and his guests. But he was a man who built things. The unraveling of human beings, their ethics, their motivations and their morality were but the detritus left in the wake of his progress.

Mr. McAdams followed in Flagler's steps, his head held high and extending handshakes to those seeing off the travelers with manners as cordial and confident as always. He did not notice Byrne until his daughter veered away from his side and headed in the direction of the Pinkerton.

Byrne stood his ground when Marjory approached, her green eyes holding his, any shame buried, if it indeed ever existed.

"I'm off for the city, then, Michael," she said as if leaving a mate at summer camp. He kept all emotion out of his face.

"Do you have the deed to the former Styx land with you?" he said. It was the first time he'd seen her stumble.

"I have no idea what …"

"Kiss my Irish ass," Byrne said. "You've got Danny's valise and the papers to the property. Did he sign them before you got to the meeting, or did you hold the pen in his dead hand to make his mark?"

Marjory McAdams stood silent, gathering herself, perfecting her words before she spoke. Byrne took it as a victory, but only for a few seconds.

"You have no idea, Michael, how it is to live in second place behind men who become rich and richer off your expertise and off your talent," she said.

"True," Byrne said and nothing more. Let them talk, just like on the streets.

"I'm sorry for the demise of your brother. He was actually a charming man in his own way."

She raised her chin even higher.

"He was not as demure as you when it came to lovemaking, and his business acumen was impressively aggressive, though in many ways flawed."

Byrne could imagine his brother in the same circumstance as he, standing naked with Marjory in the cool Atlantic. Danny would have taken what he wanted from this she-devil. She could delude herself all she wanted.

"So you screwed him and then tried to screw him," he said, matching her crudeness.

"My father knew Daniel was shopping the binder to the Styx land to the highest bidder. He knew the value. He had helped Mr. Flagler acquire most of this land himself."

They always have to justify when they're caught, Byrne thought, no different from any pimp, scofflaw or pickpocket on Broadway.

"Others found out about the deal," she said. "That ass Pearson, snooping through the telegrams. Then Birch wanted his share for lending my father the money to pay your brother's price for the binder. When I saw Roseann Birch heading into the Styx that night, I knew they were going to double-cross us. I was supposed to meet Daniel myself an hour later, when the fair across the lake was in full swing."

"But Mrs. Birch was only avenging a stain to her honor," Byrne said.

Marjory lowered her eyes. "And so she did. Daniel was dead when I followed her into the woods that night. I heard the gunshot. I saw her run. She did not see me."

"But you saw Danny's body."

"Yes."

"And his valise?"

"It was just lying there. I found it," she said, a schoolgirl claiming finder's keepers.

"So you had it all. And paid nothing for it," Byrne said. "Why set the fire?"

"I pulled his body under the shed." She looked past Byrne's shoulder, seeing something in the night. "I smashed my lantern against the wood frame. I was only trying to burn away the signs of what had occurred, for everyone's sake, even the Birches. But the kerosene, it just, just … I never meant to destroy people's homes."

A tear had actually begun to form in her eyes. An actress to the end.

"Bullshit," Byrne said. "Your interest in Shantice Carver was only to make sure she hadn't seen you out there once you'd stolen the valise. You tried to get her away before she could talk and then weaseled your way between her and anyone who might interrogate her. You were protecting your own ass."

"I was protecting my father!" she said, raising her voice and letting in perhaps the first true emotion that he'd seen in her. "He needs someone to protect him, he needs a strong woman to watch out for him. But you wouldn't understand such a thing, Mr. Pinkerton! You wouldn't understand what families have to do for each other."

Byrne watched her eyes, wet and angry and so naïve about the world of people who lived outside her own sphere.

"Everyone has a father," he said. "And when I get back to New York, yours will help me find mine, dead or alive. Your money, the Birches' money and influence, will help me whenever I need it. I'll rattle your skeletons until I'm satisfied that my family is reunited, even if it's in death. That is what happens when you do business with the devil."

When she looked into Byrne's face, she saw something that scared her, the young woman who was never scared of anything.

"And remember, ma'am, my brother was a very sound and able man. Be sure you're not carrying part of my own family with you back to New York."

Chapter 25

Late season. One could feel it in the rising humidity, the warmer nighttime temperatures, the bundles of cloud in the west. In the afternoon, water vapor would rise from the heating soup of the Everglades until the clouds turned dirty and dark and could hold no more. As they moved east, lured by the cooler air over the ocean, the afternoon showers would come.

Today there was a gathering at the beach; the allure was a unique baseball competition. Carlos Santos, it was said, had been cajoled into challenging the mighty Pittsburgh Pirate slugger John Peter Wagner—in Florida to convalesce from a leg injury at midseason—to a test of batting prowess and strength. Such a showdown had never occurred before, and there were more than a few discussions of the propriety of pitting a white slugger against a Negro in such an endeavor. But harkening back to the myopic distinction of Santos's Cuban Yankees, it was pointed out that a Latin versus a white was not unduly provocative.

So it was that Santos and Wagner were standing bat to bat on the Palm Beach Island beach. The rules had been set: Each man would face a pitcher who stood with his back to the ocean and delivered strikes to the batters over a home plate set in the sand. Each batter would receive ten pitches and have the chance to blast the ball into the sea. A set of judges standing out on the wharf would determine whose ball splashed down farthest out. Best out of ten would win.

The new manager of the Poinciana was posing as umpire and score keeper, the former manager having boarded a train north less than a week after both the Birches and the McAdamses had left the island. Judge John Born had posted a statement that "all men are equal under the law of the combined United States of America, and if a crime has indeed been committed, someone will eventually have to answer for said crimes."

Those with money had gone north to their respective homes in New York to await subpoenas that would never come. Michael Byrne had taken his brother's body back to the city and buried him next to their mother. All charges were dropped against Shantice Carver, but she was surreptitiously fired and moved back to be with her people in North Carolina.

On this day a home run derby was in progress. Women guests from the Breakers were carrying their parasols, and the men were still in their luncheon attire, with boaters shading their eyes as they followed the long arc of baseballs as they catapulted off the ash wood of the hitters' bats, rose into the cerulean sky and then fell to splash without a sound in the distance. A white flag would be raised from the pier if Wagner's shot was longer, a black flag for Santos. Nearly everyone, including the daily staff at the Breakers, was in attendance. One spectator in particular was missing.

"Where Mizz Ida?" asked one of the laundry women who had gathered under the pier in the shadows.

"She said somethin' bout getting' somethin' done down in the storage room downstairs," said the one next to her. A black flag went up, a tally changed, and Santos took the lead six to four.

"I cain't believe she would miss her boy playin' this out," said one of the housekeepers.

"No, no. Here she come now," said the first one.

The maids made a prime spot for Ida May to stand. Her work dress was smeared with some kind of heavy dust, and there was even a smudge of ash on her face, unusual for a woman known for her fastidiousness. She greeted the others, set her feet in the sand and then looked out at Santos, who was taking a few warm-up swings while Wagner was at bat. Santos made eye contact with Miss Fluery, and a silent message was passed.

The patrons on the beach were all focused on Wagner, following the parabola as the professional put his tenth ball in the Atlantic at a distance yet unmet in the contest.

Carlos Santos didn't watch his opponent's hit but concentrated instead on the sky behind them. He detected a curling spiral of black smoke rising directly above the beachfront hotel. A slight smile played at the corners of his mouth. When he approached the makeshift plate, Ida May carried a look of glowing grace as she watched her Santos. One of her underlings turned to another and whispered, "Ain't like he's the holy spirit or sumthin'." The woman next to her cut her eyes to Miss Fluery's face, knowing her colleagues' subject without asking.

"She seein' some kind of glory," she whispered back.

At the plate Santos dug his back foot into the sand and cocked his bat. He took one last look at the smoke now pouring out of the dormered windows at the rooftop of the Breakers and then faced the pitcher. The ball cruised in at a nice level speed, perfect for creating a symbiotic energy between the now powerfully turning bat and the approaching orb. The shattering sound of bursting glass giving way to a ballooning internal heat and that of hard ash on a hard, leather-wrapped baseball split their respective air simultaneously.

The patrons watched Santos's ball make a silent plop in the water, an obvious ten yards past Wagner's last attempt. Game over. Applause fluttered the beachfront air.

Ida May Fluery clapped too. Her adroit nose began to fill with the smell of dry plank wood charring in fire behind her. She did not see when the crowd's attention left the ballplayers, but their expressions of mild entertainment turned to surprise and excitement when they noticed the smoke and tongues of fire eating the luxurious Palm Beach Breakers. Ida May Fluery instead watched her boy come to accept a kiss of congratulations on his sweaty cheek. She knew by the rustle of women's skirts and the unaccustomed yelps of rich men's voices that, for one day at least, Eden was theirs.

On a clear and sunny day in 1903, the Breakers Hotel in Palm Beach burned to the ground. Hundreds of wealthy vacationers were forced out and lost their possessions to the fast-moving flames. Since it was near the end of the tourist season, many simply returned to their true homes in the North.

Less than a year later, Henry Flagler had rebuilt the hotel, and the soon-to-be-dubbed snowbirds returned the next winter. On February 1, 1904, the beachside hotel reopened to universal acclaim.

END